THE TALISMAN OF DELUCHA

Other Fiction by A.J. Calvin

THE RELICS OF WAR
The Moon's Eye
The Talisman of Delucha
War of the Nameless

The Ballad of Alchemy and Steel

Serpentus

THE CAEIN LEGACY
Exile
Guardian
Harbinger
Legend

HUNTED

WRAITH AND THE REVOLUTION

PRAISE FOR THE TALISMAN OF DELUCHA

"Calvin's prose continues to be strong, and her battle scenes are well-crafted and intense… This series is shaping up to be one with a classic fantasy feel, well-paced, well-written, with very good character work, and quite enjoyable to read."
— Author P.L. Stuart, Before We Go Blog

"This is a wonderfully compelling book. Calvin's prose is fantastic, and her battle scenes and emotional moments are both beautifully crafted and capture the different intensities."
— Beneath a Thousand Skies Blog

"*The Talisman of Delucha* truly delivers the EPIC in epic fantasy."
— Escapist Book Co.

"The Talisman of Delucha has firmly established this as a series that I love. Calvin has crafted a story in this series that has all the atmosphere and hallmarks of classic fantasy, while being entirely its own beast."
— Rowena Andrews, Author of Elior

THE TALISMAN OF DELUCHA

A.J. CALVIN

THE RELICS OF WAR
Book Two

THE TALISMAN OF DELUCHA
Second Edition

ISBN 979-8-9883193-1-3

Cover illustration and design by Jamie Noble
(www.thenobleartist.com)

Map illustration by Dewi Hargreaves (www.dewihargreaves.com)

Chapter tile illustrations by A.J. Calvin

☀ HUMAN AUTHORED

For my parents

Thank you for the encouragement you have always shown as I continued to pursue my writing journey. I know it hasn't always been easy for you, but I'm fortunate to have your continued support.

AUTHOR'S NOTE

The Relics of War series is a project that has been on-going for more than twenty years. In its first iteration, the series was not marketed. It was published only for the enjoyment of a few close friends and family members.

Fast-forward two decades. I've decided the stories are worth sharing with a wider audience. All three books have undergone a complete rewrite, significant editing, and many updates. This is the version of the series that I have always envisioned, and this is the version I am sharing with the world.

The Relics of War is meant as a series of novels for adult readers. I want to stress the importance of this statement, as there are passages that depict violence, abuse, and torture within. There is also some language that may be offensive to some. Please be advised that I do not recommend these books for a younger and/or sensitive audience.

For those who don't mind reading about some of the uglier facets of humanity, I truly hope you enjoy the series that launched my aspirations to publish.

Thank you,
A.J. Calvin

THE FIVE KINGDOMS

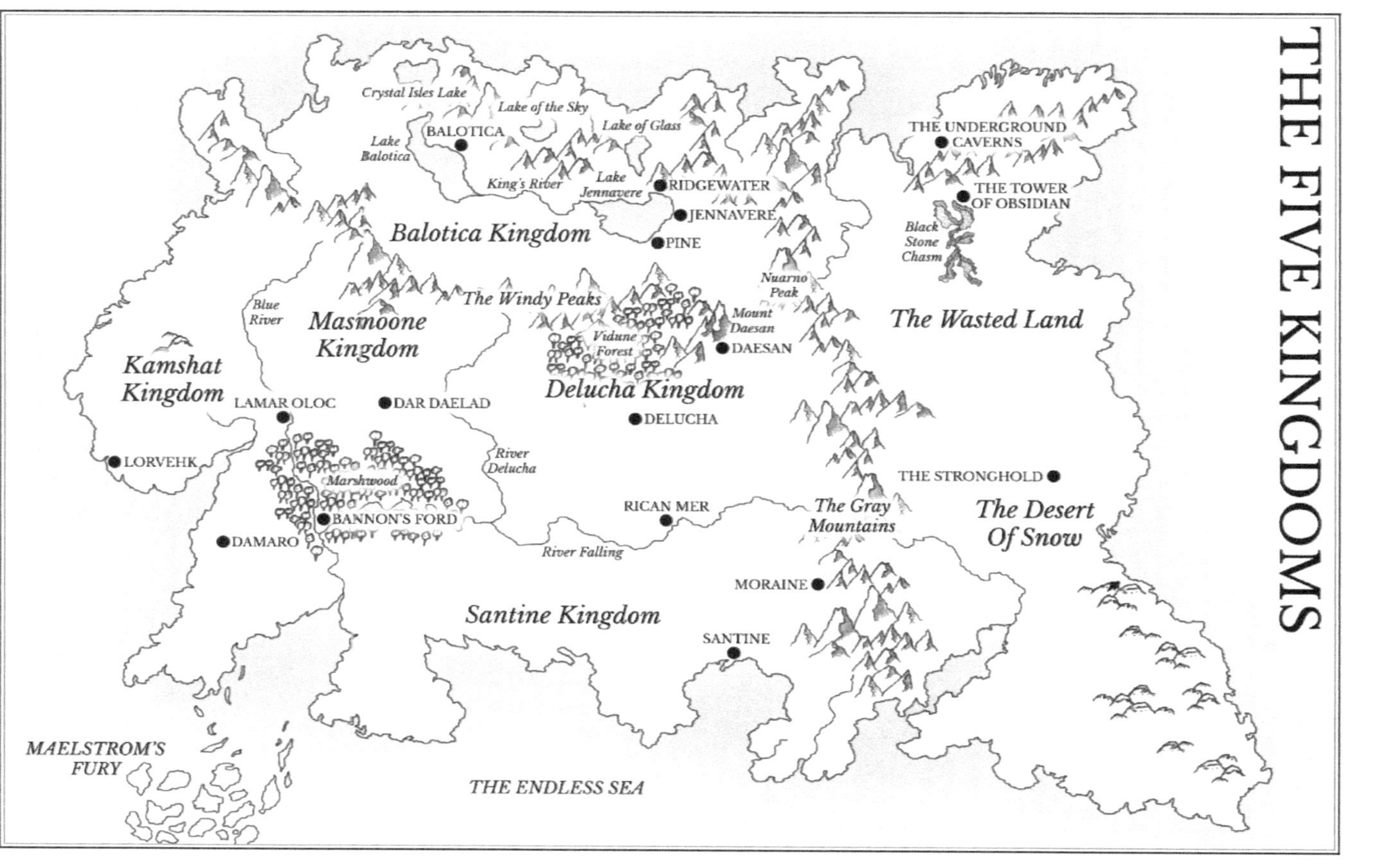

CHAPTER ONE

ARRA'S PLIGHT

Tavesin narrowed his eyes in concentration as Aziarah launched several magical attacks in his direction. The invisible shield of energy he'd erected withstood the Drakkon mage's assault; he watched with silent satisfaction as bursts of magic pelted the shield and fizzled. The other Drakkon on the rooftop observed the pair with interest and Trozyen, one of the youngest of their number, clapped his scaly hands together in approval.

"Again, Aziarah." Tavesin couldn't be certain she wasn't holding back. If he encountered the Soulless again, they would not. He was determined to be prepared.

"Tavesin, we've been at this since sundown. It's nearly midnight and you require sleep. The wizards have plans for you in the morning." Aziarah shook her lizard-like head in amusement. "Truly, I'm surprised you're not tired. Your shields are powerful, but certainly the drain—"

Tavesin crossed his arms stubbornly. "The wizards' plans are history lessons that will not help me locate Arra. If I sleep through part of Andola's lecture, I won't miss anything of importance. And no, I'm not tired. I must be certain of my skills."

"I promised your council's leader that our lessons would not interfere with theirs, Tavesin," Aziarah countered, her tone uncompromising.

"All I ask is for one more round, Aziarah. If you mean to take me into the Aethereum on the morrow, I will not be unprepared. The wizards won't help me learn what I must."

He scowled across the darkened rooftop, angry with the wizards for their refusal to assist him. Since Arra's disappearance, they'd done nothing but force him into his usual routine as though nothing was amiss. They'd been unable to search for her and had left the task to the Drakkon. Aziarah had ventured into the Aethereum several times, but upon each return, she'd found nothing that would locate the missing girl.

In his mounting frustration, Tavesin had taken every opportunity to scour the tower's library for information. The shielding technique he employed to block Aziarah's magical assault was but one shard of knowledge he'd gleaned as his resolve to locate Arra grew. He had begun to frequent the library between each of his lessons, often to the chagrin of his closest friend and fellow apprentice, Rostin.

If the wizards would not spare the resources and the Drakkon could not find her, he would take up the mantle himself. After all, he was the reason Arra had come to the Shining Tower, and if his suspicions were correct, he was the reason for her disappearance. Tavesin had made an enemy of the Soulless, and he was certain Arra had been abducted. The wizards assured him she would turn up, that she would be unharmed, but he sensed their words were meant only to placate him.

"I'm sorry, Tavesin, but you've begun to drain even *my* energy," Aziarah stated, nonplussed. "You need rest, too."

He shook his head. "One more time."

Aziarah sighed, but it was Trozyen who spoke next. "I will face you during this final assault, Tavesin, but once we are finished, you must do as Aziarah asks."

"I will. Thank you."

Aziarah's displeasure with the younger Drakkon was clear, but she stepped aside as he took her place. Trozyen was taller and more muscular than she was, and sported a crest of small, sharp spines across his forehead. Like all of the Drakkon, he was clad in leather armor.

"I will not hold back, Tavesin," he said.

"Good."

Tavesin braced himself and stared intently at Trozyen while he reformed his shield and waited for the next onslaught. He believed

Trozyen was a stronger mage than Aziarah, but due to his youth, he often deferred to her. Tavesin hoped he would prove a challenge.

Trozyen began to cast a powerful magic, one that Tavesin was wholly unfamiliar with. He could sense the Drakkon's workings, sense the ebb and flow of energy across the rooftop—another new skill he'd gleaned during his hours in the library. He reinforced his shield in anticipation; it began to shimmer faintly in response and he heard murmurs from the Drakkon observers. He ignored them and focused on Trozyen.

The young Drakkon unleashed a volley of blue-white bolts toward him. They sizzled and crackled as they shot through the air and bore down on his shield. As they made impact, they blossomed into an inferno that enveloped his shimmering barrier. Tavesin poured more magic into the shield, sensed Trozyen launch another, more powerful assault before the fiery remnants of his first dissipated, and he braced himself for the next impact. Distantly, he heard Aziarah and one of the other Drakkon admonish Trozyen, their voices filled with concern. Tavesin ignored them, his focus honed on his defense.

A blinding white light shot toward him. He recognized the magic as the same Aziarah had used to drive the Soulless away upon their first meeting. It was powerful, unlike anything he'd been faced with previously. He studied its energy signature as it closed the gap between them—there was but one way to counter it.

He poured more energy into the shield, and it began to glow blue-green around him. As the white light careened into it, Tavesin used the remainder of his energy to explode the shield outward in a harmless, yet dazzling display of color. He grinned at Trozyen even as he stumbled and fell to his knees.

Aziarah raced across the rooftop to kneel at his side. "Tavesin, are you well? Did that fool harm you? He should not have—"

He laughed, giddy with his success. "I'm fine, Aziarah. It was exactly the challenge I was seeking."

She snorted her disapproval. "Are all humans so daft as you seem to be, child? If you'd faltered for an instant, that magic could have killed you."

"I know." He looked beyond her to meet Trozyen's eyes. "He knew what I needed, Aziarah. I'm ready to face the Soulless if he appears tomorrow."

Tavesin forced his hands to remain still while he waited in the hall outside Hasnin's study. The urge to fidget and place his anxiety on display for anyone passing to see was nearly overpowering. He clenched his fists at his sides instead and hoped Hasnin's summons did not include a verbal reprimand for napping through the day's history lesson.

When the study's door opened, the Blue Sect Master emerged. She was a petite woman with dark skin and nearly black eyes, and at fourteen, Tavesin already stood several inches taller than she. She eyed him appraisingly but said nothing as she strode into the hall and went about her business elsewhere in the tower.

Tavesin frowned at the exchange, curious to learn why she'd been within Hasnin's study. Moments later, the white-haired Hasnin appeared in the doorway to beckon him inside. Tavesin entered and sat down on the empty chair facing Hasnin's writing table, while his mentor took a seat opposite him. Hasnin's table was unusually clutter-free, though he spied a stack of books leaning haphazardly in one corner of the room.

"Aziarah spoke with me this morning, Taven."

Tavesin nodded. "She wants me to enter the Aethereum tonight."

"Yes." Hasnin hesitated, as though determining the best means to deliver his next statement. "She did not come here to speak to me regarding that matter, Taven. It seems you were rather…demanding in your lessons last night."

Tavesin crossed his arms. "I had to be certain of my abilities, sir. If I encounter *him* again, I will not be beaten a second time."

Hasnin sighed heavily. "What you endured was unspeakable, Taven, but—"

"No, sir, you don't understand. You haven't faced one of them."

The words had come unbidden, a product of his frustration. Two weeks ago, he would never have imagined himself capable of standing up to Hasnin in such a fashion. Since Arra's disappearance, his mindset had altered significantly and he no longer cowered behind his former sense of propriety.

"Aziarah has informed me what transpired," Hasnin replied wearily. "I am concerned about you, Taven. It is unlike you to push boundaries in such a manner, to ignore protocol, or to be as insolent as you've been. I understand recent events have altered your perceptions—"

"Of course, they have, sir! No one is helping the Drakkon search for Arra, and—"

"Tavesin, *enough*." Hasnin rose from his seat to loom over the table. His gnarled fingers grasped the edge tightly enough they paled as his dark eyes flashed in momentary anger.

Tavesin stared a challenge at his mentor. He would show Hasnin the depths of his supposed insolence.

"As you are aware, there are no wizards amongst the Council with the ability to enter the Aethereum, with the exception of one very stubborn apprentice." Hasnin met his gaze unflinchingly. "There is little we can do to aid in the search, Taven."

Tavesin released an explosive sigh and looked away. He knew Hasnin was right, knew his anger with the wizards was somewhat misplaced, knew there was little they could do to find Arra. The knowledge did little to assuage his frustration, however, and felt compelled to continue his present course. He would do all in his power to find her and combat the Soulless he was certain had abducted her.

"I understand you've been teaching yourself several very advanced magical techniques," Hasnin continued after a moment as he resumed his seat. "Techniques that few fully-trained wizards are capable of."

Tavesin risked meeting his mentor's gaze. "I cannot sit by and do nothing, sir."

"Aziarah came to me, concerned you will push yourself too far, too quickly, and bring harm upon yourself. She told me what you accomplished last night."

"*He* won't touch me again," Tavesin replied fiercely. "And I *will* find Arra."

"Your determination is admirable, but there is a reason why we pace our students, Tavesin."

"I'm ready for the challenge, sir." He would not back down.

"I've discussed your recent visits to the library and last night's events with Mari El'Vero," Hasnin replied evenly. "The Blue Sect Master."

Tavesin's heart leapt at the news that her visit to Hasnin had not been mere coincidence. The Blue wizards were the defenders of the Council, those that specialized in shielding magics like the ones he'd employed on the rooftop. He planned to join the Blue Sect once his training was deemed complete.

"Mari has asked for some time to consider the acceleration of your studies, Taven. Like me, she is concerned at the change in your attitude of late, and we must be certain you are truly prepared for the next step."

His glower resurfaced and he peered down at his hands. "If you will not teach me, sir, the Drakkon will."

Hasnin sighed again. "I feared you would say that, Taven, and Aziarah's stance on the matter is…not in alignment with the council's. Please consider our position—and your own safety. You are young, and I don't wish to see you hurt again."

"None of us are safe, sir," Tavesin stated grimly. "The Soulless have returned. *None* of us are safe."

Hasnin was silent for several seconds before he stood. "It is time to meet the Drakkon."

Tavesin rose to follow his mentor, surprised Hasnin did not contradict his final words. The trek through the halls of the White Sect's level, and through the restricted areas of the tower beyond provided him with an opportunity to consider the wizard's lack of response.

Tavesin was right in his conviction; with the Soulless' return, none of the denizens of the Shining Tower were truly safe any longer. The Soulless he'd encountered had proven merciless and enjoyed inflicting pain. Tavesin had been targeted first because he could access the Aethereum, and later once the Soulless learned he'd stolen a relic from them. Hasnin was aware of his encounters and could not form an argument against his apprentice's words. He understood Hasnin feared for him, but there was little the aged wizard could do to sway his chosen path. Since Arra had vanished, he'd found his calling. If the wizards refused to help him achieve his goals, he would turn to the Drakkon.

They ascended the stairs toward the rooftop, pausing only when Hasnin unraveled the protective wards on the restricted levels. Tavesin scrutinized his mentor's actions as he unwound and reformed the wards; he believed he could replicate the magic involved, but kept that notion to himself. The magic used to operate the wards was supposed to remain a secret, guarded closely by select members of the White and Yellow Sects. It was best Hasnin remained unaware he had learned the trick of evaluating the magical energies involved in the workings of others.

The restricted levels were crammed to bursting with relics and artifacts of every conceivable size and shape. He could sense the thrum of energy pulsating from some as they passed, but he did not pause to study them. He'd made the same journey nearly every night for weeks, and though the objects they passed continued to intrigue him, Hasnin would not abide his curiosity. Many of the relics housed in the upper reaches of the tower were deemed dangerous, while others had unknown uses, their mysterious origins a thing of great fear amongst many wizards. Tavesin had begun to believe many of the artifacts were wasted, locked away as they were to collect dust.

"Why does no one study these things?" he asked as they climbed the final staircase toward the roof.

"Much of our knowledge was lost during the great wars," Hasnin replied. "You should know that from your lessons."

Tavesin rolled his eyes and sighed, exasperated. He'd expected the answer, but it did not serve to answer his question. "If we do not study the relics, we'll never regain the knowledge we lost."

"Tinkering with unknown magic is dangerous, even to those trained in the art of relic-making." Hasnin's tone had taken on an air of frustration. "Your point is valid, but the sentiment is not shared among many in the tower. Most believe the relics are best left alone."

"Even with the Soulless' return?" he pressed. "We should utilize every resource we have, sir."

They stepped onto the rooftop and Hasnin gestured toward Aziarah, who awaited him not far away. "It seems she has been expecting you, Taven."

Tavesin scowled, angry that his mentor refused to address his question. He may be a lowly apprentice, but he was no longer the naïve child Hasnin seemed to believe he was. His anger strengthened his resolve to take matters into his own hands.

Aziarah nodded a greeting to Hasnin, who promptly disappeared down the stairwell to leave his apprentice alone amongst the Drakkon. Tavesin pushed his grievances with the wizard aside and made his way across the rooftop. A stiff breeze was blowing, bringing with it the promise of autumn. In his aggravated state, he scarcely noticed the drop in temperature or the tendrils of dark hair that fell into his eyes as the wind tousled it.

"You are upset." Aziarah peered down at him, her golden, reptilian eyes unreadable.

"The wizards try to hold me back," he replied, then related his previous conversation to her. "Arra is in danger. I *know* it, just as surely as I know the sun will rise with the dawn. They can do nothing to help her, and you've done all that you can."

"Tavesin," she said sternly, "you cannot blame yourself for her disappearance, though your desire to find her is admirable. I have already informed your mentor that I will train you on any matter you ask of me—so long as it's in my ability to do so. He was not pleased, but I believe as you do. The wizards are impeding your progress."

Some of his previous ire melted away and he managed a tight smile. "Thank you, Aziarah. I don't believe they understand, nor do they realize what I'm capable of—"

"Believe me, Tavesin, they are aware of your power," she replied. "Your demonstrations last night did not go unnoticed. Even amongst my people, your newfound skill with shielding is a rarity. Given time and further training, you will be a force few others can hope to match."

He pondered her words for a moment. He was pleased she would continue teaching him magic beyond the realm of the Aethereum, in spite of the council's reservations. He would not be caught by the Soulless a second time. The memory of broken bones, bloodied and bruised limbs, the relentless fall of the Soulless' fists as they smashed into him time and again… He would not endure such treatment again. He was prepared, thanks to the Drakkon, and willing to risk another trip into the Aethereum in order to search for Arra.

"I'm ready, Aziarah."

She nodded and began to weave the magic that would open a portal into the other realm. He paid close attention and realized what she'd done was a simple feat but one few wizards could accomplish themselves. The magic of the Aethereum was rarely bestowed upon humans.

She began to explain what she'd done, but he shook his head, certain he could replicate the act himself. She fell silent to observe. He waved one hand and channeled his power as she'd done moments before. He grinned as another portal appeared; it shimmered blue-white in the air inches from his fingertips.

"You continue to surprise me, Tavesin." Aziarah's tone was wary.

He shrugged. "As you know, I've spent time in the library. I've learned much."

"So it seems." She gestured to the pair of portals before them. "I will meet you within."

The Aethereum appeared the same when he entered physically for the first time. The harsh quality of the blue-white light, the way his shadow seemed to pool like ink around his feet, the strange stillness that vibrated through the air—all were identical to his subconscious trips, prompted through dreams. His body felt distinctly heavier, however, and his movements felt sluggish. He turned to find Aziarah's gaze fixed upon him.

They stood on the tower's rooftop in the other realm, and where wind had blown through his hair in the physical realm, it was silent here. The sky above was awash with the strange light, while in the physical world, it had been dark and strewn with myriad stars.

Aziarah closed her portal, and indicated he should do the same.

"I feel strange," he said as the portals disappeared.

"You've grown used to entering this realm unencumbered by your body, Tavesin. You will grow used to the sensation after a time."

"Aziarah, might we go to Rican Mer? Arra and I used to meet there…"

She smiled. "Of course. It is a likely place to search, but one I am unfamiliar with."

Tavesin felt his face flush. "It's my hometown."

She held her taloned hand toward him. "Take me there, Tavesin. I will not have you travel alone and risk losing you, as we lost Arra."

He grasped her fingers and nodded. Closing his eyes, he formed the image of the small farming community in his mind, the grassy banks of the River Falling only paces away from his former home. He experienced a brief rush of sensation, as though they traveled at an incredible speed. When he opened his eyes again, he stood near the riverbank. The water was frozen in place in this strange, magical realm, but he'd come to expect such occurrences.

Aziarah released his hand and paused to take in their surroundings. Tavesin had been homesick the night he'd first come to Rican Mer while in the Aethereum. It was the same night he'd first met Arra, and they'd used the location for several rendezvous after that. A part of him had clung to the hope she would be awaiting them this night, but there was no sign of her. He swallowed his despair and focused on Aziarah.

"Your home has an aura of peace about it." Aziarah studied the small, tidy houses with their thatched roofs and neat garden plots. "Do you miss it, Tavesin? It is quite different from the tower or Dar Daelad."

He nodded. "At first, the city was a marvel, and the tower was wondrous…"

"And now?"

"I don't know, Aziarah. Sometimes I miss Rican Mer, but I don't believe I will ever fit in here again. The people here lead simpler lives than I will."

"I believe I understand."

"Aziarah, I—"

He stopped abruptly as a shuffling sound came from within the tall grasses along the riverbank behind him. His heart leapt into his throat as he spun to face the threat and he conjured a powerful shield that enveloped both himself and Aziarah. He expected trouble, anticipated facing the blurred countenance of the Soulless when his gaze landed on the source of the noise.

He had not counted on his eyes alighting on the cowering form of a red-haired girl, her face tear-stained and bruised.

"Arra!"

He was at her side, his shield gone, in an eye-blink. He sensed immediately that she was not present physically as he and Aziarah were, that she had projected her consciousness into the realm.

"Taven."

"Arra, where did you go? We've been searching…"

She sniffled and wiped at her eyes. "He took me, Taven. I…I don't know where. It's dark, windowless."

"We can find you, Arra." He glanced at Aziarah, whose expression was pained. "We can find her, can't we?" His voice rose in pitch as he clung to his last thread of hope, though he knew what Aziarah was going to say before she spoke.

"Tavesin, I'm sorry. I cannot trace her location if she is not physically here."

He swallowed the urge to burst into frustrated tears and turned to face Arra. "I will find you, Arra. I promise."

"Can you tell us anything more?" Aziarah asked gently. She knelt beside Arra and began to examine her injuries. "Gods, I do not know what's been done to you, child, but I cannot heal you, either."

Arra shook her head, forlorn. "It was a blond man. He's small, frail… He's one of *them*, Taven. His eyes…" she shuddered involuntarily. "He is Soulless."

Tavesin hung his head. It was his fault, after all. The man with the golden eyes had referred to the Soulless as Garin. Though Tavesin had never managed to get a true look at the Soulless' features, he was certain it was the same man who'd beaten and threatened him.

"I must go, Taven." Arra's voice was a bare whisper. "If he knows I've come here… I must go."

As she winked out of sight, Tavesin fell to his knees and began to sob. The frustration and fear of the past weeks overwhelmed him, and with the confirmation of his suspicions, he could no longer hold the tide of his emotions at bay. Aziarah gathered him into her scaly arms, held him as he succumbed to his suppressed pain.

"I must keep my promise to her," he whispered after a time.

"Yes," Aziarah agreed. "I will help you any way I can."

CHAPTER TWO

THE MURKOR ENIGMA

"Ah, Ravin, I'm pleased you've come."

Ravin made a half-bow to the young Deluchan queen where she was perched on a divan. A woman stood behind her, surreptitiously brushing her long, dark hair, while another sat at her feet strumming chords on a lap harp. Ravin had anticipated her summons would provide him with an opportunity to speak to her alone, but it seemed she had other designs in play.

She adjusted her heavy velvet skirts in a rustle of fabric, to better display the intricate embroidery that emblazoned its panels. He refrained from a scowl; she was deliberately making a show of their meeting for the benefit of the woman at the other end of the room.

The middle-aged Duchess of the Mers watched their meeting, a lace fan clutched in her hands. Ravin was weary of the queen's meddling in his personal life, and had no interest in the duchess or her affectations. If he didn't require his post as advisor in order to serve his own ends, he would have left Delucha and its intrigues behind weeks ago.

"You summoned me and I've come as required."

She tilted her head, a carefully formed pout upon her lips. "You make it sound as though I've inconvenienced you, Ravin. Surely, my company is not so dull that you'd wish to avoid it."

He ignored her implications. "I'd planned to check on our defenses today. Your summons delays my work."

A thin frown broke through her careful façade, an indication of her displeasure. "Very well. I'll be brief." She sat upright and motioned her companions to leave them. Both scurried across the room to resume their duties with the duchess.

"I'm listening." Ravin crossed his arms, irreverent in spite of the royal presence before him.

"I expect you to return to the courtyard tonight after supper has concluded," she informed him. "It has been several days since our last lesson, Ravin. Jasom and I require proper training. I've been lenient with you of late, but no more."

He clenched his jaw in momentary frustration. "Very well."

The queen and her consort wished to learn more of magic, and he had agreed to teach them, albeit reluctantly. He had little patience for such work; he'd been avoiding the task, and she knew it. His time was better spent fortifying the defenses he'd put in place.

"If you fail to show this evening, I'll make certain the duchess is given a key to your room." She laughed, though the sound held little warmth. "I believe she'd enjoy the premise, but I suspect you would not."

He narrowed his eyes. "It's unwise to enter my chambers if I am not present. The Aethereum is not the only realm where I've laid magical traps, Your Majesty." He lowered his voice into a growl. "If the duchess enters while I'm away, you will both come to regret it."

"Oh, Ravin, there's no need to be so sour." She smirked up at him, green eyes mischievous. "Go about your plans, if you must. I hope you'll not shirk your other duties to me."

"Gods-damn it. I said I will come." He was weary of her games.

"Good. We will be expecting you tonight."

He turned on his heel and fled the queen's solar, ignoring the protocol that insisted he must await her dismissal. He wasn't advisor to cater to her whims, though she seemed to think it reason enough to keep him on her staff. No, he'd taken the position in order to seek his revenge. He required resources, time, money—and the queen had all three in spades. He would endure her tedious summons so long as she allowed him the freedom to conduct his work and lure Dranamir into one of his many traps. He'd even settle for the capture of one of the others, but Dranamir remained his priority.

Behind him, he heard the Duchess of the Mers titter as she rejoined the queen in Ravin's wake. He muttered a curse under his breath.

Noblewomen were tiresome, petty creatures he refused to become further entangled with. For all his magical ability, Ravin had yet to formulate a method to convince them he was beneath their station. He wasn't, but if they believed it to be true, they'd cease their attempts at flirtation and leave him be. Nothing he'd said or done since coming to the palace had altered their perception of him, and the duchess was but one of the queen's many companions who had taken an interest in Her Majesty's newest advisor.

He strode through the halls of the palace, a scowl etched across his features. The servants and staff that happened upon him scurried wordlessly out of his way while he made his way to the spacious room the queen had allotted him.

Most of the palace's denizens understood his role as magical advisor, and many believed him a wizard from the Shining Tower, sent to aid the young queen. It did not make the act of performing magic in their midst any less conspicuous, and he'd rather not draw an unwanted crowd. Instead, he retired to his quarters in order to conduct his work. He did not trust the wizards, and he was certain the Soulless had spies within the palace—or at the very least, in the city just beyond. It was best that he worked in secret, away from the prying eyes of the curious.

He closed and barred his door, then opened a portal into the Aethereum. He immediately cast his senses across the entirety of the realm, a feat only he was capable of. There were a scant handful of souls within, but none marked with the corruption of the Soulless or the lesser taint of their minions in the Shadow Council. He would allow them to carry on with their business unhindered. It was likely most within his realm were Drakkon.

He thought himself outside the palace and examined the wards and traps he'd put in place weeks ago. He found no evidence of tampering, no indication that anyone had attempted to unravel them. Their purpose was to ensnare any individual that ventured near bearing the Nameless god's noxious mark. The traps were designed to first capture, then render the trespasser harmless. Even the Soulless, for all their profane power, were not immune to his machinations— particularly while they traipsed through the Aethereum.

The palace was secure, as he knew it would be. He'd used the excuse of checking his wards simply to avoid a prolonged encounter with the queen and her noblewomen, and he was loath to return to the physical realm so soon. Perhaps it was time to pay a visit to the black tower, to learn what its masters had put in place. His release from the soul-stone was no secret to them; he was certain at least one of their number would have attempted to ward their stronghold, just as he'd done for the Deluchan palace.

He thought himself to the northern edge of the black chasm that lay at the tower's feet, a vast and unseemly scar on the barren landscape's cracked surface. The Tower of Obsidian rose before him, its dark sides glittering ominously in the harsh Aethereal light. The topmost floor was guarded against intrusion in the physical realm, he noted, but there were no wards in place here. It was an oversight on the part of the Soulless, one he would exploit, given the opportunity. But now was not the time.

A presence emerged nearby. He sensed it was present only in its subconscious form, but that was not what drew his attention. The presence was gifted in the Ability, yet unlike any he'd sensed previously. Not human, not Drakkon…

He frowned, propelled by sudden curiosity. In all his years as a mage, he'd never encountered another race that harbored the Ability. Much had changed in the world during his long imprisonment within the stone, but this was unexpected. He followed the trail of the strange soul northward to the lands that surrounded the Underground Caverns and the Murkor homeland.

A solitary figure stood at the edge of the invisible perimeter that shielded the Murkor dwellings from the effects of magic. The figure was tall, wiry, dressed in shades of vibrant green and hooded in the manner of the Murkor people. The color of the garments indicated the Murkor was an alchemist if Ravin was not mistaken. The Murkor's back was to him, though he sensed the longing that emanated from the shrouded soul.

Ravin's frown deepened; he'd long believed the Murkor unable to harbor magic. He walked toward the figure and watched as it attempted to cross the unseen barrier toward the caverns. The figure stumbled backward, as though it had been physically repelled.

"You cannot enter the caverns from here," Ravin stated as he neared.

The hooded head swiveled in his direction and he caught a brief glimmer of pale eyes from within. "What is this place? I awakened here. After a time, thoughts of my home brought me to its door. Why am I forbidden entrance?"

Ravin studied him, certain the man was indeed Murkor. It was not simply his appearance, but his mannerisms, the accent in his words, his reference to the caverns as home. Not only did he harbor the Ability, but Ravin was surprised to see he was quite strong. There were indicators that he'd been given training as well, but not in his Aethereal talents, it seemed.

"This is the Aethereum," he explained. "A realm of magic that mirrors the physical world. The caverns are sealed to magic. It is why you cannot enter."

The Murkor nodded uncertainly. "It is my people's only defense against those who wish to subjugate us."

"I know your people's unfortunate history."

"History has a terrible habit of circling back on itself," the Murkor replied. "We are once again at their mercy. When I found myself here, I hoped to speak with the Kal. It seems I cannot."

"Perhaps not yet," Ravin replied. "Who teaches you magic?"

The Murkor hesitated. "I am not taught, so much as I am threatened with death if I do not comply."

Ravin nodded thoughtfully. The Murkor's words implied he was a subject of the black tower. He'd briefly considered making an offer to teach him the ways of the Aethereum—a Murkor ally could have proven useful to his plans—but it was no longer an option. He could not risk the Soulless learning of his schemes, and he was well versed in their methods of extracting information. He'd been tortured himself, branded, and made to obey, unable to withhold even the most guarded scraps of knowledge while Dranamir laughed in the background.

"While I cannot help you," Ravin said slowly, "I will give you the means to return to your body and leave this realm. It is not safe for you here."

The Murkor chuckled dryly. "Nowhere is safe, but I thank you for this unexpected kindness. I am Sal'zar."

Ravin considered introducing himself in kind, then thought better of it. "I'm afraid our meeting may place you in a rather precarious position with your overlords, should they learn of it. It's better that you do not know my name. I am no friend to the Soulless."

"I understand. I am unused to receiving compassion from your kind."

"If your only experience with humanity is from within the black tower, I cannot blame you for believing us all monsters." Ravin sighed. "Allow me to guide you out of the Aethereum. It is the least I can do for a guest in my realm."

CHAPTER THREE

THE JOURNEY AHEAD

Twilight descended upon the desert and with it a respite from the day's heat. Vardak led the others away from the Stronghold, his brief return home cut short by his brother's circumstance and his own imperative to seek the wizards in Dar Daelad.

He peered ahead but there was little to see but miles of snowy white sand, crested and shaped into broad dunes by the winds. Even in twilight, there was ample light to see by; moonlight reflected from the sand almost as readily as the sun. The desert was deceptively peaceful as darkness began to blanket the land.

Emra quickened her pace to match his, the reins of her large bay dangling from her hand. Out of respect to the Airess and Maryn, the two humans had opted to walk rather than ride. Vardak and Patak could have kept pace with the horses if they wished, even fully armored as they were. The Scorpion Men were uniquely suited for travel across the shifting sands.

"You promised answers, Vardak." Emra's gray eyes glinted with anger in the dusk light. "I've waited for our departure as you requested, but my patience wears thin."

"We were sworn to secrecy," he replied, unperturbed by her words. "I carry a relic that must be delivered to the Shining Tower, one with tremendous power—if the gods are to be believed."

She snorted. "I'm to believe the gods are involved in this mission of yours?"

He frowned and focused his gaze on the horizon. She did not understand the heavy price they'd paid simply to acquire the cursed thing that now hung on a cord around his neck. She was unaware of the gods' continued interference in his life, the terrible cost he and the others had incurred as unwitting pawns in their scheme.

The Moon's Eye was his as the gods intended, but it was useless to any without the ability to use magic. None of his people harbored the talent, nor did the Airess or the Felene who traveled with him. The two humans were warriors; Emra, a knight, and Lucas a career soldier. If either harbored the Ability, they were unaware of it. Solsticia, the celestial goddess, had indicated he ought to seek the guidance of the wizards. But that part of his journey would wait; Travin's plight must be dealt with first. The thought of his older brother, chained and enslaved to the Murkor infuriated him. His brother and the rest of his imprisoned people must be set free.

"Yes," he replied. "I may be one of Blademon's students, but the business with the relic began with Flariel. Her daughter forfeited her life to obtain it. The responsibility of delivering it to the Shining Tower now lies with me. I owe Janna that much and more."

Emra was silent for a time. "I'm sorry. I did not know."

"As I said yesterday, we could not speak of this until we'd left the Stronghold. Sevic would not allow it." He frowned at the mention of the Warleader's name. "First, we travel north to the Murkor settlement, as we agreed. I will do all I can to negotiate the release of our prisoners peaceably. Afterward, we travel to Dar Daelad."

"The hooded ones leveled an entire Balotican city," Emra said hollowly. "Do you truly believe they will negotiate?"

He chuckled wearily. "You sound like Sevic. Yes, I believe they will. Their army is on the far side of the mountains. Where the army is, the Soulless will be. Without the Soulless to antagonize them—"

"Yes, I understand. It's an opportunity for your people to be freed while my own are slaughtered."

"What can our small group hope to accomplish against the entirety of the Murkor army?" he asked, his frustration bubbling to the surface. "We are seven against thousands. I understand your anger with Sevic. He denied your request for what you deem 'true' aid."

Her cheeks flushed in the dying light. "I suppose I should be grateful that you and Patak have offered to assist us once your own objectives are fulfilled." She paused to toss her blond braid over one shoulder. "What is the importance of this relic you carry? If you truly were directed by the gods, it must be of significance."

He studied her carefully while he determined how much of the relic's story he ought to share. The humans had come to the Stronghold out of desperation, and he believed they were no friends of the black tower or the Soulless, yet the thought of divulging the relic's purpose gave him pause. Solsticia had ordered him to safeguard it and he would not disappoint the goddess in that respect. Janna had given her life so that they might use the Moon's Eye in the battle against the Soulless.

He'd met Emra for the first time only days ago. He'd had too little time to accurately judge her character.

"Vardak, if we are to help you—" she began.

He held up one hand and shook his head. "I know. What you ask is…difficult."

"Very well. Perhaps you can tell me the story of how it came into your possession," she replied. "We've a long way to travel and little else to pass the time."

He frowned and considered her words. If he did not tell her the tale, others in their party undoubtedly would.

As he began to speak, Lucas drew nearer to hear his words over the night breeze and the tread of the others' boots. Vardak began with his role in the affair, his first encounter with Janna and her volatile mother, Flariel, and their journey to Vidune Forest in search of Coreyaless. When he began to speak of Stonewall Hall, Lucas swore.

"We traveled past its entrance on our trek here. Fucking gods, even from a distance that place felt ominous." Lucas shuddered visibly in the moonlight and ran a hand through his mop of dark hair.

"Ominous is an apt description," Coreyaless agreed from behind him. "I would not care to repeat the journey."

Vardak told them of Flariel's appearance in her shrine and their abrupt departure. Maryn chimed in at times while he spoke of the Felene jungles, the southern continent, and their passage through the deadly glade filled with carnivorous plants. He told of his encounter with Blademon and the news of Travin's capture, Karmada's appearance moments after the Airess reunited on the steps of

Solsticia's temple, and the celestial goddess' role in taking them to her Sky Palace.

His heart was heavy as he spoke of Janna and her fateful decision. At twenty years old, there had been much life left ahead of her, yet she'd taken it upon herself to fulfill her mother's demands and acquire the Moon's Eye. Both Airess and Maryn concluded the story, describing the memorial the gods had held in Janna's honor.

Vardak allowed them to speak for him at the end. His final encounter with Flariel had left him melancholy, the events surrounding Janna's death continued to gnaw at him, and he wished for the hundredth time the gods would see fit to leave him be. Flariel's parting words to him indicated he'd never be so fortunate.

"Gods," Lucas breathed as the others lapsed into silence. "What manner of relic requires one to sacrifice themself simply to obtain it?"

Vardak pulled on the leather cord around his neck and drew the teardrop-shaped stone into the open. It glowed softly in the moonlight, a pale green-white. "This manner of relic," he replied gruffly.

"Solsticia did not state implicitly what it's purpose is," Coreyaless said quietly. "She indicated it was required to destroy the black tower and hinted there is more to the puzzle than this piece alone."

"Sevic ordered us to keep the relic a secret from our people," Patak added. "With good reason, I suppose. We're too near that damned tower, even here."

Vardak returned the Moon's Eye to its former location, nestled beneath his plate mail. He agreed with his brother; holding such a powerful object so near to the enemy was dangerous. Yet he'd stubbornly refused to give up on his desire to free Travin and the other Scorpion Men prisoners. Now he must carry the relic through the heart of the Soulless' lands.

"The wizards must have answers," Emra said quietly after a moment.

"I certainly hope they do," Coreyaless remarked. "The gods were close-lipped about what we must do, though they interfered enough to push Vardak along the path he now treads. In times past, they refrained from such actions."

"What has occurred to make this time different?" Lucas asked.

Vardak shrugged and focused his gaze on the horizon. It was a question he'd pondered himself and one he had yet to answer.

22

CHAPTER FOUR

DEFEAT

Aran'daj parried the axe blow with the blade of his curved black saber, but it took every ounce of his strength to hold his human opponent at bay. Aran'daj was tall by Murkor standards, tall by human standards, but the man who bore down on him had several inches in height advantage and easily outweighed him twofold. Aran'daj grimaced beneath his dark hood and shoved the man as hard as he was able. The hulking brute refused to budge, but instead leered down at him through the slats in his helm.

The sound of battle raged around them; steel clashed, arrows whizzed by, soldiers shouted, horses whinnied and screamed. A counterpoint to the cacophony was led by the Murkor alchemists as another volley of exploding stones was launched into the midst of the human defenders. They erupted on impact with a deafening boom, followed by a rain of debris and gore that splattered the surrounding battlefield.

Aran'daj narrowed his eyes and held his ground against the huge human before him, determined to survive in spite of the unfavorable odds. They'd begun their attack on Pine after nightfall, but the human defenders had been prepared for their strike. Knights had joined the battle, mounted on fearless steeds clad in as much armor as their riders. The Murkor possessed no mounted units, and the knights had rent gaping holes in their ranks. They were losing the battle, but if Aran'daj fell, there would be no one to sound the retreat, no one to ensure his people remained shielded from the Soulless' wrath.

He grunted in frustration and shoved again. He could not risk sliding his saber free for a quick strike; the human would bear down with his axe and split Aran'daj's skull. His only hope was to unbalance his foe and cause the man to stumble.

His biceps burned from the exertion. As his arms began to shake, the human cracked a humorless, gap-toothed grin. Aran'daj feared his time with Aeon was quickly coming due and there was little he could do but continue as he was, saber locked with axe in a desperate effort to prolong his existence. The human increased the pressure on Aran'daj's blade while a wicked chuckle issued from his throat.

Suddenly the man stiffened and released his grip on the axe, his laughter cut short. Aran'daj side-stepped to free his blade as the human's weapon fell to the blood-soaked earth. The man gaped incredulously at the pointed steel that protruded from his leather-clad belly, as though unable to believe he'd been skewered by the enemy only moments from his own victory. The blade was wrenched from its fleshy prison and he tumbled forward in a heap of uncoordinated limbs.

Aran'daj silently thanked the gods and saluted his black-clad savior. Jal'den nodded briefly before he turned to seek his next victim, a whirlwind in ring mail leaving death in his wake.

"Signal the retreat, Commander!" Jal'den shouted over his shoulder. "We must regroup!"

Aran'daj sheathed his saber and removed the yellow flare from his belt pouch as Jal'den's words registered. The flares were creations of the alchemists, and yellow had been decided upon as the sign for withdrawal. He studied the seemingly innocuous tube in his hands, marked only with the Murkor word for its color in their flowing script. A short, woven cord protruded from the base of the tube, and when pulled, the cord would activate the flare.

Aran'daj glanced at the field surrounding him to note he had only moments to send the flare before the next humans were upon him. He gripped the tube firmly in one hand and yanked the cord with the other. A sizzling hiss issued from the contraption before it shot skyward, a trail of blinding yellow sparks arcing in its wake.

He glanced at the onrushing humans a final time, then turned on his heel to dash through the battlefield toward safety. The drummers at the rear of the Murkor ranks began to pound a new cadence as the golden light of the flare dissipated overhead.

Aran'daj led the soldiers deeper into the Balotican mountains as they fled the massacre at Pine. The Murkor had suffered heavy casualties, though the humans had fared little better. Pine was encircled by a pair of sturdy walls, and unlike their previous targets, its defenders had been awaiting them. The addition of knights on the field and been too much for the Murkor to overcome alone.

He'd been loath to retreat. There was a high likelihood that his life would be ended in a violent and brutal fashion when the Soulless returned, as punishment for his apparent failure. He'd relayed his fears to Kama before they'd arrived at Pine, but his concerns had fallen upon deaf ears. Kama ordered the attack and Aran'daj was compelled to obey. Defiance of a direct order from the Soulless was a certain death sentence, whereas failure and defeat at the hands of the enemy might be seen as a lesser infraction. There was a small chance the Soulless would understand the overwhelming odds they'd faced at Pine, a sliver of hope that each breath would not be his last.

His dark thoughts trailed him as he guided the Murkor deeper into Balotica's rocky and unforgiving terrain. He wanted leagues between the army and Pine but he would settle for the distance they could cover before dawn colored the sky. Scores of wounded slowed their progress, but Aran'daj was not a man to leave his comrades behind. They would travel at a manageable pace for the wounded and no faster.

"Sir, we should talk." Jal'den appeared from within the ranks to fall in at his side.

He nodded. "Yes. You are my second, Jal'den—"

"No, sir," Jal'den cut in, his voice anguished. "Let's not begin in that manner. I want to believe you'll be standing here tomorrow."

Aran'daj managed a weary smile beneath his hood. He could not force himself to share Jal'den's youthful optimism. There were many things the Arms Master must know if he found himself in the position of commander upon the Soulless' return.

"We both understand our retreat will be seen as failure, Jal'den."

Jal'den growled in frustration. "I'm no strategist, sir. I won't take up your post."

"You cannot deny the Soulless, Jal'den. Not if you plan to see Sal'zar again." He sighed heavily. "I informed Kama of my concerns prior to our arrival at Pine. We spoke at length about why I believed it was folly to attack without their power to bolster our own, but our orders were already decided. He demanded the strike. You know I am in no position to argue with him."

"Why weren't they here?" Jal'den demanded angrily. "If they knew what we faced—"

Aran'daj held up one hand, and the Arms Master fell silent.

"I do not question their motives, Jal'den. If we wish to survive this war and to see the Kal's plan come to fruition, we must play our respective roles. When dealing with the Soulless, that means we act the obedient subject and do as they require. The alternative is not something I wish to dwell upon."

"We lost hundreds today, sir. Dead or lost, it doesn't matter. Scores more are wounded." Jal'den seemed to deflate with the words. "They knew this would happen."

"Yes."

Jal'den's fists clenched at his sides. "I hate feeling helpless. I fucking hate it."

"As do I, Jal'den." Aran'daj looked down to watch the churned soil and scrubby grass pass by underfoot.

"Do you believe the gods knew our paths would lead here?" Jal'den asked quietly after a time. "I can't help but think I was destined to be here, to experience this black despair. There is no other reason Blademon would have chosen me."

"Jal'den—"

"Throughout my life, circumstance has always found a means to drive us apart, Commander. I will not forfeit my life to the gods-damned Soulless, and I won't see yours taken, either. I mean to make a life with Sal'zar one day, in spite of Blademon's designs, and in spite of this fucking war." Jal'den drew himself upright and gazed skyward. "Blademon trained me at arms, sir, but he did not see fit to teach me strategy. Without you, our people are lost. So long as I draw breath, the Soulless will not touch you."

Aran'daj closed his eyes briefly. Jal'den's loyalty was admirable but foolish. If the Arms Master attempted to interfere when the Soulless decided to exact their punishment, he would fall as readily as Aran'daj.

The Murkor people were defenseless against the Soulless' foul brand of sorcery.

"Jal'den, one of us must live through our next encounter with Kama. If we both fall, there will be no one within the army to carry out the Kal's plan."

"I won't fail, Commander," Jal'den replied stubbornly.

"Gods, Jal'den, you are not invincible, and you have no means to counteract their magic!"

"They won't see me coming, sir." Jal'den chuckled mirthlessly beneath his hood. "Sal'zar gave me something, a gift from the alchemists that he'd been working on before…Before he was taken. When I saw him last, he gave it to me."

"Secrets, Jal'den? I believed we were done with that business."

"I may have spoken of *ujar'havel*, but I did not divulge everything. I was angry with you. A part of me remains so." Jal'den shook his head in irritation.

Aran'daj sighed. He understood Jal'den's position; he'd pressed for details he had no business inquiring after. Under Murkor law, Jal'den could have taken his life without repercussion or informed the Kal and have Aran'daj stripped of both title and caste. The Arms Master had done neither, but Aran'daj believed it unwise to prod him into action.

"I have apologized several times, Jal'den. I know it is not enough, but without your confession, I could not trust Sal'zar. I will forever be in your debt for keeping my indiscretions secret."

Jal'den was silent for a time and Aran'daj sensed he was brooding. Finally, he said, "Sal'zar gave me a salve that when applied to my person and my armor, renders me almost invisible. I tested only a small amount, but it works as he claimed. He could not spare more than a single bottle."

"Such a thing could prove very useful." Aran'daj considered the possibilities that presented themselves, unbidden, to his mind. "Do not waste your gift on the Soulless' return, Jal'den. Save it for a better time. We may need it in order to enact the Kal's plans."

"Fucking gods, Commander! What better time will there be?"

Aran'daj clung to the sudden hope that blossomed in his heart. "I believe an opportunity will present itself. Keep your salve, but prepare yourself for the eventuality of tomorrow's events."

He glanced over his shoulder to take in the ranks of soldiers marching through the rocky terrain, obedient and loyal to their commander and Kal. Did they share his dour outlook on the Soulless' next appearance? Would they remain to serve Jal'den once he was named commander? Would they defect and disappear into the wilds of the human lands if forced to bear witness to his own execution?

"If you are named commander, Jal'den, do all in your power to protect the others."

"I won't be, sir. You're our commander, and we will follow your lead."

Aran'daj sighed; Jal'den would not be swayed. He prayed Kama would see reason, would understand retreat had been their only option as the battle of Pine unfolded. If he failed to convince the Soulless, he feared both he and the young Arms Master would lie dead at their feet.

CHAPTER FIVE

DIVISION

Dranamir drummed her fingernails on the top of the glass case, impatient with Jannyn for his tardiness and furious with Garin for his summons. The Murkor were engaged in the battle for Pine; she and the others should have been present to ensure their victory. Yet Garin had summoned them to the tower, his disregard for the army apparent in the act.

A few paces from her, Kama folded his arms while his crimson eyes bored into Garin's. "I wish to remind you that I left our army on the brink of attack for this gathering. Where is Jannyn?"

"Yes, where *is* he?" Dranamir demanded. "I will strip the flesh from his bones when he arrives—"

"For the gods' sake, Dranamir, your bloodlust grows wearisome." Alyra tossed her head, her mane of dark hair falling loosely across her back.

Dranamir smirked; Alyra continued to play at beauty, though her days of capturing men's hearts with a single gesture were long past. When she'd given her soul to their master, Alyra's flawless bronze skin had taken on the sickly hues of decay and her lustrous black hair had thinned and become brittle. She retained her shapely figure, but her corrupted features marked her for what she was: Soulless. Of the three men, only Jannyn had been ensnared by her charms. Kama's interests lay elsewhere, while Garin was a puzzle unto himself. Dranamir wasn't certain Garin was capable of taking pleasure from anything save his clandestine meetings with their master.

"Jannyn will join us presently," Garin replied evenly. "I would not have called you here if our master hadn't ordered it. He has formulated a plan."

Dranamir continued to tap her nails on the glass while she considered his words. Their master had promised them glory; but first, the task of subjugating the Five Kingdoms and the lands beyond must be completed. It had been weeks since their resurrection and this was the first true indication he had a scheme in mind. Kama had directed the army unerringly thus far, but their conspicuous absence from the battle this day gnawed at her. Perhaps it was an opportunity for the commander to test himself, to prove himself worthy of his post. If he won the day, she would reward him. If he failed...

She smiled grimly. If the commander failed, she'd make an example of him more spectacular than she'd done for Scherok. His successor would be compelled to excel or face her unmitigated wrath. Her preferred method of extracting obedience from those she deemed lesser involved copious amounts of fear and a deluge of blood.

Near the rear of the room, footsteps echoed. She glanced over her shoulder to see Jannyn's stocky figure lumbering toward them, a scowl plastered across his grizzled face. His breathing was heavy as he came to a stop near Alyra.

"When will you have that damned relic complete?" he snarled at her.

Alyra blinked, surprised at the vehemence in his tone. "I've been assigned—"

"Before this escalates further, allow me to *reassign* your tasks, Alyra." Garin studied the pair from his position at the head of the room, an obsidian mirror in a twisted frame the backdrop to his starkly pale features. "I summoned you here at the master's behest. He has determined it is time to make our next move."

"And I have yet to receive a gods-damned replacement for the stolen relic." Jannyn narrowed his eyes, a dangerous light in their depths. "If I am to work at my full capacity, I must have one."

"Yes," Garin agreed. "Our master has come to the same conclusion. Alyra, you are to cease your explorations of the sea caves immediately and pour your energy into crafting a suitable relic for

Jannyn's use." He smiled grimly. "The master was not pleased with your lack of progress in the caves."

Without warning, Garin channeled his power. A wide, metal collar manifested itself to snap around Alyra's delicate neck. She stumbled and fell to her knees while her hands fluttered uselessly against the device. Alyra gasped and began to sob while Garin ignored her to focus on the rest of the group.

Dranamir eyed the collar with distaste. She recognized the device; it was a direct link to their master's dark psyche, a means to control even his most powerful subordinates. Alyra had been involved in the manufacture of several such relics during her time as Enlightened, and it was likely she was now caged by her own creation. The first such relic had been designed for Ravin, though she'd never been afforded the joy of seeing it put to use.

"The master has given me access to three other such relics," Garin informed them coldly. "Alyra's failure is meant as an example to the rest of you. He will not abide excuses, nor will he tolerate insubordination." He frowned imperiously at Alyra where she huddled on the tiled floor. "The collar will be removed once you've proven yourself worthy of our master's legacy."

"At least I know I'll have my fucking relic soon," Jannyn growled. He eyed Alyra with the same measure of distaste he reserved for a refuse pile.

"That is my hope as well," Garin replied. "You will have need of it. The master has ordered you and I to seek the Peace Talismans. He requires at least one, but if we can secure more, it will be a great boon to his schemes." To Dranamir and Kama, he said, "The pair of you are to continue your work with the Murkor army. I'm afraid his orders drew you away at a critical time, and the army was forced to retreat."

Dranamir watched as Kama's jaw clenched with sudden anger. "He demanded we attack Pine on this very date, then drew us away. No doubt the retreat was called due to heavy losses on our side." He muttered a string of curses beneath his breath and shook his head. "I want to know why he schemes as he does, Garin. Or was the timing of your choosing—a means to make us appear failures, as well? I've no wish to have one of those fucking collars strapped about my neck. This looks to me like a play for your own power."

Garin folded his narrow arms and met Kama's heated gaze with an icy one of his own. "I cannot administer such punishment at will, Kama. My connection to our master is unique, and through me, he is capable of exerting his power. The collars are not housed in our realm, but in his."

Dranamir lifted an eyebrow. Garin's admission was both enlightening and concerning. He was the conduit for their master's orders, but more so, the vessel of his power in the physical realm. She'd been wary of him before, but now was doubly so.

His news of the Murkor defeat at Pine came as little surprise; she did not believe their commander was as capable as Kama claimed. Her unease with Garin fueled her desire to lash out. She would make a blood-soaked example of the commander as she'd planned, if only to settle her nerves.

Kama nodded stiffly. "If the army was forced into retreat, as you claim, it's best I speak with the commander." He glanced sidelong at Dranamir. "I expect you wish to be present, as well?"

"Of course."

"There is another matter before you depart." Garin began to pace in front of the mirror, and Dranamir realized belatedly he'd chosen the location as a reminder to them. The mirror was his means of direct communication with their master. Dranamir was stronger than the seemingly frail man, both physically and magically, yet she had unwittingly become his second. Their master had chosen to tie himself to Garin more strongly than the rest, and in so doing, had marked Garin as their leader.

She glared at the realization. For all her schemes to see Alyra and Jannyn reduced to nothing, she'd failed to understand the true scope of their master's plans for his Soulless. If Ravin had been named in her stead as their master desired, she would have been his second. She'd killed him in order to attain her power. She was unable to do the same for Garin. He was Soulless; their master would protect him from her. An attempt on his life would see her reduced to the same sorry state Alyra currently inhabited—collared and subject to their master's unholy rage.

"We have all been ordered to accelerate the training of those chosen to become Enlightened," Garin stated. "Our master desires that a number of them be fully prepared and branded into his service before the next battle ensues." His eyes flicked toward Kama. "The army is to retreat from Balotica. Regroup, then refocus its energy on Delucha. It seems our dynamic with the young queen has recently changed."

Dranamir narrowed her eyes. "How so? She was to be under your charge, or his." She gestured toward Jannyn.

"Without my relic, I've been unable to travel to the palace," Jannyn snarled. "This is *her* gods-damned fault." He aimed a kick in Alyra's direction, but the sniveling wench managed to scuttle beyond his reach.

"The master considered the recent events in Delucha when he determined Alyra's punishment." Garin glanced at each of them in turn. "See that you don't follow her example."

Dranamir left the tower through the Aethereum, incensed by Garin's threats and enraged she was powerless to topple him from his position. To defy Garin was to defy the Nameless god. She would not find herself collared alongside Alyra.

She spent little time within the Aethereum and emerged into the physical world near the center of the army's hastily erected encampment. Kama had arrived ahead of her. He stood not far away, in conversation with the black-hooded commander and another Murkor. Her anger with Garin amplified her desire to see the Murkor pay for their failure, and she immediately seized her power.

She sensed Kama seize upon his own, his carefully constructed veil dissolving to reveal the true magnitude of his magic. He countered her deadly attack with a snarl; her magic deflected harmlessly into the sky, while he struck her a painful blow. She found herself sprawled on the ground and cursed herself for failing to erect a shield.

"Fucking gods, Dranamir, we cannot afford more losses this day." He cut her from the source of her power as he strode to her location. She glared up at him, but his expression remained unyielding.

"Garin stated the army's defeat was not of the Murkor's doing. If you'd taken the time to listen, rather than gloat over Alyra's punishment—"

"An example must be made, Kama."

He gazed skyward, exasperated. "As we've established, *I* am responsible for the army, and *I* will determine if such methods are warranted. Your role is to assist during attacks, nothing more."

His expression remained stony, but he offered her his hand. She sneered at him; his act of false chivalry was distasteful and unnecessary. She rose to her feet, pointedly ignoring the proffered hand, and brushed the dirt from her skirt.

"Release me, Kama."

"Do not strike at the Murkor again. I will speak with Garin if you do."

She glowered at him but nodded, his threat clear. She would not attack the Murkor, but Kama had now made himself an enemy. As soon as he relinquished the block over her power, she launched a volley of fire in his direction. It sizzled and popped in the air inches from his person, then faded from sight. He was shielded. In her rage, she'd failed to account for it.

"Are you finished?" he demanded, arms crossed.

Behind him, the pair of Murkor huddled together, fear evident in their posture. They spoke rapidly in their musical tongue. She had no doubt they discussed the spat between the Soulless in their midst. She would not allow Kama to humiliate her before their subordinates without repercussion.

"For now, perhaps," she conceded. "Do not become too comfortable, Kama. I will have my revenge, and you must sleep sometime."

Kama chuckled humorlessly. "Your gods-damned temper will be your downfall, Dranamir."

CHAPTER SIX

THE SOULLESS' SEARCH

Ravin pinched the bridge of his nose in a futile attempt to stave off a headache. Teaching was not one of his strengths, and teaching a pair of novices—particularly one as entitled as the queen—left him teetering on the precipice of madness. Her Majesty refused to listen to half of his words and bungled the rest. Her magical aptitude was mediocre at best, but her attitude inhibited what Ability she possessed. If she were not also his employer, he would have ended their lessons quickly and cut his ties to her. She would never reach what little potential she had.

Her consort, Jasom, had the sense to listen and follow Ravin's instructions. His Ability outshone the queen's, and Ravin began to understand why the Soulless had plagued him. He was gifted and with proper training might excel. Her Majesty often distracted him, however, and Ravin began to wonder what he'd landed himself in.

He needed the resources his post as advisor offered; he must remember that, no matter how trying the pair proved to be.

"Ravin, please demonstrate again," the queen said. Her eyes flicked toward the blond former farmer at her side, a coy smile on her lips.

He bit back his impatience. They were teenagers, filled to bursting with adolescent lust, unable to keep their focus for more than a handful of seconds. But *she* was the queen, and even though he was old enough to be her father, he must obey or lose his post. He grimaced and cleared his throat in an attempt to garner their attention.

Jasom faced him, a flush heating his fair cheeks. The queen ignored Ravin for a moment while her green eyes appraised the young man at her side. When she finally deigned to turn in his direction, there was no inkling of remorse in her expression. She expected he would obey, expected he would await her attention and command.

Their arrangement did more than serve him with headaches. He suffered bouts of indigestion as he grappled with duty versus need. The queen seemed oblivious to his growing distaste for her presence, infatuated as she was with Jasom Riversend.

Ravin drew a breath and prepared to repeat his previous words for the second time. Both had finally given him their full attention.

"Watch—"

He fell silent as magical alarms that only he could hear began to sound, diverting his attention. His traps had not been triggered, yet one of the Soulless had drawn near enough to trip his carefully placed wards.

"Ravin?" the queen asked, amusement mixed with concern in her tone.

"One of our enemies has come near. I must go."

Without awaiting her response, he opened a portal and disappeared into the Aethereum. He heard an indignant mutter from her as he closed the portal behind him. He cast his senses through the realm and recognized Garin's distinct signature. He'd ventured very near the palace, but had wisely remained outside Ravin's protective boundaries. His essence had traveled far westward, into central Kamshat Kingdom.

Ravin followed the Soulless' trail, intent on harm. He'd warned Garin to keep out of the Aethereum when he'd last encountered the man. He'd uncovered Garin in the act of savagely beating a child and his blood had boiled at the sight. He'd sent Garin forcefully out of his realm, imparting enough power he hoped the Soulless would sustain serious injury. Garin had not returned, to his knowledge, until now. If he'd succeeded in his ploy to injure the Soulless, Garin had obviously recovered.

Garin's foul essence led him to a maze of wine cellars. Ravin glanced about the space briefly; casks were stacked end to end along one wall, each marked clearly with the black wolf sigil of the Kamshati royal house. The Soulless were investigating palaces across the Five Kingdoms, and he must learn why.

Garin was not in the cellar but was nearby. His distinct, distorted presence, with its characteristic taint was unmistakable. Even Dranamir could not boast such darkness in her being; he was convinced Garin was more closely tied to the Nameless god than the others of his kind.

Ravin shielded himself and followed Garin's trail through the cellar and up a ladder into what appeared to be a storage room. Garin stood near one wall, his back to Ravin. He appeared to be studying something, unaware of Ravin's arrival. Ravin afforded him no warning; he struck the Soulless with several attacks simultaneously, taking advantage of the fact they were within *his* realm. In the Aethereum, Ravin's power was unparalleled.

Garin was cut from the source, forced against the wall, and spun around. Ravin crossed the distance between them in three long strides, fury etched upon his features, golden eyes ablaze.

"You and your kind are not welcome here," he snarled.

Garin struggled feebly against his invisible bonds but managed a strangled laugh. "We go…where we please, Ravin."

Ravin increased the pressure of Garin's bonds to an uncomfortable level. Garin writhed and laughed again. It was a dark sound, a sinister sound, one that seemed at odds with the frail man's appearance. Ravin glared at him and swung. His fist connected with Garin's jaw with enough force the Soulless' head snapped backwards.

"I want answers, Garin."

"Torture does not frighten me," Garin replied. "I've experienced much worse than anything you can conjure."

Ravin arched an eyebrow. He'd experienced torture at Dranamir's hands, and she was decidedly creative in her methods. The notion of taking inspiration from the woman who'd once striven to kill him disgusted him, but if it served to make his point clear to Garin, he would do so.

"Try me."

Ravin activated pain receptors across Garin's body, inflaming them to a level that caused the Soulless to cry out and convulse in his magical bonds.

"Remember, Garin, in the Aethereum, *I* am the master."

Garin shrieked as Ravin intensified his pain to a near intolerable level. A foul stench wafted through the air as he soiled himself. Ravin snarled and abruptly ceased his manipulation of the Soulless' pain response. Garin hung limply against the wall, panting as sweat ran in rivulets from his pale, distorted brow.

"Why have you defied me, Garin? Why are you here?"

Garin shook his head, stubborn to the last. "Orders," he rasped.

Ravin frowned; it was time to make his point clear. He conjured heat around Garin's body, enough to cause minor burns and small blisters, but not so much that it would leave the Soulless' flesh permanently disfigured. He meant only to inflict pain, and Garin began to writhe once more against his invisible restraints.

"Tell me, Garin. I can do much worse." He smirked. "My time with Dranamir was quite enlightening, pardon the pun."

Again, he stopped channeling the painful magic and watched as Garin slumped forward. His breathing came in ragged gasps.

"What…is your history…with her?"

Ravin chuckled mirthlessly. "Perhaps you'll learn one day, but today is not that day. Why are you here?"

Garin swallowed, his crimson eyes baleful as they met Ravin's. "The master…seeks the talismans."

Ravin narrowed his eyes. It was not the response he'd been anticipating, but he sensed no deception in the other's words. "Why?"

Garin shook his head. "I don't…know."

Ravin began to pace across the room while he considered Garin's words. It was typical of their blind god to give orders without divulging his reason behind them, and typical of his followers to act the obedient subjects without question. The Talismans of Peace were purported to be the most powerful magical relics in existence, created at the conclusion of the Time of Chaos as a means to broker an armistice between the Five Kingdoms and put an end to the centuries-long war. Ravin knew only the rudimentary legends surrounding the talismans, but if the Nameless sought them, something of their folklore must be true.

"Is the talisman why you were in Delucha?" Ravin demanded.

Garin hesitated before he nodded in resignation. "It was a…mistake to draw so near the palace… I nearly hit one of your…damned wards."

Ravin's grin was feral. "A pity you didn't. I would have settled for you falling into my trap."

"Dranamir has other orders." Garin sagged against his bonds.

Ravin suspected his exhaustion was not entirely an act, but he wasn't finished with Garin yet. "You didn't answer my last question."

Garin grimaced as Ravin moved one hand subtly. "There's no need…to continue in that manner. I will answer you."

"I'm listening."

"I went to Delucha first, knowing you were there. I believed—erroneously—that your attention would be diverted." Garin shook his head. "I hoped the queen would prove a distraction to you…I was wrong."

"And then you fled to Kamshat." Ravin crossed his arms. "If I were anyone else, I would not have been able to trace you so far. But I am not, and I *can*." He leaned toward the bound Soulless with a sneer. "I don't believe you or the others truly understand what I'm capable of. Nor does your master."

Garin narrowed his eyes and attempted to draw away. "Dranamir told me of your unusual ancestry."

"Even she does not know the limits to my power." He chuckled darkly. "You'd do well to warn the others away from Delucha, Garin. They do not possess the same level of protection from the Nameless as you, and they are vulnerable."

Garin's ashen features paled further. "No one knows—"

"I can sense what he's done to you, Garin," Ravin replied. "I'm not a fool. Striking you would be a fatal mistake, and I'm not yet prepared to depart this world a second time. If you'd been one of the others, I would have killed you upon our first meeting in Stonewall Hall."

Ravin found it interesting that Garin had not told the others of his intimate connection with the Nameless, a connection that both protected him and would one day be his undoing. Ravin smirked; he wondered if Garin knew the true extent of the Nameless' grip on his being. If Garin was unaware, it certainly was not Ravin's place to inform him of the horrendous fate that awaited him. Garin deserved that inevitable moment of terrific surprise.

"I think your time in my realm has come to an end," Ravin stated coldly. "Give Dranamir my regards."

He ejected Garin forcefully from the Aethereum in the same manner he had when he'd found the small man savagely beating the boy. Garin cried out in a shriek of momentary agony as his body was thrust through the dense weaves of magic and into physical reality. Garin's expulsion would leave him physically injured, and with luck, Ravin would not encounter him again for some time. It was a shame he was unable to kill Garin and be done with the man, but his ties to the Nameless god were strong enough that even Ravin could not hope to contend with them and walk away unscathed.

Ravin moved toward the wall Garin had been studying when he'd ambushed the man. It appeared to be solid brick and unremarkable. Another puzzle, but one he could solve another day.

He returned to Delucha and exited the Aethereum into the queen's solar. She and Jasom were no longer present, but to his dismay, the Duchess of the Mers was. She visibly startled at his unexpected entrance, then quickly composed herself and offered him an alluring smile.

"Ravin," she trilled as she strode toward him. "The queen retired to her private quarters, I'm afraid. She asked that I inform you."

He groaned internally. Of course, she'd asked the duchess to relay her message. He forced a smile and watched with dismay as a flush rose into her fair cheeks.

"Thank you, my lady. I'll go to her now."

"Please, call me Adalin." She linked her arm through his and held tightly, even as he attempted to pull away. "I'll walk with you. My quarters are just down the hall from our dear queen's."

He ground his teeth and endured her presence. He was uncertain why she persisted when he'd rebuffed her advances time and again. He believed she was married, besides. What was her interest in him? The suspicious portion of his mind wondered if she'd been planted by the Soulless, but he quickly dismissed the idea. The duchess—Adalin, he reminded himself—did not possess the guile required to achieve that level of deception.

As they exited the solar, she reveled in the act of strolling arm-in-arm with the queen's newest advisor. She made small talk and laughed too loudly at his curt replies. Her actions ensured the attention of those they passed were riveted upon them. He glowered at her and managed tight smiles for the unwanted audience. If he were a lesser man, he would have harnessed his magic and disappeared into the Aethereum once more.

When they reached the upper levels of the palace and found themselves away from the onlookers, Ravin wrenched his arm free. "Why do you insist on this farce?"

She laughed. "Oh, Ravin, it was nothing but a bit of fun. It holds no meaning for me, but it causes the queen's court to wonder. It is harmless." She paused to eye him appraisingly. "With your exotic features and your magic, every woman in court has her sights set on you."

He frowned, uncertain if he ought to believe her claims. "I have no interest in romance. I have other, more important business to attend in this life."

Her expression became pained. "That is no way to live, Ravin. Life holds no meaning without love."

He shrugged and turned away. "I must speak with the queen."

"I'll not stop you," she replied, "but if you change your mind, you know where I'll be."

He refocused his thoughts on the matter at hand and left her in the corridor. The Soulless were seeking the talismans, and though he did not know why, he meant to stop their plans before they were realized. The queen must know something of her kingdom's relic. He would acquire it before the Soulless, but first, he would learn where his search might begin. The queen should have answers.

In spite of his brusque departure from the duchess and his desire to think upon other matters, her words continued to haunt him. If revenge was no way to live, what purpose did his second chance at life truly serve?

CHAPTER SEVEN

THE ALCHEMIST'S MESSAGE

Their march had led them deep into the mountainous region that spanned the border between Balotica and Delucha kingdoms, a trek that had taken its toll on their many wounded. The able-bodied were erecting their next camp as the horizon lightened toward dawn, but those assigned to assist in the transportation of the injured would continue to pour into the camp well into the morning. A smaller contingent of healthy soldiers trailed after the wounded, burning and razing the land in their wake. When his gaze drifted northward, Aran'daj could make out a dark mass that blotted out the stars, the acrid smoke a bold reminder to the Baloticans of the Murkor presence within their lands.

A cold breeze stirred the canvas panels of tents and swirled the tiny flames of the few campfires Aran'daj had permitted. The sky remained clear but he sensed a storm brewed just beyond the horizon. He silently prayed their wounded would reach camp before the weather turned foul.

It had been two nights since Aran'daj had signaled the retreat from Pine. He believed he'd made the right call, had resigned himself to his fate as the army withdrew, but he'd been astonished when Kama stopped the female Soulless from taking his life. The two Soulless appeared equal in power, but Kama had won what would prove the first of many battles, if Aran'daj was not mistaken. Kama's actions had spared his life, but he believed Kama would demand payment in return. It was a precarious position and made his work with Jal'den and the Kal all the more delicate.

"The army requires time to regroup." Kama's voice broke him from his reverie. He turned to offer the Soulless a half-bow.

"Yes, sir. There are many wounded. Some will not survive the journey here." Aran'daj managed to keep his tone emotionless and even, despite the pain his words inflicted on his heart. It was the truth but left a bitter aftertaste.

"Yes." Kama's gaze swept the camp, as though he sought answers where none existed. "I have spoken with your Matriarch and Kal. More soldiers will be brought to this location in the coming weeks. You are leagues from the nearest Balotican city, and this place appears defensible." He turned to study Aran'daj. "Remain here, Commander. I will enlist Alyra's aid to transport those with serious injuries home to your caverns."

Aran'daj nodded uneasily; it was another act of apparent benevolence uncharacteristic of the Soulless. He was certain terrible demands would be made of him for the "kindness" Kama showed, but the Kal had ordered him to act his part. He swallowed his misgivings and met Kama's fiery gaze.

"Thank you, sir."

"Do not thank me, Commander. I do what I must to ensure our next battle ends in victory." Kama chuckled darkly. "Continue to obey as you have thus far, and I will continue to protect you from Dranamir. But if you betray me…" He trailed off, the threat tangible as it hung in the cool air between them.

Aran'daj bobbed his head in acknowledgment. "I understand, sir."

"Good. See that it remains that way." Kama smiled icily. "There is one other matter we must speak of before I depart."

"Sir?"

"We will focus our next strike on the city of Daesan, some miles south of our present location. It is a Deluchan city and sits at the base of a mountain bearing the same name. A fire mountain, Commander."

Kama gauged his reaction with a callous gaze and Aran'daj forced himself to remain still. "I will ask the alchemists to prepare accordingly, sir. We will pray Flariel does not take offense to our presence."

Kama smirked. "The fire goddess has other matters to concern herself with, but it is best to be prepared for anything. I visited Daesan during the day. I don't believe you will encounter any resistance from the locals." He laughed hollowly. "The young queen has made an enemy of us, but she fails to see the consequences of her actions. She will pay."

"Of course, sir."

"I will acquire a new map to aid in your preparations." Kama turned his attention to the far side of the camp, where soldiers continued to march in. "I will return later. I expect you to remain here until I command otherwise—and if Dranamir appears, do all in your power to appease her. She seeks an excuse to spill your blood. Do not provide one."

Aran'daj watched as the Soulless strode a short distance away and created the pale, magical doorway that would lead him elsewhere—and more importantly, away from the camp. He understood enough about the nature of the magic to know the Soulless used it as a means of rapid transportation. He wished he could prevent the Soulless from appearing in the midst of the encampment when and where they wished, but at present, he was resigned to the fact they would do as they pleased. He must remain vigilant at all times.

He awakened from a light sleep in the late afternoon. The daylight filtering through the canvas of his tent had a cold, pale quality, and he believed his previous assessment would prove correct. A storm was building overhead. The air within his tent was cool as well, and a stiff breeze rattled the tent's taut sides.

He fumbled amongst his belongings as his hands sought the thick quilted cloak he'd acquired before their departure from the Wasted Land. The garment felt unfamiliar as he drew it about his shoulders. Cold weather protection was unnecessary in his homeland, but he was grateful for the warmth it provided now. He exited the tent and made his way to the nearest fire, where he spied Jal'den's tall frame, marked by the curved, black saber he carried at his hip and the steel broadsword slung across his back.

The Arms Master gazed intently into the dancing flames and did not look up at Aran'daj's approach. Aran'daj seated himself nearby while he relished the warmth of the fire. The temperature had dropped significantly since dawn. He drew the cloak more firmly around his shoulders, then stretched his calloused blue hands toward the flames while he awaited Jal'den's greeting. Jal'den continued to gaze into the fire, his hooded face shadowed, though Aran'daj could see the light reflect from his pale eyes.

Slowly, as though he awakened from a dream, Jal'den straightened and took in the sight of his commander huddled in his cloak nearby. "Commander? How long have you been here?" His tone indicated mild surprise.

"Not long."

"I was…" He glanced at the nearby tents, at the handful of soldiers as they began to go about their late afternoon routines. He dropped his voice to a bare whisper. "I was speaking with Sal'zar, Commander."

Aran'daj rose to his feet. "Walk with me, Arms Master."

They moved away from the fire and toward the outer perimeter of the camp. Sentries patrolled at intervals, cloaks thrown around their shoulders in an attempt to ward off the bitter wind. Aran'daj walked beyond the perimeter to a small grove of pines where their words would not be overheard. Aran'daj tugged at his hood as a sudden gust threatened to pull it from his head and muttered a curse at Maelstrom under his breath. The storm god was once again threatening to unleash havoc upon the Murkor army.

Jal'den gripped his hood fiercely and scowled at the darkening sky. Aran'daj noted the swirl of familial tattoos scrawled across the back of his midnight-blue hand; the silvery ink depicted the Jal family's insignia and the origin of the Arms Master's full name. Jal'den: dawn-born son.

"Are the storms always so gods-damned relentless on this side of mountains?" Jal'den growled. "Or does Maelstrom simply wish us to suffer?"

"I wish I had an answer, Jal'den. At times, it seems as though the gods have forsaken our people."

They fell silent while the wind whipped an eddy of dust and dried pine needles around them. Aran'daj gazed skyward; the clouds above were dense and gray, thick with Maelstrom's unspent fury. The night would prove cold and uncomfortable.

"How does Sal'zar fare?" he asked.

Jal'den lowered his gaze and shook his head, his shoulders slumped with defeat. "He survives, Commander, but the Soulless are harsh masters. They have not learned of his ability to communicate with me yet. He risks too much…"

Jal'den's voice broke with emotion. He took several moments to compose himself while Aran'daj stood silently by. His thoughts drifted to Rej'amin. If he'd been granted *ujar'havel* with his own chosen partner, he wasn't certain how he would maintain the pretense of normalcy if he'd been in Jal'den's position.

When Jal'den spoke again, his voice was gruff. "I must remember that Sal'zar is as strong as I am, in his own way."

"He is resilient, Jal'den."

Jal'den managed a brief nod. "He is, and he has learned much from the Soulless. Not only magic, Commander, but the workings of their order as well. We must send word to the Kal, but I fear making a second request of Kama."

Jal'den was right to be concerned. They could not risk rousing Kama's suspicions, and Jal'den could not continue to request traveling to the caverns to oversee the army's transfer of soldiers and resources. Aran'daj sighed, his frustration unmasked.

"I agree. You mentioned Sal'zar was working on a means to contact others. Perhaps if your news can wait for a time, he will learn to do so. It is unsafe for you to risk another return to the caverns." He frowned beneath his hood. "Kama informed me that he will be moving between the camp and our home several times in the coming days. I fear his proximity to you if you bear important news from the Kal."

"I understand." Jal'den was unable to hide the disappointment in his tone.

"Did he mention anything that might help the army, Jal'den?"

"Perhaps. It seems they take their orders from the small man, Commander. The one with the pale hair." Jal'den shrugged. "He does not appear here often, but perhaps knowing Kama has his own master is of help to you."

Aran'daj smiled; if the small man gave the orders, it meant Dranamir must also obey. Perhaps his previous conversation with Kama was not as threatening as it had seemed. His heart lifted with the first tenuous hope he'd dared nurture since the army's defeat at Pine.

"Thank you, Jal'den."

He turned away, intent upon returning to the camp and the warmth of a fire when Jal'den spoke again. "There is one other matter."

He peered over his shoulder at the Arms Master. "Yes?"

"The Soulless fear what will befall them in Delucha. Sal'zar stated they weren't concerned for *us*, Commander, only themselves."

This news was of great interest, and he now understood why Jal'den had desired to speak with the Kal directly. "When you speak with Sal'zar next, ask him to learn the origin of their fear—if it is safe for him to do so, of course."

Jal'den laughed, the hint of a smile in the sound. "Your concern is appreciated. I will ask him, though it is against my better judgment. I have no doubt he will comply, no matter the danger. You will have your answer soon enough."

CHAPTER EIGHT

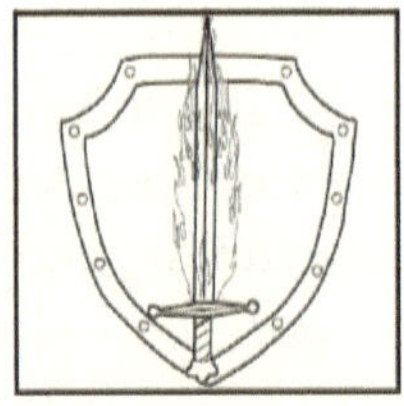

THE CALL

Emra sensed its presence long before it became visible on the horizon, a tall, black smudge that blotted out the evening stars. Her nerves screamed in wordless warning, shrieked that she ought to turn back, to flee. She shuddered and tried to ignore the blind fear her subconscious spewed forth like an erupting geyser. She recognized the dark mark against the northern horizon as the Tower of Obsidian well before the others remarked upon its presence.

Fyrmane whickered uneasily beside her, and she patted his flank absently. The war horse seemed aware of the abrupt change in her demeanor, though she strove to mask it. The fear was irrational, unwarranted. Vardak's plan to skirt the tower from a distance was solid, and there was little chance they would encounter any of its foul denizens. She repeated this to herself time and again, yet the unease would not abate.

Patak skittered to a stop alongside her and slowed to match her pace. "We'll come to the lip of the chasm soon. Luke mentioned you're not fond of heights."

She groaned. "Luke needs to keep his thoughts to himself."

He chuckled. "It's why I've come. I'll walk on this side of you, and perhaps it'll block some of the sight."

"They say it's bottomless." She shuddered again, an image of the chasm's sheer sides coming unbidden to her mind.

Patak shrugged beneath his heavy plate mail. "It's not, but I wouldn't recommend attempting a climb down. The walls are sheer but jagged and sharp. It's made of obsidian, like the tower."

She shook her head and looked away, troubled by his words. His description matched the image she'd seen in her mind. A wave of terror washed over her as she considered the implications. The sensation was akin to what she'd experienced outside Stonewall Hall, as though she'd been to the area previously. It was impossible. She'd grown up in Pine, traveled the length of Balotica during her years as a soldier and recruit, but she'd never crossed into the lands east of the Gray Mountains until recently. Her nerves continued to shriek their warning, contradicting her rational mind.

"Emra?"

Startled, she looked up to meet Patak's eyes. Concern wrinkled his brow, evident even in the darkness. She was struck again by the similarity between their two species; if she ignored the chitinous plates and scorpion body that comprised his lower half, she could almost think of him as human. An impossibly tall human, but a human all the same.

"I'm fine," she assured him and offered a strained smile. "This business with walking right past the tower has me on edge. That relic…" She trailed off and shrugged. Her excuses rang hollow to her own ears, and she was certain Patak would pick up on her evasion.

"That damned relic has my brother in a surly mood. I'll be glad to hand it over to the wizards and be done with it." He paused to study her. "Just between us, Vardak's too gods-damned serious. I suppose it suits our purposes well enough, but I miss the days when he'd smile on occasion. Since he returned with that relic, he hasn't been the same."

"I can't fault him," she replied. "The relic claimed the life of the woman he was sworn to protect, and from all accounts, she'd become a friend to him. Grief strikes us all in some manner, Patak. Perhaps this is how it manifests for him."

"Hmm." He turned to focus on the barren landscape ahead, unconvinced by her words. "Has he apologized to you, Emra? I've told him several times he ought to."

"He was merely following orders. I understand, and I can certainly relate."

They fell silent and her discomfort abruptly intensified. She clenched her free hand in response, and Fyrmane snorted as the hand that held his reins jerked unexpectedly. The sensation that she'd been to this barren, cracked wasteland previously threatened to overwhelm her senses. Her eyes found the black spot that marked the tower's location, as if drawn to it of their own accord, and a powerful wave of vertigo washed over her. She stumbled and nearly fell.

Patak was there in a flash. He offered his arm and peered at her with renewed concern. She heard Lucas shout her name from somewhere behind them, accompanied by rapid footfalls as he ran forward, his gray at his side.

"Are you certain you're well?" Patak asked as Lucas approached.

She nodded stubbornly. How could she tell this man what she experienced, without him thinking her in the grip of madness? Even Lucas would fail to believe her, and he was her oldest friend. The sensations did not make sense to her.

"I'm fine," she said again.

A look passed between the two men that indicated neither believed her.

"Why don't you mount up, Em?" Lucas suggested. "We can move some of the baggage to Dawnstar. He can handle the extra weight."

"No, Luke, I merely stumbled. It happens to the best of us on occasion."

Her tone was sharper than she'd intended, and she glowered at him in frustration. She would not be seen as weak in front of the Scorpion Men; she was a knight and had worked gods-damned hard to earn her title. She meant to prove her worth, and Lucas' suggestion—however well-meaning—would only cement her perceived frailty in their minds.

Lucas held up his hands in submission. "Suit yourself, Em. I'll head back to walk with Maryn where my head won't be nipped off."

"Luke, I'm sorry…"

He waved dismissively as he turned away to rejoin the Felene at the rear of their procession. She would speak with him later when both their tempers had cooled.

She sighed heavily and realized she still clung to Patak's arm. She dropped her hand to her side and hung her head, ashamed he'd witnessed her brief spat with Lucas.

"It's the tower, isn't it?" he asked her quietly. "It can affect people who draw near, sometimes."

She blinked and looked up at him, his dark blue eyes locked on hers. "I believed I'd imagined it."

"The Murkor claim the effects are strongest amongst people who use magic," he continued. "I have never traveled this far north myself, but I am decidedly uneasy. On edge, as though someone watches."

She nodded, though her own experience seemed more intense.

"The land surrounding the tower has seen too much death. The Murkor believe some of the spirits remain here, trapped, unable to find their way into Aeon's realm." He grimaced. "If it's true, it's a damned terrible fate."

"Yes."

"At the pace my brother has set, we'll be past the tower well before morning. Once we're away from it and the chasm, I'm certain you'll feel better." He chuckled wryly. "We *all* will."

His words proved true, at least in part. Once the tower was behind them and out of sight, Emra's sense of unease disappeared, but the unshakable certainty that she'd been there previously continued to nag at her thoughts. She remained edgy, unable to relax.

As dawn broke across the eastern sky, they made camp in the shadow of a pair of boulders. The enormous stones appeared out of place against the otherwise flat and dusty landscape. She was pleased Vardak had called a halt to their long march at that location; the boulders would provide shade during the blistering daylight hours. She was grateful for any respite from the sun, no matter how miniscule.

She apologized to Lucas a second time as they tended the horses. He laughed and shrugged away the tense moments from the previous evening, though it was clear something continued to trouble him. He stubbornly refused to admit anything was amiss, and after a time, she gave up. Perhaps it was her own guilt that tinged her perception of their exchange.

They shared a brief meal around a tiny fire before most turned in for a few hours' rest. Lucas sat beside her, and moments later, Patak joined them. The two seemed to have come to an unspoken accord, both intent on ensuring her welfare. She scowled at the campfire and pointedly ignored them. Perhaps if she made it clear she did not require their constant attention, one or both would cease their baseless worrying.

After a time, Lucas and Danness offered to take the first watch, and promised to awaken Vardak and Emra for the second. She retired to her cramped tent and kicked off her boots, though she remained fully clothed. She was restless and knew sleep would prove elusive.

She lay down to stare at the pinpricks of sunlight that seeped through the canvas above her head. She considered the strange mix of inexplicable sensations she'd experienced through the night and Patak's assertion that everyone became uneasy near the black tower. Unease, she could understand. The feeling that she'd been there previously, that she knew the area beyond her limited experience of the world frightened her. It was irrational. *Impossible.*

And the sensation had grown stronger after the tower was well behind them.

She shuddered despite the growing warmth of the morning and forced herself to relax. She closed her eyes, praying sleep would claim her.

"Ryan."

The whisper had sounded just above her head. Her eyes snapped open as a chill raced along her spine. She was alone. There was no one named Ryan amongst their party, yet… The name was familiar, somehow.

She grimaced and shook her head. She was either losing her mind or the residual foul energy from the tower continued to affect her. She prayed it was the latter. She swallowed and closed her eyes once more. Perhaps she was merely suffering from exhaustion. With sleep, a respite from the strangeness would come.

"Trillenon."

She squeezed her eyes shut. She would not acknowledge the papery voice that haunted her.

"Jessem. Arianna."

She gasped as the familiarity of the names coalesced into firm realization. The whispered names belonged to those written into the legends of the Great Wars. They were heroes, soldiers much like herself, chosen through a wicked twist of fate to bear the greatest of magical relics. The same soul, said to be cursed with rebirth, denied the peace of Aeon's realm. The legend stated the bearer would appear during times of great need when the Nameless god's threat was at its pinnacle.

She shivered and opened her eyes. The tent remained empty.

"Emra."

The whisper issued from the air inches from her face. The urge to bolt from her tent was strong, yet she forced herself into a semblance of normalcy. She sat up slowly and took the time to pull on her boots.

"Emra…"

The whisper sounded from the tent's flap. A sudden certainty came over her; the whisper wished for her to follow. She hesitated, while her skin prickled in response to the unseen energy. Slowly, she rose to her feet, compelled to obey the disembodied words. The crawling sensation beneath her skin ceased as she made the conscious decision to accept the strange summons.

She blinked in response, terrified yet peculiarly confident that the whisper meant her no harm. It spoke of destiny.

She stepped into the glare of the mid-morning sun. Lucas sat with Danness a short distance away. Their backs were to her as they chatted quietly. The others were within their respective tents, asleep and unaware of what she prepared to do.

"Emra."

The whisper led her in the opposite direction from the pair on watch. She glanced at them, briefly considered telling them of her intentions, then thought better of it. Lucas would think her unwell or mad. Perhaps she was, but she could not resist the voice's compulsion any longer. She must follow it, for good or ill. Its insistent call could not be ignored.

She left the camp, in thrall of the whispered summons. She was uncertain if she could have stopped her feet from following their current path if she'd tried. The sun beat down on her unprotected head, and sweat trickled from her brow. Her path led east across the arid landscape, and soon the boulders they'd made camp next to disappeared in the heat shimmer behind her.

"Emra."

The voice gained in strength as she traveled, transforming from a bare whisper to a conversational tone to a shout. A glimmer of metal caught her eye. She stumbled toward it as though her feet moved of their own accord. Inexplicably, she knew she must reach the object, that by placing her hands upon it the voice would cease its call, and the assault on her senses would come to a welcome end.

The glimmer resolved itself into the shape of a sword, half-buried in the ground. The hilt was plain, the guard unadorned. She knelt beside it, her hand hovering above the grip, yet she hesitated. She recognized the blade, though she'd never looked upon it before. The faint etching that traced its way along the blade twisted and swirled, an artist's representation of flames.

"EMRA."

The voice emanated from the sword. Cold dread gripped her heart as she gazed at the blade. She had been chosen, lifetimes ago. It was her blade and it sought her again. Hers was the soul denied to Aeon. Hers was the doomed soul, forced time and again to fight the Nameless god's followers.

Her hand grasped the hilt. Memories of love and loss, pain, grief, and wonder inundated her mind. They were hers, yet not hers. She screamed at the sky, the sword in her hand, as the assault continued. She must remember every detail from the past in order to combat the Soulless of the present.   Her knees buckled and she fell. Her head struck the hard-baked ground and pain swallowed her in its malefic embrace.

Memories faded to inky black as her conscious mind fled, the Fireblade clasped in her hand.

CHAPTER NINE

A FLY IN THE WEB

Mid-afternoon in the palace provided Ravin with the opportunity to enjoy a meal in relative solitude. He seated himself at a table near the hearth in the palace's lavishly furnished great hall and watched the bustle of servants as they prepared the space for the evening's meal. The queen made a point of entertaining her guests each night, keeping the staff in a state of perpetual industry. At times he envied them; their work was simple and straightforward, the interference of the nobility minimal on most days.

It was an unusual hour for someone of his apparent rank to be taking a meal, but it was what the day had afforded him. It was just as well; the noblewomen that continued to plague him were busy elsewhere and the queen's cadre of other advisors were likely closeted in their own studies. He required these moments alone, however brief, in order to align his thoughts. His latest encounter with Garin had given him plenty to consider.

He watched the servants as they moved from table to table, polishing each to a sheen. Others busied themselves on the room's perimeter, dusting the mantles, sweeping the floor, cleaning the windows that lined the wall nearest the entrance. His thoughts drifted to the matter of the talismans, a matter he'd discussed at length with the queen. She knew little of Delucha's, and nothing of its whereabouts. Instead, she directed him to the palace library and promptly found him other tasks to complete that she felt were of greater importance. He'd kept his frustration internalized. Her actions spoke of a naivete and selfishness that he knew should be addressed.

The talisman must be secured before another of the Soulless arrived in Delucha, hell-bent on taking the relic for themselves.

His attention was drawn to the hall's entrance as a pair of armored soldiers were ushered inside. He noted the blue and white livery the pair wore and the stylized snow leopard insignia that marked them as servants of Balotica kingdom. The pair strode on the heels of the portly chamberlain, whose bald head gleamed with sweat as he beckoned the soldiers to follow him. They traversed the length of the hall and proceeded toward the stairs.

Ravin sighed and stared at his plate of half-eaten food with regret. The chamberlain would be escorting the pair to the queen; it was inevitable that her advisors be summoned. He motioned to a nearby servant to clear his dishes, apologized to him for the inconvenience, and hurried to follow in the Baloticans' wake.

As he reached the solar, several noblewomen exited, the Duchess of the Mers amongst them. She flashed a smile in his direction, which he ignored. Moments later, the chamberlain scurried into the hall and beamed as he spied Ravin.

"The queen requires her advisors to attend her," he said breathlessly. "I'm pleased you're here, Ravin. Saves me the trouble of tracking you down."

Ravin chuckled. "I'll see what this is about, Dasnin. I'm certain the others will be in their studies."

"No doubt. At times I wish you were so easy to locate, but I suppose given your role, a study may not be prudent." Dasnin shrugged and tottered away to follow the same path as the duchess and her minions.

Ravin entered the solar to find the young queen perched on her favorite cushioned divan. The Baloticans stood a respectful distance away and spoke quietly amongst themselves. As Ravin neared, he could see the stain of dust and weather upon their garments, though it seemed their armor had been recently polished. One was a wiry man with strawberry-blond hair that cascaded over his forehead to fall across his pale blue eyes. The other was a woman, though her hair was cut shorter than her companion's. Her features were angular and severe, marred by an angry red scar on her left side that pinched and puckered the skin. Her eyes were a stormy gray that leveled an unspoken challenge in Ravin's direction when their gazes met.

The queen beckoned him impatiently, but waited until he knelt in front of her before she spoke in a quiet whisper. "Balotica has been attacked, Ravin. I am glad Dasnin found you so quickly. From what little they've said, it was no mere border dispute."

"The Soulless?" he asked.

She shook her head. "Perhaps you will be able to piece together their story better than I once the others arrive. They mentioned hooded ones. I'm not certain who they refer to."

"I am."

The solar door opened to admit Jadosin Corless, a man some years older than Ravin who sported the toned physique of one used to long hours in the sparring ring. Jadosin was the queen's general and advisor on military affairs. Moments later, he was followed by Dasnin and a willowy woman with pinched features and a mane of snowy hair. She was Malira Orenduss, advisor on foreign policy and relations between kingdoms. The trio knelt before the queen alongside Ravin and awaited her cue to rise.

The queen rose from her perch and indicated the advisors follow suit. Ravin took his assigned position on the queen's right next to Malira while introductions were made. The Baloticans, Cora and Daniel, had come with another soldier who had chosen to remain behind to tend their horses in the palace stables.

"We were dispatched here by order of our king, Brennan Silvermane, to request aid for our people," Cora stated. Her voice was even and carried well in the space, though her eyes darted between the queen and her advisors rapidly, an unspoken sign of her nerves.

"Repeat what you told me previously," the queen replied. "My advisors must hear for themselves what has befallen your lands."

Ravin listened intently as Cora related the devastation of Jennavere, a thriving port city with a considerable population. When she began to speak of the hooded ones and their uncertainty about who or what they were, Ravin held up a hand for silence.

"They call themselves Murkor. They live in the Wasted Land, beneath the shadow of the black tower."

Cora nodded briskly while several of the Deluchans gasped. "We suspected as much, sir. They left no survivors, but we found evidence that prisoners were likely taken. The knight in our party was sent across the mountains to appeal to the Scorpion Men for aid. We have received no further word from her since she departed."

She said more, but Ravin's attention was wrenched away from the proceedings by a mental cacophony only he could hear. One of his Aethereal wards had been triggered, and the trespasser ensnared. He closed his eyes briefly to study the sensations that emanated from his invisible trap. Each careful step he'd taken had worked flawlessly; the trespasser was not only ensnared, but cut from the source of their power and rendered senseless. They would remain in that state until Ravin was afforded an opportunity to investigate further. He refocused his attention upon the discussion at hand, no longer concerned by the intrusion.

"I advise against leaving our own border undefended, Your Majesty," Jadosin stated. "I will send an order to several northern outposts, and those men can be dispatched to Balotica. It isn't as much aid as you hoped for," he said to Cora, "but you must realize that we, too, share a border with the Wasted Land."

"Any aid is of value," Cora replied stiffly.

"We must prepare our own defenses as well," Jadosin continued, his focus once more upon the queen.

"I will draft a formal request for alliance with both Balotica and Santine," Malira added. "The Santinians must be warned of this threat if they have not been advised already."

"Dasnin, please ensure you reallocate the necessary funds," the queen said. "This matter must take precedence over all else. And Ravin, continue to ensure the palace is defended and assist Jadosin where you can. With the black tower involved, your expertise is required."

Ravin made a half-bow in response. He would inform her of the trespasser once the others were gone.

It was nearly an hour later that the queen dismissed them to go about their individual tasks. Ravin lingered, and she peered at him expectantly.

"I know something has happened, Ravin." She paused to adjust her skirts. "You were silent for a time while the Baloticans were speaking. Tell me." Her tone indicated she would abide no deception and no delay.

"Someone has stumbled upon one of my traps. I thought you should know before I investigate further."

Her green eyes narrowed, and she rose to her feet to begin pacing. "Is it one of them? One of the Soulless?"

"I cannot be certain until I enter the Aethereum to learn more. If it is not one of the Soulless, it is one of their followers. The traps are harmless to those who do not bear the Nameless' taint." His frown deepened. "I suspect this has to do with the talisman."

Her mouth tightened. "The timing cannot be coincidence. I trust you are right."

"As we discussed, I prepared a cell in the dungeons some time ago," he continued slowly. "No matter who happens to be caught in my web, I intend to drag answers from them. I request your permission to utilize the cell."

"It is shielded, I believe you said?" she asked. She paused to arch an eyebrow in his direction, though her expression remained enigmatic otherwise.

He nodded. "Even the Soulless will be rendered helpless within. I have taken every precaution, Your Majesty, and given the news from Balotica…"

"Yes, yes, I don't require a second reminder." She waved a hand dismissively. "Do what you deem best, Ravin. We can use this prisoner to our advantage."

"Of course."

He forced himself to await her dismissal, but it did not immediately come.

"Ravin, I have one further request."

"Yes?"

"If it is one of the Soulless, I would very much like to question them myself." She stopped pacing and faced him, her hands on her hips. "The Soulless will know who is responsible for Jasom's unfortunate role in my life. I want the monster who controlled his mind to pay for the damage they've inflicted."

He nodded uneasily. "If that is your wish…"

He cursed himself for his inability to foresee her newest demand. He should have accounted for it; she and Jasom had become rather close of late, despite the horrors that had brought them together. Her desire for revenge was unsurprising, but he'd failed to anticipate this turn of events. He prayed she would see reason enough to allow him to keep his prisoner until *he* deemed their usefulness at an end. A premature execution was a lost opportunity for information they desperately needed.

"It is, Ravin," she replied firmly. "You may go."

He entered the Aethereum directly from her solar, and made his way to the ward that still jangled its mental alarms through his skull. It was located within the palace kitchens. In the Aethereum, the usual bustle of staff was absent, the hearths were empty of flame, and the aromas of cooked food did not waft through the air. Instead, Ravin found the counters bare, the air odorless, and his surroundings thick with silence.

Near the stair that would lead to the wine cellars below, a stout man stood rigid, frozen in place. His features were indistinct, a clear sign he was Soulless. He was momentarily disappointed that his trap had failed to spring upon Dranamir, but perhaps this man would provide him with the details he sought.

The man remained unconscious, but Ravin would take no unnecessary risks with this prisoner. He ensured the man was cut from the source of his power and secured invisible bonds around both his wrists and ankles. In one hand, the man clutched a star-shaped box, an Aethereal relic, if Ravin was not mistaken. He plucked it from the man's grasp and slid it into his pocket. He would inspect the relic later, once the immediate danger had been dealt with. Only then did Ravin dare to touch his prisoner. Physical contact was necessary in order to transport him to the prepared location.

He willed them to the corridor outside the cell. In the Aethereum, it was awash with light, but the cell appeared as a blank, opaque space, inaccessible to those in the magical realm. Ravin opened a portal and stepped into darkness while he drew the prisoner through in his wake. He'd placed torches in the wall sconces on his previous visit, and he lit them with a flick of his wrist.

He maneuvered the prisoner into the prepared cell and shuddered as an angry buzzing sensation settled into the base of his skull. Within the sealed space, he was cut from his magic, just as the Soulless was. He ground his teeth and set to work, securing wide iron shackles about the man's wrists and ankles. Each shackle was connected to a thick chain, which in turn was bolted firmly to the stone wall.

Once finished, he scurried from the cell to lock and bar the door behind him. The buzzing subsided once he stepped outside the sealed space, and he reveled as his power washed through him. To be severed from it, even for a short time, was an immense discomfort.

He studied the man slumped in the cell. It was the first time he'd been afforded the opportunity to examine one of the Soulless while in the physical realm, and his gut twisted in revulsion at the sight. The Nameless god's touch had corrupted his very being; the man's skin was gray-green with what appeared to be decay, his dark hair was thin and oily, while the patchy beard he sported bristled and curled in turns.

This man had not undergone the same level of corruption as Garin, and he wondered what the smaller man must look like in the flesh. He'd only seen Garin hooded, and knew his eyes glowed a malevolent crimson, but nothing more. This man was not as strong in the Ability as Garin; it was a potential boon to Ravin's plans.

The man began to stir, then to struggle as he took in his surroundings. Ravin noted with distaste that this man's eyes shone with the same bloody light Garin's did, and he thanked the gods anew that he had escaped the same fate.

"Release me." The man thrashed against his chains. "Release me, gods-damn you!"

"I will not." Ravin crossed his arms and peered through the bars of the cell. "I warned Garin not to intrude in my realm and what the consequences would be if *any* of your kind failed to heed my words."

The man spat. "Garin has been abed the past two days. He is weak."

Ravin smirked, pleased to receive confirmation that his forceful ejection of the tiny man had served its purpose. "He eluded my traps. You did not."

"You're a smug bastard. Release me!"

Ravin chuckled. "No. Make yourself comfortable. When I return, you'll wish you'd never set foot in the Aethereum."

Ravin strode away to a litany of curses, all of which he ignored. When he came to the end of the cell block and the jailer on duty, he informed the man of their newest acquisition.

"He's dangerous. Do not open the cell under any circumstance. He may be given food and water, but send it through the slot." He stared hard at the man to impart the significance of his next words. "The prisoner is one of the Soulless. *Do not open his door.*"

CHAPTER TEN

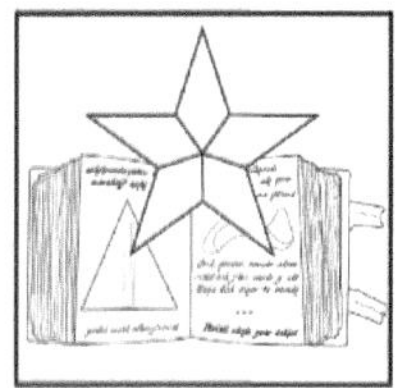

THE COUNCIL'S PLANS

Tavesin slumped in his chair, his eyes fixed on the dais at the center of the Council Chamber. It was empty, as were many of the seats in the vast, ovoid chamber. Hasnin had insisted they arrive early for the meeting the Radiant had called, which left his apprentice with little to do. His friends, Rostin and Badolo, were still on the upper floors of the tower, immersed in their own magical lessons.

Hasnin was at the chamber's entrance, in deep discussion with a pair of Sect Masters and Aziarah. He was certain they discussed him, the turn his studies had taken of late, and his involvement with both Arra and the Soulless. He'd told them everything about his forays into the Aethereum after his final meeting with Arra, everything except his encounter with the golden-eyed man. His instincts warned him divulging that secret would end badly for them both, though he wasn't certain why that would be. If his time in the Shining Tower had taught him anything of use, it was that he must trust his instincts when it came to matters of magic.

He crossed his arms and sank lower in his seat. He was exhausted. He wished the wizards had afforded him the opportunity to skip the latest meeting of the Council, but orders had been sent to every denizen of the tower and every wizard beyond its bounds. All who were able must attend.

He closed his eyes and feigned sleep while his mind continued to work. He'd thrown himself into his studies more fervently after his last encounter with Arra, determined to keep his promise to her. His mornings were spent in history lessons with the Whites, followed by an hour's respite at midday. He'd begun taking portable snacks from the kitchen and eschewing the company of his friends in favor of further research in the tower's library. His afternoons were spent in the company of Grays and Blues; both Sects had taken a keen interest in his potential.

He continued to learn new ways to manipulate his shielding ability. He could now place his impervious barriers around others, and he'd learned to concentrate the shield's energy into a single point of focus, which allowed him to strike out—his greatest defense had also become a powerful weapon. He did not inform the wizards of his newfound skills, though the Drakkon allowed him to practice when he arrived on the tower's roof each evening.

He allowed himself only minimal rest and the breakneck pace of his routine was beginning to take its toll. It had been five days since Arra had made contact, but it felt a lifetime ago. He would risk his life, his sanity, his future role within the Council of Auras, if it meant delivering her from the Soulless' grasp.

He must have dozed without realizing it. A hand fell on his shoulder and caused him to jump in his seat. His reaction elicited a peal of youthful laughter from the row behind him; he knew the source well before he twisted in his seat to meet their grins. Rostin's hand remained on his shoulder, and mischief glimmered in his dark eyes. Badolo snickered as he leapt nimbly over the chair beside Tavesin and slid into its seat. He was two years younger than the others, but it did not stop him from poking fun at Tavesin whenever he was provided the opportunity.

"You were snoring, Taven," Badolo informed him.

"I wasn't—"

"You *were*," Rostin confirmed. "We thought it best to wake you before too many wizards caught you napping." He grinned and shot a knowing look in Badolo's direction.

"You skipped lunch again, too." Badolo folded his arms and attempted to adopt a superior air. The effect failed, and the three broke into another peal of laughter.

Rostin plopped into the seat on Tavesin's other side. "Since you're always busy with important wizards and such, we thought you might have some idea what this meeting will be about."

Tavesin shook his head. "Not this time."

It wasn't long before most seats in the vast chamber were filled. Tavesin spied the group of Drakkon on the opposite side of the room; they eschewed seats and stood together near the rear wall, though he noted Aziarah was not amongst them. As their leader, he supposed she would join the Radiant and the five Sect Masters on the dais once the proceedings began.

Several minutes later, the Sect Masters appeared in the doorways that ringed the room. Collectively, the assembled wizards and their apprentices rose to their feet as the quintet walked along the aisles toward the dais. Each Sect Master was garbed in the color of their Sect, with ceremonial cloaks bearing the five-pointed star insignia of the council embroidered upon the back. As each took their place on the dais, the Radiant and Aziarah began their descent through the bowl-shaped room. The Radiant wore white, in honor of his former Sect, while his cloak was a swirl of all five colors. Aziarah wore her customary leather armor and seemed unperturbed by the curious glances she received from the humans she passed. She towered over the Radiant; he was not a tall man, but the Drakkon were considerably taller than most of their human counterparts.

"Finally," Rostin muttered.

Tavesin nodded his silent agreement, eager to learn why the meeting had been called.

The Radiant gestured for the audience to be seated. He paused for several seconds while the room quieted from the sudden shuffling of hundreds of feet before he began to speak.

"We have received dire news from Balotica," he began. His voice was magically enhanced to carry over the audience; even those in the far reaches of the room could hear his words clearly. "It seems several cities have been attacked. Many have been killed, and many others are missing. It is the council's opinion that the attacks were orchestrated by the Soulless."

A barrage of questions peppered the stage as wizards from all Sects voiced their concerns. Tavesin listened closely, though much of the discussion did not immediately interest him. There was talk of "hooded ones" and a monster in a lake, but nothing that indicated the use of magic had been involved in the Balotican attacks.

"We fully intend to support the Baloticans' request for aid," the Radiant added after a time. "Blues, Greens, and Grays will be dispatched in the morning. Those who remain here will be asked to redouble our efforts to efficiently train the apprentices. We require every trained wizard available to combat this threat—and that includes our younger members."

Tavesin heard Rostin's surprised intake of breath as another volley of questions began. "Did he—?"

"Yes!" Rostin hissed in excitement, cutting him off. "Taven, we're all going to be wizards!"

"—require the challenge," the Radiant replied to someone's question. "We will not raise any apprentice who is not fully prepared. The challenge will ensure they are. What we ask is that non-essential lessons be set aside in favor of those that will develop magical ability."

Badolo wriggled in his seat. "I believe that means no more history lessons," he whispered with a grin.

"Good." Tavesin smiled to himself; the council had finally decided to follow Aziarah's advice. Perhaps he would no longer be forced to train exclusively with the Drakkon when he wished to try some of his newfound abilities and the wizards would begin to take him seriously.

"What Sect will you test for?" Rostin whispered eagerly.

"I don't know," Badolo replied. "I've considered Yellow…"

"Blue," Tavesin replied without hesitation. He'd already proven his shielding techniques effective against the Drakkon, and he believed himself suited to the role of defender.

Rostin blinked. "You're decisive today. I think I'll test for Gray."

Tavesin nodded. He understood the choices of his friends. Rostin had a propensity toward the flashy, offensive magics, and he'd excelled in the few lessons where they'd been allowed to attempt such skills. He feared Rostin's zeal would land him both on the front lines of the coming war and in the care of the Greens. He prayed he would be proven wrong. Badolo's leaning toward Yellow was equally expected; Badolo enjoyed tinkering and would do well with the creation and study of relics.

Tavesin's attention was drawn to the dais upon the Radiant's next words. "Another apprentice went missing from the tower last night.

Given what the Drakkon magi detected in the boy's quarters, we believe he was abducted in much the same manner Arra Shannin was."

Tavesin's blood ran cold. In spite of the golden-eyed man's threats, at least one of the Soulless had been brazen enough to enter the Aethereum and snatch both Arra and this boy. The wizards were helpless against their threat; Tavesin and Arra were the only two gifted with Aethereal magic. Even the Drakkon could not prevent such incursions. They lacked the numbers to effectively monitor the magical realm. Only the golden-eyed stranger seemed capable, but he'd warned Tavesin he could not always be present to watch over the place. The Soulless possessed the power to roam as they pleased.

"Have we located either of them?" someone behind Tavesin called, her voice strident and brimming with frustration.

The Radiant looked down at his hands and closed his eyes briefly. "We know for a certainty that Arra has been taken to the black tower. She lives, but we cannot manage a rescue at this time."

Tavesin clenched his jaw. "I *will* save her," he muttered darkly. "The Soulless will regret taking her."

"Easy, Taven," Rostin whispered in a warning tone.

He glowered at the dais. "They can do nothing, Rostin, and they know it. Even the Drakkon are limited… I promised Arra I'd find a way to save her."

"That's why you've chosen Blue," Badolo stated as understanding washed over him.

Tavesin nodded. "I'm no fighter, but I will do all I can to protect my friends. I will prove to the wizards I'm capable. I will become a Blue."

CHAPTER ELEVEN

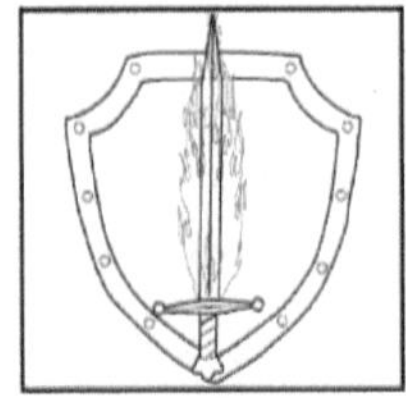

BIRTHRIGHT

Awash in a tide of unrelenting memory, the soul now calling itself Emra observed as each lifetime, each rebirth, each painful death played out before its eyes. It was helpless against the onslaught, made to watch and recall details that would undoubtedly assist in the present war.

The soul began as Camrah Varastehk, a woman born with the Ability for magic and an affinity for the crafting of relics. Camrah was taken from her native Kamshat at a young age to train in the newly constructed Shining Tower, leagues upon leagues away in Dar Daelad. The land still toiled to rebuild itself from the ages-long Time of Chaos; devastation and poverty were rampant. Her training with the wizards was exciting—and a boon to her struggling family.

During her time in the tower, Camrah learned the origin of the Time of Chaos and became convinced the Nameless god was not finished with his quest for power and destruction. It mattered not that he was both stripped of name and imprisoned by the other Immortals; the Nameless was undying, eternal. He had the luxury of time, millennia in which to orchestrate his eventual release.

Camrah seized the opportunity to ensure the world was granted a protector when the Nameless began his inevitable rumblings, deep within the earth. She crafted a relic of immense power and bound it to her soul, a weapon worthy of striking fear into the Nameless god's dark heart. When she finished her work, Aeon himself approached her. The Underworld's guardian deity admonished her for subverting him but indicated he understood her desire. He would ensure her soul would return when the world's peril was at its pinnacle.

Camrah had believed, naively, that Aeon's words meant she would be reborn a single time. She lived out her twilight years in Damaro, the capital city of Kamshat, and passed the Fireblade, as it had become known, to the royal family for safe keeping. Her soul would return to claim it years later.

The soul was reborn as Jessem Makertuk, the son of a tanner. As a child, he was unaware of his previous life. He grew up in Dar Daelad and was sixteen when the city fell under siege by the first Soulless' army. He was drafted hastily, as many young men were, and tasked with the city's defense. He bore witness to one of the greatest magical battles in recorded history while atop the wall one day; Morganus the White fought the first Soulless for countless hours, and their duel raged well into the night. Deadly magic issued from both parties as the armies from both sides looked on. The energies dwindled and fell silent in the early hours of the following morning. When the sun rose, it was not clear who the victor had been. Both Morganus and the Soulless lay dead.

The army retreated, but the Nameless was not yet finished with his schemes. He raised a second Soulless to power while Dar Daelad broke its siege protocol and life returned to a semblance of normalcy for Jessem. During the siege, something had begun to call him, an inexplicable urge that haunted his waking thoughts. He must travel west. His dreams swam with visions of a sword rimmed with fire. He left Dar Daelad one week after the siege ended and found himself in the heart of Kamshat some weeks later.

The Fireblade had been placed in the public courtyard beyond the royal palace's broad gates. The king himself had demanded it be made accessible to Camrah's long-dead soul though a contingent of guards surrounded the relic at all times. The king must be certain the soul who claimed the blade was indeed its proper owner.

Jessem's call carried him to the courtyard and into a line of hopefuls that sought a glimpse of the famed sword. When Jessem arrived at the front of the line, his hand touched its hilt reverently, and the blade responded by igniting. He fell to his knees as Camrah's memories flooded his skull.

When he awakened hours later, he found himself in a lavish guest room within the palace, tucked securely into a feather bed. The

Fireblade rested on the mattress beside him, and he understood his newfound role. He was the sword's bearer, the rebirth of Camrah's soul.

He led an army from Kamshat weeks later. More soldiers joined his ranks as he pressed eastward toward Delucha, which remained under the Soulless' thrall. It was his duty to battle the Soulless and end the Nameless god's threat. The war came to an end when the second Soulless was slain by his hand.

Jessem returned to Dar Daelad a hero and later married into the royal family of Masmoone. The Fireblade remained in the possession of that family long after Jessem drew his last breath. The Makertuks remained a fixture in the Masmoone nobility for generations, and his sons made certain their father's legacy lived on. The Five Kingdoms believed the Nameless beaten, and the Fireblade found itself housed within the royal treasury, where it gathered dust for centuries.

The Nameless was not finished, and neither was the soul's work. Its promise to Aeon would endure for eternity, or until the Nameless was defeated and made powerless.

The soul returned as Ryan Whitehall, the son of a Balotican soldier. Ryan was trained at arms from a young age and excelled in his martial training. When he was twenty-one, he set on the path to knighthood when rumors of war came to Balotica. At the same time, he began to suffer nightmares in which he fought and killed scores of hooded foes, a blade of fire grasped firmly in his hand. He attempted to shrug off the dreams, but they persisted, growing more vivid and violent as the days passed.

Seeking relief, he made his way to the nearest wizard and told them of his nightly terrors. Without hesitation, the wizard informed him he must travel to Dar Daelad. Ryan left the next day with the wizard as his guide. Two weeks later, they stood in the castle nestled on Dar Daelad's southern flank, the Fireblade once more clutched in his hand.

For the second time, the soul found itself embattled against the Soulless, and once more, the Soulless fell to its sword. Ryan did not fare as well as his predecessor, however. In striking the deathblow upon the Soulless' head, he was struck by a powerful blast of magical energy that, in turn, ended his own life.

The Fireblade disappeared from the histories with Ryan Whitehall's death, only to be located again centuries later as the cycle repeated. The soul was known as Trillenon A'ven in that age, a Santinian merchant's guard who later came to be regarded as one of the greatest heroes in legend. Trillenon's battle with that era's Soulless was described as equal to Morganus' fateful battle with the first Soulless, long ago.

The soul that wielded Fireblade found the comparison amusing. His battle was pale in comparison to the great Morganus'.

Trillenon became an adventurer and treasure seeker of sorts after the war's end. He found himself enchanted by the notion of Stonewall Hall and the hoard of magical relics it was said to contain. He formed an expedition with the foolish belief the Fireblade would protect him from Stonewall Hall's Undead. It did not, and he met his end in its twisted depths.

When the soul was next reborn, it was as Arianna Janis. Unlike her predecessors, Arianna's memories had not been erased. Dreams and nightmares played through her mind from a young age as she relived her past lives through the darkest hours of the night. When she grew old enough to travel from her home in southern Masmoone, she unerringly found her way into the heart of Vidune Forest, where she met Coreyaless. Coreyaless reluctantly agreed to guide her to the entrance of Stonewall Hall, though the Airess doubted many of her claims.

Only when Arianna emerged from the mountain with the Fireblade in hand did Coreyaless begin to believe. By that time, war had claimed much of Delucha, the Shining Tower was compromised, and Arianna felt she alone was capable of driving the Soulless out of the Five Kingdoms. Her army was written into legend, and she became the only bearer of Fireblade to defeat the Soulless without the aid of the wizards.

After the Soulless was slain and the armies of both sides began to retreat, Arianna remained in the far reaches of the Wasted Land. The histories could only speculate as to her fate.

The soul now known as Emra knew the truth. Arianna had attempted to break the cycle of rebirth in order to seek eternal peace. So many lifetimes of blood and death sickened the soul. Arianna believed the destruction of Fireblade would provide the relief she sought, but Aeon intervened. Fireblade was preserved, Arianna's life was forfeit, and the soul was thrown into another unwanted cycle of birth and death.

Pale light filtered through the tent when Emra opened her eyes. She understood what she was, what she had been through the countless march of centuries. Her hand gripped Fireblade's hilt, and she sensed its presence in her mind. Fireblade was her curse, her birthright, her responsibility.

A rustle near the tent's flap drew her attention. Patak sat studying her, his legs tucked beneath his scorpion's body. "You're awake."

She nodded and sat up, wincing as her muscles protested the action. "How long was I unconscious?"

"Two days." His blue eyes found their way to the sword in her hand. "Coreyaless recognized your blade. Or rather, the blade you found."

Emra met his gaze. "It is my blade, Patak."

"Then you're...?" He shook his head in disbelief. "Fucking gods! First my damned brother is chosen by Blademon, then this business with the relic, and now...Shit." He chuckled uneasily. "You're Fireblade's bearer."

She released the blade and crossed her arms. "I'm still *me*, Patak. I have several lifetimes of other memories crammed into my skull now, but I'm no different than I was when we met."

His eyebrows rose, and she immediately wished she could rescind her previous words. She liked Patak and certainly did not want him to fear her. If he reacted in this manner to her newfound role, how would Lucas take the news? He was her oldest friend. She did not wish to see him distance himself when she needed him the most.

"You remember...*everything?*" Patak managed. His face paled as he shook his head.

"Yes." She couldn't backtrack now.

Suddenly he broke into a grin. "Em, this is the greatest news we could have received. Do you know what this means?"

She smiled in spite of herself. His enthusiasm was contagious, and she rather liked his use of her nickname. "Tell me."

"Gods, it means we have a real chance to win this damned war! Vardak said all of the Soulless have returned, but with you here…" He glanced through the gap in the tent flap. "I ought to tell the others you're awake. They'll be pissed that I've kept the news to myself for this long."

He rose and darted outside before she formed a reply. She lifted Fireblade into her lap and gazed at the familiar weapon. It was the same size and weight as her standard sword, but if she applied her power to it, flames would spring to life along the blade's cutting edges. For a weapon of legend, the hilt was decidedly plain; only the fine etching along the blade indicated its true purpose. This relic had been a constant in each of her lives, and once again, it had returned to her.

So much of her past began to make sense as she gazed at the weapon. The sensation outside of Stonewall Hall that told her she'd been there before, her unerring sense of direction, the familiarity she'd sensed upon meeting Coreyaless in the Stronghold, her "gift" with combat skills… It was no mere coincidence. She'd been to Stonewall Hall twice. Her navigational ability was a byproduct of her magic. She'd met and befriended the Airess previously. She'd known little beyond combat for most of her past lives, and the training she'd received as Ryan Whitehall seemed to have bled through into her current iteration.

She looked up as footsteps approached. Lucas ducked into the tent, followed by Patak and Coreyaless. Lucas knelt at her side, though he did not touch her. She was keenly aware of his hesitation, and the reality twisted in her gut like a knife. Things would never be the same between them again.

Coreyaless knelt at her other side and began checking her pulse and temperature. Her hands were cool, her demeanor self-assured. After a moment, she rocked back on her heels to study Emra, while the two men watched silently.

"How do you feel, Emra?"

"Overwhelmed, but physically I'm well enough." She managed a faint smile. "It isn't the first time I've been inundated with past memories, Coreyaless. We spoke of this once before, as I recall."

Coreyaless nodded. "We did. It's unsettling to know you again… I never learned Arianna's fate, though Joshan sought to uncover the truth surrounding her—your—disappearance."

Emra looked down. "I tried to break the cycle. Aeon wouldn't allow it."

"Em, are you…I can't… What…?" Lucas stammered.

She turned to face him and felt her heart plummet. His eyes darted wildly and his face had become ashen. A fine sheen of sweat beaded upon his brow. She had no choice but to tell him the truth and hoped a brief, blunt statement would set him at ease. He clearly struggled to comprehend the enormity of what had occurred.

"Luke, this is Fireblade. I am its wielder."

He nodded stiffly in response, then rose swiftly and bolted from the tent. The sound of him retching followed moments later.

"Gods-damn it," she swore, defeated. "Why—"

"It's a difficult notion to accept," Coreyaless replied in a soothing tone. "Lucas will come around, given time. He's mentioned you grew up together, that he thinks of you as a sister. That you have been through numerous other lives is not something easily digested. Few souls are granted an exception from Aeon's realm."

"I suppose I once asked for it," Emra replied dryly. "I'd love nothing more than to end this cycle. My soul is weary of bloodshed."

"Understandably so." Coreyaless studied her for a time. "Do you require anything?"

Emra shook her head, then said, "I *am* hungry."

"I'll bring you something to eat. Don't worry about Lucas, Emra. I'll speak with him." She rose and was gone, leaving Emra alone with an uncharacteristically silent Patak.

"Please tell me you won't bolt from sight and join Luke," she said.

He moved to seat himself at her side. "No. Vardak and I grew up listening to the legends of Fireblade and its wielders. When we learned the Soulless had returned, I was certain the relic would make an appearance. It always has. This time should be no different."

"You're remarkably calm, Patak."

He chuckled. "When Vardak and Maryn found you and brought you back to camp, none of us understood why you'd left or what had happened. Coreyaless took one look at that blade and knew. Out of all of us, she was the only one who wasn't concerned over your health. Luke and I took turns sitting with you while you slept."

"It wasn't sleep, so much as it was reliving my memories."

"If the legends are true, then you remember…ah…" Patak's face flushed, and he looked away.

"What?"

"Ah, well…Luke and I spoke last evening about…your past," he stammered. "If the legends are true, then there were times you…were a man…" His blush deepened.

A laugh erupted from her throat, unbidden. "Yes, Patak. But I can assure you I am very much a woman in this life." Her smile faltered as she realized the full implication of his words. "Is that why Luke reacted as he did to the news?"

Patak nodded uneasily. "Accepting your past lives is one matter, but for him, accepting that you haven't always been…well, *you*, is another entirely."

She rolled her eyes. "Gods, he's always been such a prude when it comes to certain things. I'll speak with him—if he'll allow it."

He shrugged. "If you need to talk with anyone, I'll always be available, Em. I can't imagine this is easy for you."

She smiled. "Thank you. It's not as difficult as you might believe, Patak. I have dealt with this circumstance several times before, and Luke will come around eventually."

She hoped she was right; she didn't want to lose him from her life.

"Vardak will want to talk with you once you're feeling up to it," Patak added. "He would have come in with the rest of us, but Coreyaless wouldn't allow it." He snickered. "Vardak may be intimidating to some, but he certainly can't seem to win an argument against the Airess."

She nodded. "Fireblade—my birthright—has changed everything… When we reach Dar Daelad, I'll have much to discuss with the wizards."

CHAPTER TWELVE

MURKOR PRISONERS

Vardak watched as Lucas sprinted from Emra's tent and proceeded to vomit a short distance away. He remained hunched over for several moments, spat, then wiped his mouth on his sleeve. It was all the confirmation Vardak required to know what had transpired within the tent. Lucas hadn't accepted the notion that his life-long friend might be Fireblade's wielder and had spent most of the previous morning in vehement denial of Coreyaless' claims. The Airess had recognized the blade immediately, and Vardak believed she spoke the truth.

Lucas stood shakily and glanced through the camp. When his dark eyes met Vardak's, his face flushed with shame. He muttered darkly to himself and stalked away to tend the horses.

When Coreyaless exited the tent, she went about gathering a few items from her herb satchels and some morsels of food, remnants of their noonday meal. Danness left his post to speak with her, but Vardak was too far away to overhear their words. Beside him, Maryn shifted uncomfortably while his feline ears twitched in agitation.

"She's the one, isn't she?"

Vardak glanced at Lucas a final time before he answered. "It seems so."

"Luke hasn't taken the news well." Maryn snickered. "Patak owes me two silvers."

"The pair of you were betting—?"

"We had to do something to pass the time." Maryn flashed a grin, his green eyes mischievous. "While you were busy scowling at the landscape, we placed a few bets."

Vardak shook his head, amused in spite of himself. "Gods. I knew the two of you would become friends, but I didn't believe you'd spur each other on like this."

"Luke *also* owes me two silvers," Maryn added, undeterred.

"You're unstoppable," Vardak laughed. "You've taken coin from Patak every day since we left the Stronghold. At this rate, he'll be begging *me* to fund his poor decisions soon."

"Your brother is not as clever as he believes himself to be, and I plan to secure enough coin to buy a dagger or two during our journey. I'd like a few souvenirs to remember this strange land of yours." He shrugged. "Patak will learn eventually it's not wise to bet against a Felene."

Vardak snorted. "I doubt it."

He knew his elder brother well enough to foresee Patak giving his last coin to Maryn after a series of misplaced bets. Patak was ever the optimist, and Maryn had taken advantage of the fact.

"Do you plan to move on this evening if Emra is well enough?" Maryn asked after a moment.

"Perhaps. I'd like to speak with her first."

Coreyaless had warned them numerous times during the past two days that when Emra awoke, she may not act the same and would likely remain fatigued for some time. He would not push her to travel until she had recovered from her ordeal.

Patak emerged from her tent then and beckoned to him.

"It looks to me like you'll get your chance now," Maryn said. "I'll keep the watch."

He nodded once to Maryn and made his way to where Patak stood. His brother offered him a knowing grin. "She wants to speak with you privately. I suspect I know what it's about—" he glanced toward Maryn with a mischievous glint in his eye, "—and I expect to win back my coin."

"Gods, Patak—"

Patak cut him off with a laugh. "Go on. You shouldn't keep her waiting. I think you'll find Emra is less prickly than she was a few days ago."

Vardak raised his eyebrows in silent question.

Patak gestured impatiently toward the tent flap. "Go, Vardak. You'll learn for yourself."

The shaded interior of the tent was a welcome respite from the afternoon heat. Emra was seated cross-legged near one side with Fireblade resting across her knees. Her gray eyes scrutinized him as he entered and settled himself near the exit.

The color had returned to her fair complexion, he noted. It was a welcome change from the pale, drawn look she'd sported when they found her collapsed on the ground. Her blond hair was somewhat disheveled, and tendrils hung limply around her face where they'd escaped the confines of her long braid. She did not smile, but he sensed her former hostility toward him had lessened. Her expression remained even, revealing nothing of her thoughts.

"I've never been one to mince words, Vardak, and I won't do so now. I have a proposition for you."

"I'm listening."

She lifted the sword by its hilt and held it upright between them. He blinked and drew back inadvertently as small flames erupted from its cutting edges. He needed no further confirmation of what she truly was or what she might be capable of.

She smiled ruefully as the flames extinguished and she placed the sword across her knees once more. "In every lifetime, I find myself at the head of an army, but I've never had the mind for tactics. I have relied on others for advice. Janasu was perhaps the greatest, but he was no pupil of Blademon." Her eyes met his. "We do not command an army yet, but we will. I wish for you to take up the role of general, Vardak."

He stared at her for several moments as he contemplated her words. He'd anticipated she would speak of their need to finish his business with the Murkor and move on to Dar Daelad with as much haste as they could muster. He had not expected to be offered a prestigious position as leader of a non-existent army. He did not doubt her words; they would build one. It made sense that she would select her general before too many joined her ranks—there would be less in-fighting and posturing to quash if the soldiers knew immediately who they would take orders from.

He was honored by her trust but feared many would resent his position given his youth. That he wasn't human might also play a significant factor for some.

"You're certain?" he asked.

She nodded. "Patak said you'd be hesitant, so please listen to my reasoning. I understand that you are only twenty-four and some may discredit you based upon your age alone. But *none* of those others can claim to have trained with Blademon, nor can they boast the gift he imparted to you."

Vardak glowered at the tent flap, though Patak was outside and blocked from sight by the canvas. "Patak needs to keep his damned mouth shut."

"Don't worry, Vardak. Your secret is safe with me. If I learn he's spoken of it to anyone outside of our current group, I will deal with him personally. As will you, I'm certain."

"Yes."

"As I stated, you are uniquely qualified for this post. I will understand if you refuse, but I sincerely hope you won't."

"I'm not the only one Blademon has trained." He looked down as the words escaped his lips, uncertain how Emra would handle the news.

"I suspected as much," she replied evenly.

He looked up sharply. "Then you know from the past…?"

"The god of war doesn't always deign to teach warriors prior to a conflict with the Soulless, but this is not the first such instance he has done so." She shrugged. "There are always two—and one always finds their way into the enemy's camp. I'm certain you will face the other in the future. It is inevitable. However," she added with a pointed look, "this is the first time I am aware of that he has imparted great knowledge to one of his pupils."

"He did it as though it were an afterthought." Vardak sighed and ran one hand through his short blond hair. "I believed it was only done to guide us to the Moon's Eye."

"If he has given you an advantage over the other, we must seize it, Vardak. I want you to act as my general."

"I have never been the one to give orders, only follow them," he replied, still hesitant to accept. "I cannot promise you anything but my knowledge and my blade."

"And that is enough," she countered. "I have known many soldiers, and few are suited to become leaders. I see in you more than Blademon's gift. You would do well in the role."

Though she appeared to be only thirty-five, he reminded himself that she now had the experience from multiple other lifetimes to guide her reasoning. With the exception of Blademon himself, Emra knew more about armies and warfare than any other living being. And she wielded Fireblade.

He sighed again. "I trust your judgment. I will accept."

She grinned. "As I hoped you would. Now, we must see to freeing your people from the Murkor."

Patak was proven right in his assessment of Emra as the hours drew on and they began to break camp. She no longer seemed to fault Vardak for withholding information upon their initial meeting, and she showed a self-assurance and determination that had been absent before she uncovered Fireblade. At times she spoke of events that Vardak assumed must have occurred in the distant past, and with each revelation Lucas appeared more uncomfortable. He said little to her, though she'd made multiple attempts to speak with him after she emerged from her tent.

They departed as evening descended over the Wasted Land. Vardak took up a post at the rear of their group alongside the two Airess, while Maryn and Lucas walked a few paces ahead. Beyond them, Emra and Patak took the lead. He could hear snippets of their conversation as it carried on the faint breeze, punctuated by Patak's occasional laughter. Of everyone present, he'd been the most accepting of Emra's new role, and Vardak began to suspect his brother's interest in Emra went beyond mere friendship.

He sighed aloud. Patak had a long history with many different women, and it came as no surprise that his brother would attempt to strike up a relationship with Emra. The trouble was, she was human. Such cross-species forays were taboo amongst his people. His brother walked a dangerous line, but in classic Patak fashion, he appeared unconcerned.

"Is something amiss, Vardak?" Coreyaless asked.

He shrugged, unwilling to discuss the matter with the Airess. "I have too much on my mind."

"I suppose you do."

She resumed her conversation with Danness and he tuned them out, lost in his own thoughts. Emra's request was no longer forefront in his mind; instead, he mulled over what he must say to the Murkor once they arrived at the Underground Caverns. They would reach the Murkor homeland shortly after midnight, and his time to formulate a plan to free Travin and the others was rapidly waning. He firmly believed in his ability to convince the Murkor to release their prisoners peacefully, but the proper words continued to elude him. He'd been trained in battle, not diplomacy, after all.

A sliver of moon hung in the sky above, framed by a wreath of wispy cloud. It was well beyond its zenith by the time the group reached the rocky outskirts of the Murkor lands. A vast plateau was visible against the backdrop of stars, though it was too dark to discern the details of the landscape. Vardak had been to the caverns a few times before; he knew the entrance was within the rockface they approached. They gathered at a point that he was certain would not be visible to any Murkor guarding the cavern's gaping mouth.

Vardak clenched his jaw. He still had not formed a feasible plan, but knew this would be his only opportunity to secure Travin's freedom. Patak seemed to sense his mood and drew him aside.

"We'll both speak with them," he said. "You cannot expect to do everything yourself, Vardak."

"I'm still not certain how to go about this," Vardak admitted. He looked away, unable to meet his brother's eyes. "I've gone over dozens of scenarios, and nothing my mind has conjured seems remotely plausible. I don't know what to do."

Patak clapped him roughly on the shoulder. "I've had some time to think things over myself, you know. I have something of a plan."

He wanted to believe Patak, but he knew his brother well enough to be skeptical of his scheme. "Patak—"

"Trust me, Vardak. I ran this by Emra, and she thinks it has merit. Just follow my lead for once, and we'll see Travin freed."

Vardak released an uneasy sigh. If Emra believed Patak's plan might work, he was willing to do as his brother asked. "What is your plan?"

"You and I will approach the caverns with Danness. The others will stay here." Patak glanced toward Emra, who was speaking with Lucas not far away. "Emra believes it's best if the Murkor are unaware we travel with humans, and I agree. She does not want them to learn of Fireblade, either—or the relic you carry."

Vardak nodded in understanding. "I'll leave it with Coreyaless while we're inside. But why should Danness accompany us? He does not know our people."

Patak chuckled. "I knew you'd ask that question, little brother. Emra made a very good point regarding the Airess earlier this evening. The Murkor do not know them, but they *will* recognize Armistral's likeness in them."

"Of course."

Vardak smiled faintly, impressed. It was a brilliant ploy, one he wished he'd thought of himself. Approaching the Murkor in the company of an Airess would not only draw their attention, but it should serve to put the Murkor at ease. Armistral, the patron of the Airess race, was the god of peace and reconciliation. Danness' presence would send an unspoken message that they did not wish to fight and were there only to negotiate.

"She's remarkable," Patak said wistfully, his gaze locked on Emra though she appeared unaware of his attention.

"Patak…" Vardak wasn't certain how to voice his concern, nor if he should. Patak had always followed his own path, and he believed his words would fall on deaf ears.

Patak sighed and shook his head. "I know what you're thinking, Vardak, and you're right. It's gods-damned foolish that I feel this way about her. Even if she felt the same, it's forbidden. I'd risk exile, or worse."

"And we know very little about her, besides," Vardak reminded him.

Patak snorted. "I'd rather have this conversation with Travin. I understand your concern when it comes to our people's laws, Vardak, but you've no experience with women. Perhaps if you hadn't been taken by Blademon—twice—you might have by now. But the truth is, you don't."

Vardak scowled and crossed his arms. "Fine. Suit yourself."

It was typical of Patak to dismiss his views in favor of Travin's, but his brother's words still stung. Blademon had chosen him, and he could not have refused the god's attention even if he'd wanted to. Patak knew it and chose to use it against him.

Patak winced. "Gods, Vardak, I'm sorry. I shouldn't have—"

Vardak cut him off with his stoniest expression. "We'll discuss this later, *after* we're finished with the Murkor."

He moved away, his back to Patak even as his brother spluttered for another apology behind him. He was angry but would set his frustrations aside in order to focus on their objective. He hoped Patak would do the same. They had but one chance to free their brother and the other prisoners, and he wasn't about to waste it due to a needless spat.

A few minutes later, Vardak found himself approaching the dark entrance to the Underground Caverns alongside Danness and his brother. Since Patak had devised the plan they were to follow, Vardak remained silent when the Murkor guards called out to them. They spoke in the fluid and musical tongue of their people, a language that both Scorpion Men had been taught from a young age. Danness was unfamiliar with it, but his presence was merely for effect; he would not be required to communicate directly with the Murkor.

"We have come on behalf of Warleader Sevic, but we do not wish to fight," Patak called back. "We seek an audience with your Matriarch."

Vardak could not make out the Murkor until they were nearly standing upon them. There were four at the cavern's mouth, each clad in dark leather and ring mail, black hoods drawn over their faces. He knew the Murkor could see them easily enough in the darkness, and would not provide them with light unless they deemed it safe to do so.

"The Matriarch may not wish to see you," one of the Murkor replied. "Our people are at war."

Patak gestured toward Danness. "We come in peace. My Airess friend is testament to that."

Vardak was silently impressed with his brother's ability to seemingly charm the Murkor, and wondered idly if it was an extension of the same charm he'd used on countless women through the years. Regardless of its source, Patak possessed a way with words that Vardak himself lacked. He was grateful his brother had taken the lead despite their recent argument and busied himself with translating their words to Danness.

One of the Murkor gestured briskly while another disappeared into the gloom of the tunnel beyond. "He will send word to the Kal. The Kal will decide if you may speak with the Matriarch. You will wait here."

It was the expected response. Even during peacetime, the Murkor did not allow visitors into the caverns without express permission.

"It will take them some time to reach the Kal," Vardak informed Danness. He kept his voice low, with the hope the Murkor guards would not overhear.

"I don't fully understand the hierarchy," Danness whispered. "We asked to speak to the Matriarch, and they counter with the Kal...?"

"The Matriarch is their leader. She upholds the law and oversees their governance. The Kal is her chosen *ujar'havel*—life partner, I suppose you might call it," Patak replied with a shrug. "The term doesn't translate fully into the common tongue. The Kal is the spiritual leader but also oversees the work of the Murkor alchemists."

"In times of conflict, the Matriarch and the Kal often make decisions jointly," Vardak added, "but they tend to leave matters of warfare to their appointed commander."

Patak snorted. "Leave it to my brother to fixate on battle strategy."

Vardak glowered but made no response. He would not allow Patak to goad him into another argument.

Sensing he'd overstepped his bounds again, Patak sighed. "Gods, Vardak, I wasn't trying to poke fun at you. Perhaps you're right and I need to keep my damned mouth shut."

Vardak frowned but managed a terse nod. "All I ask is that you focus. Once Travin and the others are free, jest all you like."

Patak grinned wickedly. "You said it, little brother."

Another half-hour passed before word came to the cavern entrance that the Kal had agreed to speak with them. The soldier that bore the news held a pale, milky crystal that emitted a faint light. Its illumination was dim, but enough for Vardak and the others to see by. The soldier beckoned for the trio to follow him deeper into the mouth of the cave.

Stalactites hung from the ceiling, some large enough that the Scorpion Men were forced to duck beneath them. The cave formed a cylindrical tunnel that descended beneath the barren lands above and wound on a gentle slope toward a vast ovoid cavern.

Vardak had traveled into the first chamber on a previous trip; it was a marketplace of sorts, and he'd come with a contingent of their people to barter for Murkor goods. The journey had taken place more than a year before Blademon's first incursion into his life, when relations between their two peoples had been amicable.

The Kal met them at the base of the long ramp flanked by a half dozen red-hooded Murkor, the Kal's personal guards. It quickly became clear they would not be permitted to travel further into the caverns, but would conduct their business there. The bustle of the marketplace beyond was merely a backdrop, one they would not have the opportunity to partake in. He drew a breath to steady himself and prayed that Patak's inherent charm would win over the Kal.

Kal Aran'jandah wore a hood of shimmering copper, and a thick gold chain hung from his neck. He wore garments of soft leather, designed for comfort, and a curved black saber was sheathed at his hip. Vardak knew the Kal was aged and had never trained at arms; the saber was merely a symbol of his station.

"I believe I understand the nature of your visit," the Kal stated, "and I am pleased by your fortuitous timing."

Patak's eyebrows rose, and he glanced toward Vardak uncertainly. For all his talk of preparation, the Kal's words had taken him by surprise.

"We've come to negotiate the release of our people," Vardak replied.

The Kal nodded. "It is as I suspected." He glanced at the guards surrounding them, then motioned briskly. "I will speak with our visitors alone."

It was Vardak's turn to look questioningly at his brother. It was unheard of for the Kal to eschew his personal protectors in the presence of strangers. Patak merely shrugged as they waited for the Kal to speak. The guardsmen strode away but stopped to observe the proceedings once they were beyond earshot, while the Kal remained silent for several more moments.

"My people do not wish for this war," he informed them in the common tongue, "but we have little choice in the matter. The commander sought to keep your people as our prisoners in order to spare their lives. The Soulless wished them dead."

Vardak clenched his jaw as his stomach roiled with the news. If not for the Murkor commander, Travin would be lost to them. He owed the man a debt, though he doubted he would be afforded the opportunity to repay him properly. They were at war, the Murkor their enemies.

"The Soulless' army is beyond the mountains," Patak replied evenly. "Their attention is drawn elsewhere."

The Kal chuckled. "I am aware of their actions, and we have enough venom to last us years, if need be. Your people are of no further use to us. I will send the guardsmen to escort them here."

"You'll release them?" Patak asked, incredulous. "I expected something of a fight…"

"We have lost too much blood already," the Kal replied, "and I would not spill more in the presence of Armistral's kin. As you stated yourself, the Soulless are preoccupied. If the prisoners disappear into the night, they will be none the wiser. Your people may return home, and my people will continue upon their current path."

"And what path is that?" Vardak asked quietly. He was certain there was a deeper meaning behind the Kal's words.

The copper hood turned to fix him in the Kal's shadowed gaze. "It is the only path that will see the Murkor truly freed. Perhaps you understand. Perhaps not."

Vardak nodded, certain the Kal was working against the Soulless in some small way. Their peoples had been made enemies, but the Kal might prove something of an ally if his supposition was correct.

The Kal motioned for the guardsmen to return, then briskly issued his orders to them in the Murkor tongue. They did not question him. Each saluted in turn, and four disappeared into the busy marketplace. The remaining pair stood alongside the Kal, their midnight blue hands resting easily on the hilts of their sheathed weapons.

"It will take some minutes to retrieve them," the Kal stated. "We will await them here."

Vardak forced himself to remain still while they waited, though Patak began to pace, unable to contain his anxiety. Danness appeared to be lost in thought, his dark eyes fixed upon the marketplace and the array of colored hoods that wandered through the various vendor stalls.

When the red-hooded guardsmen reappeared at the far end of the cavern, the other Murkor near their location fell silent and ceased their dealings to watch the procession. Two dozen Scorpion Men marched in their wake, blindfolded, their hands bound roughly behind them. Each prisoner's stinger was encased in a triangular glass jar affixed to their scorpion's tail with several layers of thick rope. Most wore nothing but the blindfolds that covered their eyes, though the Murkor had allowed the three women to cover themselves with thin robes. The armor and weapons they'd borne during the skirmish were nowhere to be seen.

Vardak scanned the line of prisoners and relief flooded through him as he spied Travin's shorter, yet muscular frame near the rear of the procession. Beyond the indignity of the blindfold and the alchemists' venom jar, his brother appeared to have been treated well. None of the prisoners sported any recent injuries, and those that had been received during the skirmish looked as though they'd been tended to.

"Remove the blindfolds," the Kal ordered. While the guards worked to comply, he addressed Patak and Vardak. "We will unbind their arms and remove the venom collectors once they have been taken outside. I must ensure the safety of my people. I cannot trust your people to act peaceably, given the treatment they have received."

A few of the prisoners grumbled and snarled at the guards, but they did not attempt to break their bonds. Most appeared weary and thankful to see two of their own present to negotiate with the Kal. Vardak recognized many of the faces, but his focus was drawn to Travin. His brother smiled as their eyes met, his expression one of knowing gratitude.

A quarter-hour later, they stood beneath the vast expanse of the night sky while the Murkor unbound the prisoners' wrists and removed the glass apparatus from their stingers. The Murkor worked in silence and retreated into the caverns once their task was complete. Travin pushed past the others as soon as he was freed and wrapped Vardak in a fierce embrace.

Patak crossed his arms and feigned hurt. "I knew you favored Vardak."

Travin laughed and turned his attention to their elder brother. When they stepped apart, he said, "Pouting doesn't suit you, Patak. I am grateful to you both. We all are," he added with a glance toward the others.

"Sevic was reluctant to allow us to come here," Patak replied. To Vardak's relief, he spoke in a low tone that only he and Travin could hear.

"You cannot fault him, Patak. Sevic only does what he believes is best for our people." Travin sighed and ran one hand through his raven-dark hair. "Nevertheless, seeing your ugly face tonight was the best thing we've encountered in weeks." He smirked at Patak, who laughed half-heartedly.

"Vardak was the reason Sevic finally relented," Patak replied. "Well, Vardak and the humans."

Travin frowned. "Humans? Are they looking to free their people as well?"

"What?" Patak asked at the same time Vardak said, "There are human prisoners here?"

Travin looked between them, his expression worried. "The Murkor have hundreds of human captives in the depths of the caverns. Most are made to work the water wheels or sent into the mine shafts."

"Fucking gods, Emra will be livid." Patak shook his head helplessly. "We didn't know, Trav."

"Perhaps we introduce everyone and allow Emra to make a decision regarding her people," Danness said quietly from behind them.

Vardak startled; he'd forgotten the Airess was present. "Yes. That's likely the best course of action." He beckoned for Travin and the other prisoners to follow as they made their way toward the rocky outcropping where they'd left Emra, Coreyaless, Lucas, and Maryn.

He wasn't certain the Murkor would welcome them a second time, and doubted they would allow the humans entry without a proper escort. He would assist Emra if she decided to attempt further negotiations with the Kal, but he held little hope the humans would be freed. The Kal had allowed the Scorpion Men's release only because it aligned with his own mysterious goals.

CHAPTER THIRTEEN

THE QUEEN'S COMMAND

Ravin winced as the pounding on his door repeated for the second time. It wasn't yet dawn. He'd been with the queen and Jasom until past midnight in another futile attempt to train Her Majesty in the ways of magic, he'd managed perhaps two hours of sleep, and he was irritable. The urge to strike at the unwary perpetrator that had undoubtedly been sent by the queen was strong. He grimaced and sat up in the tangle of his bedsheets.

"Give me a gods-damned moment!" he bellowed angrily.

The pounding mercifully ceased as he slipped from his bed. The clothing he'd worn the night before lay in a crumpled heap beside the wardrobe. It was wrinkled and smelled of the wine Adalin had spilled on his trousers as she'd regaled him with a story he no longer recalled. She had a habit of becoming animated while she spoke, and with a goblet in hand, she proved a messy dinner companion.

He ignored the soiled clothing and pulled open the wardrobe in search of something suitable to wear. Though the cabinet was filled to bursting with garments, many were simply not to his taste and he refused to wear them. The queen preferred her retainers in velvet and embroidered satin, a show of opulence he was loath to partake in. He located a pair of plain black trousers and a simple white shirt with laces at the collar.

He dressed quickly and paused to gaze at his reflection in the mirror before making his way to the door. Purplish smudges were visible beneath his golden eyes, a blight across his otherwise blemish-free bronze skin and a clear indicator of his exhaustion. His dark hair was mussed and had grown a bit longer than he'd prefer, and he was in need of a shave. He ran his hands through his hair in an effort to tame its curls, but the effort was wasted. The queen might reprimand him for his lackluster appearance, but it was she who had awakened him after too little sleep, and he was in no temper to argue with her. His appearance would suffice.

He pulled open the door to the corridor to find one of the palace's many pages fidgeting outside his room. The boy could have been no more than ten, and he was clearly nervous at having been sent to fetch Ravin. It was no secret amongst the servants that he was the queen's advisor and a powerful mage, as well. He supposed his status must seem intimidating to the boy.

He summoned a wellspring of patience that he did not feel and resigned himself to the situation. "I apologize for my earlier words to you. What does Her Majesty need of me at this early hour?"

The page peered at him uncertainly for a moment before making his reply. "I wasn't sent by the queen, sir. The jailer sent me. He said it's important you meet with him, sir."

Ravin frowned. The jailer wouldn't summon him unless something had gone awry with their Soulless prisoner. The notion soured his stomach.

"Thank you," he told the page as he strode past. His mind was already engaged, seeking solutions to the myriad problems the Soulless prisoner may have created. The page was promptly forgotten.

Ravin encountered few others as he made his way toward the staircase that descended toward the palace's holding cells and the dungeon below. A handful of servants were about, but it was too early for most. The quiet corridors and vacant rooms were reminiscent of the palace he recognized from the Aethereum, at odds with the bustle of activity that would ensue within a few hours' time.

When he arrived in the jailer's cramped quarters at the base of the stairs, he found a trio of royal guards barring his passage. His previous concern transformed itself into bitter anger; the jailer had summoned him not due to the prisoner's actions, but the queen's.

The jailer peered from behind the three, his face pale and lined with worry. "Let him through, men. Let him through."

A single torch illuminated the room; its light cast flickering shadows throughout. Ravin noted a sheen of sweat on the jailer's brow, and the right side of his face twitched periodically as the guards complied. The man was nervous, and with good reason. Ravin had explicitly ordered him to allow no one—not even the queen—into the dungeons without his express consent. The Soulless prisoner was dangerous even when cut from the source of his magic.

Ravin fixed the man in a fierce glare. "Where is she?"

"I'm sorry, sir. She's the queen…I cannot deny her."

Ravin closed his eyes briefly in order to rein in his temper. "My orders were for *her* safety, beyond all others. I will not ask you again. *Where is she?*"

"She went into the dungeons, sir." The jailer stared at his feet, unable to meet Ravin's eye as he shifted uncomfortably.

"You're a gods-damned fool and as incompetent as they come."

Without waiting for a reply, he spun around and pushed past the guards a second time. One attempted to block his passage, but Ravin was in no temper for the man's naïve show of loyalty to his monarch. He seized his power and pinned the guard against the wall. The man's face drained of color while his eyes widened in surprise.

"Your queen is in greater danger than any of you lackwits seem to realize," Ravin snarled. "Do not stand in my way."

He strode into the narrow corridor and did not release the guard from his invisible bonds until he was beyond their line of sight. His path was lit by a few strategically spaced torches, and the inhabitants of each cell were clearly visible. The jail was at half capacity; the occupied cells harbored criminals awaiting judgment for crimes that ranged from theft to murder. Most of the prisoners were soundly asleep, though a few peered at him with interest as he passed. A few of the jailer's men were making their rounds, and they nodded to him warily. He ignored inmates and guards alike as he made his way to the stone steps leading to the dungeon below.

A second guarded checkpoint awaited him at the base of the steps, and it was there he caught up with the queen and her escort. Unlike the jailer, the man tasked to oversee the more dangerous prisoners housed in the dungeon had blocked her passage. She was furious with his denial, her jaw set and eyes hard. There were three royal guardsmen with her, but there were five men with the dungeon master. Ravin stepped between the two parties swiftly once he arrived, fearing if he did not, the queen would order her men to attack the others. It would prove a senseless battle, one that must be prevented.

He made a half-bow to the queen, whose eyes narrowed with suspicion at his sudden appearance. "Your Majesty, as I've warned you previously, the prisoners housed on this level are extremely dangerous. The man in the customized cell in particular."

She waved one hand at her guards. "I did not come here unescorted, Ravin."

"Yet you put yourself and them at risk." He crossed his arms, done with the pretense of niceties. "The Soulless prisoner is not a man to be trifled with, even cut from the source of his power as he is. You should not have come here without me. It was irresponsible."

She straightened at his words, incensed, and rose to her full height. Even so, she did not reach the level of his shoulders.

"Do not overstep your position, *advisor*," she hissed.

"Then stop being a damned fool and heed my advice." He frowned down at her, unyielding. "If you walk down that hall without someone who understands the magic in place around that cell, you risk becoming entangled in it yourself. I guarantee the Soulless will not hesitate to pounce upon such an opportunity. He may be unable to use his magic, and he may be shackled to the wall, but he can still inflict damage if he desires it. If you insist on this shortsighted adventure, then at least have the sense to allow me to accompany you."

Her green eyes were like chips of ice. "Very well. We'll discuss your behavior later, Ravin."

He ignored her implied threat; he would level some of his own once they were in private. She might believe she was in control, but he would remind her that without his magic, the Soulless currently chained in the dungeon would have free reign of the palace. She would see reason, or he would leave her service—and take his magical precautions along with him.

He nodded to the dungeon's guards who immediately stepped aside to allow them passage. When he glanced at the queen, she motioned for him to take the lead.

"I want this prisoner to answer my questions, Ravin." Her tone was clipped with anger, but Ravin had anticipated her ire.

"And what questions might those be?" he asked over his shoulder. He suspected he knew what she would say and was not disappointed.

"I need to know what the Soulless plan. I must know why they seek the talismans. If he refuses to speak on his own, you are capable of…forcing him. That is true, isn't it, Ravin?"

He swallowed his unease as her words once again reminded him of Dranamir. Perhaps his influence would divert her from following a similar path, provided she did not send him packing due to insubordination.

"Your guards are capable of inflicting as much pain on the man as I am," Ravin replied.

She laughed coldly. "I did not request this of *them*, Ravin. I asked it of you."

He ground his teeth in frustration. She tested his loyalty and his resolve, but the prisoner *was* Soulless, and likely deserved far worse than Ravin would unleash upon him. "If that is your command…"

"It is. He will answer my questions truthfully, or he will suffer the consequences. Do not hold back in your dealings with him, Ravin, or you'll regret it as well."

Ravin kept his focus on the path ahead and considered his options. She could do little to harm him that he could not magic himself out of, but her words served to remind him of his purpose in Delucha. He planned to use his position as advisor to gain the resources necessary to oppose the Soulless—and Dranamir. Without his post, it would take far longer to carry out his plans. He grimaced; he had no choice but to comply with her wishes, no matter how distasteful they proved to be.

The Soulless crouched at the rear of his cell, his malevolent, crimson eyes locked upon Ravin as they approached. He made no move to rise. His expression twisted into a sneer as he took in Ravin's companions.

The queen stepped alongside Ravin and peered into the cell, though she wisely kept her distance from its bars. "Who are you?" she demanded.

He ignored her question and smirked at Ravin. "I see your royal pet doesn't know me. A shame, since it was I who sent the pretty blond boy to her bed."

The color drained from her face as she whirled to face her guards. "Leave us," she ordered, her tone strained with the effort required to control her anger.

"Your Majesty, I advise against—" one began.

Her hand lashed toward him faster than he was able to react. The sound of her palm striking his face echoed in the stone corridor, and he blinked at her in stunned silence.

"Leave us," she repeated.

A dangerous light had entered her green eyes, and Ravin prepared to intervene on the guardsman's behalf. He would not allow her to harm them, no matter the threats she'd leveled at him moments before. He seized his power as a precaution, felt the magic suffuse his being while its seductive song whispered to him. He had the power to level the palace if he desired, but there was no reason yet to do so.

To his relief, the guards bowed to their queen and backed away. She whirled around in a flurry of velvet and lace and glared at their prisoner. Ravin maintained his hold on the magic flowing through him; the queen's actions left him decidedly uneasy.

"You are responsible for the mind-control," she said.

The prisoner leered up at her. "I would have taken you for myself, but what fun would that have been? I'd rather live vicariously through someone younger and more attractive, someone even a queen would be unable to resist. I'd say he served his purpose quite well. As I recall, you rather enjoyed his affections. Or shall I say, *my* affections?"

"Kill him, Ravin."

"If you wish to learn what the Soulless plan, I advise he remains alive. He cannot provide the information you seek from beyond the grave," Ravin replied.

Her fists clenched and unclenched at her sides, and Ravin began to wonder if she meant to slap him as she had the guardsman. He made a mental note to ask the dungeon's keeper to post additional sentries along the corridor to ensure that no one entered without Ravin's consent a second time. He did not believe the queen would resort to murder, but the ice in her gaze gave him pause.

"Very well. You will live," she informed the prisoner, "but you will answer my questions. If you do not, Ravin will inflict pain of a magnitude you cannot imagine."

The Soulless eyed them warily, his gaze lingering on Ravin. "I know of you. Garin informed us of your return, and Dranamir nearly took his fucking head."

Ravin arched an eyebrow at the admission. He was surprised Garin had told the others, and if Dranamir had challenged him, she was unaware of the full bond Garin shared with their overlord. Interesting.

"You will censor your language," the queen ordered.

The Soulless smirked and shook his head. "As you wish. What tale shall I regale you with this fine day, my lady?" He mocked.

"Who are you?" she demanded.

"Ah, an easy question to start. The history books refer to me as The Butcher."

She motioned impatiently to Ravin, her intent clear. He frowned, but resigned himself to the role of royal torturer for the day. As Ravin's magic inflamed the man's pain receptors, he began to writhe in his chains.

She bent toward the bars, a sadistic light in her eyes. "Your name."

Ravin swallowed his growing anxiety as he realized she enjoyed watching the man's pain. Even though he was Soulless, he'd anticipated she would have little stomach for the aftermath of her orders. He'd been wrong and was troubled once more by the notion that she shared distinct characteristics with Dranamir.

"Jannyn," he hissed.

"Good. That wasn't difficult, was it?" She waved her hand at Ravin, and he ceased his assault.

Jannyn slumped against the wall of his cell, his breaths coming in ragged gasps. "The others will come for me."

Ravin snorted. "The others likely don't know where you've gone, and based on my history with three of your number, I doubt they'll waste their time searching."

"Why were you in Delucha?" the queen pressed.

Jannyn glanced at Ravin before forming his reply. "Garin and I were tasked with acquiring the talismans. Delucha possesses one."

"We know this." Ravin crossed his arms. "Why does the Nameless seek them?"

Jannyn shrugged. "Garin is the one who speaks to our master. You ought to interrogate *him*."

Ravin's smile was grim. "I have, and he's likely still recovering from our encounter. You mentioned he was abed upon our first meeting— I was the source of his injury. You won't fare as well."

"Wait!" Jannyn pleaded. "I tell you the truth. I don't fucking know! Our master doesn't seem to speak with anyone but that gods-damned little shit, and he's the one who relays our supposed orders. Garin's powerful, and I'm not fool enough to cross him."

"Are you certain he has useful information, Ravin?" the queen demanded. "My patience wears thin, and we may have a better use for this cell—"

"Wait, I'm not done," Jannyn begged. "I can tell you of our master's plans for the army. I can tell you what I know of the others and of the Enlightened. I can tell you—"

"Enough," she replied icily. "Ravin will visit you to extract the information I require. But know this: If you fail to comply, or if I learn you have lied to him, you will die. I will make certain it is a very public affair."

Jannyn nodded hastily. "Of course, my lady. I will do as you require, so long as it means I'll keep my head."

"Good." She turned to Ravin, her demeanor as frigid as her eyes. "You will continue this business later. We have other matters to discuss this morning."

He trailed her along the corridor and did not speak until they were well away from their prisoner. "You cannot trust his final words, Your Majesty."

She smirked up at him. "I'm well aware of that, Ravin. He is Soulless, and he is the man who landed Jasom and I in our current predicament. Thanks to him, the guards are now aware of what transpired, and I will be forced to announce my condition sooner than I'd planned. I'd rather you kill him and be done with this business, but as you made it clear earlier, I ought to trust my advisors. Do not make me regret the decision to do so."

Ravin managed a half-bow, taken aback by her words. He'd believed he understood her demeanor well enough to anticipate her actions, but this morning had proven him wrong on several fronts. He'd witnessed a side of the queen he hadn't believed existed.

"He will prove useful to our plans," Ravin assured her.

"See that he does. I'd hate to lose such a valuable resource—and an advisor as well."

CHAPTER FOURTEEN

BROTHERS

"You're not returning to the Stronghold, Vardak?" Travin attempted to mask his surprise and confusion with a show of mild curiosity, but both of his brothers saw through it.

The three stood on the outskirts of their ramshackle camp at a distance from the others. As the day waned into evening, their shadows loomed long across the barren ground. It had been three nights since their departure from the Underground Caverns. During that time, they'd been given little time to speak privately. Much of it was Patak's doing; he was a constant presence at Emra's side.

"We can't," Vardak replied. He looked away, his thoughts on the relic hidden beneath his breastplate.

"He's right," Patak added as his gaze slid toward the blond figure of Emra as she emerged from her tent. "Sevic ordered us to Dar Daelad, and that was before she found that damned sword. We have…" He shifted his focus to Vardak. "You should tell him, little brother."

"We were ordered to secrecy, Patak." He was reluctant to recount his tale again. Once had been enough.

Patak rolled his eyes. "Travin's not a Murkor spy, and you're a stubborn ass."

"Patak, it's fine," Travin interjected. "If Sevic ordered you both into secrecy, it was for good reason. I won't force either of you to disobey the Warleader."

Vardak nodded silent thanks to Travin. "If you want to know the details, mother can tell you."

Patak smirked. "It wasn't about Sevic's orders. That was merely a convenient excuse." He ran one hand through his hair and sighed. "I suppose I understand. You went through hell on Flariel's account with little to show for it."

"I'd wondered about your journey, Vardak. I had plenty of time to think while I was shackled to the cave wall and processed for venom by the Murkor." Travin scowled toward the horizon. "At least that ordeal is over. The others can return home. Dakna will understand my desire to accompany you."

Vardak exchanged a pointed look with Patak. His oldest brother understood the root of his sudden concern and cleared his throat awkwardly. "You need to return home, Trav."

"Of the three of us, you're the least likely to follow Sevic's orders," Travin replied, nonplussed. "You'd best have a damned good reason for that demand."

"Trav," Vardak cut in, "it's Dakna—"

"You're going to be a father," Patak said at the same time.

"What?" Travin shook his head in disbelief before his face slowly broke into a broad grin. "Gods-damn it, Patak, when were you going to tell me? This is wonderful news!" Abruptly he threw one arm around each of his brothers and laughed loudly.

"Why must you blame me?" Patak asked, feigning hurt.

"There are days I'm convinced Vardak's vocabulary consists of less than ten words, but you're chatty as a cactus wren. Besides, as the eldest, it's your duty, isn't it?" The grin remained plastered across Travin's face.

Vardak allowed the jibe to pass; it was typical banter between his brothers, and he had no grounds to argue Travin's point. He'd spent the past three nights walking at the head of the group alone, lost in his thoughts, or with Maryn and Lucas as they plotted the best course through the Gray Mountains. Travin had spent plenty of time with Patak—when Patak wasn't fawning over Emra. He wondered if the pair had discussed Patak's unorthodox attraction to the human knight, but if they had, it seemed Travin was unconcerned.

Travin released them both and stepped back to study them. "I suppose your reason for my return home is sound enough, Patak. I wish you would have informed me sooner."

"It slipped my mind, Trav."

Travin smirked. "Yes, I *know* what's been on your mind. Mother won't be pleased."

Patak's smile faltered and he turned away. He crossed his arms and stared into the growing darkness for several moments, then said, "Vardak said as much, too. But tell me, Trav, when you met Dakna, did you know you were meant to be with her?"

Travin sighed. "Yes. I cannot imagine my life without her."

"Then you understand."

"Patak, this business of yours is different," Travin replied in a warning tone. "Dakna is one of our people. Emra is human. What you seek is forbidden. You'll be exiled—if Sevic doesn't take your head first. If you consider nothing else, think of what this will do to our mother."

"If Emra will have me, my decision is made," Patak growled.

"Fucking gods, Patak! You haven't spoken to her yet?" Travin was stunned.

"She's had other matters on her mind."

"Did it occur to you that she may not reciprocate your affections, brother? You may be throwing your life away on nothing more than a daydream." Travin shook his head in disbelief and turned to face Vardak. "Please tell me you'll talk sense into him after I'm gone."

"I've tried. He insisted he'd rather speak with you since I have too little experience." Vardak shot a glare in Patak's direction; he was still bitter at their previous exchange.

Travin released a sigh. "Gods, Patak. For once in your life, please listen to reason."

"My decision rests with her," Patak replied stubbornly. "I won't allow our gods-damned outdated laws to stand in my way."

"I will have to tell mother," Travin said again.

Patak's expression softened and he nodded in understanding. There was pain in the depths of his blue eyes, along with fear and a desperate longing. "I know."

It wasn't yet midnight when they came upon the faint, weather-worn marker that directed travelers southeast toward the desert and the Stronghold. It was there Travin and the other Scorpion Men parted ways with Vardak and the others. Their goodbyes were brief, and Travin promised he would give their regards to Dakna and their mother.

Vardak watched as they disappeared into the darkness, pleased that he'd proven Sevic wrong and the prisoners were freed. They had been unable to do the same for the humans imprisoned in the caverns, and in spite of Lucas' protests, Emra had refused to pursue their release. They lacked the numbers to mount an assault, and as she'd pointed out numerous times, it would draw the Soulless' suspicions if the Murkor gave up too many prisoners without good cause. Lucas had spent his time in avoidance of Emra, which played into Patak's interests.

When he turned away from his departing people, Vardak noted the others seemed to have been waiting for him. He'd hoped to remain at the Stronghold to bolster his people's defenses during the war, but the gods and the Warleader had conspired against his plans. His path lay far to the west, in Dar Daelad.

Wordlessly, they began to trace their own route westward toward the looming shadows of the Gray Mountains. They'd decided to follow the merchant's road through the long-abandoned mines which would take them into Santine Kingdom beyond. He was capable of navigating the twisted passageways, thanks to Blademon, and Emra had claimed she was knowledgeable as well. The mines presented their own unique dangers, but it was quicker to venture through them than it would be to attempt crossing the mountains. There was also the matter of autumn, and with it, foul weather in the heights.

Lucas fell in beside him after a time; next to him was the dapple-gray horse that carried many of their supplies. "It's always difficult to walk away from your home."

Vardak nodded. "I'm grateful to you and Emra for agreeing to help us free Travin and the others. Without you, Sevic would never have allowed us to undertake the journey." He sighed. "I wish I were joining them."

"I know. I've felt the same nearly every time I was dispatched from Pine. I became a soldier with the dream of becoming a knight—the same as Em. The reality is I miss my home every gods-damned day, and I failed one of the three trials required to make knighthood. I wish I'd taken my uncle's advice and become a tanner, like him." He shook his head, and his eyes found Emra's silhouette in the darkness ahead. "Perhaps if I'd stayed in Pine, I'd have a family of my own now. Instead, I chased the dreams of my friend and put my own aspirations aside."

"You chose Emra over yourself?"

Lucas chuckled dryly. "Yes. I always have. There was something about her that drew me, for good or ill. As I see it now, it was her connection to that damned sword."

"Finding it changed her," Vardak replied quietly.

"Hmm. Not as much as you seem to believe, Vardak. It's given her a confidence that she sometimes lacked before, but she is much the same. The greater change has come from her hours spent with your brother." Lucas' tone grew hard. "Between us, if Patak does anything to hurt her, he'll regret it."

Vardak shrugged uncomfortably. "Travin and I both tried to speak with him about his attraction to her. He's stubborn and won't see reason, even when faced with exile."

Lucas appeared stunned. "Exile? Why—"

"My people don't approve of pairings with humans—or other races, for that matter. Our ancestors may have been human, but we are no longer." He sighed. "Travin is compelled to tell our mother, and she will be forced to inform Sevic. I'm certain you can see where that will lead, even as an outsider."

Lucas scowled and placed one hand across his face for a moment. "Gods, Emra doesn't know. In spite of her lifetimes full of memories, I doubt she's had much interaction with your people beyond the battlefields. She would never lead him on if she was aware of the cost."

"Patak made it very clear what he intends," Vardak replied, "and he's aware of the repercussions."

"You fear what this will do to him, to your family."

"Yes."

Patak's actions would affect himself and Travin, their mother, and Travin's unborn child. They would lose respectability in the eyes of many, all because Patak was convinced he'd fallen in love with a human.

Vardak wasn't certain his brother truly loved Emra; he had a lengthy history of wooing women only to break his ties a few weeks later. Yet Patak had approached this relationship differently than his others. He was more hesitant, less confident, and his temper had proven more volatile when the topic of Emra surfaced. Perhaps he felt differently, after all.

"I'll speak with Em," Lucas promised. "I'm not certain it will do any good, but it's the least I can do. I'm overdue for a chat with her, in any case. It's time I faced the reality of who she is and accept it, rather than avoid her and pretend nothing has changed."

CHAPTER FIFTEEN

A TEST

"There you are. I should have known."

Tavesin looked up from the scroll he'd been reading to find Rostin smirking at him from across the polished oak table. Tavesin had spent the entirety of his morning in the tower's library, poring over several texts in search of new ways in which to rescue Arra. Bookcases ran from floor to ceiling around the perimeter of the room, and dozens of shelves filled the spaces between. Every shelf was crammed full of books, scrolls, maps, and pamphlets on a thousand different topics, though all were related to magic in some way. A handful of tables were interspersed between them, most occupied by fully-trained wizards. Tavesin was the only apprentice at work that morning.

It was a day designated as a respite from studies; apprentices were given one per week, but Tavesin often lost himself in the library on such occasions. It was unusual for Rostin to set foot within the massive room unless prompted to do so, and his presence came as a surprise.

"What is it, Rostin?" he asked as he pushed the scroll aside.

"Hasnin was seeking you," Rostin replied with a shrug. "Most likely it's your business with the Drakkon again. What are you studying, Taven?"

"I'm trying to learn better ways of protecting myself in the Aethereum. Aziarah suggested the library might have some resources, but I've found nothing so far." He rose from his seat and stretched. "Is Hasnin in his study?"

"That's where he said he'd be." Rostin chuckled. "I've been relegated to the role of errand-boy for my greatest friend, while he takes all the glory."

Tavesin rolled his eyes. "If you're accepted as a Gray, you'll have more glory than I ever will."

"There is still time to change your path, Taven." Rostin flashed a grin. "Imagine the two of us on the battlefield, taking down the Soulless one by one…"

Tavesin shook his head, amused, as they began to make their way out of the library. "I'd rather become a Blue. Someone will need to make certain you're protected. As I understand it, Grays are all offense. Without a Blue, they're vulnerable."

Rostin cast a sidelong glance in his direction and broke into a grin. "Are you offering your protection, Taven? I'm honored."

"We can still be on the field together," Tavesin replied with a smile. He was less enthusiastic than Rostin when it came to the notion of battling the Soulless, but he would protect his friend if given the opportunity to do so.

"Hmm, I suppose that's true enough. The Soulless won't know what they're in for when we're finally allowed to face them." Rostin snickered. "I've finally been granted lessons with some of the Grays. I'll be starting tomorrow."

The two discussed their future plans and lessons as they ascended the tower toward the White Sect's floor and Hasnin's study. Rostin harbored grandiose aspirations for himself, while Tavesin's were decidedly more subdued. He meant to save Arra from the Soulless, but his future remained hazy beyond that singular goal.

"If you're not kept busy for the remainder of the day, Badolo and I were planning to visit the market," Rostin informed him as they reached the door to Hasnin's study. "We'll wait until mid-afternoon if you'd like to join us."

Guilt at sequestering himself in the library gnawed at him, and though he didn't particularly care for visiting the market, he decided he ought to make time for his friends. If the Soulless continued on their present course, they would be afforded little opportunity to do so in the future.

"I'll join you if I can," Tavesin promised.

Rostin grinned. "It's about time you spent some time in the sun, in any case. You're starting to resemble the Undead!" His laughter echoed along the corridor as he departed while Tavesin shook his head, bemused.

Tavesin drew a breath and rapped on the door. When it opened moments later, Hasnin's wizened countenance peered at him from within. Behind the aged wizard, Tavesin spied the slightly younger features of the Radiant, perched upon the only available chair.

"Good, you've arrived." Hasnin waved him inside impatiently and swiftly closed the door behind them.

Tavesin remained standing near the door while Hasnin made his way around his cluttered desk. The Radiant did not stand, but his dark eyes studied Tavesin closely. Tavesin resisted the urge to fidget under the council leader's scrutiny.

"It has been brought to my attention that you've progressed significantly in your studies of late," the Radiant began. "Your long hours in the library have been well spent, it seems."

Tavesin swallowed, uncertain of the direction the conversation was headed. "Yes, sir."

"And your talent for Aethereal magic has been honed, as well?"

Tavesin nodded. "Aziarah tells me there is little more she can teach me."

The Radiant and Hasnin shared a knowing look before the Radiant refocused on the nervous apprentice at the door. "Do you believe you require Drakkon oversight to venture into the magical realm, Tavesin?"

The Radiant's dark eyes bored into him as he awaited a response. Though Tavesin knew he was prepared to face the Aethereum's dangers alone, he'd refused to ignore Aziarah's advice after his final confrontation with the Soulless named Garin. He'd learned much since that terrible night, yet fear had rooted him firmly to the zone of relative safety at Aziarah's side. He drew a breath, knew the answer he must give, but remained uncertain of the consequences.

"I don't require it, sir, but I prefer it."

The wizards shared another knowing glance, and Tavesin began to wonder at the true reason behind their meeting. Something was afoot, something he was not privy to.

"Think of this as a test, Tavesin," the Radiant said slowly. "If you agree to our proposed plan, your challenge date will be set. You have proven yourself ready in a number of areas, but we believe you must learn to overcome your fears in order to succeed. Have you chosen a Sect to challenge for?"

Tavesin's stomach made several somersaults with the Radiant's revelation. He understood the implications; they would ask him to enter the Aethereum alone, to carry out a task of their design, and in exchange, he would be granted the opportunity to prove himself worthy of becoming a Blue. A part of him was determined and prepared for anything they might have in store. The other part cowered, terrified of another encounter with the Soulless.

He remained frozen for several long moments while he sorted through his tangled thoughts. He came to the conclusion that there was only one path forward. He must learn to confront his fears if he wished to become a wizard.

"Blue, sir."

"Ah, Virano will be disappointed, but I believe I understand your decision." The Radiant leaned back in his chair and smiled. "We ask that you venture into the Aethereum and learn all you can of Arra's whereabouts. It may take some time. I have already informed the Drakkon that they must limit their lessons with you to one per week. You have other priorities to fulfill, Tavesin."

He nodded while struggling to keep the dismay he felt from showing in his expression. The Drakkon had helped him test his newfound skills when the wizards had refused to do so, and he had come to respect them for their knowledge and willingness to aid him. To be limited to one night per week with them was a disappointing blow.

"Are you willing to accept this test, Taven?" Hasnin asked carefully. "I believe you are up to the challenge, but if you are not ready, we will accommodate your decision."

It was an opportunity to locate Arra, and if it meant he would be granted his challenge sooner, he would accept the task. Once he was named wizard, he would no longer be forced to endure the restrictions of an apprentice.

"I'm ready, sir," he replied without further hesitation.

He would find Arra—and prove himself to the council.

Tavesin met Rostin and Badolo an hour later. The two were thrilled that he'd decided to join them on their brief excursion into the city, but Tavesin's mind was occupied with thoughts of what he must do. His heart wasn't in the journey, and it didn't take long before the others picked up on it.

"Taven," Badolo said as they skirted a merchant's cart and dodged a cluster of guards on patrol, "what did your mentor have to say?"

Tavesin hesitated, then realized he had not been warned to keep his business a secret. After all, he may need his friends to watch for his return from the Aethereum and fetch help if things went awry. In a subdued tone, he relayed the conversation that had unfolded in Hasnin's study.

Rostin gaped at him. "They'll set your challenge date if you do this?"

"Yes."

"And you've agreed to it?" Rostin asked, dumbfounded. "Taven, I know you care for her, but after what happened the last time—"

"I didn't know half of what I do now," Tavesin replied, cutting him off. "There is little else Aziarah can teach me of the Aethereum, and my shields are stronger than any fully-trained Blue can boast. I'm ready. If no one else will search for Arra, then I will."

Badolo shrugged uncomfortably. "No one else *can* search for her, Taven."

"All the more reason why I must do this."

"Gods, Taven, this is madness." Rostin shook his head. "I know I'm not usually the voice of caution, but what if *he's* there? Can you truly withstand one of the Soulless?"

Tavesin's thoughts flashed to the golden-eyed man he'd met and the ease with which he'd ejected the Soulless from the realm. Aziarah had taught him the magic required to perform the same feat, and he believed he could replicate it. His shields were powerful. He would not be taken unawares a second time.

"Yes, I believe I can."

"But alone, Taven?" Badolo asked, his dark eyes wide with unspoken fear.

"Do I have a choice?" he countered. "No. Someone must find Arra, and it may as well be me."

Rostin muttered under his breath and shook his head, but the pair mercifully allowed the matter to drop. He understood their concerns, but if Hasnin and the Radiant both believed he was up to the challenge, then he would not disappoint them. He owed it to Arra to find her and rescue her; it was his fault she'd been taken, after all.

As they entered the crowded marketplace at the heart of Dar Daelad, it quickly became apparent that Badolo had orchestrated their excursion. His desire to join the Yellow Sect had prompted him to conduct research of his own, and he sought several non-magical components for a device he planned to create. He would say nothing of what his future creation was meant to do, only that he believed it would assist the wizards in the coming war. Tavesin found himself trailing in the smaller boy's wake as he deftly navigated the maze of merchant stalls and wagons.

Badolo acquired an assortment of dried herbs, a small dagger, several strips of cloth in various shades, a pair of clear glass marbles, and a round mirror the size of his palm. The last item cost a hefty sum, but Badolo produced the coin with a grin for the surprised merchant. Tavesin had never seen so much gold in one person's hand.

As they began to wend their way back toward the tower, Rostin released a low whistle. "Do you come from a family of merchants, Badolo?"

The smaller boy laughed. "No. I suppose I've been harboring a secret from you. I know Taven won't tell anyone, but I'm not certain about you." He grinned playfully, though his dark eyes were serious.

"I am sworn to secrecy," Rostin replied with mock-humility.

Badolo laughed again, then peered at each of his friends in turn. "The truth is, I am the youngest son of Darehn Lorvehk."

Tavesin frowned; the name meant nothing to him. Rostin's eyes widened in surprise, and he openly gaped at Badolo.

"What is it?" Tavesin asked.

Rostin rolled his eyes in Tavesin's direction. "You truly *don't* pay attention in our history lessons, Taven. Badolo is royalty! A prince!"

Tavesin found himself staring at his friend in stunned silence. He would never have guessed Badolo was royalty, but some of his friend's mannerisms began to make sense. Unlike Tavesin, a farmer's son, and Rostin, who rarely spoke of his family, Badolo had lived a life of luxury prior to his journey to the Shining Tower.

"Shh!" Badolo hissed. "It's a secret, Rostin!" He glanced at the passersby warily, but none seemed to have overheard Rostin's outburst. "I came to the tower under orders from my father that no one should learn of my identity. I've defied him by telling you, so you must keep this to yourselves."

"Why would a prince join the Yellow Sect?" Rostin mused quietly.

"I am choosing Yellow because it interests me. There is no other reason," Badolo replied testily. "I am the only Lorvehk in several generations gifted with the Ability, and my father was pleased to learn of it. I'm also the youngest of nine which means I'll never have claim to the throne. My father believed that of all his children, I am the best suited to follow my own path. I will become a wizard, and I've found I rather enjoy creating with my hands. I was not given the opportunity for such endeavors while I lived in the palace. Yellow suits me."

Rostin smirked as Badolo finished speaking. "I believe I understand why you speak as you do at times. For all your secrecy, you can't shake your upbringing."

Badolo glowered at him. "I am trying, Rostin. I must fit in, and I cannot let anyone know my true identity. Even the Radiant doesn't know. To him, I am Badolo Shansehk, the son of a Kamshati nobleman. It is a lie, but one I must continue perpetuating."

"We will keep your secret," Tavesin promised and shot Rostin a meaningful glance. He knew Rostin meant well, but his friend had a penchant for gossip.

"Yes," Rostin agreed hastily. "Now that you've told us, perhaps you'll let us in on the details of your magical project?"

Badolo snickered. "Not today, Rostin."

As the trio entered the tower's gardens, Tavesin decided it was time to make his request. "After supper is finished tonight, I believe I need your help."

Badolo studied him carefully, and nodded. "Name it, Taven. I will assist if I can."

"As will I," Rostin added.

"Thank you." Tavesin paused to consider his next words. "I plan to enter the Aethereum. I need someone to await my return, and if I don't come back by a set time, you must inform Hasnin."

Rostin looked down uneasily. "You still mean to go through with this madness?"

"Yes."

"I will watch for your return," Badolo stated as Rostin released a heavy sigh.

"We both will," Rostin agreed grudgingly. "I may not like it, but it is your decision, after all."

They gathered in the room Tavesin shared with Rostin after supper was finished. Tavesin impressed upon them that he would return before midnight. If he failed to meet his self-imposed schedule, one or both of his friends would seek Hasnin. Once he was satisfied they were in agreement, he created a portal into the Aethereum and left the physical realm behind.

He cast his senses through the area as Aziarah had taught him, but sensed no one. Nevertheless, he created an invisible shield around himself as a means of protection from magical attack. He wasn't certain, but he believed the Soulless might be capable of cloaking their presence within the Aethereum based on some of the texts he'd read.

He traveled first to Rican Mer, the last location he'd encountered Arra. Again, his senses told him he was alone. He wandered through the empty streets of the village he'd once called home and paused to stop outside the tiny wooden hut he'd grown up in. It would be a simple matter to exit the Aethereum and pay his family a visit, but he risked missing Arra's arrival if she appeared. His family must wait.

He was certain she would travel to Rican Mer if she were able, but as time passed and midnight drew near, there was no sign of her. Despair threatened to overtake him while guilt gnawed at his gut. She'd been weak and injured when he last spoke with her, and she'd claimed her time in the Aethereum was limited. She feared discovery by the Soulless, and rightly so.

Tavesin grimaced at the thought of what pain Garin must have inflicted upon her. He'd experienced first-hand the physical damage the man was capable of.

Minutes from midnight, Tavesin shook his head sadly and returned to the tower. Arra had not come, and without her he was uncertain where to begin his search. Though his friends welcomed him back with relief and joy, he could not share in their enthusiasm. Arra had not appeared, and that boded ill for them both.

CHAPTER SIXTEEN

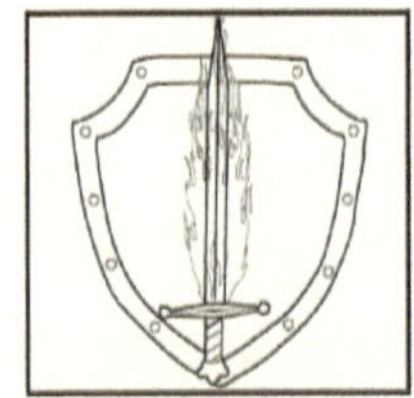

FIERY INTERFERENCE

Emra emerged from her tent just as the dawn began to tinge the sky in shades of rose and pale gold. Patak stood at the western edge of their campsite, his gaze fixed upon the dark opening in the mountain's side that marked the entrance to the mines. None of the others had emerged from their tents.

Since the reclamation of Fireblade, her nights had been plagued with nightmares and visions of battles long past. Sleep proved elusive more often than not, and though she was weary, she would press on. There was little else she could do, and she'd learned in her previous life that attempting to defy her fate was futile. Aeon's designs would not be thwarted.

She made her way toward Patak, who glanced over his armor-clad shoulder when he heard her approach. He offered her a smile, and in spite of herself, she felt her heart flutter. He was damned attractive. After speaking with Lucas, however, she knew she ought to repress the burgeoning feelings she harbored for the tall, muscular warrior. It had grown more difficult to push them aside as she'd come to know Patak better. She didn't want to hurt him, but she could not allow him to face exile on her behalf.

"Good morning," he greeted her.

"I suppose it is," she replied as she came to stand beside him. Though she was tall for a woman, her head did not reach the level of his shoulders. The Scorpion Men were veritable giants when compared to their distant human cousins.

His smile faltered, and his gaze returned to the cavernous opening carved into the mountain. "More nightmares, Em?"

"When you have memories from six lifetimes flooding your head, it's inevitable." She sighed. "Even more so when most of those memories are unpleasant."

He ran one hand through his short blond hair. "Gods, I wish there were something I could do to help you."

An idea sparked in her mind then, and she smiled faintly. Perhaps there was a way, after all…

"I believe there is," she replied quietly. "Lucas has been avoiding me, and I could use someone to speak with. Someone who is willing to listen, yet who can also be trusted to keep my secrets."

He turned to look at her once more, an unconcealed yearning in his eyes. "Emra, are you suggesting that I…?"

"You are easy to talk with, Patak, and I've learned enough about your people in the past few weeks to know I can trust you implicitly."

Patak smiled uncertainly. "Friendship, then? I can accept that."

"I know of your brothers' concerns." She bit her lower lip while he sighed heavily, but she pressed on. "I won't see you exiled for me, Patak, but perhaps this arrangement can…circumvent those laws. I need a confidante, and against my better judgment, I want you at my side."

His smile broadened with her words. "Then we have an agreement, Em."

"Good." She returned his smile and wished she could offer him a better arrangement. He was several years her junior, he wasn't human, but she could not deny the attraction she felt for him. Friendship must suffice, no matter how strongly her heart ached for more.

As she considered what she wished to tell him first, she heard a loud crackling sound from the campsite behind, followed by a string of vehement curses. She turned to find Vardak near the campfire, flint and tinder in hand. Instead of sparking a flame, it seemed he'd summoned Flariel. The fire goddess' body was humanoid in form, though her flesh appeared molten and much of her torso was wreathed in a violent swirl of flame. Her incandescent gaze was fixed on Vardak and her expression was furious.

"Oh, hell," Patak whispered beside her. "This won't bode well."

She nodded a silent agreement and watched as the scene unfolded before them.

"I believed my instructions to you were clear," Flariel began. "Your delay has displeased me, Vardak, and you shall answer for your failure."

Her voice rang loudly through the campsite. Within moments Maryn and the two Airess peered from their tents to see for themselves what the source of the commotion was. Maryn shook his feline head and muttered several curses under his breath. Lucas appeared behind Flariel, his eyes wide while he gaped at her. The goddess ignored her mortal audience with the exception of the man who had seemingly drawn her ire.

"I was unaware you'd given me a deadline, Flariel." Vardak crossed his arms defiantly and scowled at the goddess.

"Your brother walks a dangerous line," Emra whispered to Patak.

Patak chuckled. "Vardak is weary of the gods' interference in his life. I can't say I blame him, but I certainly wouldn't provoke one of them. Least of all Flariel."

"You were to take the relic directly to Dar Daelad." Flames cascaded along Flariel's body in a dangerous display of anger. "Instead, you have remained here, wasting precious time."

"And I believed I'd made it clear to you and Blademon that my first priority would be to free my brother from the Murkor," Vardak growled. "If you knew anything of how a family truly operates, you might understand."

Flariel's glare was intense, but Emra was impressed when Vardak met it unflinchingly. It was further proof she had chosen wisely when she'd asked him to take up the role of general.

"He may have gone too far," Patak murmured uneasily.

"It is fortunate that both Blademon and Solsticia seem to favor you," Flariel hissed. "I should burn you to ash for your insolence."

Vardak appeared nonplussed. "Why have you come, Flariel?"

"To inform you there is another path you ought to consider," the goddess replied. "The only mage with the power to wield the Moon's Eye in Dar Daelad is a mere child and untrained. He may be recruited, but the Council of Auras will resist your efforts. However, there is another."

"I'm listening."

"My eldest sister has attempted to keep his existence to herself," Flariel continued, "but she was forced to divulge her secret to the rest of us a few hours ago. He is the greatest mage of this era, and he has no love for the Soulless. You can find him in the Deluchan palace. You will know him by his golden eyes."

"Then you believe we ought to travel to Delucha, rather than Dar Daelad?" Vardak asked.

Flariel laughed coldly. "No, Vardak. I suggest *you* travel to Delucha." Her incandescent gaze lifted to pierce Emra. "Fireblade's wielder must continue on her path to Dar Daelad. If you visit Ukase's temple while there, Aeon may be amenable to a visit."

"You claim there is a wizard in Dar Daelad that may be recruited," Vardak began, only to be cut off by Flariel's next heated words.

"There is, Vardak, but he is a child. I have given you two possible routes to follow, and you may choose as you wish. However, the mage in Delucha is a certain ally, whereas this child in the Shining Tower is an unknown." She folded her arms and fixed him with an unyielding stare. "Be certain you choose the best path, Vardak. The fate of many depends on your actions."

Before he could respond, Flariel vanished in a plume of smoke and ash. Vardak lifted his gaze toward the sky and clenched his fists at his sides.

"I'd best go speak with him," Patak said quietly. "We'll have plenty of time to talk later, Em. At present, my brother needs me, whether he'll admit it or not."

Emra nodded. "I understand family, Patak. Go."

He flashed a final smile at her and skittered away.

She knew family dynamics better than most, she reflected as she watched him approach his younger brother. Six lifetimes gave her an insight few others could boast, nor comprehend. Even the Airess, for all their longevity, did not fully understand. In each life, she'd experienced a different family life. Some had been wholesome, some contentious, but all had been meaningful. In her current existence, she had no siblings—Lucas was the closest she had, and they were not kindred by blood. In other lives, she'd known brothers and sisters both. Yes, she understood Patak's desire to guide and protect his youngest brother, and she would not stand in his way.

"It's proving to be an interesting morning," Lucas said from beside her.

She startled at his sudden presence and turned to face him.

He chuckled. "You won't give up on him, will you, Em? I suppose that's your business—and his."

"I've always had poor timing, Luke." She sighed. "I should be focused on our journey to Dar Daelad and what I must tell the wizards."

Lucas smirked. "It will be another two weeks at least before we reach the city, Em. I won't fault you for seeking a diversion in the meantime, but…Please be careful. You're my oldest friend, and Patak's likeable enough. I'd hate to see either of you hurt."

"Gods, if he was human this would be far easier."

"You were never one to take the easy route, Em." Lucas grinned. "I'm glad I finally decided to speak with you yesterday. I've missed this."

"As have I, you senseless fool," she replied with a laugh. "I'm not so different than I was before."

"I realize that now."

"I'm glad you're here, Luke. I doubt any of the others would have understood this business of mine as readily as you have."

Lucas grunted. "I don't fully understand it, Em, but I'm with you no matter what transpires. And if he makes you happy, I'll not stand in your way. I still maintain the Scorpion Men are a bit terrifying, even after we've come to know them."

"They're not so bad." Emra's gaze flicked to Patak. He was still in conversation with Vardak, a mischievous grin on his face.

"Says the woman who can't keep her eyes off one of them." Lucas grinned even as she turned to shove him playfully.

"In all my lives, love has always been fleeting," she said quietly after a moment. "I had a family of my own once, but it was not a match borne of love. Perhaps this time, my fate will be different."

Lucas shrugged uncomfortably. "Em…"

She shook her head. "I'm sorry, Luke. I know my talk of past lives makes you uncomfortable, but it's my reality." She sighed. "When we reach Dar Daelad, I'll take Flariel's suggestion and visit the temple. If Aeon is willing to speak with me, perhaps this life will be my last."

Lucas crossed his arms, his expression a cross between horror and uncertainty as he studied her. She realized her words had done nothing to set his mind at ease.

"Gods-damn it, I'm terrible at this," she muttered. "Luke—"

"No, Em, don't apologize. As I said, I don't understand this business, but I *am* here for you." He glanced toward the Scorpion Men and added, "As is he."

She followed his gaze to find Patak and Vardak were making their way toward her. Patak smiled as their eyes met, while Vardak growled something under his breath. His words only served to make Patak laugh.

"Have you made a decision, Vardak?" she asked once they were near.

He nodded. "Flariel has given me a choice, and to my mind, Dar Daelad still seems the better destination. No doubt she'll return to berate me regardless of the path I follow."

"I'm pleased you'll remain with us," Emra replied. "I plan to begin recruitment once we're in Santine. Your presence will be welcome."

Patak snickered and elbowed Vardak. "That's right, *General.*"

Vardak's eyebrows rose as a faint smirk crossed his lips. "I'll have no insubordination from you, brother or not."

Patak threw his head back and roared with laughter. "I never thought I'd see the day when I'd be taking orders from my youngest brother."

"You won't be," Emra cut in. "You'll both answer to me directly."

Beside her Lucas shook his head in amusement. "Knowing Em as I do, you'll wish you were reporting to him, Patak."

"I'm not so bad," Emra replied defensively.

Lucas snorted. "Trust me, Patak. She's a task-mistress at the best of times."

Patak shrugged, a knowing smile upon his lips as he studied her. "I'm willing to take my chances."

CHAPTER SEVENTEEN

MURKOR SCHEMES

Aran'daj parried the blow aimed at his hooded skull with his saber and muttered under his breath. His reactions were too slow and his strength was waning. He grimaced and shoved at his adversary's broadsword with as much might as he could muster to little avail. In front of him, Jal'den chuckled darkly and continued to press his attack. The Arms Master was quicker, stronger, and had the distinct advantage of years' worth of training with Blademon himself.

"The Kal has released the Scorpion Men," Jal'den informed him in a low tone. He slid the blade of his broadsword along the edge of Aran'daj's saber and pushed the commander away.

Aran'daj drew a breath and braced himself for the next assault. The deadly dance the pair had engaged in was designed as a show for the other Murkor soldiers, but served the dual purpose of allowing the two to discuss matters without being overheard. A dozen paces away from them, Kama stood impassively observing the affair. The Soulless had been a constant presence in their camp since the night Aran'daj had been spared from Dranamir's wrath.

As their blades collided again, Aran'daj muttered, "And what of the human prisoners?"

Jal'den spun, his broadsword a whirl of deadly steel as he struck at the commander's right flank. Aran'daj maneuvered and parried the strike, breathing heavily.

"They remain, sir," Jal'den replied with a weary chuckle. "You're not bad for a soldier who has seen little action in decades."

Aran'daj ground his teeth and attempted to shove Jal'den away, but the Arms Master held his ground. "Fucking gods, you're strong," he panted.

Beneath his hood, Aran'daj was slicked with sweat, despite the chill mountain air that surrounded them. Their match had only lasted several minutes, but already the exertion of keeping pace with Jal'den was beginning to take its toll. Aran'daj was not one to back away from a challenge, but it was becoming apparent he was no equal to the young Arms Master. Aran'daj was nearly twice Jal'den's age.

"Tired, commander?" Jal'den eased the pressure he applied against the commander's saber. Aran'daj heard the grin in his voice and shook his head stubbornly.

"We're not finished yet, Arms Master."

Jal'den danced away and swung again as Aran'daj struggled to recover. As their blades clashed again, he felt the reverberation of the blow deep within his bones. He knew Jal'den was holding back. Silently, he thanked the gods they were merely sparring and the younger man had no intention of inflicting injury. Jal'den was a force unto himself on the battlefield, as their campaign through Balotica had demonstrated.

"Sal'zar mentioned the Kal has begun to set his plan in motion."

Jal'den struck another three times in succession, his movements measured for Aran'daj's benefit. Aran'daj blocked each strike and tried to ignore the ache in his shoulders.

"Did he provide you with details?"

Jal'den growled and pivoted, his blade arcing upward toward Aran'daj's gut. The commander cursed under his breath and parried again. His wrists screamed; the blow had more force behind it than he'd anticipated.

"Sal'zar would say only that we would speak in person when our time comes, Commander." Jal'den's frustration was apparent as he whirled away and prepared for another assault.

Aran'daj shook his head and allowed his saber to fall upon the frosted earth, his hands raised in defeat. "You win the day, Jal'den."

Jal'den lowered his broadsword and tilted his head to one side, contemplating his next move. "Good fight, Commander." He glanced at the ring of soldiers that surrounded them and said, "Will anyone else challenge me? I'm not finished."

Aran'daj stooped to pick up his saber and sheathed it as he made his way into the ring of bystanders. Another young warrior entered the space he vacated, prepared to try his skill against Jal'den. Aran'daj doubted the Arms Master would hold back for the newcomer as he'd done for their commander. Their match had lasted as long as it had for the sake of information, and there had been little this day.

"You held your own better than I'd expected, Commander," Kama's voice stated from behind him.

Aran'daj turned to face the gray-faced, corrupted countenance of the Soulless. "I am no equal to Jal'den in combat, sir."

"Nevertheless, your performance was impressive. You are an example to the soldiers under your command." Kama stared down his long nose at the commander, his crimson eyes unreadable. "I begin to understand why the Kal selected you for this post. It was not merely your knack for strategy."

"Yes, sir." Aran'daj was uncertain of what he was expected to say.

"I will make certain Dranamir does not make a second attempt on your life. So long as you continue to impress, you have little to fear from me—or the others."

Without waiting for a response, Kama strode away. The other black-clad Murkor soldiers gave the Soulless a wide berth as he passed, and Aran'daj heard the unsettling sound of Kama's dark laughter drift toward him on the wind.

Aran'daj released a sigh of relief at Kama's departure. Each direct encounter he survived with the Soulless was a victory for himself and his people. He wished he knew more of the Kal's plan to subvert them, but perhaps his continued ignorance of the scheme was all a part of the overall strategy. What Aran'daj did not know could not be divulged to their enemy, even if he was faced with torture. And torture was an ever-present possibility.

He turned to the sparring circle in time to see Jal'den hand his challenger a swift defeat. The Arms Master sheathed the broadsword across his back and offered his hand to the fallen soldier, who accepted it with some chagrin. Another pushed their way into the circle, intent upon testing their luck against Jal'den as the first disappeared into the crowd. Jal'den shook his head.

"I'm finished for a time. The commander and I have a battle strategy to prepare."

Aran'daj smiled beneath his hood; they'd made no such plans, but it was as good an excuse as any to continue their previous conversation. With Kama occupied elsewhere for a time, it was wise to make the most of the situation. Given their proximity to the Soulless' next intended target, it was a plausible explanation for their actions.

Jal'den fell in beside him, and the pair began to make their way toward the center of the encampment and Aran'daj's command tent.

"There is more, Jal'den?" Aran'daj asked as they ducked inside. The tent was marginally warmer than outdoors, and a respite from the biting wind was welcome.

Jal'den peered around the tent for a moment, though they were alone. When he spoke, his voice was a bare whisper. "When Sal'zar returns to us—and he assured me he will—he plans to mark some of our soldiers. Those sympathetic to the Kal's plan."

"What did he mean by 'mark,' Jal'den? And for what purpose?" Aran'daj feared the Soulless' actions if they suspected the Murkor schemed against them.

Jal'den shook his head. "I don't know, Commander, and he refused to tell me. Me, of all people, he should be able to trust! Have I failed him?"

"No, Jal'den," Aran'daj replied in an attempt to soothe Jal'den's anguish. "He withholds information to protect you."

Jal'den seemed to deflate. "It is *my* duty to protect *him*," he said sullenly.

"Perhaps it is time to accept that you must protect one another."

Jal'den was silent for some time before he straightened and made his way toward the tent flap. "It goes against my nature, Commander. I am a warrior, a defender. Sal'zar is brilliant, but he is hapless with a blade."

Aran'daj smiled sadly beneath his hood. "Sal'zar is an alchemist and now learns the ways of magic. He is not defenseless, Jal'den, and perhaps he understands the stakes of our situation better than we can claim to."

"I hope you're right, Commander."

Jal'den disappeared outside, leaving Aran'daj to study his table full of maps alone.

CHAPTER EIGHTEEN

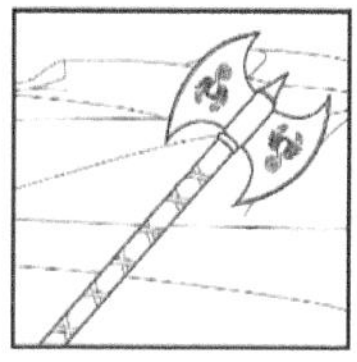

THROUGH THE MINES

"I'll light a torch once my eyes adjust," Maryn whispered into the darkness. "It seems magic only works when the wielder is awake."

Vardak had grown accustomed to the faint magical illumination Emra provided them during the day's journey into the mines, but once she'd fallen asleep, their group was plunged into a gloom so absolute he could see nothing. He was immeasurably thankful Maryn had offered to take up first watch with him; the Felene's eyesight was remarkable.

They had traveled to the first waypoint, where a series of ancient symbols were etched into the smooth stone walls. The symbols were reminiscent of those he'd encountered in Stonewall Hall. Thanks to Blademon's imparted knowledge, he knew the direction they must travel once morning arrived. Or what passed for morning in the tunnels that wove like a spider's web leagues beneath the Gray Mountains, he corrected himself.

"Thank you," Vardak replied in kind. "I'm effectively blind."

Maryn snickered, and Vardak heard him shuffling through the camp. "Fortunately for you, feline eyes can see in this murk. I will be just a moment."

The torch flared to life, its flickering light casting irregular shadows across the chiseled walls. Maryn held it above his head as he picked his way around their sleeping companions to rejoin Vardak. His striped, orange ears twitched as he grinned up at the much taller Vardak.

"Where would you be if I'd remained behind in the jungle?"

Vardak chuckled quietly. "Fumbling about, and praying to any god that might listen that I'd successfully light that torch without setting the rest of our campsite on fire."

Maryn grinned mischievously. "That, or Flariel would have done it for you."

Vardak scowled into the darkness beyond the torchlight at the mention of the goddess' name. "She came near enough this morning."

"I don't envy you, Vardak. My brief conversation with Aeon while we were in the Sky Palace was enough to last a lifetime, and you know what they say about the Underworld's caretaker…"

Vardak chuckled dryly. "I certainly don't want to garner *his* attention."

"Exactly."

Behind them, Lucas stirred in his sleep and mumbled incoherently. Vardak exchanged a glance with Maryn, and the pair fell silent as they resumed their vigil. They had traveled several miles through the mines over the course of the day, and the others needed their rest. He would not interrupt it further with idle banter meant only to pass the time. Maryn was of a similar mindset.

After a time, Vardak tucked his legs beneath himself to sit upon the cool stone floor. The soft crackle of the torch's flame and the occasional stirring of the others as they tossed in their sleep were the only sounds to be heard. He anticipated their watch would prove uneventful, but he kept his battle axe at hand as a precaution. The merchants that traveled between the Five Kingdoms and the Stronghold often told tales of monsters in the mines. Their stories often sounded too fanciful to be true, but after his experience in the southern jungles, he'd come to appreciate the potential for truth in such accounts. It was best to be prepared for the unexpected.

The remainder of their watch passed uneventfully, and Vardak was content to pass the torch to Patak and Danness. Even so, it took him some time to relax enough to drift into sleep. When he was awakened several hours later, he sensed it was morning, though the darkness around them remained unchanged. They huddled around a small fire Emra had conjured and took a brief meal before they departed. The ancient symbols directed them onto the left-hand path.

Vardak took up a position at the rear of the group alongside Lucas. Maryn took the lead, utilizing his superior night vision to warn the others of what lay ahead. They passed through another three waypoints during the day's journey, and he sensed the tunnels gradually begin to wend their way downwards, deeper into the earth. The air grew stale, and the temperature increased to a stifling level that even he and Patak struggled to contend with. They spoke little as each battled their own brand of misery within the depths.

As they approached a fourth waypoint, Vardak could sense the others' flagging desire to press on. The heat, coupled with the miles they'd journeyed, were taking a toll on everyone. Emra peered at the markings on the wall and grinned.

"It indicates that way," she said, then pointed along a tunnel that rose steeply upward from their present location. "I believe if we continue even a short distance, we'll escape this infernal heat. I don't recall it being this gods-damned hellacious in here before," she added in a quieter tone.

Her last statement elicited an uneasy glance from Lucas, who quickly diverted his gaze. Vardak hoped the man would come to terms with his long-time friend's new role soon; his hesitancy to admit Emra had memories that spanned centuries was growing tiresome.

"We'll continue up the tunnel for a short distance," Vardak agreed. Beneath his plate mail, his torso was slicked with sweat, and his energy waned. He was certain the others felt the same, but they would all sleep more soundly in a cooler environment.

There was a mumble of agreement before they began to move forward once more. Vardak glanced at Lucas as they brought up the rear, intent on addressing the man's misgivings.

"It isn't her fault she has other memories," he stated quietly.

Lucas startled, then smiled sheepishly. "I know, but at times I'm not certain if I'm speaking to her or to someone else. Fucking gods, when I say it aloud it makes no sense." He shook his head and looked down. "Then there's this business with her magic. Some pieces of our collective past I now understand. It's how she was able to navigate to the Stronghold unerringly, and why she reacted oddly as we passed Nuarno Peak. I suppose what bothers me the most is that she knew nothing of any of this for thirty-four years, and then she found that damned sword. One touch, and she is suddenly not simply Emra. She is five *others*, as well."

"And yet, she is not," Vardak countered. "She is Emra, with additional memories and experience to guide her. She is not so different from me, with Blademon's gift of imparted knowledge."

Lucas seemed to deflate. "I hadn't considered it that way. You're right, Vardak. I'm being a fool."

"I didn't say that—"

Lucas cut him off with a laugh. "You didn't have to." He shook his head again. "When she named you General, I'll admit I was envious of you. You're a decade younger than we are, and from Patak's account, untested in true battle. I wanted to believe Emra made a mistake in choosing you, but I think she saw beyond your age and inexperience. Your training with Blademon had little to do with her final decision."

Vardak shrugged uncomfortably. "I made the same arguments to her when she offered the post."

Lucas grinned. "Knowing Em, she ignored them and gave you ten other reasons why you ought to agree."

"It may not have been ten, but it was enough."

"And you've proven your earlier point, as well. She *is* much the same."

Lucas' gaze drifted forward, seeking Emra near the head of their column. She walked between Fyrmane and Patak; in spite of their obvious fatigue, they seemed to be engaged in friendly banter.

Lucas sighed. "She's in love with him, you know. She promised she would make certain your brother does not face exile, but I'm not sure she'll be able to keep her word."

Vardak frowned. "And Patak is unconcerned. He has always followed his passions, no matter the repercussions for the rest of us."

"Perhaps given who Emra is, your people will reconsider their stance?" Lucas asked hopefully.

Vardak shook his head. "You've met Sevic. It would take an act of the gods to sway him."

They fell silent and followed the others as the tunnel bent sharply ahead. A cool draft of air washed over them once past the curve, and Vardak found himself silently grinning. The change in temperature was a welcome respite from the sweltering heat they'd endured for the past several hours. The others had stopped, and it quickly became clear Emra intended to make camp.

After a few moments of discussion, it was decided that Lucas and Patak would take first watch, followed by Vardak and Emra on second. Coreyaless distributed dried fruit and nuts to the others, while Maryn dug some dried jerky from within his pack. The Felene was a strict carnivore, and the diet of the others was a constant source of amusement for him. Vardak would have liked something more than fruit and nuts, but until they reached the city of Moraine on the other end of the mines, he must abide with what they had.

Despite their exhaustion, the group's spirits improved with the cooler environment, a meal, and the prospect of rest. Vardak reminded Patak to awaken him in four hours' time before he removed his armor and lay down to rest. It seemed he'd only closed his eyes when his brother's rough hands shook him awake once more.

"Sleep well?" Patak asked with a grin.

Vardak rubbed the sleep from his eyes and pushed himself up with a groan. The stone tunnel was uncomfortable, and he'd been locked in the same position for several hours. A few paces away, Lucas stood sentinel, a torch in hand to ward off the ever-present darkness.

"I slept," Vardak replied dryly and began to don his armor.

"I doubt you'll need that," Patak informed him. "It's been quiet."

Vardak shrugged and continued with his task, his desire to be prepared outweighing his wish for comfort. Patak shook his head, bemused, and moved to awaken Emra. Vardak hefted his battle axe and slung it across his back, then moved forward to stand beside Lucas. Lucas stared down the tunnel they'd ascended a few hours previously, then turned to face Vardak.

"As Patak said, it's been quiet. He's unconcerned, but…" Lucas shook his head. "Something feels off, Vardak. Be wary."

"Don't worry, Luke, we will," Emra chimed in as she came toward them. She flicked her wrist, and a pale, yellow illumination enveloped their camp, its light steady compared to the dancing of the torch's flame.

"I suppose you won't be needing this." Lucas smirked and doused the torch. "Wake us in four hours, Em."

"Of course." She leaned back against the wall and studied Vardak for a time, her gray eyes unreadable. Only after Lucas and Patak had settled themselves and seemed to be drifting into slumber did she speak again. "Do you trust your brother's assessment of the night, or Luke's?"

He knew she was not asking out of mere curiosity. It was another test of his character as she sought confirmation that she'd made the correct decision when naming him General. He pushed aside his misgivings and opted to give her the truth, as he saw it.

"It would be unwise to dismiss Luke's concerns, and Patak has a habit of believing the best of every situation he finds himself in." Vardak crossed his arms and gazed into the darkness beyond the edge of the magical light. "Either may be right, but I'd rather remain vigilant."

"A cautious approach," she replied and drew herself upright. "Do you believe the tales about monsters in the depths?"

"After what I've seen in Stonewall Hall and the southern jungles, I will not discount the possibility."

She nodded thoughtfully. "An open mind will prove beneficial when dealing with the atrocities of the Soulless."

She fell silent, and he found himself relieved that he seemed to have passed her latest assessment. Perhaps she was merely preparing him for what lay ahead. There would undoubtedly be many who questioned his ability and his competence, regardless of his history with Blademon.

"I expect it will take us another two days to reach the exit—" Emra began, but fell silent as they both heard a tapping echo from the corridor beyond the light's reach. She drew Fireblade from its sheath. Flames erupted along its cutting edge as the relic responded to her touch.

Vardak reached for his axe and unsheathed it as he strained his ears for further sound. Moments later, it came to them again, a dry, ticking sound, not unlike that made by his own people as their chitinous legs moved across stone. None of the Scorpion Men, with the exception of himself and Patak, had been given clearance to leave the Stronghold. The sound continued for several seconds before it abruptly ceased. To his ear, there were many legs involved, and if they belonged to his people, there were a sizeable number of them. The abrupt halt, however, gave him further pause.

He glanced at Emra as he adopted a defensive stance. Whatever was making its way toward them would be revealed with its next movement, and he did not believe they would encounter Scorpion Men. This was something else entirely.

She donned her shield and stood ready, the white snow leopard depicted on its surface gleaming dully in the faint light. "I had to mention the damned monsters," she muttered under her breath, before calling over her shoulder loudly, "Lucas, Patak, awake!"

The ticking sound came to them again as the others began to stir into wakefulness. Patak mumbled incoherently even as the source of the noise moved into the light. A long, chitinous body supported by dozens of pairs of legs snaked into view, its length so great that its hindquarters remained enshrouded by the shadows beyond. The legs were jointed and sported numerous sharp bristles. The creature's head was insectile; it sported a pair of long antennae and two large pincers that glistened with what Vardak assumed was venom. It was eyeless, a creature born and adapted fully to the dark beneath the mountains.

"Shit," Patak muttered behind him as he began to scramble for his armor and broadsword.

The creature skittered nearer, drawn by the sounds within the camp. It reared up, pincers gnashing violently at the air, and released a rattling hiss. Vardak held his ground and prepared to strike if it came within his range. Adrenaline coursed through his veins and activated the venom glands at the base of his tail, though he suspected it would do little against this foe. The creature was reminiscent of the centipedes they sometimes encountered in the desert, which were immune.

"By Aeon's hairy ass, what is that?" Maryn gaped as he took up a position between Vardak and Emra. He held a long-bladed dagger in each of his furry mitts, his green eyes riveted upon the creature.

As if in response, it scuttled closer and hissed again. It was almost within striking range, though the end of its long body remained beyond the edge of the light.

"I'd advise to aim for its eyes, but it has none," Vardak stated.

He scanned the creature for obvious weak points, but could detect none. Smooth plates interlocked across its expanse, forming a natural suit of armor. It reared up again and gnashed its pincers in warning. As he observed its movements, an idea came to him.

"Strike into its mouth if you can!"

It lunged in his direction, its aim guided by the sound of his voice alone. He side-stepped and swung his axe as the creature's pincers missed him by a thread. His blade struck the side of its eyeless head but failed to penetrate the thick scales. It backed away slightly and hissed.

Emra strode forward, Fireblade ablaze in her hand and Patak on her heels. He'd managed to don his armor during the few moments in which the creature had been focused on Vardak. Now, he adopted a defensive stance at Emra's side as she began to slash at the creature's legs. Her magically-enhanced blade inflicted damage where his standard steel had failed.

The creature reared again as it prepared for another strike, this time in Emra's direction. Vardak glanced at Maryn as it opened its mouth wide.

"Now!" he cried.

Maryn threw both of his daggers in succession, his aim true. One struck the creature in the roof of its gaping maw, while the other lodged itself within its throat. Its hiss became a strangled rattle as it began to shake its head violently from side to side. Its movements failed to dislodge Maryn's blades, and Emra took the opportunity to drive Fireblade through its broad body as it writhed in anguish. Its head fell to the stone floor with a crunch. Yellow ichor pooled from the severed ends of its body.

"Good aim," Emra said to Maryn as she backed away from the carcass.

Maryn grinned. "Now the question is, who will volunteer to help me retrieve my blades?"

Vardak chuckled and motioned toward his brother. "We'll help you with that, Maryn. I doubt the creature's venom will affect us."

Patak snorted. "I'm less certain, but we're more suited to the task than the rest of you." He shook his head and peered at the lifeless creature. "By the gods, I hope we don't come across any more of these."

CHAPTER NINETEEN

DRAKKON RESOLVE

It was the fourth night in a row that Tavesin entered the Aethereum while Rostin and Badolo awaited his return to the physical realm. There had been no trace of Arra and no indication the Soulless had returned to the realm. A part of him desperately hoped the golden-eyed man would find him again, but Tavesin did not know the man's name. Without that information, it was impossible to locate his one-time savior.

He knew where Arra was held, but he dared not venture there again. He'd forced himself to appear a short distance away from the black tower on his second night of futile searching, only to discover the tower's denizens had erected a number of magical traps. He'd studied them carefully for a time to learn more of their construction, and realized the traps were not designed to ensnare the unwary visitor—they were designed to kill. His fleeting hope of a valiant rescue was immediately dashed.

This night, Tavesin returned to Rican Mer with the expectation that he would once again return without news of Arra. He trudged between the farmhouses, his head down as he failed to combat his despondency. His despair consumed him, and soon it became difficult to maintain the thin magical shield he'd deployed upon entry into the realm. It sputtered and flickered around him in a cascade of brilliant blue light that outshone the Aethereum's strange illumination.

In spite of his heavy heart, Tavesin vowed to return each night until he formulated a plan or until he encountered Arra again. He would not disappoint the wizards, and he would not leave Arra to the

Soulless' whims if he could help it. The trouble was, he lacked direction, and the tower's library contained little information on the Aethereum. He was at an impasse.

Time crawled by as he continued his vigil. His hope waned as midnight drew near, and he began to doubt Arra—or anyone else—would appear that night. In his frustration, he would have welcomed the entrance of one of the Soulless and the chance to test his newfound skills. A strike against one of their number would have given him a sense of redemption, and perhaps achieve vengeance for Arra. Yet no one arrived; it was another night wasted.

He sighed heavily and prepared to depart for the tower. He paused to scan the homes of Rican Mer a final time when motion caught his eye near the riverbank. A flash of coppery hair in the harsh light lifted his spirits, and he sprinted in its direction.

"Arra!"

She lifted her head slowly and turned her face toward the sound of his voice. He stumbled and fell to his knees alongside her, aghast at the change wrought in her features. She was thin to the point of frailty, her body marred by bruises. Some, like the one that blemished her right cheek, were dark purple-blue. Others, like those visible on her wrists, had faded into a sickly yellow-green hue. Her eyes, once vibrant and filled with life, were now glassy, her spirit broken.

His voice caught in his throat. "Arra! Gods…I wish there were a way to save you…" His eyes stung with unshed tears.

Tentatively, she reached toward him. Cold fingers touched the side of his face. When she spoke, her voice was hoarse. "Do not blame yourself, Taven."

"How can I not? If it wasn't for me, you would still be safe in your home, far away from the tower and the Soulless…"

"You are a true friend." She dropped her hand and began to cough, a wracking sound that tore at his heart. When the fit passed, she shook her head, tangled strands of hair falling over her face.

"Is there anything I can do?" he asked. "I can return, fetch Aziarah—"

"There is little she can do, Taven. My hurts cannot be healed while my body lies within the black tower. The Soulless cannot stop me from coming here in this manner, but they have caged my power in the physical realm. I cannot bring myself here, as you have."

Each word was a knife to his heart. He was unable to help her, unable to confront the Soulless in their domain.

"Arra, I will do everything in my power to save you."

"Do not make promises you cannot keep, Taven." Another bout of coughing consumed her as she crumpled to the grass.

"Arra!"

"Forget me, Taven. You deserve to *live*, as I cannot." Tears spilled from her eyes, and she managed a faint smile. "Save your energy for the Soulless. War is coming, and I will not live to see it. Goodbye, Taven."

"No!" The tears that had threatened began to run down his cheeks as she winked out of existence.

He howled into the void; anger coupled with helpless frustration served to fuel the sound. Grief overcame him after a time while guilt gnawed at his mind. He dissolved into sobs, unable to muster the energy to return to the tower. His shield faltered and dissipated, leaving him vulnerable, but he no longer cared. Let them come—his failure was absolute.

He lost count of the minutes he'd spent in the Aethereum, but knew it was well beyond the agreed-upon hour of his return when he finally came to his senses. He was unsurprised when Aziarah's voice broke the silence that had grown in the wake of his grief.

"Tavesin, what has happened?" She was at his side in an instant, concern etched into her reptilian features.

"Arra," he whispered, and blinked away a fresh wave of tears. "She's dying, Aziarah, and I can do nothing to save her."

A half-hour later Tavesin found himself back in the physical realm, surrounded by a trio of Drakkon, Rostin, and Badolo. None of the wizards had been summoned; Rostin explained when he'd gone to seek Hasnin, his study had been empty, so he'd signaled Aziarah instead. Rostin had learned a few tricks himself over the course of the past weeks, and had sent a vibrant flare of light skyward from the tower's garden. Moments later, a pair of Drakkon had arrived to investigate, then left to inform Aziarah.

Tavesin now sat with his back against the trunk of a tree in the tower's garden. The trees and flowers surrounding them were vibrant and lush, in defiance of the autumnal breeze. The air was cool but not cold, in spite of the early hour. Clouds blanketed the sky overhead and obscured the stars. Rostin sat to his right, Badolo to his left, and the Drakkon stood a few paces away from them. Trozyen appeared troubled, Aziarah flustered, and the third, a female that Tavesin did not recognize, scowled toward the tower.

"I'm displeased with the route the wizards have steered your education, Tavesin." Aziarah began to pace restlessly before the others while her wings ruffled with agitation.

Tavesin shrugged indifferently. "They did not give me another choice, Aziarah, and I've prepared myself for the Soulless as best I can."

Her expression softened momentarily. "You are more prepared than most, Tavesin, but that is not what upsets me. Does your mentor not understand the impossibility of the task he's saddled you with? Does the Radiant?"

"They seized on his desire to see the girl freed," the other female replied. "I doubt they care if he completes the assignment successfully or not. If he passes their test too quickly, they will be forced to make good on their promise to him—and I do not believe they are prepared for that eventuality."

"Do you mean the wizards have set Taven up to fail?" Badolo asked in disbelief.

"If he succeeds, they must allow him to undergo his challenge. It would make him the youngest wizard in the tower's history—a thing that may not sit well with many of your council's elders. If he tries and fails to deliver upon his task, they will delay his challenge and avoid further controversy." She gestured toward Aziarah. "We have discussed their motives at length, and are of the opinion the wizards have done great harm to your friend, Master Lorvehk."

Badolo stiffened as she spoke his name. "How did you—?"

Trozyen chuckled. "Lyveria possesses the gift of past sight. It is why she joined us when we ventured here. The wizards can hide nothing from her."

"Nor can you, young prince." Lyveria winked in his direction. "Do not worry. The Drakkon will keep your secret."

"There must be something we can do," Rostin stated. "I don't want to see Taven fail, and if you're right about the wizards' motives, what they've done is unfair."

"There is much we can do." Aziarah spoke with conviction. "I want the three of you to return to your beds. In the morning, skip your scheduled lessons and make your way here. My people will teach you what you ought to be learning from the inept fools that run your council. The Drakkon will ensure the three of you will be trained appropriately for the battles to come. If the wizards deign to offer you the challenges they've promised, so be it. If they do not, we will make certain they regret their decision to deceive you."

Tavesin looked up, hope blossoming in his heart for the first time in weeks. "Aziarah…"

"I am finished playing their senseless games, Tavesin." She tossed her head and fluttered her wings in agitation. "Your council will learn the error of their ways, one way or another. I expect to see the three of you by mid-morning."

CHAPTER TWENTY

SEEKING THE STONE

"You are Deluchan, if I'm not mistaken." Ravin feigned boredom with his prisoner and picked at his nails. "I'm certain you know more than what you've divulged to the queen."

"I told you days ago that I don't fucking know where the talisman lies." Jannyn glared sullenly from within his cell. "I was sent here to seek that answer when I landed myself in your gods-damned trap."

"Then you're of no use to me."

Ravin shifted his gaze to examine the man shackled within the cell. The guards had been ordered to treat him fairly but to remain at a safe distance from the bars. The Soulless was provided food and drink, clean water and soap every two days in which to bathe, and a chamber pot. Given their instructions, the delivery and replacement of these items had fallen to Ravin. He alone was equipped to deal with their prisoner, and he'd begun to time his interrogations to coincide with the unsavory chores.

"Wait, I promised I had more information, and I do."

"The queen may be interested in your battle plans and other schemes," Ravin sneered. "I am not."

It wasn't true, but Ravin wanted to see the man squirm.

"You *will* be interested in this," Jannyn promised. "Garin was ordered to bring you to the tower—unscathed. Our master has plans for you."

"Your master will not have me." Ravin frowned at him in disdain, though within, his rage smoldered. "I'm aware of Garin's orders. He's attempted to act on them several times, and he's failed. He will *continue* to fail." He leveled a cold stare at the Soulless. "Tell me something I don't already know, or your time here is finished."

"Kama was set to lead the army into Delucha," Jannyn blurted.

Ravin's eyes narrowed, and he leaned forward until his forehead nearly touched the bars of Jannyn's cell. "If I find you have lied to me…"

Jannyn shook his head adamantly, eyes wide. "I heard her order, and I speak the fucking truth! His target was Daesan! Go into the Aethereum and see for yourself."

"Don't worry, I will. But not this instant." Ravin straightened and glowered down at the cowering Soulless. "How did you plan to search for the talisman if you did not know its location?"

Jannyn ground his teeth in frustration but remained silent.

Ravin smirked; he'd been anticipating the man's swift change of demeanor. "Clearly, you know something." When the Soulless continued to hold his tongue, Ravin said, "I have no qualms when it comes to extracting information from your kind."

Jannyn released a sigh and gazed at him sullenly. "Prior to my untimely demise and recent resurrection, I was seeking this kingdom's talisman to further my own goals. It's why the Nameless assigned me this task. He is always aware of our actions."

Ravin studied him for a time. He believed Jannyn spoke truthfully, even if he continued to skirt the topic.

"I'm aware of your god's hold over you. Continue."

"You must understand, my death occurred at least four hundred years ago, if my calculations are correct. The information I was acting upon may not be valid any longer." Jannyn eyed him nervously.

"I'm willing to take a risk," Ravin replied. "Speak, or I'll allow the queen to make good upon her threat."

Jannyn swallowed hard. "If I am killed, the Nameless will never forgive my failure. Please…"

"He was once the god of death. I imagine forgiveness is not in his nature."

"No. It will be an eternity of torture worse than even you can inflict."

Ravin crossed his arms, growing tired of Jannyn's hesitation. "Then speak, you gods-damned fool."

"I traced an ancient text to this palace's library." Jannyn deflated at the words. "It speaks of the talismans, their creation, what they may be used for… All the knowledge you seek is within that book, but I don't know if it's still there."

"That wasn't difficult, was it?"

Ravin channeled his power and held Jannyn firmly in place while he unlocked the cell door. He pushed the bucket of water, which was no longer warm, a rag, and a bar of soap from the corridor and into the cell with a swift current of air. The items stopped inches away from Jannyn's shackled form, and he released the man only when the door was secured once more.

"Must this fucking humiliation continue?" the Soulless moaned.

"No. I'll leave you to your ministrations," Ravin replied acidly. "Perhaps when I return, I'll have further questions for you."

Jannyn rolled his eyes. "I can't say I'm looking forward to our next meeting."

The palace's library was housed on the main floor, at the end of a little-used corridor hung with fraying tapestries. He reflected on his interactions with the young queen since his arrival in the palace and resigned himself to the notion that the Serales family had likely held little regard for the literary treasure trove in their possession.

The library's heavy wooden door was propped open just far enough to allow him entry. As he stepped inside, he was greeted with a daunting sight.

Books were shelved from floor to ceiling along each wall, and dozens of rows had been erected in between. Books were piled atop books, scrolls were crammed into nooks, texts and tomes of numerous shapes and sizes filled every conceivable space. A narrow aisle ran from the door to a dusty oaken table and an empty hearth on the far side of the room. A half-melted candle in a metal holder was perched on one corner of the table. Fine filaments of cobweb hung from the wax taper and extended to the floor. A single high window with a cracked pane provided dim illumination to the room.

Ravin shook his head in astonishment. It was evident that no one had entered the space in years, and it was unlikely anyone in the queen's employ would know the system of organization in the space—if indeed there was one. There was a tremendous amount of knowledge stored in the library, wasted by the kingdom's present regime. It would take weeks to sift through the books without some inkling of where he might begin his search.

Dust plumed into the air as he crossed the room toward the table. "Gods, they've squandered what they have here. And for how many years?"

The motes dancing in the pale daylight gave no response. He scanned the innumerable rows of texts again, overwhelmed by the task he faced. Where to begin?

"There you are." The queen's voice carried over the stale air, her tone bemused. "When one of the servants informed me you'd gone this way, I laughed at her. No one has come here in generations."

"Clearly." He did not turn to face her, and the ensuing silence told him she was irritated by his lack of interest in her presence.

"I have no interest in dirtying my skirts to cross this room," she informed him.

He frowned and turned away from the shelves to face her. "What do you want?"

Her dark eyebrows rose as she bristled at his tone. "An update. I know you've been to see our prisoner again."

"He provided me with two items worth investigating," Ravin replied evenly. "A book once resided here that may lead me to the talisman, but I do not know where to begin."

"I will send servants to assist you. The gods only know when this room was last used, and it is in need of a good cleaning." Her expression soured as she spied the cobweb near the table. "And the second item?"

"He claims the Soulless plan to attack Delucha. He mentioned Daesan."

She sniffed imperiously. "Daesan is a poor target. The fire mountain has deterred their attacks in the past."

"Even so, I mean to investigate the truth of his words."

A sadistic gleam entered her green eyes. "I hope it is a false trail meant only to delay our progress. The man deserves to die."

"While I am in agreement, he remains useful alive," Ravin reminded her.

"That remains to be seen. I will send a dozen servants to aid your search, Ravin. Keep me apprised of your progress." She turned in a swish of silk and disappeared into the corridor.

He moved to the nearest row of books and began to scan the titles. Even with the aid of servants, many of which he was certain would be unable to read, it would take days to locate the tome he sought. He prayed the book was still within and his search would not prove futile.

He would find Delucha's talisman before the Soulless claimed it as their own, then use the relic against them. In the meantime, there was the matter of Daesan to consider.

CHAPTER TWENTY-ONE

THE NAMELESS' THRALL

Days spent amongst the initiates left Dranamir in a foul temper. The handful of would-be Enlightened that showed true aptitude with magic pleased her, but the scores of others that fumbled about tried her patience. She would have purged the ranks of the unworthy weeks ago had her master allowed it. He had not. In fact, he'd ordered her explicitly to teach them without making bloody examples of the failures. A disappointment, and one Alyra had grown fond of bringing up.

Thoughts of the once-beautiful vixen soured her mood further. Even collared, Alyra continued to find opportunities to goad her. The Nameless had forced his will upon Alyra, and she complied with his orders dutifully. It seemed those orders did not extend to her interactions with the other Soulless. With each remark, Dranamir's desire to be rid of the other woman increased. She would find a way; it was only a matter of time.

She scowled at the ranks of initiates as they practiced shielding and attack techniques. They worked in pairs, one on defense, the other on offense, while Dranamir and Alyra looked on. Alyra strode amongst them, her head held high and her expression imperious. She paused at intervals to offer encouragement or advice.

Dranamir stood at the front of the room, arms crossed. She was aware of each success the initiates made as well as each mistake. The latter she made special note of; those initiates would be dealt with later. She could not kill them, but she was allowed to inflict pain, a reminder that they must strive to do better. There were only a handful who demonstrated near perfection, and she paid close attention to their actions. They would be the first to undergo initiation rites, should they continue to impress.

Her attention was diverted as a man botched the fire magic he was attempting to cast. Rather than send it hurtling toward his assigned partner, a gout of flame erupted inches from him. He staggered backward, horrified at his mistake. He stared aghast at his red and blistering hands from a face whose eyebrows were singed away.

Dranamir's furious gaze skewered him in place as she strode toward him. The other initiates scurried aside to allow her passage, which was fortunate for them. She would have thrown anyone in her path violently aside.

The man swallowed while his eyes darted across the room in search of a savior that would never come. Dranamir locked him in position but restrained herself from further action until she stood a single pace from him. Despite the mild burns on his cheeks, his face grew ashen.

"Fire is a useful tool when properly managed." Her voice rang across the room. The gathered initiates remained still and silent, fearful and expectant for her next words. "When mishandled, fire is a dangerous beast."

Behind her, Alyra sighed in disapproval. "Be wary of our orders, Dranamir."

She smirked at her quarry, helpless in the air before her. "Our orders stated we may not *kill*. They said nothing of torture."

She reached toward him and prepared to strike him with an onslaught of pain, when a summons rang obtrusively through her mind. She blinked in momentary frustration and dropped her arm. Garin's timing was deplorable, but the summons could not be ignored.

"It seems our presence is requested," she hissed through clenched teeth. "Be certain you tame your unruly flames before our next meeting, else I will make an example of you."

She spun on her heel and stalked toward Alyra. The other woman had opened a portal into the Aethereum to facilitate their travel to the tower's topmost floor. Alyra wore an amused expression, as though she enjoyed the interruption to Dranamir's planned violence. Dranamir fixed her in an icy gaze as she stormed through the opening. A day would eventually come when she could make good on her promise to remove Alyra from the Soulless' ranks—it was simply a matter of biding her time.

She traveled to the top of the tower and emerged into the physical realm without waiting for Alyra's arrival. Moments after her own portal closed, the other woman emerged from another, a glare pinching her features. Garin and Kama were already there; the smaller man paced near the mirror, while the tall Kamshati stood impassively toward one side. Kama appeared to be less pleased with the summons than Dranamir was. Jannyn was nowhere to be seen.

Garin stopped pacing after their arrival and turned toward them, his pale features grim. "I've just spoken with our master, and it seems there are two matters of import we must discuss."

Dranamir folded her arms and frowned at him. His constant posturing was wearisome.

"Then speak," Kama growled. "Your timing, as usual, is gods-damned abominable."

Garin ignored the outburst and continued, unperturbed. "Our master has deemed Alyra's punishment sufficient."

He waved a thin wrist in her direction, and the collar snapped open. It vanished before it reached the tiled floor while Alyra beamed. Tears leaked from her crimson eyes and she sank to her knees in supplication.

"Please tell our master I am grateful to have pleased him."

Dranamir rolled her eyes at the sickening display. "Have you no shame?"

"You do not know what it's like to wear the collar, Dranamir."

She smirked. "And I never will. Unlike you, I don't fail in my tasks."

"Enough," Kama snarled. "I did not leave our army on the brink of reaching Daesan to listen to the pair of you bicker." His gaze flicked toward Alyra, then landed on Dranamir. "We've all been made fully fucking aware of your temper and your tendencies, Dranamir. The incessant reminders do nothing but increase my desire to see you brought to your damned knees."

She met his gaze unflinchingly but made no response. It seemed their previous argument and his subsequent display of power over her, had emboldened him. She wondered if he still harbored anger for her attempt on the Murkor commander's life, or if he'd simply lost interest in his pursuit of her. It mattered little; she was accustomed to working alone, and she would not be caught off her guard by him again.

"The arguments do not further our cause," Garin stated into the tense silence. "The other matter I summoned you here for is far more troubling. Jannyn is missing, and even our master is unable to locate him."

"What?" Alyra gaped, her eyes wide. "That's impossible."

"There are only two scenarios he believes would prevent him from locating Jannyn," Garin replied. "The first, and most likely, is Jannyn lies on the brink of death."

"No," Alyra moaned. She began to rock on her heels while fresh tears spilled from her eyes. "He cannot be…dying…"

"Afraid you won't find another man to entice into your bed?" Dranamir asked venomously.

"What is the second scenario?" Kama demanded irritably.

"Jannyn is in a sealed location, veiled from our master's sight." Garin looked at each of them in turn to impart the gravity of his statement. "There is only one mage capable of creating such a space, and the master last tracked Jannyn into the Aethereum."

Dranamir ground her teeth together as a blinding rage consumed her. "Ravin."

"Yes."

"You should have left him to rot in his self-imposed prison," she seethed.

Alyra rose to her feet and stared between the pair, stunned. "Ravin is alive?"

Dranamir sneered at the other woman. "I'm surprised he chose not to inform you. He's told everyone else."

"Given your unfortunate history with Ravin, the master felt it best that you remained ignorant of his return," Garin replied.

Alyra's eyes narrowed. "The master felt it was best, or you, Garin?"

Garin shrugged and chose to ignore her question. "Ravin is our enemy. The master ordered me to locate his soul-stone and resurrect him, with the belief Ravin would be disoriented upon awakening. I was to subdue him and return him to our order. I was…unprepared for his strength."

Dranamir snorted. "You miscalculated, and now we must all deal with the consequences of *your* failure. Why did the Nameless not collar you, Garin? Inept as she is, Alyra did not unleash a creature that may prove to be our downfall. *You did.*"

Garin straightened to his full height and pulled the collar of his shirt down to reveal his collarbones. Beneath each was scrawled a single word in the language of the ancient race, known only as the builders. The letters were sinuous, as though painted with a flowing hand. The word translated to "thrall".

Dranamir's rage evaporated, leaving dread in its wake. Garin would never be collared as Alyra had been; the magic that bound him to the Nameless had achieved the same effect without the need for a relic. He was their god's puppet, to be used as their master deemed necessary. Garin had relinquished his free will in order to become Soulless. Devout as she was to serving the Nameless, she would never have agreed to a similar arrangement.

"Now you understand my position," Garin stated coldly. "When I speak, it is with our master's authority. When I act, it is as his hand in this world. Do not question me, Dranamir, for in doing so, you question *him.*"

"Apologies." The word was like bile in her throat, but she would not endure being collared. It must be said.

Garin nodded tersely and adjusted his collar to cover the marks once more. "Ravin's threat is palpable. Our master has ordered that none of the initiates venture into the Aethereum and that we limit our visits there to necessity only."

"And what of Ravin?" Alyra asked.

"I will deal with him," Garin replied. "I believe I have learned of a means to disarm him."

Dranamir scowled. "I hope you plan to destroy him, Garin."

"His fate is not mine to decide. I will do as our master commands."

CHAPTER TWENTY-TWO

AN UNLIKELY PARTNERSHIP

Ravin ground his teeth and glowered at the tabletop. With his news that the Soulless' threat had been confirmed and the Murkor army was indeed moving upon Daesan to the northeast, the queen had called an emergency session with her advisors. She explained the situation, then promptly vacated the premises to allow her advisors to deal with the problem.

Her apparent disregard for the unfolding problem rankled, and the reason for departure even more so. She claimed she had "business" with Jasom Riversend. He knew what business she referred to; it only served to lower his opinion of the young monarch further.

"I will dispatch a message to Balotica immediately," Malira stated into the silence that had descended over them in the queen's wake. "They asked for our aid to combat this threat, but it seems they have succeeded in driving the enemy into our lands."

"Are the ambassadors from Balotica still within the palace?" Jadosin asked gruffly.

Malira shook her head. "They left three days ago."

"Hmm." Jadosin stroked his iron gray beard as he contemplated his next words. "I will issue new orders to the soldiers that were sent northward, but they may not receive our message in time to stave off the threat."

Ravin's frown deepened. His priority was the talisman, but he was in a position to assist the others. The queen's flighty concerns be damned.

"Give me your messages," he said without looking up. "I will deliver them personally. I can reach both locations far faster than your messenger birds."

"We would be in your debt, Ravin," Malira replied.

He shrugged noncommittally. "You owe me nothing. When it comes to the Soulless, I will do everything in my power to thwart their plans."

"With your magic, perhaps you can transport the soldiers nearer to Daesan?" Jadosin asked hopefully.

Ravin chuckled humorlessly. "I may be powerful, but I cannot perform such a feat without assistance. I can deliver your message and pray your men can reach Daesan in time to turn the tide of battle."

"Perhaps the Shining Tower can be of aid?" Malira suggested. "I have contacts in Dar Daelad."

Ravin knew Aethereal magic was a rarity amongst those born and blessed with the Ability. The likelihood that even a pair of wizards possessed the talent was miniscule. He shook his head as yet another reason struck him.

"You may contact the wizards if you wish, but I'm not certain they will welcome the notion of working alongside someone like myself."

She sighed. "Perhaps you're right. I will pen a message to Cedric Hightower in Balotica and leave my correspondence at that. I thank you for your aid in this matter, Ravin."

He managed a tight smile, unused to such praises. "I'll be in the library. Find me there once your messages are prepared."

He rose from his seat and strode from the room as the others continued their discussion on matters of palace defense. His input was unnecessary; matters of food stores and weaponry, diplomacy, and protocol were not within his purview. His departure would also allow him precious time to further his search for the kingdom's talisman, and time was a commodity in short supply.

Since the previous afternoon, the library had been dusted and swept, the cobwebs dispatched, the window cleaned, and the hearth cleared of debris. A fire blazed merrily in the hearth upon his arrival, candles adorned the table, and several of the palace's literate staff perused the shelves in search of the text Ravin sought.

He stepped inside as Adalin, Duchess of the Mers, swept into view on the opposite end of the room. He groaned audibly. The sound was not lost on her, and she offered him a knowing smile.

"Our young queen said I might find you here, Ravin. I must say, I'm impressed with the collection. Who knew the palace held such a wealth of knowledge?"

"Did she also tell you I wished not to be disturbed?" he asked, unable to mask his irritation.

"Oh, she did, but I assured her I would be of assistance. I *can* read, you know." She beckoned him toward the shelf she'd been browsing when he entered. "I believe I may have found something, Ravin."

He doubted her words and made his skepticism clear in his expression.

"It cannot hurt you to take a look," she snapped as her previous cheer morphed into exasperation. "You may be a great mage with power beyond reckoning, but you are as witless as any man I've met. Bullheaded, too." She placed her hands on her hips and fixed him with an impatient glare. "If you've failed to notice, there is no one from court about to flaunt you to. I came to assist, and I believe you ought to do me the service of looking over what I've found."

"My time is—"

"Valuable, yes. I'm aware. Or were you about to say it's limited?" She smirked. "You're not as mysterious as you believe yourself to be, Ravin, and I'm not about to leave until you've acknowledged my discovery."

He sighed loudly and made his way across the room. The woman was determined to remain a thorn in his side.

"Such flair for the dramatic," she chided him as he came to stand at her side. "And I thought you would not tangle yourself in the games of the noble court."

"I'm gods-damned frustrated at the interruption," he snarled, flustered by her words.

"Then perhaps this will soothe your temper."

She winked at him conspicuously and removed a thin, leather-bound volume from the shelf. The spine was worn and cracked with age, and the front cover was tooled with the design of an eagle with its wings spread. It was the insignia of the Deluchan royal house, but he did not understand the significance of the book she'd chosen. He raised his eyebrows, nonplussed.

She growled in irritation. "The scribes of the royal house once recorded the greatest secrets of the kingdom in books such as this one. The tooling is very old, if you care to look closely." She traced one fingernail along the eagle's outstretched left wing. "The age of this volume coupled with the insignia told me immediately that its contents are important."

"And are they?" He continued to exude skepticism.

She flipped the book open to a page near the end. "This is a catalog of the library's contents, from King Valsen's reign." She tapped her nail against a single line near the middle of the page. "This, my friend, is the title of the book you've been searching for."

The Relics of Peace: The Talismans. S36,14.5.

He stared at the line for several seconds, then looked up at her. "Does the book still reside here?" His voice was breathless as he attempted to rein in his excitement and the false hope that accompanied it. Too much time had passed since the catalog she'd found; it was an impossible notion that the book he sought would be found in the same location. And yet, the library had sat untouched for generations…

"The numbers written at the end of the title indicate its location amongst the shelves. There is a book on that shelf, but I don't know if it bears the same title. Come."

She closed the book and replaced it, then took his arm firmly in her own. She led him to another bookcase at the rear corner of the room, a pleased smile upon her lips. He spied another book, partially extracted from the highest shelf, before she pointed toward it.

"I was about to seek a step-stool when you arrived. That is the location indicated by the catalog, but I cannot reach it without assistance." She gazed up at him. "You will have no trouble, Ravin."

"Do you believe it's the book we seek, Adalin?" he whispered.

She arched one dark eyebrow in amusement. "A few moments ago, there was no mention of 'we'. I could not read the words printed on the cover. Given the state of this room only yesterday, I believe there is a good chance it *is* your book, Ravin. Delucha's monarchs have a long tradition of ignoring their own history."

"I've noticed," he replied dryly, but grinned at her in spite of himself.

"I don't believe I've ever seen you smile, Ravin. Gods, you're a heartbreaker when you do." She shook her head and looked away from his gaze while carefully extricating her arm. "We should see about this book."

He frowned, puzzled by her sudden change in demeanor. He'd done nothing but share a moment of enthusiasm with the duchess, but perhaps whatever had occurred would steer her away from further meddling in his affairs. He rose onto his toes in order to reach the indicated tome. A shower of dust rained upon them as he pulled it free and turned it over to examine it further. It seemed the servants had been unable to reach the shelf during their time spent cleaning.

"By the gods," he whispered in awe as he scanned the peeling front cover. "I don't know how you discovered that catalog, but I owe you my thanks, Adalin. The whole of the kingdom owes you its thanks."

"This thing you seek—is it truly so important?" she asked.

He spun toward the table and answered as they walked. "Any relic the Soulless seek must be secured. I will not have the talisman fall into their hands."

He placed the heavy volume on the table and carefully opened the cover. The pages within were yellowed and the ink faded, but it remained legible. The paper was rough and brittle under his hands.

He glanced at the duchess, a faint smile of anticipation alighting his features. She blinked uncertainly in response. He ignored her strange reaction and focused his attention on the book once more. It was strange; he thought she'd be pleased to know her meddling had helped achieve something of such importance. It was another item that she might lord over the other noblewomen at court, yet Adalin had become almost reticent.

He turned the first page of the book gingerly. "Have I said something to offend?" he asked quietly while he scanned the text.

She laughed uncertainly. "No, Ravin. You've shown a side of yourself today I didn't believe existed. The dour, scowling man with enchanting eyes has been replaced by one capable of smiles and joy. A man I am wholly unfamiliar with."

He snorted and turned another page. "If I seem dour, it is because I detest politics and intrigue. And I've been mired in both."

"Why do you remain as Tamarin's advisor if you hate the post?"

"My post is a means to an end," he replied. "Nothing more."

"What end, Ravin?"

Her tone was suspicious, and he looked away from the text to peer at her. "The only end I seek to achieve is the destruction of the Soulless. Namely, Dranamir."

Her face paled, and she shuddered visibly. "You would draw them into a fight? That's madness, Ravin."

He shrugged and returned to his perusal of the tome. "It's why the talisman is important. Without it, I cannot defeat them."

"Does the queen know of your plan?"

"Yes, though she's a constant source of delay. Hmm…" He trailed off as a passage drew his attention. "Gods-damn it."

She leaned over his arm to better read the page he'd stopped on. "There are catacombs beneath the palace? And this relic is guarded by traps?"

"Twelve of them," he confirmed. "Would the queen know anything of these catacombs, Adalin?"

"Perhaps, but I doubt it. Her mind is set upon childish desires, and her kingdom's history is not a priority." Adalin stepped back and crossed her arms with a frown.

Ravin studied her for a time, once again perplexed by the new side of her he was witnessing. "You care deeply for the history of this land."

"Yes. And our rulers have ignored it for generations. It is why you fascinate me, Ravin. The queen let slip some of your past…"

He ground his teeth together to stifle a growl. "Of course, she did."

"If her tales were true, you alone have the knowledge and power to make good on your schemes."

"That remains to be seen," he replied. "There is much yet I must prepare for."

"Allow me to help you." She offered him a genuine smile, the first of its kind. "I can compile the information you require while you are away tending to your other duties. The queen will not miss my presence—she's grown quite fond of Jasom and spends much of her time with him."

Ravin searched his mind in vain for a reason to deny her. Their close proximity in the days and weeks to come was certain to cause a stir amongst the nobility, but more importantly, he feared her involvement would place her at risk. If his plans failed, he had no doubt Dranamir would seek out anyone he'd associated with. Her next words shattered what remained of his resolve.

"I have studied history since I was a girl, Ravin. You can use my help." Another smile appeared on her lips, less certain than its predecessor, yet beautiful all the same.

He sighed in resignation. "Very well. But please keep our true business to yourself…What we do is dangerous, Adalin."

She laughed softly. "Not to worry. I can concoct enough juicy gossip to make even the Soulless believe I'm nothing more than a titillating diversion for you."

He felt his face flush in response, another reaction he'd long since believed himself incapable of. He cleared his throat uncomfortably as she continued to laugh.

A knock sounded on the doorframe, mercifully distracting him from the duchess. He looked up to find Jadosin, a pair of sealed scrolls in his rough hands. The queen's military advisor stood rigidly while his eyes flicked between Ravin and the woman at his side.

"My apologies for the intrusion," he said. "I have the messages, Ravin. Malira's is here." He gestured toward one of the scrolls with his free hand.

Ravin strode across the space, immensely relieved at the interruption. Adalin's presence had begun to evoke thoughts he felt were better left ignored. "I'll deliver these immediately," he promised as he took up the scrolls.

"You've proven yourself a man of your word," Jadosin replied evenly. "I'll trust these reach our men and Balotica's leaders quickly." His gaze flicked behind Ravin toward Adalin's location and back. "You have my thanks, Ravin."

As Jadosin departed, Ravin shook his head, flustered. It seemed Adalin was already making good on her promise of gossip, and she'd uttered not a word. The rustle of silk warned him of her approach, but he did not turn to acknowledge her.

"I must go."

"I heard, Ravin. I will continue our work while you're away. We are now partners, after all." She touched his arm lightly before she withdrew.

He shook his head in order to clear it before he created a portal into the Aethereum. He glanced over his shoulder before stepping inside; Adalin was bent over the text, engrossed in its contents. It was an unlikely partnership, but one he found himself anticipating. There was more to the duchess than he'd believed.

CHAPTER TWENTY-THREE

DAESAN

Aran'daj was slicked with sweat in spite of the cold and the flurry of snow that swirled around him. His breath puffed in icy clouds as he slashed and parried his way across the battlefield steps behind Jal'den.

The Murkor had come upon Daesan the previous night, but under orders from Kama, they waited to attack until noon the next day. Even so, the city had been unprepared for the assault, and the Murkor had taken the walls within an hour. At Aran'daj's command, they streamed through the city, dispatching the remnants of Daesan's defenders. Those deemed suitable for labor in the caverns were subdued and taken to the Murkor encampment hidden in the hills a half-mile from the city.

Beyond the eastern ramparts, the dark countenance of Mount Daesan loomed ominously. Thin tendrils of smoke issued from its lopsided cone, the harbinger of Flariel's wrath. Aran'daj eyed the mountain warily as the army progressed through the city at its foot, but it seemed it was not in danger of imminent eruption. To his mind, it was a victory nearly equal in measure to the overthrow of Daesan.

Jal'den's broadsword flashed silver and crimson as it arced through the air to cleave a human skull. The path of destruction left in his wake was incomparable, and the Arms Master appeared tireless. Aran'daj kept pace with him, but only just. Battle and conquest were the games of younger men whose stamina would not fail them.

"I plan to return to the caverns with the prisoners," Jal'den informed him as he yanked his blade free. "The Kal must know how we fare."

Aran'daj was faced with his own assailant, a gray-haired, toothless man wearing mismatched leathers who bore a meat cleaver. The commander deftly deflected the man's first, clumsy strike, spun to disengage his blade, then sliced it across the man's abdomen. The man's apparent age slowed his response, and Aran'daj used it to his advantage. The man doubled over and fell to his knees while the cleaver clattered to the cobblestones at his side. Aran'daj was uncertain if the wound would prove fatal, but without swift treatment, the venom imparted from the black metal would consume him.

He stepped away from the fallen man and pursued Jal'den. "Is it wise to return again, Jal'den? We've spoken of this."

Jal'den's black hood nodded once, tersely. "If I do not return as I have in the past, the Soulless may believe something is amiss. If I continue to act as I have previously, I will not draw their suspicion."

Though his logic was sound, Aran'daj could not allay his fears. There was too much at stake, and he knew too little of the Kal's schemes. The loss of Jal'den as an asset would not only cripple his battle plans, but it would strike a significant blow to the morale of the soldiers. He could afford neither.

They rounded a bend and were confronted with a group of shackled humans being led away by a pair of green-clad alchemists. Jal'den stopped abruptly, for which Aran'daj was grateful. He needed a moment in order to catch his breath. Aran'daj turned around slowly and noted the regiment that followed in their wake was no longer engaged.

Jal'den sheathed the broadsword across his back. When he spoke, Aran'daj could hear the grin in his voice. "It seems we've crossed the whole gods-damned city, Commander. What are your next orders?"

"Assist the alchemists with the prisoners," Aran'daj panted.

He sheathed his own blade and gestured toward the others, silently relaying his orders. Several dozen broke away from the group and jogged in the direction of the prisoners. Aran'daj smiled beneath his hood; the attack had been successful. He was certain Kama would be pleased, and he would keep his head another day.

He motioned for Jal'den to accompany him as he embarked on the return trip across Daesan. The soldiers had their orders, and he was confident they would be followed without his presence to oversee them. He was weary, cold, and needed time to speak with Jal'den alone.

"You're certain a return to the caverns is wise?" he asked again as they trudged through Daesan's blood-soaked streets.

"Wise or not, I must go," Jal'den replied with a shrug. "Sal'zar has not yet learned how to contact anyone else. Yesterday, he gave me a message that I must relate to the Kal. He has not been granted permission to leave the tower, or he would have gone himself."

Several blocks to the south, a loud crack sounded. Moments later, Aran'daj witnessed bricks and planks of wood erupt high into the air.

"Exploding stones." Jal'den nodded in approval before he seemed to deflate. "Gods, I wish he were here."

"You will be reunited, one day." Aran'daj forced a measure of conviction into his tone, though they both knew the future was uncertain. He could not help but empathize with Jal'den and hoped his words would eventually prove true. The Arms Master and the alchemist forced him to recall a time more than two decades past that continued to tear at his heart.

"I will continue to pray you are right, Commander." He drew a breath and exhaled slowly. "Is there anything you wish me to tell the Kal?"

"He must learn of our victory today," Aran'daj replied thoughtfully while he considered his next words. "Tell him I believe the easy victories are nearing an end, Jal'den. We may require more troops in the coming months. More supplies will be needed, along with the support of our craftsmen and alchemists."

Jal'den tilted his head slightly. "Sir? What aren't you telling me?"

"We have won this day, Jal'den. Savor the victory while you can."

He would not tell the Arms Master he feared the next battle might prove his last. He would not burden Jal'den with his mounting concerns. The Soulless pushed them toward an unattainable goal, and even Kama's power could not protect him from the others of his kind indefinitely. The woman, Dranamir, wanted his head—and would have it if he so much as twitched in her presence.

"Commander." Jal'den's tone was firm. "If I am to relay your message, I must know its meaning. The Kal will demand answers that I cannot give."

"I require time to consider my answer, Arms Master." He nodded ahead, toward the city square and the looming form of Kama. "Return to me in the camp, Jal'den. We will speak again once your work is finished within the city."

Jal'den saluted and strode away, his movements stiff. The Arms Master exuded frustration but was wise enough to follow the command without further question. Aran'daj watched him go, then refocused on the Soulless ahead. Kama's back was to him, but he was certain the man knew of his approach well before the sound of his boots announced his arrival.

"You have done very well, Commander." Kama's corrupted, graying flesh twitched into a feral grin. "Daesan has fallen; its defenders lay broken and bloodied in the streets. Another victory to offset the troubles you faced in Pine."

Aran'daj stiffened at the mention of his failure. His heart began to race, and he drew a shaky breath in a vain attempt to quell his fear. "Yes, sir."

Kama chuckled darkly. "Be at ease, Commander. Savor the victory while you can."

His throat constricted as Kama repeated the words he'd spoken to Jal'den. The Soulless had overheard their conversation, though if he suspected Aran'daj of conspiring against him, he made no mention of it. Aran'daj swallowed and clenched his fists at his side to hide their trembling.

"The Arms Master is right to question you, but I admire your resolve to shield your troops from reality." Kama clasped his hands behind his back as he continued to observe the line of human prisoners that now trudged through the street ahead. "They do not know how tenuous your position truly is. The request for additional troops and supplies is wise. Will the Kal provide them?"

"I believe he will, sir."

"Good. I'd hate to be forced to make an example of you simply to encourage his compliance."

Aran'daj fixed his gaze on the prisoners and their Murkor escorts. "Jal'den asked to return to the caverns to relay my message."

"I assumed so." Kama turned to peer down his long nose at Aran'daj. "Alyra will arrive this evening to help with the transport of the prisoners."

"Thank you, sir."

Kama sneered. "Do not thank me yet, Commander. Our next target is Delucha City, and it will prove to be the turning point in your career. We will face others who can channel magic there, and one in particular is far more dangerous than even I can claim to be."

"Perhaps I ought to ask for more than the standard number of alchemists to assist us," Aran'daj replied carefully.

"I suggest you do. We will need every advantage we can muster."

It was evening before Jal'den found his way to the commander's tent. Aran'daj had spent an hour or more praying to the patron god of their people, Ukase, to guide his next actions. He knelt at the center of his tent, his head bowed, the maps and orders scattered across his table ignored. The tiny brazier at his side provided a semblance of warmth against the frosty air, and he'd allowed it to burn down to mere coals while he asked the gods for insight.

He did not turn to look up when Jal'den entered, and was surprised when the Arms Master knelt beside him to join in the silent ritual. He wondered if Jal'den also prayed to Ukase, or if his entreaties were reserved for Blademon's ears.

It was sometime later that Aran'daj rocked back on his heels and stood. He stretched the stiffness from his muscles, then went about adding wood to the dwindling fire while Jal'den concluded his unspoken petition.

"He overheard us, Jal'den. You were right, and you must return to the caverns." He feared to elaborate and hoped Jal'den understood the full implications of his words.

"Of course, Commander."

"While you are there, tell the Kal we require as many alchemists as can be spared. We will soon face the wizards."

"Yes, sir." Jal'den turned toward the door.

"And Jal'den? Ask the Kal… Ask my grandfather to deliver the message he's kept for me. It goes to Rej'amin. I may not be granted the opportunity to deliver it myself."

Jal'den nodded slowly as understanding came over him. "Now I see. I hope you are wrong about the next battle, Commander. For the sake of our people, I hope you are wrong."

CHAPTER TWENTY-FOUR

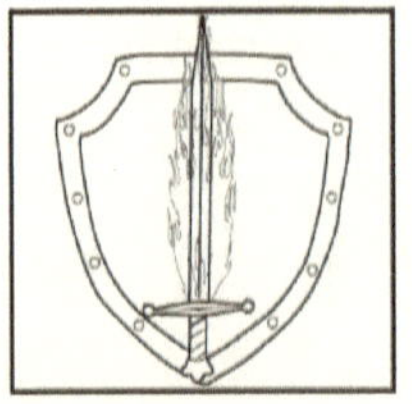

MORAINE

Not for the first time that afternoon, Emra was grateful to the pair of Scorpion Men who had accompanied her into town. She was weary from their long trek through the mines, yet elated to feel the sun on her face and the wind in her hair once more. She'd made the decision to journey into the city of Moraine after they made camp in the forest not far from its outskirts, intent upon gleaning insight into the minds of the people—she had an army to gather and a war to wage against the Soulless, after all. She'd asked Vardak to accompany her, and Patak refused to be left behind.

She led the way to the city's central square, where she planned to make her first of what would prove to be many speeches. Flanked by Patak and Vardak, she drew stares. Their people rarely ventured beyond the mountains, and to spy two of them at once was an oddity to behold. The tall, armored woman between them was the true spectacle, however. Emra smiled with amusement at the gasps she elicited when she drew Fireblade from its scabbard and held it aloft. It was a legend, a beacon even the greatest of skeptics could not ignore. That she was its wielder was immediately evident to those gathered as flames licked along its exposed blade.

The growing crowd of spectators pressed toward her, eager for a better look, but the brothers held them at bay. Vardak stood immobile, his arms crossed as his eyes scanned the throng. His tail shuddered as he assessed the humans for any potential threat, and she noted the glisten of venom at its tip. His axe was sheathed across his armored back, but he did not require the use of the weapon to prove deadly.

On her other side, Patak shifted and skittered, unable to contain his anxiety. He wore a shield on his left arm and bore a mace in his right hand. Between the two, she doubted anyone would dare to approach without her consent.

She placed her free hand on Patak's arm. He glanced at her with a nod and seemed to relax. It was time to say her piece. She channeled a trickle of magic in order to amplify her voice over the noise of the jostling crowd.

"I believe many of you recognize my blade."

A rapid hush fell over those gathered and she took a step forward, brandishing the weapon. The flames that danced along its edges swirled in response while gasps escaped some of the onlookers.

"It is the Fireblade. Those who know their history will understand what this means."

A multitude of voices rose up in response, some in awe, others in anger. She expected nothing less; in each life, the reaction to her presence had been similar. She allowed the locals to express their opinions for a few moments before she addressed them further. She knew what she must say and braced herself for the inevitable backlash.

"I am gathering an army. The Soulless have returned to torment our world once more, and we must stand in defiance of them. We must stand in opposition to the Nameless god they serve. Only together can we hope to achieve victory. Already, the city of Jennavere in Balotica has fallen to their schemes. We must not allow them to continue their conquest."

Demands, queries, jibes, and cheers erupted from countless mouths around the square. The noise was deafening, the individual voices lost in the wash of sound.

"Gods," Patak hissed. "Half of them seem ready to join us, while the other half are poised to run us out of town. Is it always like this?"

"Yes," she murmured. "It will become easier as people begin to commit to our cause and our numbers swell. I'm glad you and Vardak are along today."

Patak snorted and shifted uneasily. "I don't like this, Em."

"Give them a few moments to sort their thoughts," she advised gently. "My appearance with the blade is unsettling to many and confirms their worst fears."

He released a breath and nodded once. She was grateful for his presence and the trust he placed in her words, but she could not allow herself to become consumed with thoughts of him. Not now; it was not the place nor the time. She must focus on the throng that surrounded them, anticipate their actions, allay their misgivings, and act the part of leader that she'd been destined to become—time and again.

She amplified her voice once more to address the crowd. "For those who wish to volunteer their services, my camp can be found along the road in the forest west of your fine city. We will await you there."

She turned away from the throng and sheathed her iconic sword as anxiety gripped her heart. Each time, she'd felt the same. Beginnings were the most difficult, but once she established herself, recruiting would become simpler. The first to follow Fireblade's wielder were always the thrill-seekers and those seeking refuge from a life they wished to flee. Those who considered themselves level-headed would join later. In all her years and lifetimes, the nature of the human psyche was one of the few constants she could rely on.

"We're not prepared for an influx of people," Vardak stated as they departed the square.

"We are more ready than you may realize, Vardak. This is not my first foray into building an army."

A twitch of a smile crossed his lips. "No, I suppose it isn't."

"I plan to speak with the others once we return. Each has a unique talent that can be put to good use, and if they are amenable to my recommendations, we'll have everything sorted and running smoothly in no time." She grinned. "Your role has already been decided, Vardak. I have no doubt you are up to the task."

His flicker of good humor faded. "Fucking gods, I hope you're right," he muttered under his breath.

On her other side, Patak laughed. "Who better to lead than Blademon's protégé? And what would you have of me, Em? The keeper of your secrets has not been informed of this particular scheme."

She laughed in spite of herself, pleased once again to have him at her side. "With my announcement today, I will become a target," she replied seriously. "There will be those seeking to aid the Soulless, those wishing to find glory, those with a misplaced sense of righteousness guiding their hand. I learned a rather harsh lesson long ago and was nearly killed by an assassin. Until that day, my hubris led me to believe I was invincible. I am not."

Patak frowned. "You didn't answer my question, Em."

"I need someone I can trust implicitly to ensure my safety while I rest." She peered up at him with a meaningful expression. "I ask that you act as captain of my personal guard."

"Shouldn't that role fall to Luke?" he asked uncertainly.

"No, Patak. I have another job in mind for Luke—if he'll accept it."

They arrived at their small campsite a half-hour later. Emra called the others together while Vardak paced along the perimeter, his eyes fixed upon the road. While he anticipated the first of her recruits to arrive at any moment, she doubted anyone would until the following morning. It required time to pack one's belongings and say goodbye to loved ones. She would not contradict him, however, and was grateful for his vigilance. It allowed her to focus fully on the next task at hand.

"I have a proposal for each of you," she began, taking a moment to look each of her companions in the eye. "Recruits will be joining us soon, and our numbers will only continue to grow as we march toward Dar Daelad. This is a good thing, but I cannot run an army alone. I am requesting your help, if you are willing."

"You know my answer, Em," Lucas replied without hesitation.

"We have followed Vardak this far," Danness added. "Coreyaless and I decided to assist him, and our decision has not changed."

"I came at Aeon's behest," Maryn stated with a grin. "I'll do my part."

She smiled, relieved at their responses. "Luke, I'll begin with you. You have a way with horses, and even though you're a poor jouster, you're damned good in a fight."

He snorted. "You had to remind me…"

"I want you to lead our cavalry. You will coordinate with Vardak when the time comes. Ours will not be the only horses in the camp for long."

"Em, you're certain?" he asked, astounded.

"I am. You have the skill—and my trust."

He grinned. "Then I suppose I'd best prepare myself before your, ah…recruits begin to arrive."

She turned to face Maryn next. "Vardak informed me you were a watchman in your homeland, and I am aware of your keen eyesight. We will require a rotation of soldiers to take up the watch each night, and as our numbers grow, more will be needed. I would like you to take up that post."

Maryn flashed another grin. "I will not disappoint you."

"You will also coordinate with Vardak," she added before he turned away.

"It'll be like nothing has changed," Maryn quipped.

"Coreyaless, you won't be the lone healer to enter our camp, and the others will need direction. You took up this role previously, and I hope you will consider doing so again."

Coreyaless did not smile, but her tone was warm. "I'm surprised you didn't bring the matter up sooner, given our last campaign together."

Emra shrugged; the answer was simple. "It slipped my mind. I've had much to consider."

"Indeed." Coreyaless shifted her gray-eyed gaze to Danness. "And what role would you have my partner perform, Emra? Our people are not warriors."

Emra smiled. "I've noticed how closely Danness monitors our supplies. Every army requires a quartermaster."

"It is merely habit after years spent traipsing through the jungle," he replied. "I will not have us run out of food or water."

"Then you accept?" she pressed.

"Yes, I will take up the mantle. I must discuss the horses' needs with Lucas."

"Speak with Vardak, as well," she suggested. "We must all work together, and it is for that reason I've asked this of you. We have done well so far, but greater challenges lie ahead."

CHAPTER TWENTY-FIVE

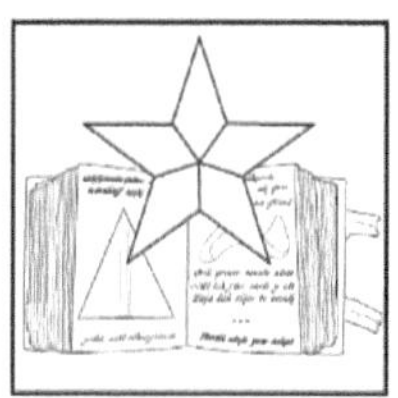

SELECTED

Tavesin grinned and caused his shield to flare outward in a brilliant display as Rostin's carefully timed attack met his defense squarely. The air sizzled where the two magics collided, and the scent of ozone permeated his nostrils. Rostin narrowed his eyes and prepared to strike again as Tavesin reformed his shield.

"I believe that's enough for one day," Aziarah stated firmly. She came to stand between the two boys, a pleased smile on her reptilian face. "You have both progressed quite well in the past weeks."

Tavesin beamed at the praise as he allowed his shield to dissipate. He could have continued for some time, but Rostin had grown fatigued by his efforts to thwart his friend's powerful defenses. Aziarah was right to put an end to their sparring for the day. Rostin needed rest—no matter how much he might protest—and it would be growing dark soon, in any case.

His gaze drifted toward the trees a short distance away, where Badolo sat between two other Drakkon. He was hunched over a metallic device, his hands moving deftly across its surface; it glowed softly in response to his touch. Badolo had been secretive about his project, but it was clear to Tavesin he was constructing a relic of some sort. Badolo would tell them its purpose, given time.

"I'm not done, Aziarah," Rostin complained.

She fixed him with a knowing expression. "You are, child. Do not overtax yourself. I've told you before—"

"—it's dangerous," he finished in a disappointed tone. "I only wish I could keep up with him."

Tavesin looked away from his friend's pointed stare, decidedly uncomfortable. He knew he was much stronger than Rostin, but he'd chosen to follow a different path. They were not in competition—at least, none that Tavesin was aware of.

"Each being gifted with magic is blessed with a different aptitude for it," Aziarah replied evenly. "Tavesin is far stronger than most humans could ever hope to be, Rostin. It is fortunate for us all that he met me when he did, else the Soulless might have conscripted him. It is why they've taken such interest in your friend." She turned to face Tavesin. "Even I cannot hope to match your power, child. You are exceptional."

Tavesin stared at the ground between his feet, his face flushed with embarrassment. He disliked the attention; he simply wanted to be on equal ground with his friends, to be *normal*. Since his first accidental journey into the Aethereum, he'd been considered anything but typical.

"It is nothing to be ashamed of," Aziarah said gently. "Others in your position would take the opportunity to flaunt their newfound gifts. That you do not speaks much about your character."

"I will do what I must to save Arra," he mumbled with the hope Rostin could not overhear his words.

"I know, child. Now," she said with a note of authority, "the two of you ought to be off to your supper. Take Badolo along with you, or the boy will never eat. I've rarely seen anyone become so absorbed in their work."

Rostin snorted a laugh. "We'll make certain he eats, Aziarah."

"Good. I will see the three of you in the morning. And Rostin," she added as he turned away, "be certain to bring your blade tomorrow. Jerizyen has deemed you ready for true combat training."

Rostin's eyes lit up with excitement. "No more practice blades, then?"

"That is for him to decide, but I suggest you bring your weapon in any case."

Rostin flashed a grin and beckoned for Tavesin to follow him. They made their way to Badolo, who paid them no heed for several seconds. Unable to hide his impatience, Rostin began to pace behind their younger friend.

"Give me another moment," Badolo said without looking away from his work. "I'm nearly finished."

Tavesin watched with interest as Badolo wove his magic. He understood the basic machinations in process, but the weaving and details Badolo imparted into his work made little sense to him. It was unlike any magical construct he'd studied previously. He wondered again just what the young prince was crafting under the tutelage of the Drakkon.

When Badolo abruptly ceased channeling his magic, Tavesin understood his work was complete, though he was unable to decipher the object's purpose. Badolo beamed at the nearest Drakkon mage and offered her the device. She studied it carefully for a time, then nodded in satisfaction.

"This is a wonder. We shall put it to good use in the days to come."

Badolo stood and grinned at his friends, pleased with himself and the praise he'd received. "Let's find supper."

"What was that?" Tavesin asked, his curiosity unsated.

"I know you were spying on me, Taven," Badolo replied with a shrug. "Were you unable to unravel my process?"

Tavesin sighed; he wished there was a way to shield his prying from Badolo, but the younger boy always detected it. Most of the wizards were unaware of his newly acquired ability, and those who knew could not sense it. Only Badolo and a few of the Drakkon had managed to catch him "spying" thus far.

"No. It was a jumble. I couldn't understand what you did."

Badolo chuckled to himself. "Katyara says few are gifted in the magics necessary to create relics from nothing, as I have done. She told me the magic I work appears foreign to others, as though I speak a different language entirely." He grinned at Tavesin. "For all your probing about, I'm rather pleased you're unable to replicate what I've done."

Beside him, Rostin snorted. "Taven is powerful enough. Gods, I wish I had your stamina! You weren't even winded, and I..." Rostin glowered and kicked at a loose stone in their path. "There must be a way to condition myself. I won't be left behind!"

Tavesin blinked, startled by the outburst. "Rostin, I'm sorry—"

Rostin laughed dryly. "It's no fault of yours, Taven. I am frustrated that of the three of us, I am the eldest, I was the first to the tower, and I am the *last* to prove myself worthy."

"You aren't last," Badolo pointed out. "None of us has 'proven' ourselves to anyone yet. We are learning—all of us."

"Besides," Tavesin added, "Aziarah told you to bring that saber you've been bragging about for two weeks to your training tomorrow. You aren't behind anyone, Rostin."

Rostin crossed his arms and tossed his head, undeterred. "I'll never be as strong as either of you."

"In my book, Taven is a freak of nature," Badolo stated with a grin. "You cannot compare yourself to him, Rostin. And I am no fighter, as the two of you are. When the wizards go to war, I will likely be left behind, no matter my status."

The trio fell silent as they reached the tower's entrance doors and made their way inside. The vast anteroom bustled with activity as wizards and apprentices scurried about their final tasks of the day. They made their way toward one of the spiral staircases that would lead them to the second floor and the kitchens.

"Do you truly believe they'll do it, Badolo?" Rostin whispered after a time.

"Who, and what, Rostin?"

Rostin sighed impatiently. "The wizards. Do you believe they'll go to war? You grew up in a palace. I'm certain—"

"Ssshh!" Badolo hissed and glanced frantically around them. "You're a terrible secret keeper, Rostin."

"I don't believe anyone overheard him," Tavesin said as he scanned the faces around them.

Badolo frowned at Rostin. "Watch your words. I came here under a false name for my own protection, and I won't have you ruin it. My father would have your head, Santinian or not." Badolo closed his dark eyes for a moment and gathered his composure. "You are right, however. I have contacts in the tower who keep me apprised of the decisions being made by the Sect Masters and the Radiant. I send word to my father when I learn of important events."

"Then you know." Rostin shot him a knowing look.

"I know they have made no official decision," Badolo replied.

Tavesin was unsurprised, yet disappointed. Word had come from Balotica that the kingdom was under attack, the wizards had acknowledged the Soulless' return, and Arra's disappearance was a clear indicator that the Shadow Council was prepared to weaken their opposition by any means necessary. He understood enough of the tower's bureaucracy to know that any decision would take weeks or months to achieve, even under the present circumstances. He preferred the Drakkon's straightforward approach to matters.

As they entered the kitchens, the trio were met by a contingent of wizards, Hasnin amongst them. Tavesin recognized the Blue, Gray, and Yellow Sect Masters, but the other two wizards he was unfamiliar with. He glanced at Rostin, then Badolo. Both appeared as uncertain as he was.

Mari El'Vero, the Blue Sect Master, stepped forward and ushered them toward an empty table in one corner of the room. She was no taller than Badolo, but clearly the leader of the group in spite of her petite frame and small stature. Once the group was seated, she clasped her dark hands in front of her and peered at the three boys, studying each in turn.

"The Drakkon have kept us apprised of your progress," she informed them. "You excel in your studies, and it is clear each of you has chosen the Sect you wish to challenge for."

Tavesin swallowed hard, his eyes wide. He knew what would come next. He had longed for this moment, yet now that it had arrived, he found himself both elated and terrified. An apprentice was allowed to challenge twice, but no more. Most did not meet the expectations during the first challenge, particularly those selected at a young age. The second attempt was successful for perhaps half of those selected. Those who passed were named wizards, while those who failed were blocked from their magical ability and sent on their way. Tavesin could not imagine a worse fate—to lose his power forever, knowing how close he'd come to achieving a place amongst the wizards.

Mari's eyes met Rostin's. "Rostin Ver'An, you have been selected to challenge for the Gray Sect."

Rostin sat rigid in his seat, his dusky features growing slightly ashen with her proclamation. "I am honored," he rasped.

She indicated the stern Kamshati to her right, with his wild mass of white hair. Virano Rinsahk was aged, his hands gnarled, but he retained a fierce gleam in his dark eyes. "Virano will schedule the date and time of your challenge. Prepare yourself accordingly."

Mari's eyes fell upon Badolo next. "Young master Shansehk, you have been selected to challenge for the Yellow Sect." She pointed to the woman on her left who bore similar features and coloration. Tavesin knew they were sisters, though Mari seemed the elder of the pair. "Lilyna will schedule the date and time of your challenge."

Lilyna leaned forward, a warm smile on her lips. "If you pass—and I'm certain you will—you will be the youngest wizard the council has seen in many generations. The Drakkon have indicated you have a wondrous talent."

Badolo flushed slightly and looked down at his hands. "Thank you. I will do my best."

"Which brings us to you, Tavesin." Mari's eyes bored into his, and he resisted the urge to squirm beneath her scrutiny. "You have been selected to challenge for the Blue Sect. Rumors of your power have reached throughout the tower, and I must say, I was quite impressed with your sparring match this afternoon."

Tavesin swallowed hard. "You…you were there?"

She smiled. "We have all stopped by from time to time since the Drakkon took over your training. We could not be certain you were prepared to challenge otherwise."

"I won't disappoint," Tavesin promised despite the sudden eruption of butterflies in his stomach.

"I don't believe it's in your nature to do so," she replied. "I will schedule the date and time of your challenge. Continue to prepare yourself, Tavesin. We all understand the magnitude of your power. Of the three of you, yours will prove the most difficult; we have very high expectations of you."

Tavesin looked away and clasped his hands tightly to prevent them from visibly shaking. He heard the sound of chairs scraping against the floor as the wizards rose and departed, but he paid them no heed. His mind whirled, his heart raced, the world spun. It was the moment he'd been waiting for, the moment he'd been dreading.

"Well," Badolo said quietly once they were alone, "I was not expecting this today."

"Nor was I," Rostin replied in a shaky tone. "Taven, are you alright?"

Tavesin shook his head, uncertain. "Perhaps it's fortunate you aren't as strong as I am, Rostin."

"I don't believe the wizards know *half* what you are capable of." Badolo peered at him with a faint grin. "You will surprise them, Taven, and you will become a wizard. You'll see."

He shrugged and wished he possessed a fraction of the confidence his friend seemed to have. "I hope you're right because I cannot afford to fail."

CHAPTER TWENTY-SIX

A ROYAL WEDDING

The library had become Ravin's oasis, the sole location within the palace where he could work without interruption for hours. With Adalin's help, he had uncovered more details about the magical traps that awaited in the catacombs below, and after some late-night investigations, they'd located the entrance to the subterranean labyrinth that sprawled beneath the palace grounds.

When they were alone, she maintained her distance and gave him space; in spite of his initial protestations, they worked well together. Once an observer happened upon them, however, Adalin adopted her court persona and clung to his side. Their guise was necessary, but it turned his stomach all the same. He loathed being the subject of court gossip, and he could scarcely walk five steps outside of the library without overhearing some scrap of whispered conversation regarding his "affair" with the Duchess of the Mers. It was maddening.

He shook his head to clear it of his unwanted thoughts and skimmed the passage he'd been studying for the dozenth time. It spoke in detail of eleven of the traps he must dismantle, but the twelfth was omitted from the page. He flipped the page with a scowl, well aware the remainder of the tome was blank. Why was the last obstacle not mentioned? He turned the page over again with a growl.

"Snarling at your book won't change its contents, Ravin." Adalin peered around the corner of a shelf wearing an amused expression.

He sat back in his chair and ran one hand through his hair. "I won't venture down there without knowing fully what awaits me. There must be something more…Somewhere."

"That is why I've continued to peruse the shelves. We will find what you seek, Ravin."

"Gods, I hope so. With Daesan fallen, it's only a matter of time before they're on our doorstep." His glare landed on the open tome before him. He was certain there was something within the book that he'd missed. "Damn it. It must be in here."

He hunched over the volume once more, scouring the passage for the answer that continued to elude him. After several moments, Adalin's carefully manicured hands appeared across the brittle pages, blocking the faded text from view. He sat up sharply and scowled.

"Ravin, we have both looked over that page a hundred times. It's not there. We must move on or make do with the knowledge we have uncovered so far." She leaned over the table, her head dangerously close to his own.

She was right, but he was reluctant to admit it. "I'm certain I've missed something."

"And I'm certain you're more stubborn than any other man I've met." Her words were tempered with a smile. "Perhaps we could both use a break. It's nearly noon, and we've been in here for hours."

His mood soured further at her words. "I'd rather not—"

"You must, Ravin. The queen had an announcement to make, if you recall." She stood upright and placed her hands on her hips. "You're a royal advisor. Your presence will be expected. By hiding away in here, you'll only make the rumor-mongers more ravenous."

He groaned and pushed away from the table. He'd forgotten the queen's offhanded comment regarding her news to the kingdom, and Adalin was right. By missing such an event, he would draw more unwanted attention.

"I cannot argue with your logic, though I sorely wish I could."

As he came around the table, she took his arm in her own and led him toward the door. "I knew you were a man of reason. It's merely a matter of breaking through your mulish demeanor first."

"Did Her Majesty give you any insight into what this announcement will hold?" he asked.

"Not directly, though Catalin informed me Jasom's family arrived late last evening." She smirked up at him. "I suspect the queen plans to marry him. If I were twenty years younger, I suppose I'd find him

175

attractive, though he cannot compare to *you*." She tittered flirtatiously, and it was only then he noted the pair of servants studiously cleaning a window ahead.

He suppressed a groan. "Must we do this?" he whispered.

"Would you rather the staff learn the truth?" she countered.

"Gods-damn it. Fine." He forced a semblance of a smile onto his face, and they passed the cleaners in silence.

"My company isn't so bad, is it, Ravin?" she asked after a moment. He was startled by the uncertainty he heard in her tone.

"No," he admitted, "but this deception we play at… I'm certain even a false affair will have repercussions, should your husband learn of it."

She sniffed. "My husband died three years ago, Ravin. It was a hunting accident. I was his third wife, and stood to gain nothing from his estate, which is why I found myself here." She pierced him with a knowing gaze. "It is noble that you worry over my reputation, but I am old enough to make my own choices and accept the consequences, thank you."

"Your title—"

"—Will be gone once the late duke's son marries." She waved her free hand dismissively. "There will be no jealous husband barging into your quarters in a blind rage, Ravin. Even if there were, I'm certain you would handle the situation without my help. The duke was no wizard, nor was he a warrior."

He released a breath, relieved. "I wish I'd inquired about this sooner."

"I'm surprised you didn't know." Her hand tightened on his forearm as they rounded a bend in the corridor and more of the palace's staff came into sight. "We must play our parts, Ravin. This game benefits us both. Now, smile."

He did as she ordered and nodded in greeting to those they passed as they traversed the corridor to the palace's great hall. Adalin waved and gushed to the other noblewomen, all the while clinging to Ravin's arm possessively. Many returned her smiles with venom in their eyes. Her game was not harmless, nor was it without consequence.

After one particularly hostile gaze, he bent his head to speak into her ear. "That one will prove trouble if you aren't careful."

She turned to look up at him with a seductive gaze. "I know, Ravin," she purred as she continued to perform her self-assigned role. "If I'm not mistaken, you're beginning to care." Her voice was low, meant only for his ears.

His smile faltered as a flush rose into his cheeks. "I'm…I'm not certain."

She laughed and turned her attention to the onlookers once more. "I won't press you, Ravin. Take your time."

A moment later, they entered the great hall and were quickly ushered to seats by one of the chamberlain's assistants. The queen was descending the staircase at the far end of the room, and mercifully, the attention of the others was quickly diverted to the young monarch. Ravin sank into his seat and disentangled his arm from the duchess' grasp, relieved he was no longer the focus of the palace's collective stares.

The queen wore a gown of ivory and pale gold adorned with pearls and topaz. The golden tiara that had once belonged to her mother was perched atop her mass of dark hair. At her side was Jasom, garbed in similar finery. She rarely made state appearances with the young Balotican in tow; Ravin was keenly aware of the whispers that swirled through the room in response to his presence. As she reached the base of the steps, she paused to allow the conversation to cease, then took Jasom's hand in her own.

"I have gathered you here today in order to make a grand announcement," she stated with a smile. "In one week, I shall wed Jasom Riversend. His family arrived yesterday. They approve the match."

Adalin leaned toward him and spoke into his ear. "*Her* family would never have agreed to it. Perhaps it's fortunate for our young queen they're now with Aeon."

Ravin arched an eyebrow but made no reply as the queen continued.

"There will be much to do to prepare for the ceremony, and we shall all be kept very busy. A royal wedding is a grand affair, and I will not disappoint my subjects." She beamed at the audience before taking her seat at the center of the head table.

The room erupted into conversation around them. Ravin winced at the noise and wished himself anywhere but within the great hall at that moment. Once his presence was noted by the others packed into the space, he would be bombarded with questions—questions he had no answers for. The queen had not confided in him regarding her plans to marry the young Balotican farmer she seemed so taken with, though he understood her desire well enough. She would be unable to hide her pregnancy much longer.

Adalin grasped his hand. "Perhaps we shall take our meal in the courtyard?"

He smiled, relieved, and allowed her to lead him out of the noisy room. "Thank you," he said quietly once they were in the corridor.

"I may enjoy teasing you, Ravin, but I don't like to see your discomfort. We'll eat, then return to the refuge of the library."

He sequestered himself amongst the musty books for the next week, using his mission to acquire the talisman as an excuse to avoid the queen and the whirlwind of retainers, craftsmen, nobility, and curiosity-seekers that had descended upon the palace. The queen made good on her promise of a grand affair.

The great hall was transformed into a glowing attraction as two massive crystal and steel chandeliers were installed, adorned with dozens of ivory candles apiece. The tables were polished to a bright sheen, the chairs were cleaned and their cushions mended or replaced. New tapestries were unfurled along the walls, depicting the young queen and her betrothed in what Ravin assumed would be their wedding day finery. Hundreds of flowers were acquired and arranged from as far away as Santine Harbor, where the days were yet warm.

Contingents of palace servants marched through the halls at intervals, armed with feather dusters, buckets, and cleaning rags. Even his private quarters were not exempt from their thorough disinfection of the palace. He returned each evening to fresh sheets on his bed, a spotless fireplace, and pristine windows.

The only room in the complex that seemed untouched by the queen's demands was the library. She did not believe the nobility and myriad visitors to the palace would find anything of interest in the long-disused corner of the palace, and Ravin did not contradict her.

He was pleased to have that single sliver of normality amongst the chaos the wedding announcement had sown.

Another week of research brought him no closer to unraveling the mystery surrounding the twelfth pitfall of the catacombs. He began to suspect he would never learn how to disarm it unless he ventured into the tunnels himself. When he managed a brief audience with the queen two days prior to her ceremony, she vehemently denied his request. It must wait until after her wedding.

Her behavior continued to irk him. Daesan had fallen, the Soulless were within the bounds of Delucha kingdom, and she was concerned only for her appearance. If it came to light that she was carrying Jasom's child before they were wed, it would be the scandal of the century, but the acquisition of the talisman was far more important in his eyes. Without its power, he was certain the palace would fall; the Soulless were aware of his location and would prepare accordingly. If he did not prepare in kind… He tried not to dwell on the inevitable outcome.

When the date of the ceremony arrived, Ravin found himself inexplicably swarmed with a group of manservants whose sole purpose was to ensure the queen's advisor looked his best during the festivities. Ravin swallowed the urge to barricade himself within an impenetrable magical shield only after one of the men indicated they'd been sent at the duchess' request. With that revelation, he grudgingly allowed them to select an outfit, trim his hair, and carefully shave the dark stubble from his cheeks. He would endure the tiresome ministrations for Adalin's sake but for no one else. Her assistance combing through the library had proven invaluable; he owed her this indulgence, no matter how ridiculous it seemed.

When they had finally finished with him, Ravin assessed himself in the wardrobe's mirror. The garments he wore were comfortable and aligned with his personal style rather than the queen's overtly flamboyant tastes. Dark gray trousers and a matching jacket embellished with a touch of scrollwork embroidery in golden thread, blackened leather boots, and a simple white shirt. The colors complimented his dark complexion, and he was forced to admit he cut a dashing figure. Adalin would be pleased.

"The duchess is expecting you in her quarters," one of the men informed him as they prepared to leave.

He thanked them for their trouble and made his way toward the palace's eastern wing. He ignored the whispers that plagued his passage as he sought the duchess' rooms. The staff seemed to know he'd spent the past two hours under the care of Adalin's people—it was another thread added to the complicated tapestry of their false affair. A young maidservant greeted him when he knocked upon the duchess' door. After several moments spent ogling him and blushing furiously, she darted inside to inform Adalin of his arrival. He was left alone in the corridor, perhaps his only respite from the festivities for the remainder of the day.

He walked to the window across from her door and peered outside. It overlooked the palace's main courtyard; from his vantage point three floors above, it resembled a kicked anthill. A swarm of humanity scurried across the space as final preparations were made for the royal wedding. The sight made his skin crawl. He'd never been one for crowds.

"Ravin?"

He tore his gaze away from the window at the sound of her voice. Adalin wore a gown in shades of gray, a swirl of golden embroidery across the bodice. Her dark hair had been pulled up into an elaborate twist, while glints of topaz sparkled amongst her tresses. Similar gems hung suspended on thin gold chains from her neck and earlobes. She was stunning.

He gazed at her for several moments, uncertain what he ought to say. It had been far too many years since he'd last involved himself with a woman—even if their involvement was merely a farce. He felt compelled to tell her something, but words eluded his grasp. She walked toward him with an uncertain smile upon her lips. A genuine smile, he noted with a measure of surprise.

"I hope you don't mind that I asked the staff to match our costumes."

He glanced down at his jacket and chuckled, making the connection for the first time. "I hadn't noticed. It's part of our game, is it not?"

"Indeed."

He offered his arm, and she accepted without hesitation. Prompted by the trio of servants that exited her quarters, he said, "You are beautiful." It may have been a part of their ploy, but he meant it.

"Thank you." She smiled up at him, mischief in her eyes. "How much of a stir would you like to cause at this event, Ravin?"

He arched an eyebrow warily. "What do you have in mind?"

She laughed. "Nothing terrible. I expect we shall be seated together, given the rumors we've birthed. I simply would like a dance or two from you when the time comes."

"I suppose I can oblige." He offered her a grin. "After everything you've done to assist me, it's the least I can do."

"You're enjoying yourself more than you let on." Her fingers squeezed his forearm gently. "Perhaps life at court isn't so bad?"

"I'll admit, it has its perks."

When they arrived in the great hall, Adalin was proved correct; the chamberlain had arranged for them to be seated together. A swirl of whispers followed their progress as they were led to their assigned places, and he overheard several comments regarding their matching attire. Her ruse was working better than he'd anticipated, though he remained uncertain of what she stood to gain. Perhaps it was merely status, perhaps attention. Regardless, it furthered his own agenda, and he no longer found it necessary to complain.

It was another hour before the proceedings began, heralded by a brassy flourish from a group of trumpeters. Ravin rose to his feet, Adalin clinging to his arm, as the processional began. A priest from the nearby temple of Armistral entered first, garbed in a flowing white robe. Behind him strode a dozen pairs of young nobles from throughout the kingdom, each dressed in golden silk trimmed with ivory lace.

Ravin grimaced at their attire, thankful Adalin had the foresight to arrange simpler garb for himself. He watched as each pair parted ways at the front of the room; the women moved to the left and the men to the right, forming a long line on either side of the priest. Several paused to preen before the gathered audience, clearly pleased with their role of superficial importance in the day's affair.

Another brassy fanfare sounded as Jasom entered the room. He strode along the aisle with carefully measured steps, and though he appeared outwardly calm, Ravin noted the pallor in his cheeks and the strain that tightened his eyes. The boy was terrified.

"Poor child," Adalin whispered. "This must be overwhelming for him."

Ravin nodded his agreement. Jasom was about to be elevated from a mere farmer to the husband of a queen. Lacking noble status, his title would merely be consort; he would never rule, but his every action would be scrutinized for the remainder of his days. Ravin did not envy him.

As Jasom reached the dais and paused to straighten his ivory jacket, the musicians began to play once more. Strings overtook the trumpets as the young queen entered the room in a dazzling gown of ivory silk studded with diamonds and pearls. Three women trailed in her wake, their sole purpose to adjust and straighten the gown's long train. The queen appeared radiant as she marched toward the dais and the man who was to become her husband.

"She basks in this attention." Adalin's low whisper was tinged with bitterness. She stood on her toes to speak into his ear. "The girl must know there are more pressing matters at hand than her wedding ceremony."

Ravin shrugged. "It was not for lack of trying on my part."

The priest motioned for the audience to be seated, and Adalin took the shuffle around them as an opportunity to speak a final time. "I know, Ravin. Between us, she is a fool who will bring ruin to this kingdom."

Ravin's thoughts turned inward while the priest conducted the ceremony. He agreed with Adalin's assessment of the queen and their current situation, and resolved to venture into the catacombs to begin his investigations as soon as he was able—the queen's desire to keep up appearances be damned. The talisman must be located, and time was against him. He would secure it no matter the cost. And against her orders, if need be.

He would not allow the Soulless to overtake Delucha, and he would show Dranamir the magnitude of her error when she'd attempted to take his life. But in order to do so, he must acquire the talisman.

After the conclusion of the ceremony, Ravin found himself dragged throughout the vast room as Adalin made small talk with the other guests. He resigned himself to beginning the search the following day; his absence during the festivities would be too conspicuous.

A six-course feast was presented as the sun began to set. Adalin chatted to those seated nearby, but he said little. Instead, he picked at his food and continued to mull over what must be said to the queen. Obtaining the talisman was imperative, and she had stalled him far too long.

As the final dishes were cleared away, the queen and her new husband descended from the dais to a space that was cleared near the center of the room. The musicians began to play while the pair began to dance. Ravin watched them spin and whirl about the room, eyes locked upon one another, unwavering. Both smiled, content in the moment despite the restless audience surrounding them.

Adalin grasped his hand beneath the table and leaned into his arm. "I hope you don't plan to renege on your promise, Ravin."

He chuckled. "I'm a man of my word. If you wish to dance, then I shall dance."

"Good. It may be the last opportunity for frivolity we have for some time."

Polite applause erupted through the room as the newlyweds finished their turn on the floor. Other couples began to rise from their seats to take up places in their stead. Ravin stood and offered the duchess his hand. "Shall we?"

CHAPTER TWENTY-SEVEN

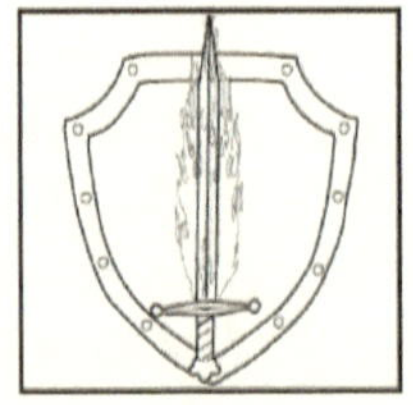

THE RADIANT

In all but one of her lifetimes, Dar Daelad had remained a constant, a relatively unchanging cityscape that sprawled across the otherwise sparsely populated plains at the heart of Masmoone Kingdom. The shimmering, opalescent tower at its heart, visible from several miles away, was the beacon that drew wizards and scholars alike. Even after more than two centuries, the familiarity of the scene that greeted Emra as they passed through the city's sculpted gates was a welcome sight.

She sat astride Fyrmane while Patak skittered along at her side. He stood slightly taller than her steed; between the two, the crowds parted to make way. Patak drew stares, but he largely ignored them; Vardak had warned him he would prior to their departure from camp. He sported his heavy plate mail and carried his two-handed sword across his back. Though she'd tried to convince him the weapon was unnecessary, he refused to escort her to the tower unarmed. It was his duty to protect her, after all.

"Gods, there are so many people," he muttered as they rounded a bend in the road. "I'm beginning to think all human cities are this way. How do you stand it?"

She managed a smile. "It has always been this way, Patak."

"I suppose you must have felt the same in the Stronghold. There are a great many of *us*, but we do not spread across the land as humans do."

"My visit to your homeland was truly the first." Emra shifted slightly in her saddle. "I was not afforded the opportunity in other lifetimes."

Patak fell silent for several moments as they navigated toward the marketplace. "Has Lucas finally come to terms with your…past?"

"He is no longer avoiding me, but he doesn't like to speak of it." She sighed. "I am thankful he agreed to lead the cavalry. The Santinians were certainly eager to join us. I'd not anticipated our numbers to swell as quickly as they have."

Patak snickered. "My little brother has his work cut out for him."

"As do you," she reminded him.

He grinned. "Is it truly work if I enjoy it?"

His near-constant proximity, coupled with his mannerisms made it increasingly difficult for her to ignore what she felt for him. In some of her lives, she'd found love. In others, she'd chosen to keep her distance; the fear of losing those she cared for had been too great. In this life, she was leaning toward love.

Her thoughts returned to their last conversation with Flariel, and the goddess' suggestion that Emra ought to seek Aeon while they were in Dar Daelad. If she could convince the wily god to end her cycle of rebirth, to give her the peace her soul craved, then perhaps this life would hold more purpose for her. It would be her last, and she would make every moment count.

She smiled as her eyes met Patak's. She wanted no regrets in this life.

His grin broadened before he looked away. It dissolved into a grimace as the sight of the crowded marketplace, swarming with people, came into view. "Gods, this is madness!"

She reached out and touched his armored shoulder. "They'll move aside once they take notice of you. And if they don't, Fyrmane is adept at forging a path through crowds."

The horse whickered in response. He was a beast born and bred for battle and rarely allowed anyone near him but Emra or those close to her. He'd accepted the Scorpion Men readily, as though he sensed kindred spirits, but humans were another matter. Fyrmane had a history of kicking and biting to get his point across. She hoped it would not come to that, but the throng ahead was dense and seemingly oblivious to their presence.

Patak squared his shoulders and moved a few steps ahead of Fyrmane. "I won't have him nipping at the unwary, Em. I'll see us through."

Fyrmane snorted with indignation. Emra patted his neck and guided him with her knees as they followed Patak through the marketplace. "We both know you're the best horse a knight could hope for."

Fyrmane held his head aloft at the praise, though his eyes shifted warily amongst the humans that surrounded him. Ahead, Patak managed to make a path easily enough, given his stature. The crowd thinned significantly once they were past the market and on the broad, tree-lined boulevard that led to the Shining Tower's door.

Patak slowed as their destination came into clear view, his blue eyes wide with wonder. The tower rose high above the metropolis, its opalescent exterior glimmering in an array of colors in the morning sun. Surrounding the tower's base was a lush garden filled with leafy trees and flowers of every variety imaginable. Even in autumn, the blooms flourished, thanks to the magic that sustained them. The intervening centuries had done little to change the tower and its grounds, Emra noted with satisfaction.

"Vardak did not come here when he was in Dar Daelad," Patak said in a hushed tone. "Gods, it's wondrous. This is the work of magic?"

"Yes." Even from a distance, she could sense the forces at work within the structure's foundation. Ancient magics that had at one time fascinated her greatly kept the tower and its grounds pristine.

"How many times have you visited this place, Em?"

She smiled sadly as memories enveloped her. In her first life, she'd been a wizard, living out her life within the shimmering beacon that loomed before them. In others, she'd made the journey to Dar Daelad in order to seek the wizards' aid. All except for her last life, she amended. During Arianna's time, the Council of Auras was corrupt and filled with the Soulless' spies.

"Many times, Patak, though this is the first in my current life."

"Has it always looked as it does now?"

She was grateful for his acceptance of her past, thankful she'd crossed paths with him. Few others, beyond the long-lived Airess, had ever understood. "Very little has changed. It's comforting, in a way."

She dismounted as they neared the broad, arching doorway that led inside the tower, then handed Fyrmane's reins to Patak.

He shook his head adamantly. "No, Em. I'm not about to let you out of my sight."

"I'm in no danger here," she replied evenly. "Besides, I must travel up the tower. As much as I'd like you at my side, I know your people don't manage stairs well, and *he* will be nothing short of a terror inside the tower," she added with a gesture toward Fyrmane.

Patak growled in frustration. "I did not accompany you only to be left behind. It's my job to make certain you're safe, Em."

"I'll be fine. If I don't return by noon, then you may scour the tower in search of me." She reached up to touch the side of his face. "I appreciate your concern, Patak, but we are in no danger here."

He closed his eyes, sighed, then nodded reluctantly. "If noon arrives without you, I'll tear this damned place apart with my bare hands if need be."

She dropped her hand and offered him a reassuring smile. "It won't come to that, Patak." She glanced at Fyrmane. "Make certain he behaves."

As she turned away, Patak muttered, "I've been relegated to the role of equine nursemaid, it seems." Fyrmane snorted loudly in response.

She smiled at the exchange and strode through the door, one hand on Fireblade's hilt. She studied the five-pointed star set into the anteroom floor, each point marked by a different color to signify the five Sects of the council. Arched doorways led away from the anteroom, while three broad staircases spiraled up the sides of the room toward the second floor. A number of people crossed the anteroom on business of their own, and few paid her any mind. When last she'd been in the tower, the office of the Radiant had been on the third floor, behind the vast chamber the council used for its largest gatherings.

She made her way toward the nearest staircase. A middle-aged woman paused at its base to study her, dark brown eyes locked upon her own. Emra knew the woman was a wizard; she could sense the other's power and the tentative probe of magic that sought to understand her further. Emra opened herself to the woman's wordless investigation. It would expedite her business if she was not forced to explain who and what she was time and again.

The woman's eyes widened and fell upon Fireblade's hilt at Emra's waist as the color drained from her face. "By the gods, you've returned."

"I must speak with the Radiant."

The woman nodded and beckoned for Emra to follow her. Her hands shook, and she glanced furtively toward Emra several times as they ascended the stairs. Emra sighed; it was a reaction she'd come to expect over her many lifetimes, though it remained a source of irritation. It was rare that she'd encountered anyone who truly understood her position and accepted it without question or a semblance of fear. Her thoughts flashed to Patak, and she smiled briefly. He was one of the few.

She followed the woman to the third floor, then around the long, curving corridor that led to the Radiant's personal study. The woman said nothing during their journey, but found her voice as they stopped in front of the study's closed door.

"I'll inform him of your arrival."

Emra crossed her arms and leaned against the smooth stone wall. She watched the woman knock on the door, her fist tapping out a predetermined cadence as it made contact with the aged wood. Emra feigned indifference, though her curiosity was piqued at the wizard's use of a signal to the leader of her council. She wondered at its significance as the door rapidly swung open and the woman stepped inside, disappearing from her sight.

It was mere moments before the door opened again, and the woman stepped into the hall, her face ashen. Behind her, a stocky, middle-aged man with the pale features and dark hair that marked him as Deluchan filled the doorway. He spoke quietly to the woman, who nodded rapidly and scurried away. Once she was gone, he crossed the hall to stand before Emra and offered his hand in greeting.

"I am Berasin Jarens, Radiant of the Council of Auras."

She accepted his hand and shook firmly. "Emra Castledowns."

She sensed his magical probing, and endured another silent investigation of her Ability and its connection to the relic she wore on her hip. As the council's leader, she would allow him this final round of confirmation, but her patience wore thin. There would be no other wizards allowed access to her mind. His eyes narrowed momentarily, though his reaction to her presence was more subdued than his colleague's had been. Once he was satisfied, he motioned that she should follow him.

He led her through the open door to his study, closing it swiftly behind them. The space was tidy and sparsely decorated. A polished oak table occupied the center of the room, with a number of matching chairs. A single bookcase lined one wall, though it was largely empty.

"Please, sit. We have much to discuss."

Emra took the chair nearest the door while he sat down across the table from her. "You must know why I'm here."

He cleared his throat nervously. "Yes. In truth, we were beginning to fear your reappearance would not occur. The Soulless are—"

"I'm well aware the Soulless have attacked Balotica," she replied. "I was in Jennavere hours after their army moved on. They left no one in their wake, though I suspect many were taken as prisoners." She eyed him with steely resolve. "Rumors state that the previous five have returned. Can you confirm it?"

"I, ah…" He looked down and swallowed uncomfortably.

"I will not tolerate games from your council," she replied. "In my last incarnation, I could not trust those within these walls. I stood against the Soulless without the aid of the wizards then, but I cannot do so now if all five of them have indeed returned."

"We believe they have."

His words confirmed her fears, and she knew she must inform the others in her camp of the development. That they had taken so many prisoners from Jennavere alarmed her. It would be a conversation neither Patak nor Vardak would enjoy. Her stomach roiled at the prospect.

"As I said, many were taken prisoner. If Dranamir has returned, this bodes poorly for those in captivity."

He frowned in confusion. "I'm afraid I don't understand."

She sighed in frustration. "Then listen carefully. During the first Great War, Dranamir—the first Soulless—made no attempt to hide the atrocities she committed against the prisoners of war. Thousands were killed by her hand, and those that managed to survive were forever changed. Their humanity was stripped from them. There are a pair of Scorpion Men in positions of command within my army. Do you understand the source of my concern?"

He nodded stiffly. "Yes, of course. Do you believe Dranamir will attempt the same feat a second time? My understanding is that it took vast amounts of energy—"

"Dranamir was the only Soulless I have not faced personally, but by all accounts, she was the most heartless of the lot. Given what I know of her character, she will do it again if we fail to stop her first." Emra sat back in her chair and studied the man across from her. He was terrified at the implications her presence brought, and doubly so at the turn their conversation had taken.

"Do you believe she will seek to control them, as the histories claim she did during her rule of the Shadow Council?"

Emra shook her head. "Safeguards have been put in place for the Scorpion Men. They will not face subjugation a second time. The human prisoners they currently possess are not protected in the same manner. We cannot allow history to repeat itself if we're in a position to prevent it." She sighed. "My general and the captain of my personal guard are both Scorpion Men, and they will not take this news lightly."

"What would you have me do, Emra?" he asked quietly. "There are many within the council who would readily join you. I will not prevent them from doing so, if that is their choice."

"I'm pleased to hear it. We will need as many able wizards in this fight as can be mustered."

"Will you remain in Dar Daelad long? I will inform the council of your arrival—and your request for aid."

"I'm not certain," she admitted. "I would prefer to remain here until spring, to gather more soldiers during the winter months before marching eastward. I cannot guarantee that will be the case, however. There are other forces at work, as well."

She understood Flariel would likely make another appearance, though whether it would be to provide information or simply to antagonize Vardak was yet to be seen. The Moon's Eye was key to something of the goddess' plans, yet its purpose remained mysterious. Perhaps Vardak would uncover more when he made his own visit to the Shining Tower.

"There always are," Berasin replied grimly. "If my accounts are correct, your army is camped a few miles north of the city?"

"It is. Any who wish to oppose the Soulless are welcome to join me there." She rose from her seat and turned toward the door. She paused at the threshold and glanced over her shoulder. "I hope your council has not been infiltrated by the enemy, Berasin. If we are to prevail, trust is paramount."

"I understand."

She nodded. "Then I will await those who wish to oppose them."

She left his study and hurriedly descended the tower. She had much to discuss with Patak while they returned to camp, and little of it good.

CHAPTER TWENTY-EIGHT

INTO THE CATACOMBS

Ravin was feeling particularly devious as he rapped his knuckles loudly on the door to the queen's private chambers. It was moments after dawn on the morning after her wedding. She'd forced him to delay long enough, and he would wait no more; the catacombs must be dealt with and the talisman secured.

Beside him, Adalin shrugged in discomfort. "You could have sent her a message. This is cruel, Ravin." Despite her words, she smiled faintly.

"I'd rather she hears the news directly. She won't be pleased with the intrusion or my insistence on beginning the work today, but there is little she can do to stop me." He eyed the duchess with interest. "I'm still uncertain why you've insisted on coming along."

"If something goes amiss down there, you'd be alone. I won't stand for it."

She looked away and busied her hands by smoothing a perceived wrinkle from her garments. She was dressed as if for riding to allow for greater freedom of motion while they navigated the tunnels beneath the palace. It was a wise choice, he conceded. They knew of the traps, but there was a chance more would await them than anticipated from their studies. The texts were ancient, predating even Ravin's first visit to Delucha.

Ravin raised his fist to knock a second time, but paused as the sound of shuffling was heard on the other side of the door. It opened a crack to reveal Jasom's blond head and bleary eyes, his hair tousled.

Ravin smirked as a glimpse of the boy's bare shoulder appeared in the gap behind him.

"Ravin? Gods, what time is it?"

"The time is irrelevant." He suppressed a laugh. "I came by to inform Her Majesty that I'll be going into the catacombs today. I'll have no further argument from her—or you—on the matter. This business must be done."

Jasom blinked several times, then stifled a yawn. "Very well. I'll tell her."

When he closed the door, Ravin offered Adalin his arm. The pair quickly departed; Ravin did not want to become mired in a senseless debate with the queen, and the longer he loitered in the hall, the greater the likelihood she would appear. She would hinder his progress no longer.

He led Adalin through the quiet corridors and down two flights of stairs to the main floor. They passed few others due to the early hour. Those they encountered were part of the staff; maids were busy scrubbing floors and polishing furniture, servers carried trays laden with steaming breakfasts between the kitchens and the private quarters of the nobility, and armored guards stood sentinel at various points along their route. Their journey was not questioned until they descended a final staircase toward the jail and its holding cells.

Adalin gripped his arm more firmly as a trio of guards moved to block their path.

"It's standard procedure," he whispered to her. Her grip remained firm as his words failed to relieve her anxiety.

"Advisor," one of the guards said by way of greeting. "Are you here for the prisoner again?"

"Not today. I have business in the catacombs."

The man's eyebrows rose. "Strange business, that. I'm certain you have good reason to visit the place." He motioned to the others. "Let the advisor and his lady through."

Adalin released his arm once they were beyond earshot of the guards. "It seems our ruse has worked well enough if even the jailers believe we're involved." She laughed softly; the sound echoed off the bare stone walls ahead.

Ravin flashed a grin. "In spite of my initial reservations, we make a fine team."

He led the way through several empty corridors toward a rusted iron door. He'd come to this place once before, after they'd uncovered the location of the catacombs' entrance. He glanced at Adalin as he placed his hands upon the ancient handle.

"I haven't been through this door. I don't know what awaits us on the other side."

"Open it, Ravin. Don't keep me in suspense."

The door swung open with a groan of rusted hinges. A narrow stair curved into inky darkness that the torchlight from the corridor failed to penetrate. A faint, musty odor wafted toward them on a current of cool air. Ravin suspected it had been many years since anyone had ventured into the lightless realm beneath the palace.

"Gods, it's dark." Adalin shuddered beside him.

Ravin channeled his magic and flicked his wrist. A soft yellow light enveloped them, bright enough to illuminate their path.

"I should have taken up with a mage long ago. Tricks like this are quite convenient."

He chuckled. "This is but a simple feat, Adalin. Any half-trained novice can make themselves a light." His good humor dissipated as he considered what lay ahead. "There are complex wards in the depths, if the book you uncovered is to be believed. Unraveling such magic may tax even my abilities."

He stepped into the stairwell and began to descend, Adalin at his heels. "You speak as though you possess great power, Ravin."

"Yes." He would not elaborate unless she pressed him for details. His magical prowess and his lineage were not topics he readily discussed without good reason.

At the base of the stairs, they were met with a long corridor lined with shelves. Countless bones were stacked neatly along each for as far as the magical light penetrated the gloom. The bones were yellowed with age but smooth, as though they had been polished. Most appeared human, though Ravin noted several elongated skulls that appeared Drakkon in nature. The musty odor was stronger here, and he wrinkled his nose in discomfort.

Adalin peered carefully at the nearest remains. Ravin had expected her to react adversely to their new environs, but she was engrossed in her examination and seemed not to mind the macabre display nor its accompanying stench. The duchess continued to surprise him.

"I read about this place some years ago," she said quietly. "The bodies were placed here during the Time of Chaos, though the records were unclear why it was done. So much history was lost during that era. It's a shame."

"I was not expecting to find this," he admitted before moving on.

She straightened and quickened her step to keep pace with his longer strides. Adalin chuckled softly. "The place is called the catacombs. What *were* you expecting, Ravin?"

He shrugged; she made a fair point.

The passage continued before them relatively unchanging for some distance. He could make out what appeared to be a solid wall at the end, but their route did not bend. It simply stopped at the wall as though the builders of the catacombs had suddenly given up. Ravin suspected the wall was not what it seemed.

He examined the pitted stone surface carefully as they approached. Words were chiseled into its heart, and a series of fanciful depictions of common animals were carved beneath them. He scowled as he read the text; it was a riddle, and one only a scholar of Deluchan history could decipher.

> *Daresin, the first of his name*
> *Believed himself above the hawkers*
> *He tamed a beast, noble but vain*
> *And used it as his marker.*

Helplessly, he turned to Adalin. "I wasn't prepared for—"
She moved swiftly past him and pressed firmly on the image of an eagle in flight. His eyes widened with concern. They had both pored over the book in the library countless times. A wrong maneuver on their quest to unravel the talisman's location would land them both in Aeon's realm.

"Adalin …?"

She tilted her head to the side as a low, grinding sound issued from somewhere far below their present location. She smiled knowingly. "It was a simple matter, Ravin. Or rather, it was simple for someone with knowledge of Deluchan history."

Before she could continue, the wall swung inward with a rumble. A fine cascade of dust and debris tumbled from above as the passage was revealed for the first time in over a millennium. The burst of air that enveloped them from beyond smelled stale and stagnant.

"Do you see?" she asked cheerily. "Daresin was the first Serales to take the throne. He was our monarch at the time the talismans were supposedly forged. The reference to the hawkers and the noble beast relate to his love of eagles. He had a pair of them, or so the stories tell, and often took them into the fields to hunt game. I'm certain you have noticed the royal house still bears the eagle as its insignia."

"When were you going to inform me you weren't merely an interested party, but a scholar as well?" Ravin was unable to mask his astonishment, but he was grateful she'd insisted on accompanying him. He would have been left stymied at the first junction without her.

"If you hadn't been so determined to avoid me until recently, perhaps we could have discussed this sooner." Her smile was warm. "It's no surprise to me that a Santinian-born mage would have little knowledge of Deluchan history, and I suspected you would have need of it. There were vague references in that book, if you recall."

"It seems I am in your debt. Again."

She laughed. "Then I shall ponder what to ask of you while we continue our journey." She gestured toward the ancient corridor ahead. "Lead on, Ravin. If memory serves, the next few barriers should be magical in nature."

Beyond the first obstacle, the corridor was smaller in diameter, the stone roughly hewn and uneven underfoot. There were no skeletal remains to adorn the walls in this portion of the catacombs; the path was devoid of decoration as it spiraled gently downward. Ravin cast his senses through the area, seeking evidence of their next obstacle, and was met with nothingness. Either they had a significant distance to travel, or the wards had been shielded from his magical sight. He assumed the latter and remained vigilant.

He wasn't certain how long they traveled the winding corridor. The stone remained unchanging, the only indications of progress the ache in his feet and the inexplicable sensation that they were deeper beneath the earth than they had been when they'd entered. The air remained still, and plumes of dust followed in their wake, stirred from a centuries-long rest by the passage of their boots.

He saw the seal that blocked their passage long before he could sense the magical weavings that formed its essence. It was shielded, as he'd surmised. It spanned the width of the passage, a semi-transparent green-yellow barrier that glowed fainter than his own manufactured light. He motioned for Adalin to remain at a distance while he approached the construct warily. He was within arm's distance before he passed beneath its invisible shield and could finally sense its nature.

He closed his eyes as he assessed the craftsmanship employed, his mind following each strand of magic as it wove through the larger tapestry. It was complex and fascinating, a thing of beauty for anyone gifted enough to appreciate its nuances. He traced the threads to their origin, then outward once more to their endpoints. It must be unraveled in reverse of its creation.

"Ravin?" Adalin's voice was hushed.

He gestured for her to remain where she was but did not open his eyes, lest he lose his place within the seal's intricate weaving. "Give me a moment, Adalin. I must concentrate."

She released a pensive sigh but said nothing more.

He worked swiftly, and unerringly unraveled the magical strands that held the seal in place. It had lasted centuries, its design remarkable even to his mind. It was a shame he must destroy it in order to obtain the talisman. As the last of the seal's tangled tapestry was undone, a low grinding sound resonated from within the earth beneath his feet.

He sought Adalin when he opened his eyes, and she wordlessly made her way to his side. "The magic in this place is unparalleled."

"It is said the wizards of old possessed greater power than those of our age."

"I'm not certain it has anything to do with lost power," he replied as they began to walk once more. "It feels to me as if there is lost knowledge, lost artistry... The technique employed to form that seal was unlike any I have encountered before, yet it took little power to dismantle it."

"Tell me something, Ravin," she said slowly. "You admitted earlier that you are very powerful, yet after some prying, I can find no trace of your name connected to either the Shining Tower or Santine. Surely a man with your ability would be well known by his country, if not the Council of Auras."

He bristled at her admission. "I was unaware you were spying on me."

"The queen ordered me to learn what I could of her newest advisor. I agreed to the work long before I came to know you, Ravin. If I'd refused, she planned to send me away. We've already discussed my situation." She sighed. "If she learns I've told you, she *will* make good on her threat."

He glowered into the darkness ahead, angry with her for misleading him, angry with the queen for her mistrust, and angry with himself for failing to anticipate the ploy. He said nothing in response and quickened his pace.

"Gods, Ravin, I'm sorry. Truly, I am."

He spun on his heel, forcing her to stop abruptly in front of him as he rounded on her. "Why now, Adalin? Why, after all of this time parading me about the palace, do you finally decide to reveal the truth? If you—or she—had merely asked, I would have been forthcoming." He shook his head and turned around, unable to look at the duchess further as fury overtook him. "Gods-damn it, my work here is no game."

He strode ahead and heard her pace quicken to keep up with him—and the light that surrounded him.

"I've wanted to tell you for days, Ravin, but I feared your reaction. It seems I was right to be concerned."

He nearly collided with the invisible magical box that loomed in their path and he swore. He backed up a few paces to study the obstacle, his anger quickly draining away. Perhaps he'd been too hard on her; she was trying to protect herself and keep her position at court, nothing more. An order given by the queen was as law.

"What is it?" she asked timidly. She hovered behind him, fearful of coming too near.

He grimaced, guilt roiling in his gut. "A trap. One I nearly stepped into." He shook his head, irritated by his lapse of concentration. "The queen ordered you to spy on me, and I suppose I should not have been taken by surprise by the news. She schemes against her other advisors in much the same fashion."

She took a tentative step forward. "Ravin—"

"You won't find mention of me, Adalin, and I'm not prepared to share my history if I know it will find its way back to the queen. I will tell you what I've told her: I did not train with the wizards, and the Soulless have made an enemy of me. I am my own man."

He assessed the trap before them and dismantled it within seconds. It was not the beautifully complex weaving the seal had been but would have resulted in instantaneous death had he stepped within its unseen confines. He shook his head again with a frown.

"Too close," he muttered.

"I'm sorry," she said again. Her voice cracked, and he turned around to find tears streaming from her eyes.

His resolve shattered, and the last vestiges of his anger evaporated. "Gods, now I'm the one who's sorry." He reached toward her, but something held him at bay. "Adalin…"

She looked up as he dropped his hand to his side. "I've been a fool, Ravin. It wasn't the first time she asked me to surveil one of her inner circle, but it was the first time I've allowed myself to befriend her target. You are…not what I'd expected, Ravin." She wiped at her eyes and managed a tremulous smile. "I must give her something soon, else I will be sent away. I have nowhere to go."

"Then allow me to help. I should not have lost my temper with you—the orders were not of your making." He drew a breath and offered his arm to her. When she stepped forward to take it, he said, "How well does Her Majesty know geography?"

Adalin snorted. "As well as she knows her library."

"Then tell her I'm from Tarren Haven."

He cast his senses through the area, though he knew it would do him little good until they came upon the next obstacle. He would not be caught unawares a second time and put Adalin at further risk.

She was thoughtful for a time. "The name is unfamiliar to me, Ravin."

"Tarren Haven no longer exists, but it was my first home."

"What happened to it?"

He shook his head. "The honest answer is, I don't know. I'm certain one of the library's books will have mention of it, but they'll not be recent volumes."

She frowned up at him. "You aren't making sense."

"Perhaps one day I will share my story with you, but now is not the time. I…Oh…"

He stopped as a shadow passed across the boundary of his light. The rasp of scale upon stone greeted his ears, and he wondered what sort of being was about to reveal itself. There were very few creatures capable of withstanding the passage of so many years without magical alteration. He recalled what he'd learned of Dranamir's atrocities during the First Great War, and knew it was plausible the thing hiding in the shadows might be the victim of similar modification.

Adalin peered toward the edge of the light as though transfixed while her fingers dug into his forearm. "Should we continue?" she asked in a breathless whisper.

Whatever the creature was, he could sense nothing of it. Like the previous obstacles, it was shielded from his magical sight. He nodded once, and together they eased along the passage toward the source of the sound. Adalin shuddered as another dry, papery rustle issued from beyond the reach of the light.

"It has the sound of a snake," she hissed uneasily. "I cannot abide snakes."

He channeled his power and formed a shield around them as a precaution. She jerked her hand away, startled, and stared at him with wide eyes.

"It won't harm you," he promised.

"I wasn't concerned about safety. I felt…" She shook her head and glanced at her hands. "I believe I felt your magic pass through my hand. It was unsettling."

A low growl emanated from the corridor ahead as the light revealed a creature unlike any Ravin had encountered previously. It was easily as large and powerful as the bears that roamed the Gray Mountains, though it was covered in gray-green scales. An eyeless head with unsettling humanoid features swiveled in their direction, as if it could sense their presence without the use of sight to guide it. It moved on all fours and backed against the curve of the wall as another low growl issued from its thick throat.

Ravin froze, uncertain if the creature planned to attack. He was near enough to sense it had not been manipulated by magic; its otherworldly form was its natural state. Beside him, Adalin stood rigid, the color gone from her face.

"What is it?" he asked of Adalin, praying she had uncovered something in her studies of the catacombs. Before she could respond, the creature hissed and began to speak.

"It?" the creature rasped. "It has a name."

Ravin had not counted on the creature harboring intelligence. He swallowed once and struggled to mask his astonishment. "Forgive us," he replied evenly. "We have not encountered any of your kind before."

"Have you come to undo the magics in this place?" it inquired.

Ravin eyed it warily. He suspected a trap, though the question seemed harmless enough. "Yes."

It reared onto its back legs and roared loudly, the sound reminiscent of an angry bear. "I agreed to guard the talisman. Only those who prove their worth may pass."

"A gatekeeper, Ravin," Adalin whispered. "The book spoke of several."

The creature made a garbled hissing sound that Ravin realized belatedly was laughter. "I am Yox. The lady is correct."

Ravin nodded. He understood what he must do; the gatekeepers existed for the sole purpose of evaluating the character of those seeking to gain entrance into the deeper levels—and the talisman beyond. He drew a breath and outlined their need. He explained the return of the Soulless and their desire to obtain the talisman for themselves.

"And what will *you* do with such a powerful relic?" Yox demanded, tilting its blind head.

"I will defend this land," Ravin replied without hesitation. "I will drive the Soulless and their army from Delucha, then I will pursue them to the ends of the earth if need be. I will hound them until all five lie dead at the Nameless god's feet."

Adalin grasped his arm as Yox lumbered forward. It stopped a hair's breadth from the pair and sniffed at the air. "You possess the resolve. You possess the strength."

A low rumble issued from the depths that caused the floor to quake momentarily. Yox sighed expansively and fell to its knees.

"You may pass," it stated as its body began to convulse.

Ravin watched in horror as the ancient gatekeeper tumbled onto its side, its life's purpose fulfilled. Adalin turned to gaze up at him, tears sparkling in her eyes.

"It lived alone for countless centuries, waiting for someone to come," she whispered. "Now that we have arrived, its life is spent."

"We won't allow its long vigil to have ended in vain," he replied, his gaze on Yox's unmoving form. "Find peace in Aeon's realm, gatekeeper."

CHAPTER TWENTY-NINE

THE CHALLENGE

Tavesin's hands trembled as he descended the stairs. His summons had been issued and he was expected to embark on his challenge at once. Hasnin walked on his left, Aziarah on his right. The steps led to a level beneath the tower's main floor, an area designed specifically for the purpose of the apprentice's challenge. He could sense a difference in the design of the walls and floor as they neared the bottom; this portion of the tower was magically reinforced, shielded from outside influence, and tempered to withstand even the greatest of magical assaults from within.

Tavesin's heartbeat accelerated as he made the realization. The wizards and the Drakkon both had indicated he must demonstrate his abilities and withstand the trials his challenge presented. It was only now, as he journeyed into the depths below the tower, that he understood the full implications of their words. In order to succeed and be named wizard, he could not hold back. The notion of failure terrified him.

He clenched his fists to hide the tremors in his hands as they stepped into a small antechamber at the base of the stairs. A broad, arched doorway filled the opposite wall, and a small, magically-powered light shone from within ornate lanterns on either side. Mari El'Vero stood in front of the door, garbed in her ceremonial blue robes that marked her as Sect Master. She smiled at Tavesin's approach, though he failed to muster one in return. His nerves would not allow it.

"It is rare that we test an apprentice so young, but you have shown great promise, Tavesin." Mari gestured to the doors that blocked his passage. "It has been many years since an apprentice with your strength has graced the tower, but with such strength comes great difficulty. The challenge is designed to test your resolve, your Ability, your dedication, and your character. Each apprentice faces a different set of obstacles within, determined by the assessment made upon entry."

She paused to study him for a moment, dark eyes scanning his face. Tavesin resisted the urge to squirm and maintained eye contact.

She nodded, satisfied with what she perceived within his gaze. "The door opens into a vast chamber. The chamber is an enormous relic, tempered by years of students like yourself channeling their magic within. The relic is autonomous. It will determine your character the moment you pass through the doors, and it will test you to the limits of your Ability. What you experience within may be very personal in nature. We will not ask you to speak of your experience, though you may if you wish to. The choice will be yours alone."

Tavesin drew a breath, though it did little to calm his nerves. "And if I fail?"

"You will be permitted another month to prepare yourself and hone your skills. At the end of that time, you will be summoned here again." Mari looked down, her expression pensive. "Those who cannot endure their challenge after a second attempt are severed from their magic and sent home. It is dangerous to allow half-trained apprentices to continue working their craft. Long ago, the council allowed it, but too many died as a result."

The same had been explained to him previously. Tavesin could not imagine his life without magic now that he had studied in the tower and learned much of the craft. Losing his power would be akin to losing his sight or his hearing.

"I won't fail."

"If you succeed, the relic will resonate with its counterpart in the Radiant's study. We will discuss the outcome of your challenge once you have finished, then summon you. You will be inducted into the Council of Auras—if your trial proves successful. The induction serves four purposes, Tavesin. Do you recall what those are?"

He nodded once. "I will be sworn to uphold the edicts of my chosen Sect, the Blue. As a Blue, I will be a defender of the people and the council. I will be sworn to render aid to any who seek it, if it is within my ability to do so. I will become an oath-bound enemy to the Soulless, the Shadow Council, and those who follow them. I will be sworn to obey the Radiant's call to arms should war descend upon our Council."

Hasnin's hand fell upon his shoulder, a sign his aged mentor was pleased with the recitation. Aziarah peered down at him, her reptilian gaze penetrating. She did not smile, but she bobbed her head once in acknowledgment. He understood from his time amongst the Drakkon that her people held a similar ritual for their would-be magi, though with fewer rules to bind them at its conclusion.

Mari moved aside and held her arm aloft in a gesture of welcome. "I deem you ready to proceed, Tavesin Drondes. At the conclusion of your challenge, you shall be named a Blue, or you shall be required to test again in one month's time."

Her words were ceremonial but served as a reminder of his goal. He could not rescue Arra without becoming a wizard and gaining the freedom associated with the title. He ignored the churning of his stomach, squared his shoulders, and stepped forward.

"I'm prepared to accept my challenge."

"Then gods be with you, Tavesin, and may Solsticia bless you with her favor this day."

"Good luck, boy," Hasnin murmured, while Aziarah said, "I will see you in the garden when you're finished here, child."

Emboldened by their words, he strode toward the door. He lifted his hand toward the handle and hesitated for a heartbeat before he grasped it between his trembling fingers. He drew a breath and pulled it open, and his eyes were met with darkness. Hasnin had prepared him for this moment, yet taking his first step into the unknown was terrifying.

The image of Arra as he'd last seen her, broken and battered, flashed through his mind. He would not fail her.

He released his grip on the handle and stepped across the threshold. The shadows enveloped him while a stifling silence descended over him. He was momentarily blind as the door clicked shut behind him, sealing him inside until he had proven his worth.

After a few moments, a pale light appeared, glimmering a short distance ahead. Instinctively, he moved toward it. The light resolved into a candle at his approach; the flame danced and flickered in a wind he could not feel. The air around him was warm and still, as though the world held its breath in anticipation of his next move.

The sound of footsteps in the darkness drew his attention, and he turned toward the sound. The footfalls were slow, measured, purposeful. Ominous.

Tavesin narrowed his eyes and created a shield around himself, prepared to face the danger that lurked in the shadows. A thin man appeared, his face drawn and his skin pale, as though untouched by the sun for decades. Thin tendrils of pale blond hair clung to his skull. The eyes that stared balefully at Tavesin were crimson and glimmered in the darkness. Tavesin recognized the Soulless before he stepped fully into the light.

Garin had taken him unaware once in the Aethereum; it would not happen a second time. Not in the physical realm, not in the Aethereum, and not *here*, in the chamber of his challenge. This Garin may have been a magical construct, but Tavesin was certain he was no less dangerous than the real being.

His previous anxiety evaporated. Rage coursed through him as his eyes met those of his tormentor and Arra's captor. He held it at bay; his mind required clarity and focus. He braced himself for an attack that did not immediately come.

"You'll never have her, little rat. She is mine."

"You're wrong." Tavesin glared defiantly at the Soulless, his words bolstered by his fury.

Garin smirked and examined his fingernails, feigning boredom. "I recall our last meeting clearly, little rat. Had your savior not happened along, you would have found yourself at my mercy indefinitely." The crimson eyes flicked upwards to scan his face. "It seems you've learned a trick or two since that time."

Garin thrust one arm toward him. Violet sparks sprang to life to careen through the air toward Tavesin. A small part of his mind cataloged the action and the magic employed for later analysis while he poured more energy into his shield. He would endure and prove to Garin—or whatever this truly was—that he was no longer the hapless child who had stumbled into the Soulless' trap.

The violet sparks erupted into blue-white flame as they buffeted his shield, then ricocheted erratically in several directions. He strengthened his shield further to create a faintly shimmering barrier a hair's breadth from his skin. He narrowed his eyes and prepared for the next assault.

A low moan issued from behind him, and Tavesin glanced in the direction of the sound. Arra knelt paces away, her face swollen and bruised as tears of blood leaked from her eyes.

In his periphery, Garin motioned and struck again. A beam of gray-white light issued from his hands, but rather than direct it at Tavesin, he launched it toward Arra.

Tavesin reacted without thinking; he expanded his shield swiftly to cover Arra just as the beam reached her location. The magic employed in the attack was more powerful than any Tavesin had encountered previously, and it took a tremendous effort to hold his shield intact. The beam glanced off its intended target and into the gloom.

Tavesin crossed the distance to Arra and knelt at her side while he assessed the damage Garin had done to his shield. He expended more energy to repair and strengthen it, then turned to glare up at the Soulless.

"You won't have her."

Garin laughed coldly. "I can perform this dance all day, little rat. The question is: Can you?"

Tavesin rose to his feet and stood in front of Arra protectively. He wasn't certain if he was truly as strong as the real Garin, and in his challenge space, he could not sense the other's power. His mind informed him he could not because this Garin was not *real*. He steeled himself and prepared to endure the next onslaught.

"I will match you stroke for stroke." Tavesin clenched his fists. "You will not have her."

A wicked smile stretched the Soulless' pallid features. "Then we shall dance, little rat."

CHAPTER THIRTY

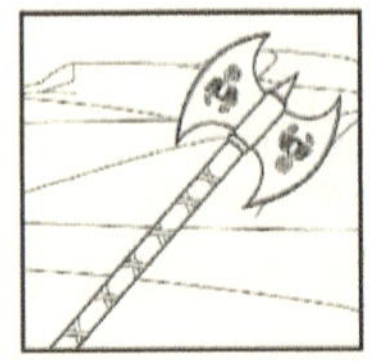

THE DRAKKON'S OFFER

Vardak opted to make the journey into Dar Daelad alone, in spite of Patak's protests. Emra seemed to understand he required time to himself in order to sift through his thoughts and swiftly overruled Patak, to his brother's astonishment. He knew what to expect from human establishments from his time with Emra's growing army, and could navigate Dar Daelad well enough without a guide. He'd been to the city once before, on that seemingly long-ago day with Janna.

Thoughts of her twisted his gut. He was plagued with guilt in spite of the many assurances others had given him that he was not at fault. She'd given up everything in order to obtain the Moon's Eye while he'd wallowed in indecision. He kept her final message to him amongst his private belongings and reread it on the dwindling occasions he had a few moments alone. He carried out Flariel's demands not for the goddess, but to honor the memory of her daughter.

Though he had not traveled to the Shining Tower on his previous journey into the city, he located it easily enough. It soared high above the other structures and most roads led toward where it loomed in the city's heart.

He had little experience with wizards beyond his dealings with Emra and the handful of others that had joined her since her visit to the tower the previous day. She'd quickly taken charge of the magic wielding folk within her growing camp, leaving Vardak to focus on matters of military importance. The solitary journey into the city had served to clear his mind, but he was now faced with the prospect of approaching the wizards with the matter of the Moon's Eye.

He paused at the outer edge of the lush garden that surrounded the tower's base, uncertain how he ought to begin. Emra had indicated the Radiant may be of assistance, despite her misgivings about the man. She'd found him only moderately helpful with her own matter, and Vardak believed his was of equal importance.

Movement drew his eye as he contemplated his next move. Several red-scaled Drakkon moved beneath the canopy of a broad-leafed tree that had not yet shed its greenery in preparation for winter. Among them were two teenaged human boys garbed in shades of brown. He understood enough about the wizards' hierarchy to assume the pair were apprentices. It was curious to see the Drakkon in the heart of a human settlement, and on the ground, no less.

He focused on the open door of the tower and began to make his way across the garden. The Drakkon were not the reason he had come.

He was nearly to the door when one of the Drakkon approached, a female; if he judged their people correctly. She stood nearly as tall as he did and lacked the small horns that adorned the heads of some of the larger members of her group. Dressed in leather armor, a mace at her hip, she strode up to him with questions in her hazel eyes. Her leathery wings were folded along her back, and she appeared at ease.

He studied her warily. He had no experience with the Drakkon to guide his words. They did not make the long journey to the Stronghold to trade with the Scorpion Men as so many other peoples did.

"You are not the same man who accompanied Fireblade's wielder here yesterday."

He shook his head. "That was Patak." He offered her his hand in greeting. "I'm Vardak."

She took his hand. "Aziarah. I lead the Drakkon mages." Her eyes scrutinized him, and he held her gaze, unflinching. "Come, I believe we have much to discuss, Vardak."

He hesitated. "I require an audience with the Radiant."

She snorted. "And I assume he'll be as much help to you as he was to Emra." She glanced around the garden, then lowered her voice so only he could hear her next words. "I can sense the relic in your possession, and I can help you. I don't believe the wizards can."

He nodded. Her words mirrored Flariel's; she had impressed upon him the importance of traveling to Delucha, rather than Dar Daelad.

He had ignored the goddess, partly out of spite, and partly because she hadn't forbidden him to continue along the same path as Emra.

"Come," Aziarah said again.

This time he followed her without question. She led him beyond the cluster of other Drakkon toward a secluded grove of evergreens. Some of her people watched their passage curiously, and the two human boys openly stared. They were young, and it was likely the first time they had encountered one of his people. He'd become accustomed to the stares he received during their travels, and it no longer bothered him as it once did.

Once within the grove, he said, "Can all mages sense the relic?" The notion that others had taken note of the object he carried unsettled him.

She chuckled. "No. Very few learn the talent to detect such items."

Relieved, he nodded. "You said you might be of help, but the wizards—"

"Yes," she replied swiftly, cutting him off. "The relic you possess harbors vast power. I do not know where you found it, or what its purpose might be, and perhaps it's best I don't know. If you seek a wizard with the strength to handle such an object, there are none within the tower." She frowned then said, "Perhaps I misspoke. There are none in the tower *yet*."

Again, he was forced to recall his last conversation with Flariel. "An apprentice?"

"Yes. He is as much my apprentice as he is the tower's. The boy is gifted beyond any I've encountered before—and that says much." She smiled faintly. "He is undergoing his challenge at present and will be named wizard should he prove himself adequately. I have no doubt he will succeed. But tell me, Vardak, why did Emra not bring this relic herself? It would have saved one of you the trip."

"It's a long story."

"I'm listening." She made a point of sitting down on the ground and folded her wings carefully behind her. "Sit and tell your tale. The others have little need of me as they work with the boys."

"Who are they?" he asked as he folded his legs beneath him.

"The older of the two—the Santinian—is Rostin Ver'an. He shows much promise with combat magic, and as such, must also learn to properly wield a blade. The other is Badolo. He harbors nearly as much power as the apprentice we were discussing previously, though his Ability is suited to the creation of magical devices." She eyed him with amusement. "I will answer no further questions until you answer mine."

"That's fair."

He paused a moment to collect his thoughts, then began. Aziarah listened quietly as he spoke while her eyes gleamed with interest. She refrained from interruption and did not question him until he concluded his story.

"I'm not certain if you are blessed or cursed, Vardak," she stated when he finished. "First Blademon, then Flariel, then Solsticia… Most of us are considered fortunate to have a single interaction with a god in our lifetimes."

He scowled at the ground. "Based on my last interaction with Flariel, cursed is the more apt description."

"And this relic you bear is truly the Moon's Eye? It is legendary among magical creations for its purported power."

He tugged on the cord around his neck and withdrew the small, teardrop-shaped stone from beneath his armor. Each time he looked upon the relic, the knife in his heart twisted a bit more. Janna's sacrifice must not be forgotten.

"It is, and it came to me at great cost."

Aziarah was silent for several moments. "Yes. I had hoped to shelter Tavesin from the coming war as long as I was able, but your coming here…" She shook her head and trailed off. "He is young and naïve to much of the world's machinations, Vardak. But he possesses the power to wield your relic where no others within his council can."

"And what of your people, Aziarah?" He tucked the relic back into its customary hiding place.

"I am the leader of the Drakkon magi, Vardak. If even I lack the strength, none of my people can help you."

He sighed and looked away. He must place his trust in a half-grown boy, or blindly follow Flariel's advice and take the relic to Delucha. He knew nothing of the other mage, and Aziarah had volunteered nothing. Perhaps she did not know whom the Fire Maiden referred to.

"When Tavesin has finished his challenge, I will speak with him. Once he is named wizard, he will no longer be forced to obey the missives of his elders, with the exception of the Radiant. He may be willing to help." She chuckled softly. "Knowing him as I do, it is unlikely he will turn you down, Vardak. How long do you plan to remain near the city?"

"We have made no formal decision, but Emra is considering we remain until spring. Travel will become difficult as the days grow colder and the weather foul." He shrugged. "I am unused to the drastic changes in seasons this side of the Gray Mountains experiences. The timing of our next move will be her decision."

"Of course." Aziarah rose swiftly, and he stood to join her. "I'm glad we have spoken. When Tavesin makes his decision, I'll accompany him to your camp."

CHAPTER THIRTY-ONE

THE LAST BUILDER

Adalin met him outside of his quarters with the dawn. She carried a plate of fresh bread, butter, and honey in one hand, and a cloth-covered basket in the other. She smiled, mischief in her eyes.

"I've brought breakfast, Ravin." She handed the plate to him, then indicated the basket. "And luncheon, as well. We were unprepared yesterday."

"Our lack of food was the least of it." He beckoned her into his room and set the plate atop the wardrobe table.

She took a crust of bread and slathered it with honey. "Your meeting with Her Majesty didn't go smoothly?"

"No." He took a bite and frowned, his gaze seeking the room's single window. The glass was streaked with rain, the sky a threatening shade of bruised purple-gray. The stormy scene matched his mood.

A messenger had awaited him upon his return to his quarters the previous afternoon, bearing a terse summons from the queen. When he'd arrived in the solar, she'd proceeded to berate him for several tedious minutes. His decision to inform her in person of his plan to enter the catacombs had been a mistake. She'd been furious at the early morning awakening, and her temper had been soured further when she realized his plan. He'd endured the tirade and informed her he intended to return each day until he obtained the talisman.

"You will not," she'd seethed. "I have not given my permission."

"Unless you want to hand your kingdom and your palace to the Soulless, you won't stand in my way."

He would remember the sound of her hand striking his face long after the pain faded. Despite her fiery reaction, she conceded the kingdom's future was more important than her desire to approve of his doings. His own ire sparked, Ravin had been unable to stop himself from worsening the situation.

"I don't require your approval, and I won't gods-damned ask for it." He had stormed out of the solar as she raged at his back.

He told Adalin the abbreviated version of events while they breakfasted.

"Be wary of her, Ravin. She may be a privileged child, but she will become dangerous if you goad her too far." Adalin popped a final morsel of bread into her mouth and gave him a pointed look. "At least your skin is dark enough I cannot see the imprint of her hand."

He shrugged indifferently; it wasn't the first time a woman had slapped him, and he was certain it wouldn't be the last.

"Once I have the talisman, I won't need to maintain my post as advisor any longer. I'll remain here if need be, but my path must take me elsewhere eventually."

Adalin's expression became pensive and she looked away. "Then perhaps we ought to be on our way."

As she picked up the lunch basket, Ravin created a portal into the Aethereum. He studied Adalin carefully, weighing how much he ought to tell her of the realm against the risks of leaving her in ignorance. It was not the first time he'd opened one in her presence, and she immediately understood its purpose.

"If it were as simple as teleporting ourselves to the catacombs, why didn't you do so yesterday?" she asked. "I am still footsore."

"I cannot travel to a location I know too little about," he replied. "It's unsafe, and if I cannot visualize the space properly, I'll go nowhere. I can transport us to the place where we turned back yesterday, but no further." He offered his arm and she took it, questions in her eyes. "Once we step through, you must hold onto me no matter what occurs. You don't have the Ability, Adalin. Without it, I cannot locate you if we become separated. This shortcut we take is very dangerous, and I—"

He stopped himself, stunned that he'd nearly admitted he didn't want to lose her, despite their argument from the previous day. Instead, he shook his head and offered her a strained smile. "I may be powerful, but even my Ability has limits. Don't let go."

She flinched as they entered the Aethereum and the harsh, blue-white light met her eyes. Ravin tightened his grip on her hand, fearful she might inadvertently disengage.

"I thought you merely opened a door to somewhere else and were there." She blinked at their surroundings. "This looks like your room in the palace, yet different. Where are we?"

"The Aethereum." He knew she would have dozens of questions, but he was not prepared to answer them at present. "I can travel instantaneously to other locations while here."

She nodded and her fingers tightened on his own. "Then let's not waste any more time."

He nodded, noting the ashen hue her features had taken while she continued to squint through her lashes. The light was affecting her, and there was little he could do to spare her the discomfort but to conclude their travels quickly. He imagined the darkened corridor where they'd left Yox's body the previous day. They arrived precisely where he'd intended in the span of an eye-blink.

Adalin gasped. "By the gods, Ravin, this should not be possible."

He chuckled. "Very few mages can access the Aethereum. Fortunately for us, I am one of them."

He opened a second portal, created a magical light, and together they stepped into the darkness of the catacombs. He was strangely pleased that he'd managed to impress the duchess.

She released a sigh of relief and dropped his hand. "I cannot abide the light in that place. I felt as though my skull would split at any moment." She set the basket on the floor and massaged her temples. "Does it not affect you?"

Ravin considered her words and his countless excursions through the Aethereum. He could not recall experiencing the adverse effects she described, but perhaps he was attuned to that other realm. It had originally been created for his use, after all.

"No, it doesn't. We will take the long route back to the palace when we've finished for the day." He frowned, concerned. "Are you well, Adalin?"

"My head is clearing already. Shall we?" She took up the basket with a bright smile, though he detected discomfort in the depths of her eyes.

"You're certain?"

She groaned. "Yes, Ravin. I'm not as fragile as I seem, and I won't have you treat me as such. Come."

"Very well."

They gave Yox's corpse a wide berth and continued along the corridor in silence. Ravin contemplated the shift in his arrangement with the duchess as they walked, surprised at the sudden and inexplicable turn it had taken. As he'd begun to accept her ploy for the sake of court appearance, she'd begun to reveal a different facet of her personality. She was a genuine, forthright woman with a keen intelligence he'd long believed lost amongst the nobility. He understood now, after her revelation of the previous day, the lengths she'd gone through simply to keep her place in the palace. Without her façade for the sake of the court, the queen would have dismissed her long ago.

Perhaps, he reflected, her motives were not so different than his own.

The seal appeared in their path before the light touched it, and he knew immediately it would take more time to unravel than the first had. As they neared its shimmering surface, he noted there were three distinct threads woven together to form a dense tangle of magical energy. He must work to unwind each in turn, switching between threads as necessary in order to disable it without bringing harm to himself or Adalin. A single wrong maneuver could prove devastating.

She leaned against the wall as he set to work. He could feel her eyes fixed on him. He wondered what she was thinking and if she understood the enormity of what they hoped to achieve. Obtaining a talisman was a feat no one in history had managed since the date their safeguards had been set in place. The traps and seals, wards and gatekeepers had withstood the turn of countless centuries.

Until now.

He felt the final thread in the seal untwist and dissolve. He smiled and opened his eyes, the barrier that had spanned the width of the corridor gone.

"You made quick work of that." Adalin stood upright and approached.

"Did I? It's difficult to tell when I focus on tasks of this sort. I'm not fully aware of the passage of time."

She smirked. "Clearly. When you disabled the previous--what did you call these constructs?"

"Seals."

"When you disabled the previous seal, it took you nearly an hour. This was a matter of minutes."

He frowned thoughtfully. This seal had been far more complex than its predecessor; it should have taken him longer to unravel. After a moment, he shrugged and gestured that they should continue their journey. The puzzle of elapsed time was one to be dealt with another day.

It was another hour before Ravin discerned a faint sound from somewhere ahead. It was an intermittent, metallic jangle reminiscent of links of chain being pulled across the stone floor. Yox had been a gatekeeper and untethered. Though frightening in appearance, Yox had not been a threat. Whatever lay next in their path was dangerous if the builders of the catacombs believed it required restraint to keep in line. Ravin wasn't certain he wanted to learn what manner of beast would be unveiled when his magical light penetrated its shadowed prison.

He cast his senses forward into the gloom but could uncover nothing of their next obstacle. Another long rattle echoed from the walls, and Adalin shuddered visibly. Her eyes sought his, wide with fear. He wished he could reassure her that all was well, that there was nothing lying in wait in the gloom ahead, prepared to pounce upon them given an opportunity. Instead, he shrugged helplessly. They would learn what lurked in their path only when they drew near enough for his light to uncover it.

Another metallic rattle careened off the walls, much nearer than the previous one. Ravin paused warily, though he could see nothing of the sound's source. He motioned for Adalin to walk behind him with the hope he might protect her should their next encounter prove hostile. She arched an eyebrow, disapproval written across her features.

"I don't know what lies ahead, Adalin."

"And we shall face it together," she replied stubbornly. "We had an agreement, Ravin."

"So we did." He scowled ahead, angry with himself for yielding to her earlier demands. She may not be fragile, but she was vulnerable to the workings of magic. "I cannot protect you if you insist on accompanying me in this manner."

She laughed softly. "A few weeks past, you wanted nothing more than to escape my presence. Now, you act the noble hero."

"Adalin..."

"No, Ravin. I've made my decision and have accepted the consequences that may arise. We will face this together."

Reluctantly, he nodded. "Whatever lurks ahead is not far."

The chains became visible first, coiled in a great heap near the center of the corridor. Ravin followed the links with his eyes into the shadows beyond the reach of the light. Each link in the chain was nearly as long as his hand and as thick as his thumb. He paused to examine the coil of chain, keeping a wary distance. He could sense nothing magical in the area; the chain was ancient and flecked with rust, but not imbued with unseen power. The size of the chain concerned him, however. It would take great strength to break free of such bonds without the aid of magic.

As if in response to his inner musings, the chain rustled and began to clink against the floor. A faint rasp accompanied the chain's slackening, as though parchment were being unfurled just beyond the edge of his light. He peered into the darkness with wary anticipation. Moments later, the source of the sound soared into view on large, bat-like wings. It sported a furry muzzle, lupine in form, and long blade-like fingers protruded from the ends of its wings. A length of chain was secured around its midsection and another around its throat.

Ravin shouted in wordless warning and shoved Adalin toward the nearest wall while simultaneously summoning a shield to protect them both. He recognized the creature as one of the ancient builders of Stonewall Hall. The builders had been cursed by the Nameless god during the Time of Chaos, fated to roam the depths beneath Nuarno Peak without respite as wraiths for eternity.

It alighted atop the coil of chain and tilted its head as it scrutinized the two humans in its presence with eyes like polished onyx. Ravin studied it in turn; it was no wraith, but one of the builders in corporeal form.

It bared its small, sharp teeth. "Humans are ever meddling." Its voice was little more than a dry croak, unaccustomed to speech after centuries of disuse.

"Another gatekeeper?" Adalin whispered into his ear.

He shook his head. A gatekeeper would not be tethered as the builder was. This was another matter entirely.

"Why did they imprison you here?" Ravin asked, hoping to draw the builder's attention away from their purpose in its unorthodox lair.

It fixed its dark eyes on him, unblinking. "*They* did not. I volunteered."

"Why are you chained?" Adalin demanded. "A volunteer should receive better treatment."

"Entitled human," it replied, though Ravin detected amusement in its tone. "The chains do not restrain me. They protect me."

"I'm afraid I don't understand." Adalin placed her free hand on her hip and leveled one of her best no-nonsense stares at the builder.

"The one you call Nameless was not always so. He was once powerful, the patron god of my people." The builder tilted its head in the other direction and fell silent for a time. When it spoke again, its voice was a well of sorrow. "I lost count of the years long ago, but I am certain even you are aware of the curse we suffered at his hands. The chains I wear were forged by Aeon himself. I was spared the misfortune of my people until the time arrived when someone returned to this dark realm seeking the relic at its heart."

Adalin inhaled sharply while Ravin nodded in understanding. "I am well aware of the curse, friend. I've been inside Stonewall Hall."

"Then you know why I volunteered to remain hidden in the shadows."

"Yes." Ravin looked away, heart heavy as he considered the builder's plight. It had been faced with an eternity of mindless horror, losing itself to the ravages of the Nameless' malice as a blood-seeking wraith. He did not blame it for seeking an alternative, even if it meant centuries trapped within the confines of the lightless catacombs.

"We encountered Yox," Adalin said quietly. "Will your fate be the same as his?"

The builder's face twitched in a semblance of smile. "If I choose to open the path before you, I shall perish as Yox did. I've had many years to contemplate my decision and am content with my inevitable fate. Do not despair; I will not share the fate of my people. Aeon will embrace me and welcome me into his realm when my service has finally come to an end."

"I assume you wish to know why we've come," Ravin replied.

"No. That was Yox's purpose. He sought *why*. I seek *how*."

Ravin frowned. "What do you mean?"

The builder tittered. "The relic in the depths is powerful. Yox believed your purpose was suitable, and it is not my purpose to question its judgment. I wish to know *how* you plan to use it once it falls into your possession." Its eyes glittered with anticipation. "My people were the greatest of all magic wielders. I can sense your power, mage, and I have met few who can claim to rival it. The last keepers will assess your power, but you will impress even them. My question remains: *How will you use the relic?*"

Ravin gazed at the builder impassively. "In war," he replied evenly. "The same god who has cursed your people seeks to destroy all others. I will thwart his plans at any cost."

"I did not expect honesty from you, mage." The builder sighed heavily and turned to face the gloom beyond the edge of the light. "Humans often attempted to subvert my people. We were too different from your kind. We were feared."

Ravin blinked with surprise, but it was Adalin who next spoke. "On behalf of our ancestors, we apologize. Humanity has always been flawed."

"Follow me. I will open the way."

The builder met a similar fate to Yox. Ravin consoled himself with the fact that they'd been afforded the opportunity to thank it before its passing. He prayed its soul would find peace once it reached Aeon's realm.

"Did it speak true, Ravin?" Adalin asked quietly after a time.

"What do you mean?"

She shrugged uncomfortably. "You've alluded to your power several times, and I believed you were merely boasting. But it said—"

"Once we're finished here, I will tell you my story, Adalin. You have my word." He sighed and shook his head, disturbed by the implication. "I'm an anomaly amongst humans."

There were few people who knew the truth of his past, and he wished to keep it that way. He supposed Adalin deserved to learn it; she had shared her own secret with him, after all.

"I will hold you to your promise, Ravin."

He smiled faintly. He harbored no doubts that she would.

They continued on their journey for another hour, then stopped to rest and devour the contents of the basket Adalin had absconded with from the kitchens. Bacon sandwiches with a sharp, yellow cheese and a bottle of mead they quickly drained. Fortified and energized after the meal, Ravin was eager to press forward. The thick buzz he experienced from the mead dulled the sensation of sorrow that had settled upon him after the builder's sacrifice. Adalin smiled readily and took his arm as they descended further into the depths.

It was not long afterwards that they came across the next obstacle in their path. It was a simple ward, though cleverly hidden by a cloak of shielding magic. Ravin dismantled it with ease and his spirits lifted further.

Adalin stumbled as they continued and fell against his side with a peal of girlish laughter. "Perhaps the mead was a mis...mistake." She giggled again as he attempted to steady her.

Through his own golden haze, Ravin grinned. "I've made worse."

"Gods, don't smile like that, Ravin. Your beauty ought to be a crime."

He blinked at her slowly, the words taking their time to coalesce in his brain. "It was my mother's doing, you know."

She snorted. "I could say the same for my looks."

"Hmm." She stumbled again, and he steadied her against his side. "Don't fall, lady duchess. We've a long way to go."

"You're drunk, Ravin." She giggled. "As am I."

"Perhaps...Perhaps we ought to return," he suggested. It was a struggle to speak coherently, and he would need his wits should they encounter any other gatekeepers or traps.

"You did well enough with that ward," she countered.

He grinned again in spite of her previous admonition. "I did, at that. Perhaps one more challenge, lady duchess? Then we shall return."

"Agreed."

A half-hour later by his estimate, they encountered a bricked wall in their path. At its center was a smooth bronze placard with several lines of text etched into its surface. Without reading the words, he understood it was another riddle, likely rife with Deluchan history. He slumped against the wall and sat down, then gestured grandly toward Adalin.

"I believe this is your specialty, lady duchess."

She shook her head and laughed. "I rather like this side of you, Ravin."

She studied the placard for a time. He knew he ought to be alarmed when she swayed on her feet, but he could not summon the energy to rise to his feet on his own. To his relief, she righted herself. Her lips moved, forming silent words as she read through the lines.

She shook her head slightly, then brightened. "Ah, this refers to Castelin's reign...And this...Yes, it's the stag." She peered at Ravin. "The mead was a mistake, and I wish you weren't Santinian."

"Did you solve it?" he asked, unconcerned though he knew he ought to be.

"I believe so," she replied with a slow smile. "If I choose the wrong tile, what will happen? I can't think properly at present."

"Death." He shrugged. "I trust you, Adalin."

"I'm responsible for our s-sorry state," she pointed out. "You shouldn't."

"The mead will be our secret." He pushed himself to his feet and sauntered to her side. "Perhaps we return tomorrow to choose the correct tile...?"

"It's the stag," she muttered emphatically. Before he could stop her, she pressed the corresponding tile and stepped away from the wall. "Smile, Ravin. If I'm wrong, I want to see it...one last time."

He raised his eyebrows and grinned as the wall began to grind slowly open. "It seems we're in luck, lady duchess. This won't be the last smile you see." Emboldened by the effects of the mead, he winked at her conspiratorially, then belatedly realized what he'd done. He flushed, embarrassed at the lapse in his character. "I think we ought to return…"

"Mmm, yes." She leaned into him as he summoned a portal, then grimaced. "Perhaps our return trip will prove enough to bring me back to my senses. Though you…" She giggled again and patted his cheek. "I rather like the relaxed Ravin the mead has brought about."

CHAPTER THIRTY-TWO

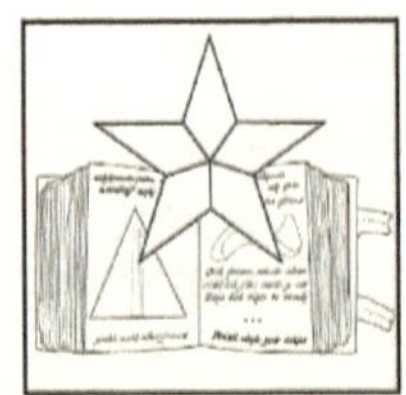

THE YOUNGEST WIZARD

When the doors of the challenge chamber opened of their own accord, Tavesin was too exhausted to appreciate that his trial had come to a successful end. He stumbled toward the opening and the soft light that spilled through it, beckoning him toward his future and a welcome respite from the arduous ordeal. He stumbled forward on legs made weak from hours on his feet, his mind numb with fatigue.

A pair of silhouettes appeared in the doorway, temporarily blocking the light from his weary eyes. He forced one foot in front of the other, slowly marching toward them. Did every would-be wizard struggle as he did once their challenge was concluded? His mind was wreathed in fog, and the thought flitted away as quickly as it had come.

The silhouettes resolved themselves into Mari El'Vero's petite form and Hasnin's gnarled countenance. Hasnin offered his arm in support as Tavesin stumbled across the threshold. He mumbled his thanks, only distantly aware of Mari's next instruction. His mind grappled with her words for several seconds before he understood.

"I must confer with the Radiant, and together we will determine the final outcome of your trial. A meal will be taken to your room, Tavesin. Eat, then rest." She smiled in understanding as he managed a weak nod. "A summons will be brought to you once our decision is made."

He leaned against Hasnin's arm as they made the long journey from the tower's sublevel to its ninth floor. He remembered little of the journey later and nothing of what his meal had consisted of, though he recalled it had been the best food he'd ever tasted. He promptly fell asleep on his bunk as soon as Hasnin departed.

When he awakened again, Rostin was perched on the edge of his own bunk on the opposite side of the room. His friend flashed a grin in his direction and leapt to the floor.

"What was it like?" Rostin asked, his dark eyes alight with curiosity.

Tavesin sat up and groaned with a shake of his head. "Exhausting. I've never expended so much energy so quickly." He was reluctant to speak of the ordeal; it had rekindled his fears for Arra's safety and his desire to see her rescued. He glanced toward the room's single window and noted golden daylight shone beyond its panes. "How long was I asleep?"

Rostin shrugged. "Hasnin informed us you were finished not long after midday. It's not yet evening, so a few hours, I suppose." A slow grin spread across his face. "One of the Scorpion Men came to speak with Aziarah today. He's likely still with her, and she asked that you speak with her once you were ready."

Tavesin stretched and forced himself to rise. His brown apprentice garb was rumpled from sleep, but in his excitement, he did not care. "I wondered why Aziarah wasn't outside the chamber when I emerged, but I was too tired to ask where she'd gone."

As they descended the tower, several wizards nodded to him as they passed, knowing smiles on their faces and intrigue in their eyes. Tavesin nodded uncertainly in return; news of his challenge must have spread through the tower, though its outcome remained unknown. He hoped he'd impressed Mari and the Radiant enough to be granted his blue cloak and the rank of wizard. He'd poured every ounce of his magical reserves into the battle with the construct's Garin.

Rostin snickered as they stepped into the tower's vast anteroom and another pair of wizards eyed Tavesin. "You'll be a celebrity if you're raised, Taven. I'm not certain I'll be able to cope with your ego."

Tavesin flushed and looked away at Rostin's teasing. "You won't be far behind."

Rostin chuckled. "Perhaps not, but I believe Badolo will challenge before I do. I need more practice in physical combat before the Grays will allow me to test."

Despite his cheerful façade, Tavesin could see the disappointment in his friend's expression. That Rostin had been the first to enter the tower and was the eldest of the three, yet the last to challenge, weighed heavily upon him. Tavesin wished there were something he could say to lift Rostin's spirits, but he could think of nothing that might suffice.

A light breeze ruffled his hair as he stepped outside and into the late afternoon sunlight. Not far away, he spied the Drakkon. It was clear they'd been awaiting his return with Rostin, and several of their number made their way toward the tower's arched entrance, Trozyen amongst them. Tavesin could not immediately locate Aziarah.

Trozyen greeted them with a smile. "Aziarah's been expecting you for some time. Her visitor has been eager to depart, but she's managed to convince him to stay until he's met with you." He glanced at Rostin. "With *both* of you, that is."

Rostin's expression was skeptical. "Why would he wish to speak with me?"

"I wasn't privy to the details, Rostin, but Aziarah has another scheme afoot—and it involves both of you, wizards or not." Trozyen beckoned to them and began to lead the way toward a dense grove of evergreens.

Tavesin glanced at Rostin curiously and received a shrug in return. They followed Trozyen, pausing to wave at Badolo in greeting as they passed. He was engrossed in the construction of another device but spared a moment to return their gesture with a grin. As they neared the grove, Tavesin spied a narrow footpath that wound between the trunks into its shaded heart. Trozyen stopped at the edge of the trees.

"They're within."

Tavesin grinned at Rostin, unable to mask his excitement. He'd heard tales of the Scorpion Men, but had never before encountered one. Rostin returned his grin with one of his own. The pair darted between the trees, eager to meet Aziarah's visitor.

Tavesin skidded to a halt as they came to a clearing within the trees. Aziarah stood on one side, while her visitor loomed on the other. Tavesin gaped at him; he stood taller than most of the Drakkon and cut an imposing figure in his plate mail. The handle of a large weapon poked above one of his broad shoulders. Tavesin couldn't help but feel unsettled as he studied the man's human torso and head attached to the scorpion's body just below his waist. The man's scorpion half was unarmored, yet sported dark brown chitinous plates that were easily as thick as the plate mail encompassing his upper half.

Beside him, Rostin swore under his breath. "Gods, he's enormous. I'm glad he's on *our* side."

Tavesin nodded a silent agreement, unable to tear his eyes from the man even as Aziarah spoke and began introductions.

"Tavesin, Rostin, this is Vardak."

Vardak lifted his blond eyebrows as the pair continued to stare. He crossed his arms with a long-suffering expression. "Aziarah has spoken highly of you both."

"Tavesin is the young wizard who you've journeyed so far to meet," Aziarah said to Vardak. "Rostin is the one who might benefit from your particular expertise."

Vardak focused his blue-eyed gaze on Rostin first, and Tavesin was relieved his turn under the giant's scrutiny was delayed. "Will the wizards allow him to travel to our camp for training? I cannot spare time away on a regular basis. Already, I've been gone too long."

"I will speak to them on Rostin's behalf," Aziarah replied smoothly. "I'm certain the travel can be arranged."

Rostin squirmed. "What training, Aziarah?"

"Vardak has agreed to train you at arms," she replied. "It is a high honor to be trained by one of Blademon's people."

Rostin gaped, and his gaze darted between Vardak and Aziarah. "I…I'm to train…with *you*, sir?"

"If you wish it," Vardak replied evenly. "If not, I'm certain the Drakkon will continue your education."

"I'll pack my things now, if that's what it takes." Rostin grinned. "If I'm to match Tavesin's progress, I need to become better with my blade."

"We will speak with your mentor after we finish here," Aziarah interjected firmly. "Once she is in agreement, we will arrange your travel to the army's camp."

While Rostin quivered in excitement, Tavesin was rooted by anxiety as Vardak shifted his gaze to assess him. Tavesin wasn't certain why Aziarah believed he could help the tall warrior; he did not need combat training as Rostin did, nor did he want it.

"You are the strongest wizard within your council, according to Aziarah."

Tavesin swallowed hard. During his stay in the tower, he'd come to realize he was more powerful than most fully-trained wizards, but he'd never considered himself to be the strongest. He glanced uneasily at Aziarah. She shrugged in return and indicated silently that he ought to speak.

"I...I don't know, sir. I'm strong enough to have been granted my challenge." He resisted the urge to fidget under the scrutiny.

"I know what it's like to be chosen for something beyond your understanding," Vardak replied in a gentler tone. "I was little older than you when Blademon apprenticed me. What I ask...It will change you, Tavesin." He sighed and raked one hand through his hair. "I hoped I'd never place a child in this position, yet I am here, asking a mere boy to take up a burden that should belong to his elders."

"His elders cannot rival his Ability, Vardak," Aziarah whispered. "Tavesin is the one Flariel sent you to find."

Tavesin's mind reeled; why was the goddess interested in him?

Vardak's expression was troubled as he pulled on a cord that hung around his neck. A small, green-white stone emerged from beneath his armor, gleaming in the last of the sun's rays. Tavesin gasped as he studied the gem. It was a magical relic. Now that he was focused upon it, he could sense its energy, poised to burst forth at the proper call.

"Gods," Rostin breathed. "Badolo would tie himself in knots to see this."

Tavesin nodded and tore his gaze away from the stone. He looked up at Vardak. "What is it?"

"The Moon's Eye." Vardak tucked the relic into its hiding place once more. "The gods are keen to have it delivered to a mage capable of using it to fulfill its true purpose. If I am to believe Aziarah, that mage is you."

"What purpose?" Tavesin asked. "I know nothing of this relic."

Vardak scowled at the ground. "The gods did not deign to tell me. I brought it to Dar Daelad with the hope one of your council would know."

"Perhaps there is something in the library," Aziarah cut in. "Emra indicated she wishes to remain nearby until spring. It will give Tavesin an opportunity to research the history of your relic, Vardak."

He nodded thoughtfully. "Yes. In the meantime, I'll keep it with me. Flariel will have my hide if it falls into the wrong hands."

The sound of approaching footsteps drew their attention. Tavesin turned to find Hasnin emerging from the trees. His aged mentor nodded a greeting to Aziarah and Vardak before settling his gaze on Tavesin.

"The Radiant summons you, Tavesin."

A wave of anxiety gripped his heart, and he glanced at Aziarah, seeking reassurance. She smiled kindly.

"Go, Tavesin. We will speak again later."

He glanced a final time at Vardak before turning away to accompany Hasnin back to the tower, secretly relieved to be away from the imposing warrior. He understood his hesitancy toward Vardak was borne of irrational fear, but it was one he could not shake. Once they were beyond the copse of evergreens, he released a long sigh.

"I'm certain the Radiant bears nothing but good news for you, boy," Hasnin replied, mistaking the expulsion of air as a sign of Tavesin's nerves.

Tavesin didn't correct him. He was ashamed to admit he feared Vardak and the terrible possibilities his people represented for humanity. He fell silent as they crossed the garden and reentered the tower, contemplating his perceived weakness and the implications it held for his future. Aziarah was certain he was meant to wield the relic Vardak carried, though Tavesin harbored many doubts. He rarely compared his own burgeoning power with that of the other wizards and could not confirm her assertion. He was merely fourteen; the notion that he was stronger than the remainder of the wizards in the council was ludicrous.

Hasnin led him to the tower's second floor. They took the circuitous route along the perimeter of the council chamber toward the Radiant's study. The corridor was empty save for Tavesin and his mentor; their footfalls echoed loudly against the tiled floors. When the Radiant's door came into view, Tavesin's heart leapt into his throat. The outcome of his challenge would soon be revealed, and he wasn't certain he was prepared for the news no matter which way the decision had fallen.

Hasnin stopped at the door and peered at Tavesin, his expression a mixture of melancholy and pride. "I'm afraid I cannot announce you this time, Taven. You'll need to knock and guide yourself inside."

"Sir?" His voice sounded small to his own ears, fearful, the bold declarations he'd made to the Garin of the construct forgotten at present.

"If you wish to become a wizard, you must act the part, Taven." Hasnin touched his shoulder in an attempt to reassure him. "You have nothing to fear from this meeting. I'm certain of it."

Tavesin swallowed his anxiety and nodded. "Thank you, sir."

Hasnin smiled. "I don't believe you'll need to refer to me as 'sir' any longer, Taven. I'll await you here."

Bolstered by Hasnin's encouraging words, he rapped his knuckles against the heavy oaken door. It opened moments later to reveal Mari El'Vero, garbed head to heel in her ceremonial Blue Sect Master garb. She smiled warmly and ushered him inside.

The Radiant sat behind his tidy desk, the ceremonial multi-hued cloak that marked his position draped across his shoulders. He rose slowly at Tavesin's approach.

"Welcome, Tavesin."

"Thank you, sir."

"We have reviewed the outcome of your challenge. There is but one conclusion that can be made."

He stooped low to retrieve a parcel hidden beneath his desk. Tavesin gasped as he realized what the Radiant held in his hands, and his heart thudded painfully in his chest. The Radiant held the carefully folded length of blue cloth toward him, and with trembling fingers, Tavesin plucked it from his grasp.

"It has been several centuries since a wizard of your caliber graced our council, Tavesin," he said quietly. "It is my honor to name you a wizard on this momentous day."

"And it is mine to accept you as one of my Sect," Mari added from behind him. "Welcome to the Council of Auras, Tavesin Drondes, wizard of the Blue Sect."

CHAPTER THIRTY-THREE

THE KAL'S PLOT

Aran'daj studied the scout's crude map silently, memorizing its details with his pale eyes. The army was moving across the vast grasslands of northeastern Delucha, leaving a trail of smoldering ruins in its wake. Daesan had been its first victim, followed by several small farming communities. It seemed there were a handful of farmsteads in their path, but no further settlements for some time. It was a relief; the soldiers needed a respite from the bloodshed and time to mend their wounds.

Aran'daj believed they had another week's worth of marching before they came to the outskirts of the kingdom's capital city, provided the weather continued on its presently mild course. It was autumn; he did not believe they could trust Maelstrom to hold his temper much longer. Storms were inevitable as the world cooled toward winter and the storm god began to stir. He prayed the skies would remain clear and the winds fair.

"We will continue for another hour, then make camp."

His words were met with murmurs of appreciation by the nearby lieutenants. If Jal'den had been present, he'd have made a show of issuing the orders, serving to boost the soldiers' morale in the process. Aran'daj lacked the charisma of the Arms Master, but he retained the loyalty of his people nonetheless.

He'd come to rely on Jal'den during their campaign and felt his absence poignantly. He prayed Jal'den would return unscathed from his secretive mission to meet with the Kal, prayed the Arms Master came bearing positive news. A small part of him yearned for a reply from Rej'amin, though he doubted his long-lost partner would be afforded the luxury of penning a response. To Rej'amin's *ujar'havel,* such correspondence was forbidden, no matter the contents of the message Aran'daj had asked Jal'den to deliver on his behalf.

He pushed aside his thoughts to focus on the path ahead. Open plains of knee-high grasses swayed in a light breeze, the stalks limned in silver from the moonlight. The army spread out behind him, rank upon rank of mail-clad Murkor armed and prepared to strike down any opposition. Since their departure from Daesan and the smaller settlements, they had encountered little resistance. It puzzled him. It was as though the people of Delucha were unconcerned by—or unaware of—the Murkor presence in their lands.

They made camp at his signal. A swatch of the tall grass had been trampled flat in the army's wake, and any pursuing forces would have little trouble locating them if they had a mind to do so. Aran'daj tasked the lieutenants with setting a watch and patrols. He doubted they would be attacked during the daylight hours, but he would remain vigilant. The moment he or his soldiers became lax would be the moment of their downfall.

Aran'daj did not immediately rest once camp was set and his tent prepared. He placed several maps in the center of the space; some depicted the region, others nearby cities, and a few were sketches prepared by his forward scouts. He paced, restless as he considered his next move.

The sun was well beyond the horizon when a black-clad soldier ducked into his tent. He saluted and stood expectantly near the exit while he waited for Aran'daj to acknowledge his presence.

"Do you have news?"

"Yes, Commander. Jal'den has returned." The soldier shifted uneasily. "The Soulless did not remain in camp. He transported Jal'den, then left immediately. The Arms Master asks for an audience, sir."

Aran'daj smiled beneath his hood. "I will speak with the Arms Master. Send him in."

"Yes, sir."

Aran'daj watched the soldier disappear outside before he turned to collect the maps that lay strewn across the tent's floor. He was still tidying the space when Jal'den entered.

"Commander."

Aran'daj grinned, though he knew Jal'den could not see his expression. It was a relief to have the Arms Master in camp once more. "Arms Master."

"Kama returned to the tower. He claimed to have pressing business." Jal'den chuckled. "It's just as well he's not here. We can speak freely."

"What news from the Kal?" Aran'daj was eager for word and further instruction. Jal'den's lengthy sojourn to the caverns had left the commander in a state of frustrated anxiety that could only be assuaged by the receipt of news from their homeland.

"He has a plan." Jal'den lowered his voice and glanced over his shoulder toward the exit, as though he feared they would be overheard. "It's a bold idea, one that I believe will be our downfall if it fails. But I can see no other way out of our present situation." Jal'den sighed heavily. "Perhaps you will have further insight, Commander."

"Tell me."

Jal'den began to pace the length of the tent, his strides swift and movements rigid with agitation. "The Kal hopes to carry out his plans when the army returns to the Wasted Land for the winter. Sal'zar is to 'recruit' sympathetic soldiers to his cause. He…" Jal'den's voice broke, and he shook his head.

Aran'daj understood that Jal'den's next words would reveal the source of his anguish. "You fear for him."

"Yes." Jal'den's voice was strained. "Sal'zar is to take the sympathizers with him once we deem their numbers sufficient. He will signal them, but the Kal would not provide further details. He would not allow me to accompany Sal'zar when he leaves. I am *ordered* to remain with the gods-damned army, Commander," he added bitterly.

"I'm sorry, Jal'den." He could provide little else to the Arms Master as consolation for the news and his perceived loss. "I know you'd rather be at his side."

"The Kal believes my perceived loyalty to the Soulless is paramount—as is yours."

Aran'daj nodded. He understood the Kal's plot more thoroughly, perhaps, than did Jal'den. If it appeared the commander and Arms Master were unaware of the scheme, the Soulless would not retaliate against the Murkor people as a whole. Only those involved—those like

Sal'zar—would become targets. Jal'den was right to be concerned for his partner; Sal'zar would be placed at greater risk than most soldiers pressed into the front lines of battle.

"Have you spoken with Sal'zar?" he asked gently.

Jal'den nodded, dejected. "He volunteered to take point in the Kal's scheme. When I demanded to know why, he said it was *his* turn to protect *me*." A strangled growl escaped his throat. "Fucking gods, Commander! I don't want to picture life without Sal'zar in it."

"I understand your pain," Aran'daj replied quietly, his thoughts once more revolving around Rej'amin.

Jal'den fell silent. After a moment he squared his shoulders and faced Aran'daj. "You do, perhaps better than any other I've known, Commander. I have long known my uncle's tale, but my mother never mentioned the name of his forbidden love. When you spoke his name to me outside Daesan, I pieced the story together."

"It is why I chose the path of *drajak'ven*."

"I delivered your message to him." Jal'den seemed to brighten. "He said he could not risk sending you a written reply, but he asked that I tell you something on his behalf."

His hopes soaring for the first time in weeks, Aran'daj straightened in anticipation. "What did he say?"

"He's kept his word to you. He said you would understand his meaning." Jal'den paused for effect, then said, "He called you his *ama na jalan*."

Love through eternity.

Aran'daj smiled beneath his hood. "Perhaps one day, during this war or when age takes me, we will find one another in Aeon's realm. Our mothers were not as understanding to our desires as yours was, Jal'den—but his message is welcome. I thank you."

Jal'den nodded. "Your words have given me strength, Commander. I will see Sal'zar again—one way or another."

"If we play our roles well—all of us—then you will see him at the conclusion of this war."

Aran'daj would ensure Jal'den survived, even if it meant his own life would be forfeit in the process. The Arms Master was young and deserved to experience all that life had to offer. He would do everything in his power to make certain his words to Jal'den would be upheld.

"I'll pray to the gods you are right, Commander. And I'll pray that the Kal hasn't sent our people to their doom with this ploy."

"We must seize this opportunity, Jal'den. It may be our only chance to subvert the Soulless and regain our freedom. I will play my role, and you will play yours. As you stated earlier, there are no other options available to our people." Aran'daj sighed. "The Kal has chosen not to inform us fully of his plans for our own safety. The less we know, the greater the chance we will survive if his schemes fail."

"I understand. I don't have to like it," Jal'den groused.

Opting for a change of topic, Aran'daj asked, "Did Kama indicate when he would return?"

"No. He said only that he would be back prior to our assault on Delucha City. How long does that give us?"

Aran'daj returned to the neat stack of maps he'd left near the rear of the tent and rifled through it. The map he sought was near the bottom of the pile, a carefully lined depiction of Delucha kingdom. Aran'daj was no cartographer, but he believed this map had been drawn by the hand of a master. He withdrew it and knelt to spread it across the center of the floor.

He pointed to an area within the grasslands that he believed was their present location. "We are here, and we must travel here." He traced his finger along his chosen route to the city drawn on the map. A fanciful castle adorned the artist's carefully penned script. "I estimate we have another two weeks, provided the weather holds."

Jal'den stooped to inspect the map. "I'll pray that Maelstrom holds his foul temper. The sooner this battle is over, the sooner we will return to the Wasted Land. I mean to speak with Sal'zar in person before he attempts his folly."

"Do not be so harsh, Jal'den. You said yourself that he does this for you."

Jal'den rose with a feral growl. "This gods-damned war! If not for Shan'tar and his fucking stone, none of this would have happened." He kicked aimlessly at the floor and began to pace once more.

"While I'm in agreement with you, we cannot change the past." Aran'daj stood slowly, his knees protesting the action. "We must make use of the time we have. I'll make certain you return after the next battle, and I'll do my damnedest to see you reunited with Sal'zar. You have my word, Jal'den."

Jal'den paused to stare at him, and Aran'daj wished he could see the expression on the other's face. When he spoke, Jal'den's voice was firm. "I appreciate your kindness, Commander, but you'd best not do anything rash in order to keep your promise. I won't be able to carry out the Kal's orders without your guidance."

Aran'daj smiled sadly. "I will do as I've always done, Arms Master. I will do what is necessary."

CHAPTER THIRTY-FOUR

WRAITHS IN THE DARK

Dressed and eager to begin the day's work, Ravin propped the door to his quarters ajar as he awaited Adalin. Eight of the twelve obstacles had been cleared from the route to the talisman, and he was confident the final four would be unraveled by day's end.

He went to the room's window and peered through the foggy glass at the bustling courtyard below, watching the various merchants and craftsmen scurry about in the early morning light. None were aware of the relic buried deep beneath their feet, nor of its significance in the defense of their city and kingdom. He envied them their ignorance; they were free from the concerns that plagued his waking hours and haunted his dreams.

A light tap on the door drew him from his reverie. He turned to find the duchess, garbed not in her riding attire, but in a formal gown. He raised his eyebrows in silent question as she placed a basket carefully atop his wardrobe.

"Her Majesty has ordered me to accompany her today." Adalin's tone was bitter. "I felt I owed it to you to come in person, Ravin. I suspect she means to interrogate me about our time together."

Ravin shrugged indifferently. "What will you tell her?"

"I was hoping you would provide me some insight." She dropped her gaze, her expression strained. "I believe I mentioned this before, Ravin, but I'll say it again. I consider you a friend, and I loathe the idea of spying on you for the sake of a spoiled teenager's whims."

Ravin smiled to himself; he'd come to respect Adalin in spite of his initial misgivings. Her words stirred a wave of admiration within him, a sentiment he'd rarely experienced since his reawakening in Stonewall Hall.

"Tell her what you will of the talisman," he replied. "She is aware of my goal, and I'll not have anyone stand in my way—least of all her."

"She seeks details of your past, Ravin," Adalin reminded him. "You've shared precious little during the many hours we've spent together. I fear she'll make good on her threats if I cannot provide her with something of value."

Ravin raked his hand through his hair with a sigh. "That girl will be the death of me," he growled, "but for your sake, you may tell her of Tarren Haven. I've already agreed to that."

He began to pace as he considered what more he was willing to share. Much of his past was clouded by his final months amongst the Enlightened, a period of time he wished to keep hidden. If anyone learned the truth of his past, he would lose his credibility, the trust he'd built, and would very likely be marked for execution by the queen. His power would allow him to elude her, but he didn't relish the notion of a life spent in exile and obscurity. His purpose was to correct his mistakes, to destroy the Soulless, and eliminate the threat they posed to his person. It was a selfish goal, wrapped in the noble guise of protecting Delucha from the army that was marching toward it.

An idea struck him then, one that might solidify Adalin's precarious position as well as deter the queen from prying further into his past.

"Tell her I've had several run-ins with the Soulless—in addition to the night I spared her from their grasp." His grin was feral and failed to reach his eyes. "Insinuate that I've told you *her* secrets, Adalin. Yes, the dear queen was involved in far darker dealings than she'd like the world to believe."

Adalin's eyes grew wide and her face paled at his words. "The Soulless? Ravin—"

"How do you think she and Jasom came together? He wasn't a visitor to the palace, and prior to his arrival, she wouldn't have given the poor boy a passing glance. He's a farmer, Adalin. *Beneath her station,* as so many of your cohorts in court are fond of whispering." Ravin crossed his arms. "Jasom was not at fault for his actions, but they were not brought together by the usual forces. They were *forced* together by the Soulless."

She swallowed and seemed to steel herself. "If I mention any of this…Gods, Ravin, she will either throw me in the dungeons or she will attempt to buy my silence. I'll pray for the latter."

"Perhaps if you insinuate that I've grown fond of you, she'll abandon any notion of punishment." He smiled knowingly. "She knows less than a fraction of my power. If she harms you, I will ensure she comes to regret it."

"I made the right decision when I confessed to you. I'm fortunate I've made you an ally rather than an enemy."

He nodded once. "Thank you for bringing my lunch, Adalin. I'll return to the library once I'm finished in the catacombs today."

"I will seek you there, if my time with the queen ends favorably." She looked away and drew a breath. "If it does not, I will find a means to inform you of my fate."

Ravin returned to the location of the second historical riddle and studied the placard for the first time. The reference was vague, and only someone with vast knowledge of Deluchan history could have managed to solve it. It was a testament to Adalin's intellect that she'd done so—and under the influence of mead, no less. He shook his head, amused and frightened by the memory; there would be no more drinking while traipsing through the catacombs.

He moved quickly through the darkness and came upon a vast ward not long after he'd begun the day's journey. Unlike the seals he'd dismantled previously, the ward could not be unraveled. Only a mage with a great deal of power could hope to penetrate this manner of defense. He smiled grimly; he was one such mage.

He channeled a great blast of energy toward the ward. As the two magical forces collided, a sound like the shattering of glass resounded through the corridor. Ravin sensed the dissolution of the ward before its physical manifestation faded from his sight.

He continued his journey, the silence that enveloped him broken only by his footfalls. The quiet set his nerves on edge. He realized belatedly he missed Adalin's company, if not her questionable taste in beverages.

After an interminable amount of time, the corridor opened into a spherical chamber large enough to envelop the palace far above. The path ended abruptly three paces from the chamber's edge. The walls were smooth and slick, carved from a pinkish-gray stone.

Ravin strengthened the illumination of his magical light until it reached the far side of the chamber, where the path resumed. He scanned the space for a stairwell, a series of handholds—anything that might see him securely to the opposite side. There was nothing save the smooth stone.

He frowned, stymied in his progress, and looked down while he considered his options. A rough patch on the floor near the path's end drew his eye. He edged forward, unnerved by the sheer drop before him, and carefully knelt down to examine the anomaly. Ornate script was etched into the floor.

Only those blessed of Solsticia will find the way. The goddess watches over all realms of magic.

Ravin's frown deepened into a scowl. He understood the meaning well enough; Solsticia was the goddess of all things celestial—magic included. Those blessed by Solsticia were the mages of the world. The reference to the realms unsettled him, however. She had told him long ago the Aethereum was created *for him*. Either she'd lied to him, or she'd enlisted the services of her sister to breach the bounds of time in order to create this obstacle.

He sighed and shook his head. He didn't believe Solsticia had lied to him; she'd created the Aethereum as a refuge for him when the Nameless' cronies had begun to overtake the Enlightened. A lie would have served no purpose—and why would a goddess deign to spin falsehoods to her only son? The implications unnerved and frustrated him, but his questions were best left for another day. He could not call upon Solsticia outside of a shrine, in any case.

He rose carefully and created a portal into the Aethereum. As he stepped through, he was met with the sight of a graceful stone bridge arcing over the chasm. A pair of handrails spanned its length, decorated with intricate scrollwork.

He snorted, unable to mask his irritation. The gods had played a role in the creation of the talisman's resting place, Solsticia foremost amongst them. He was certain his part in obtaining the talisman had been planned from the beginning, and he detested the notion his path had been preordained by his mother. He'd wrangled his freedom from the clutches of the Nameless god, only to find himself mired in another deity's schemes. When next he found time to visit a shrine, he planned to have words with her.

He crossed the span quickly and exited the Aethereum once he reached the opposite side. He glowered over his shoulder at the void in the midst of the path a final time, then with a shake of his head, pressed on. His mother had never been free with her answers, but this was a matter he would not permit her to evade.

After another span of time spent striding through the dark, his anger began to fade into mere displeasure. The gods did as they pleased with little regard for the mortals entrenched in their schemes. His mother was no exception.

He'd promised Adalin on more than one occasion that he would share his tale with her one day. He began to wonder if her attitude toward him would change more from the revelation that he'd once been a member of the Council of Enlightened, or from the confession he was Solsticia's son. He valued her friendship and prayed it would not disintegrate when he finally gathered the courage to divulge his past. Ravin had never made many friends in his life, though he'd made plenty of enemies. He didn't want to lose the strange bond he'd formed with the duchess.

A faint glimmer of light caught his eye as he rounded another wide bend in the path. It moved and danced in the manner of torchlight, but the coloration was altogether wrong; the flickering illumination ahead had a decidedly bluish cast. He approached slowly, certain he was nearing the location of the talisman's final gatekeeper.

The path broadened to reveal a square chamber. Dozens of small sconces lined the walls, each flickering with ethereal blue flames. He sensed the powerful magic that infused the space and knew instinctively the chamber had been designed as a trap. He edged his way toward the room's center, uncertain what awaited him.

A sudden rush of energy enveloped him, and before he had time to react, Ravin found himself blocked from the source of his magic. In the same instant, the flames guttered and died, leaving him powerless and blind in the sudden darkness. He'd arrogantly entered the catacombs without a weapon, and his only means of defense was the wicker basket he carried that contained his noon-time meal.

He stood frozen in place as whispers began to issue from the gloom. Each voice was distinct, yet all harbored an otherworldly timbre he'd only heard once in his lifetime. The strange resonance was akin to the god Aeon's voice. Ravin shuddered at the memory; he'd incurred the god's displeasure during the conversation and had defied his orders, besides. He prayed whatever he'd stepped into at present was mere coincidence, and he would not find himself facing the Underworld's guardian deity.

"He's a mage," a low voice stated from his left.

"And Santinian, by the looks of him," a second added, this one from his right.

"Alone." The third voice was softer, feminine in nature, and seemed to be directly in front of him.

"Why have you come, stranger?" The voice possessed a dangerous edge, as though the speaker was both suspicious and irascible.

If the voices belonged to the final gatekeepers, Ravin's only option was to be forthright and truthful as he'd been with their predecessors. He drew a breath, keenly aware of his vulnerability, and braced himself for their reaction.

"I've come for the talisman."

"She said you'd come one day," the low voice replied.

"Of course, you have," the female voice stated dryly. "There would be no other purpose to your presence in the dark depths beneath Delucha. Only great need would drive someone into our realm."

"Or greed," the suspicious one added. "A Peace Talisman would fetch a hefty sum."

"Let him speak," the second voice hissed, irritation in its tone.

"I'm seeking the talisman to combat the Soulless."

When he was met with silence, Ravin realized the owners of the voices might not understand the significance. The first of the Soulless did not emerge until centuries after the talismans were purportedly created.

"The Soulless are servants of the Nameless god," he continued. "They seek to destroy Delucha, and I intend to stop them."

"Alone?" the feminine voice asked incredulously.

"No." Ravin peered into the darkness but could see nothing of his interrogators. "There is another who was helping me through the catacombs previously, but she was…otherwise engaged today."

"I harbored doubts a Santinian-born mage would have understood the history enmeshed in these walls," the second voice replied, while the low voice chuckled.

Ravin bristled. "My nationality means nothing in the face of the destruction the Nameless seeks to sow. I'll admit, I came to Delucha without purpose, but I've since found one. There are few capable of the power I wield—and I will stand against the Nameless and his Soulless puppets, with or without your help."

"Prickly," the cantankerous voice stated.

"He does not lie," the low voice added. "His power is vast."

"The Eshmere Stone, as the talisman is properly called, was not meant as a tool of war," the second chided. "Its power will overwhelm and consume even the strongest of mages if not handled appropriately."

"I'm no novice." Ravin was unable to mask his irritation. He was well aware of the risks inherent in the use of magical relics and did not require a lecture from the unseen questioners.

"He speaks the truth again." The low voice's tone had become interested.

"So he does," the second conceded grudgingly. "I am loathe to allow passage to a Santinian."

Ravin clenched his jaw in frustration. Why were these entities concerned about his lineage? His desire to defeat the Soulless—and Dranamir—ought to be sufficient.

"The wars are long ended," the female replied. "Delucha and Santine made peace long before we came to this place. It was our purpose to protect the stone, and we have served the celestial goddess well. I am in favor of allowing his journey to continue."

"As am I," the low voice agreed.

A hiss of frustration escaped the second voice. "My trust is not so easily gained."

The surly voice spoke from its location behind Ravin. "Our vigil has spanned centuries. Time has forgotten us. I will allow his progress if it means I can achieve my eternal rest. I will welcome Aeon's embrace."

The second growled in response.

"Surely you don't wish to continue wandering the shadows?" the female demanded bitterly.

"He is Santinian."

"I'm not well versed in ancient history," Ravin interjected, "but I don't believe our kingdoms have been at war in more than a thousand years. My ancestry should play no part in this decision. I've no control over who my father was."

"Agreed," the low voice replied. "We were tasked to judge *intent* and *power*, not lineage."

The second voice sighed wearily. "Very well. But know this, mage: You cannot acquire the talisman alone. The final barrier will thwart your efforts."

"Then I'll be certain my associate returns to assist me," Ravin promised. "She is a historian and—"

"Her intelligence will not serve her there," the low voice interrupted. "If she is unlike you, then perhaps she will prove useful."

Ravin scowled in confusion. "What do you—?"

Another whirl of energy overtook him, this one more powerful than the first. He gasped and fell to his knees as he was buffeted by the invisible onslaught. A moment later, the block on his power dissolved, but the blue flames did not reappear. He grasped his power hungrily, as though he'd been denied its presence for days rather than minutes, and conjured a magical light.

The chamber was empty and still, the previous sensation of magic that imbued its walls gone. He rose unsteadily to his feet and grimaced as the world tilted precariously before his eyes. The onrush of energy had taken its toll on his body; he needed rest.

He summoned a portal into the Aethereum and stumbled through. He would return to his chambers, sleep off the sudden bout of fatigue, then seek Adalin as he'd promised. Though the voices had departed before his final question was answered, he intuited that he would require her help to cross the final barrier.

245

CHAPTER THIRTY-FIVE

FLARIEL'S DEMAND

Vardak paused at the base of the ramp that ran alongside the twelve steps leading to the entrance of Ukase's temple in Dar Daelad. From his vantage point, the enormous columns supporting the peaked roof shone starkly white in contrast to the inky shadow the roof cast over the broad double doors. When last he'd set foot within the temple, Janna had accompanied him. He recalled her bubbly enthusiasm as they embarked on their journey to seek the Moon's Eye; even at the end, when she'd made her final, fateful decision, she'd remained optimistic. Her life had been cut far too short.

"It's never easy facing memories of those we've lost." Emra's words were gentle, understanding.

He nodded once and glanced over his shoulder at Patak, who stood behind them. His older brother had become a fixture about Emra's person since she'd named him the captain of her guard, and though he had no business in the temple himself, he'd refused to be left behind. Patak was contemplative and uncharacteristically silent, his gaze fixed on Emra. He appeared unaware of Vardak's glance.

"She should not have felt obligated to sacrifice herself," Vardak replied as a new set of memories flooded his consciousness. Flariel's rage at Janna's memorial, her refusal to listen to reason, her insistence that Vardak was to blame… He had enough to consider with Emra's army. Flariel merely complicated his life further, a fact the goddess seemed to relish.

He shook his head in irritation. "It's past time I spoke with Flariel."

"You can postpone the inevitable only so long," Emra agreed. "I feel much the same when it comes to my meeting with Aeon."

They ascended the ramp to be greeted by the same priestess Vardak had met on his first visit to the temple. A flicker of recognition passed through her eyes, but she made no comment on his present company or Janna's absence. While Emra made introductions, the priestess' expression shifted from mild curiosity to stunned reverence.

"I must speak with Aeon," Emra concluded, her expression unreadable, "and Vardak requests an audience with Flariel."

"Of course," the priestess breathed. She took a moment to smooth her white skirts and collect her wits; it was clear Emra's visit had come as a shock. "Please, follow me."

Vardak walked behind Emra and the priestess as they entered the temple, Patak at his side. Patak gazed at the stone columns that adorned the anteroom in mild wonder. After a moment, he shook his head, an amused smirk on his face.

"Ukase's temple is grand, but I prefer Blademon's," he whispered to Vardak.

"I felt the same when I first came here." Vardak shrugged. "And again when we arrived in Solsticia's temple."

Patak grinned. "I enjoy these rare times when I find myself understanding you, little brother."

Vardak lifted his eyebrows, nonplussed. "We're more alike than you'll admit, Patak."

They followed the priestess into an adjoining corridor, where she promptly stopped in front of a lacquered door. "Do you require assistance, Emra?"

Emra shook her head. "This is not my first conversation with one of the gods. I know well how to summon him."

Patak shifted uneasily and glanced at Vardak. "I'd like to…" He gestured at Emra.

Vardak nodded in understanding. "I'll meet you here once I'm finished." He didn't add that he was likely to emerge from his encounter with Flariel scorched, the cinders of her wrath smoldering between the plates of his armor.

He faced the priestess who led him to the matching door across the hall. "Do you require assistance, Vardak?"

He hesitated briefly, then nodded. "In the past, the Fire Maiden sought *me* out."

"I will summon her, then depart for your privacy." The priestess opened the door and gestured that he should precede her. "Few contact Flariel, though I suspect this has much to do with your previous visit here."

"Yes."

He entered the room to note it was identical to the one he'd found himself in upon his first encounter with the Fire Maiden and her daughter. It was windowless and largely unfurnished, save for the large oval table that took up much of its interior. The tabletop was inlaid with a polished smoky-hued mirror. He stood aside as the priestess placed her hands upon the mirror and whispered fervently.

The mirror's surface flickered with shards of light, trapped within its depths like miniscule bolts of lightning. It was several moments before the glass shimmered brilliantly and Flariel appeared, swathed in flame. Her molten countenance turned purposefully in Vardak's direction. Her expression was steely as her luminous eyes met his.

She lifted one arm and pointed at the door. "Leave us, priestess."

At hearing the acid in her words, Vardak had no doubt he was about to receive a scathing reprimand. He faced her stoically and said nothing while the priestess vacated the premises.

"Did I not make myself clear when last we spoke?" she demanded, the flames around her swirling dangerously close to the room's ceiling. "You were to seek the mage with power enough to wield that stone, and I find you in Dar Daelad." She sneered and leaned forward, towering over him.

"I've found a wizard with the capacity to use it." He met her gaze unflinchingly; he would not be cowed by Flariel, goddess or no.

"A child." She tossed her head, the fiery locks casting embers through the room in their wake. "He is powerful, but he cannot compare to the mage in Delucha."

He opened his mouth to argue, but the glare she leveled at him caused him to reconsider.

"I will not be defied again, Vardak. My pain remains raw." She paused to study him as a sand viper might study the mouse it was planning to strike. "You will travel to Delucha without delay. The child may accompany you if he wishes, I suppose. You will seek the mage and acquire his assistance."

"I have an obligation—"

"To the wielder of Fireblade. Yes, I'm very much aware of that, Vardak. You can resume your duties once you've finished this errand for *me*."

He ground his teeth in anger but swallowed the words he would have liked to say. He could not hope to win an argument with Flariel.

"I need more information about this mage."

"He won't be difficult to find. He acts as advisor to the queen." Flariel tossed her head again, and a shower of sparks fell upon the table's mirrored surface. "Find him. Explain the relic you bear and impress upon him the importance it holds." She reached into the flames that ensconced her body and withdrew a sealed metal cylinder. "Give him this, as well. If he questions you about its origin, tell him it comes from his mother. He will understand."

She tossed the cylinder toward him and he caught it deftly. "What is this?"

"A message. As I said, *he* will understand. *You* do not need to." She frowned at him before disappearing in a shower of errant sparks.

He shielded his face with his free hand and groaned at the empty room. He doubted Emra would be pleased with the goddess' meddling and his forced departure from the army. He would speak with Tavesin once they returned to camp, though he remained uncertain if the boy would agree to travel with him. Tavesin had slowly begun to overcome his initial fear of the Scorpion Men, but he remained skittish. Rostin would be sorely disappointed; Vardak could not take him from Dar Daelad until he was named wizard. The Council of Auras would never allow it.

He frowned at the silver cylinder and made his way into the corridor. Emra and Patak awaited him; his brother gazed at Emra longingly while she smiled up at him. It seemed neither were concerned with the potential for Patak's exile, and Vardak was weary of reminding Patak of the risk.

He cleared his throat as he approached the pair. Emra straightened, while Patak sighed in disappointment.

Emra tilted her chin toward the cylinder in his hand. "What did Flariel have to say?"

Vardak grimaced and looked down, unable to meet her gaze. "She ordered me to Delucha."

"Yes, Aeon ordered me there, as well."

His head snapped up at her words. "Aeon, too? What's happening in Delucha?"

Emra chuckled dryly as they began to make their way toward the exit. "That's the question, isn't it? If even the gods fear this war, there are forces at work far greater than our own."

Vardak nodded in silent assent. The notion that the gods feared the outcome of the war was unsettling. He glanced over his shoulder as they exited the temple as a sudden desire to speak with Blademon gripped him. The war god understood his people's needs—and his own—far better than Flariel or Aeon did.

"The journey should take us no more than ten days, even with the army," Emra stated. "Dar Daelad and Delucha City aren't terribly far apart. I've made the journey with more soldiers in less time."

"Well," Patak said with a grin, "it seems we're going to Delucha. More adventure awaits."

"I suppose it's good one of us is pleased at the prospect," Vardak groused. "I'd hoped for a respite from the near-constant travel and time to better train some of the newer recruits."

"They'll learn how to handle themselves, Vardak," Emra replied. "If they don't…" She shrugged, as though the outcome couldn't be helped.

His gut twisted at the insinuation. Many of the humans that had joined them were young and zealous, but untested in battle. Emra had named him their leader; he was ultimately responsible for their fate. He shook his head but made no reply.

"That's a bit callous, Em," Patak stated.

"It's the truth. Time is not on our side, Patak—unless you've spoken to Minora without my knowledge?"

Patak chuckled uneasily. "No. I'll leave the business with the gods to you and Vardak. I'd only manage to piss them off with a failed attempt at humor."

"Then you need to understand the reality of our situation, bleak as it may seem." Emra softened her tone and offered him a sad smile. "At times, I forget you're unused to war, despite your culture and your brother's training. Most of my memories are plagued by it. I suppose my words came across as rather heartless."

"I'll do all I can for our soldiers, Emra," Vardak promised, cutting into the conversation before the pair managed to forget his presence entirely.

"I know, Vardak. That's a large part of the reason why I chose you for your role."

CHAPTER THIRTY-SIX

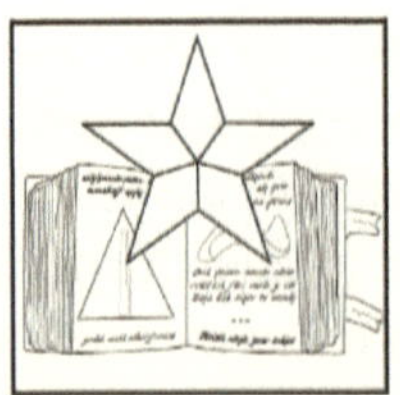

WHISPERS OF WAR

It felt as though weeks had passed since he'd last seen Arra. Tavesin entered the Aethereum as often as he was able, though given the upheaval of his life in recent weeks, his visits had been infrequent and often brief. He ached to see her, if only to tell her he was working on a plan to free her. He prayed her absence was due to lack of opportunity and that she still lived.

It was early afternoon when he finished his latest sparring session with Trozyen on the outskirts of the sprawling army camp. The usual crowd of onlookers began to disperse, and Tavesin made it clear he was departing for his tent, though he did not indicate what he planned to do once there. Most of the observers were soldiers unfamiliar with the workings of magic. Tavesin's impressive displays of energy had drawn their attention from the outset. At first, he'd been decidedly uncomfortable with the notoriety; many of the soldiers were rough and vulgar, and he was a mere child amongst them. After they began to understand the power he wielded, he gained the respect of some and the fear of many others. The latter often gave him a wide berth.

He threaded his way through the camp toward the small cluster of tents that belonged to the wizards pledged to the Fireblade's cause. Tavesin was the sole Blue amongst their number, but there were a dozen Grays and nearly as many Greens. A pair of Yellows had accompanied Badolo, who refused to remain in the tower when Tavesin, Rostin, and the Drakkon were with the army. Tavesin was uncertain if they intended to stay when the army began to move, or if they planned to return to the tower.

He spied Rostin near the tents with the dark-haired Balotican named Lucas. When Vardak was unavailable, Lucas often took charge of Rostin's combat lessons. Tavesin waved at his friend as he passed and received a brief nod in return before Rostin focused on Lucas' next instruction. It was just as well; he meant to search for Arra while he had a few hours' time to himself. He would speak with Rostin later.

Tavesin ducked into his tent and removed his cloak. The Aethereum was a realm without weather; he would have no need of the extra garment. He steeled himself and created a portal at the center of his tent. He stared at the faintly luminous blue oval that appeared at his command, unable to force himself to step through it for several seconds. He feared the consequences of entering the magical realm without the support of the Drakkon, but they were otherwise engaged. If he was to utilize this opportunity to search for Arra, he must go alone.

He drew a breath and stepped through. Energy crackled against his skin as he breached the barrier between realms, but the sensation faded as soon as he was through the portal. He waved it away and peered around the unsettled, flickering construct that comprised his tent in the Aethereum. He understood the instability was due to the temporary nature of the dwelling; permanent structures appeared no different between the physical realm and the magical.

He closed his eyes and envisioned the riverbank near Rican Mer. If Arra was in the Aethereum, she would be there. A brief rush of air caressed him as he traveled to the location. When he opened his eyes, he stood a few paces from the riverbank. The water was frozen in place, a crystalline statue with a coppery hue that filled the rocky riverbed. He turned from the sight and peered into the quiet village. There was no movement, no indication that anyone was present.

Unable to conceal his bitter disappointment, he looked at the ground beneath his boots and sighed heavily. Arra was nowhere to be seen. He cast his senses through the area but detected no one. His despair became palpable, an acrid taste at the back of his tongue.

He made his way to the nearest home and sat down with his back against the outer wall. He would remain in the Aethereum for several hours, or until Arra appeared. He doubted she would come, but he refused to abandon the final, tenuous strands of hope he clung to.

He maintained his vigil for over an hour before the sensation that someone was near tickled at the base of his skull. He rose to his feet silently and produced a defensive shield; he prayed the newcomer was Arra but feared it was one of the Soulless. He traced the source of the sensation to a copse of trees some distance along the riverbank and west of his present location. He willed himself forward, each step tainted with dread.

A faint rustle in the otherwise still grasses told him his magical insight had not led him astray. He froze as he reached the trees, terrified of what he might find concealed beyond their broad trunks.

"Hello?" His voice lacked the conviction it had when he'd faced the construct-Garin within his challenge. To his mind, he sounded like the frightened child he was striving to leave behind.

"Taven?"

His heart leapt at the sound of Arra's voice, cracked and sullen as it was. His previous fear gone, he raced through the trees to find her kneeling in a thick clump of dried grass at the river's edge. He knelt beside her, reveling in the knowledge that she was still alive.

Her face was bruised, one eye swollen nearly closed. A deep laceration followed the edge of her scalp, and another cut split her upper lip. Her reddish hair hung limply around her battered features. Carefully, he drew her into a gentle embrace, wary of hidden injuries she may have sustained.

"Arra, I'm here."

"Thank the gods," she whispered. "I prayed I would find you today. One of them must have taken pity on me."

"Arra, I'm…"

He stopped abruptly, the realization that she was a prisoner of his sworn enemy stilling his words. How much could he risk revealing to her about his plans, his rank, the army?

"I'm glad to see you," he said finally, opting for caution. If the Soulless learned of the army or his plan to free her, the world would suffer for it.

If she noticed his brief hesitation, she ignored it. "I came because he let slip something of great importance, Taven. You must know. Tell the wizards, the Drakkon…Tell anyone willing to listen."

"What did he say?" Tavesin was certain she referred to the pale man who had plagued him time and again, the man the trial chamber had forced him to confront: Garin.

"Their army moves upon Delucha. The Soulless seek to overthrow the queen and claim the crown for their own."

He nodded, the urgency of the situation clear. "I will tell the Drakkon. Arra…I…"

"You must go, I know."

"I wish I had the ability to mend your hurts," he replied quietly.

She managed a strained smile. "I do, too, but we both know your path lies elsewhere. Go, Taven."

By the time he returned to camp, Aziarah was already awaiting him. She paced just outside the entrance impatiently and spun to confront him as soon as he stepped outside. She eyed him knowingly.

"I won't ask where you've been, since I believe I know. We must talk, Tavesin, but not here."

She turned swiftly and began to lead the way through the camp. He increased his pace to a trot in order to keep up with her longer strides.

"Aziarah, she was there," he panted after a moment.

"I see."

"Where are we going? I have news I must tell you. *Important* news. Emra ought to know, too."

Aziarah peered down at him. "It happens we are going to her command tent. The Radiant is here, among others. They also have news but would not share it until all members of their council were present."

Tavesin resisted the urge to squirm in discomfort. "How long were you waiting?"

"Long enough." She sighed. "Perhaps your news will assuage their tempers, but the Radiant was quite disappointed that you weren't here."

"If I'd known they were coming, I wouldn't have gone." He kicked at a loose stone in frustration. "I'm glad I went. At least I know Arra's alive."

"For a man who is charged with the welfare of his council, your Radiant has shown a distinct lack of concern for her," Aziarah growled. "That is a matter for another day, however. Their news—and yours—must be shared."

They paused outside the command tent as two human soldiers scanned their persons for obvious weapons. Aziarah was made to relinquish the mace and dagger at her belt. Tavesin had learned it was common practice for Emra's personal guard to make such requests on his first day in the camp. He was grateful the pair on duty this afternoon were human and not one of the intimidating Scorpion Men. Despite Rostin's assurances, Tavesin could not overcome his initial, irrational fear.

Satisfied, the guards waved them inside. Tavesin found himself in the company of a half dozen wizards, the Radiant, and the Green Sect Master. Emra stood at the center of the gathering, Fireblade sheathed at her side. Behind her loomed Vardak and his friendlier brother. Lucas and the strange feline sentry stood opposite the wizards with the two winged Airess. At their entrance, Emra nodded in silent greeting.

"Now that we're all gathered, I would like to say my piece," the Radiant stated. His dark eyes were ringed by shadow, his brow creased with worry.

"Very well," Emra replied.

"We received word from one of our own in Delucha," he continued. "Daesan has been overrun and lies in ruin. The Soulless' army cuts a wide swath through the land and burns everything in its wake."

Emra peered over her shoulder at Vardak, and a silent communication seemed to pass between them. "We are aware there is trouble in Delucha," she said after a moment. "We were preparing to give the order to move this very afternoon. I will not allow the Soulless to claim Delucha."

Tavesin chewed at his lower lip and glanced up at Aziarah. Her gaze was fixed on Emra, but when Tavesin gripped her scaly hand, she looked at him sharply. "Arra mentioned Delucha, as well," he whispered as the Radiant began to discuss the logistics of moving wizards along with soldiers.

Aziarah nodded in understanding but did not interrupt the exchange immediately. She allowed the Radiant to finish before she stepped forward.

"I believe young Tavesin's delay holds some further importance to the current proceedings." She glanced at him pointedly; it was clear she meant for him to speak.

He swallowed, nervous in the face of so many important adults. "I…I went into the Aethereum. I was seeking Arra, and I found her."

"The girl who was kidnapped?" Emra asked, her gray-eyed gaze shifting to pierce his.

He nodded. "She's hurt. I'm not a healer…" He shook his head and drew a breath. "That isn't important. She told me they were planning to attack Delucha, that they plan to take the crown for their own."

Emra whirled to face the Radiant. "Did your contact mention the direction the army travels?"

"South…and west."

"They make for the capital city," she stated. "We must leave with the dawn if we hope to reach it in time. Will your people be ready, Radiant?"

"Only those who are already in your camp. I will urge the rest to make haste."

"And your apprentices who study with the Drakkon? Will they remain here, or return to the tower?"

Tavesin tensed at her words. He could not imagine embarking on such a journey without Rostin at his side.

"They have not completed their challenges," the Radiant stated uneasily. "It would be dangerous—"

"I believe they ought to make the decision for themselves," Aziarah interrupted him, her tone unyielding. "They are both more capable than most of your fully-trained wizards could ever hope to be, and young master Ver'an could use further instruction with his blade."

Her words were met with an approving nod from Vardak.

"It is without precedent, Aziarah," the Radiant argued.

She frowned, unimpressed. "Then create one. If they wish to remain with the army, their skills will prove quite valuable."

"I will speak with them," the Radiant replied, defeated. "I would like to speak with all of my council before I depart."

Tavesin's heart leapt at the exchange. He had no doubt Rostin would join the army, but Badolo was an unknown. His skill with creating magical devices could be utilized anywhere, and there was the matter of his lineage to consider. Tavesin wasn't certain the young prince would risk himself on the battlefield.

"I'll collect them," Lucas offered quietly before he ducked out of the tent.

Vardak crossed his arms and peered at the Radiant, his expression unreadable. "I spoke with Flariel this morning. She indicated a 'mage' resides in Delucha, one who acts as advisor to the queen. What do you know of him?"

The Radiant shook his head in bewilderment. "I'm afraid I know nothing of this." He looked to the Green Sect Master for guidance, but the younger man merely shrugged.

Vardak scowled at the tent's canvas floor. "It's as I suspected. Flariel has sent me on another gods-damned errand with few clues to follow."

Tavesin didn't know Emra's general well enough to offer his sympathies, but he understood from Vardak's expression that he was frustrated with his predicament and the goddess' role in it.

"It will not be difficult to seek an audience with the queen's advisor," Emra assured him. "We know enough to locate him."

At that moment, Lucas returned with Rostin and Badolo in tow. Rostin peered around the tent with interest, while Badolo gaped, wide-eyed.

Emra motioned to her people. "We all have much to do if the army is to move out with the dawn." She glanced at the Radiant. "We will leave you to discuss what you must with your council—and the apprentices."

Beside him, Aziarah gripped his shoulder firmly but gently. "I must bring word to my people, Tavesin. We can speak once you are finished here."

As the others filed out of the tent, Vardak paused to speak to Rostin in a low tone. Tavesin was unable to hear the exchange, but Rostin glanced warily at the wizards and nodded emphatically at

Vardak. A faint smile graced the warrior's lips as he followed the others outside.

"Do you truly plan to defy the collective wishes of the council, sir?" the Green Sect Master asked quietly once the wizards found themselves alone.

"Aziarah made valid points, and though I'm loathe to break protocol, I believe it is in the best interest—"

"This is madness," one of the Grays interrupted. "Sir, when the tower learns of your decision, they'll have your head."

The Radiant lifted his hands, fingers splayed in a gesture meant to seek a break in the conversation. When no one spoke again, he said, "I understand, and I stand by my previous words." He turned his gaze to meet the trio of boys huddled near the exit. "Rostin, Badolo, you are untested, unchallenged, and yet I ask you to make this decision for yourselves, as if you were named wizard."

One of the Greens groaned in displeasure, but the Radiant ignored the outburst. "The council is aware of the power you both possess, and I ask that you consider traveling with the army when it leaves tomorrow. If you choose to remain in the tower, you are welcome to do so—but the choice is yours."

Rostin grinned. "I'm leaving with the army."

Badolo looked away and appeared introspective. Tavesin knew the decision would be more difficult for the younger boy, but he secretly hoped Badolo would choose to travel.

"I don't believe my father would agree to my departure from the tower," Badolo said quietly, "but we must all do our part to stop the Soulless. Besides, my father isn't here." He glanced at Tavesin and Rostin in turn. "The three of us have studied and trained together. It wouldn't be right to abandon you now."

Tavesin grinned, a mirror of Rostin's expression. He'd hoped both would accompany him to Delucha, and they had not disappointed him.

"You will report to Radosan," the Radiant instructed, drawing the trio's attention. He gestured to the Green Sect Master on his right. "Master Cerandess is the only Sect Master assigned to accompany the army, but the skills of a Green will be needed. Tavesin," he said, "it will be your duty to ferry messages between the army and the tower, should the need arise. Your Aethereal magic will be put to good use."

"Yes, sir," Tavesin replied, startled that he'd been singled out.

"Rostin, you will continue your studies with the warriors in the camp and the Grays that travel with you. Badolo, the same holds true for you, but you will study with Aziarah's people." The Radiant's smile faltered at the mention of her name. "When it is deemed you are both ready to challenge, perhaps Tavesin or one of the Drakkon can find the time to escort you to the tower."

Rostin nodded, and Badolo mumbled, "Yes, sir."

The Radiant turned to face the other wizards. "As for the rest, you know your roles. I must return to the tower and face the consequences of my actions today."

Tavesin was awake long before dawn began to paint the eastern horizon. He packed his satchel with the handful of personal belongings he possessed and exited his tent. Many others were awake and moving about the camp as the sky slowly lightened. Soldiers donned armor, cavalrymen saddled horses, craftsmen bundled their tools. Tents were torn down and stowed, fires were doused, quick breakfasts were washed down with tea or sour ale.

Once Tavesin had readied himself, he walked to the perimeter of the camp and gazed southward toward Dar Daelad in the distance. The tall gray-white walls that encircled it shone faintly in the pre-dawn light, while the tall tower at its heart shimmered in a dazzling array of color. The Shining Tower had become his home during the past several months, and he found himself saddened by his imminent departure.

He sighed and turned away. He traveled with Emra's army for the sole purpose of one day rescuing Arra from her plight. If he was granted the opportunity to defeat Garin in the process, all the better. The tower would be there to greet him when he returned.

CHAPTER THIRTY-SEVEN

INITIATION RITES

"Will no one volunteer?" Garin's voice thundered through the room, his anger embodied in the question.

Alyra fell to her knees with a gasp while Dranamir met his rage unflinchingly. From the side, Kama watched the spectacle unfold with an amused smirk plastered across his angular features; his duty was to the army, not to the deplorable task of training the recruits. In times past, Dranamir relished the task of initiating the worthy into the ranks of Enlightened, but this matter was abhorrent. The Murkor weren't supposed to possess the Ability, and now one of their number had proven himself worthy of initiation. It was distasteful, a blight on their council.

"Are you finished?" Dranamir demanded, one dark eyebrow arched in amusement. "I believe *you* were tasked to assist us in this matter as well, Garin."

Garin's pale lips curled in distaste. "I will have nothing to do with the Murkor abomination unless our master forces the task upon me."

"He is strong," Alyra replied hollowly from her obeisant position on the tiled floor.

Dranamir snorted. "Garin's little display was mere child's play."

"I wasn't referring to him." Alyra climbed to her feet and straightened her skirt. "The Murkor is very strong. I don't believe I can oversee his initiation."

"An excuse," Dranamir scoffed. "Unless you truly are as pitiful as you appear?"

"It's true, Dranamir." Kama smirked at her. "I called him away from the army for this purpose at our master's request. I assessed his potential."

"The duty is yours, Dranamir," Garin added. "I will not sully myself for a lesser species. Think of it as payment for the loss of the previous three you took into the initiation chamber."

Dranamir leveled him with her coldest glare. "Perhaps the next time you wish them to *survive*, you'll pair them with Alyra's bleeding heart. I do not suffer the weak."

"Nevertheless, the Murkor is yours." Garin shrugged indifferently. "If he fails to survive, I'll consider your advice for the next set of recruits."

Dranamir scowled but refrained from striking at Garin. She'd been wary of him since his revelation regarding his bond with the Nameless, and Kama was undoubtedly seeking a second opportunity to overpower her. She would reserve her anger for the Murkor's initiation, where she would be unchallenged.

"It would be useful if at least *one* were available to assist the army in Delucha," Kama stated dryly. "At the commander's current pace, the army will be upon Delucha City within a fortnight. As the capital, it's heavily defended." He frowned at Dranamir. "That you've made an enemy of the queen does not help matters."

She narrowed her eyes. "She is not the true threat in Delucha City."

"Yes, Ravin." Garin's tone was bitter. "Kama is right. We need as many Enlightened at Delucha as can be initiated. The recruits are more valuable alive than as fodder for the wildlife."

"Then pray for them, Garin. The Nameless will protect those worthy of his brand."

Dranamir located the Murkor's quarters near the base of the tower and rapped loudly on the door. It was nearing midnight; she knew of all the tower's residents, the Murkor would be awake. When he answered the summons, Dranamir peered up at the tall figure shrouded in vibrant green. The glint of his pale eyes was visible beneath his deep hood. Behind him, the room was dark.

"You are called to your initiation," she said without preamble.

She studied him, gauging his reaction to the news. He nodded once, but nothing in his demeanor gave her an indication of what he felt. She wished she could peer beneath his hood to see his expression. She knew enough about the Murkor to understand such an act would be considered a violation akin to physical assault, and the prospect was tantalizing.

"Do you know who I am?" she demanded impatiently, enraged by his silence.

"Yes. I am prepared to answer the call."

There was no discernable fear in his tone, no hesitation. The Murkor was proving a puzzle, one that Dranamir meant to solve. He would reveal his true nature to her, or he would die as the others had before him. Such was the way of Enlightened initiation.

"Follow me."

She turned from his door and began to descend the spiral of steps toward the tower's anteroom below. She heard the soft click the door made as the Murkor closed it behind him, followed by the sound of his footfalls on the steps as he obeyed her command. They did not speak as she led him across the anteroom's polished obsidian floor toward a pair of unembellished, black lacquered doors.

She paused to extract an equally plain iron key from the pouch at her belt. The key was merely symbolic; the doors could be opened only by an Enlightened bearing the dark brand of the Nameless god.

She held the key loosely in her hands and faced the hooded Murkor. "You are the first of your kind to enter this sanctum. If you wish to emerge, prepare yourself now. I've been forced to kill three of the others this week, and I won't hesitate to do the same for you if I find your skills lacking."

Again, he gave no outward reaction to her words. "I am ready."

His voice was calm, unwavering, though she detected a strange note in his words. Resignation, perhaps? His stoic façade infuriated her.

"The initiation consists of a duel. We will battle without interference while Garin oversees the match from the balcony above."

She paused to frown in displeasure. In her first tenure in the tower, she'd been the one to monitor the duels. Garin's bond with their master elevated his position above her own. It rankled, but there was nothing she could do to remedy the situation at present.

"Garin will determine when—or *if*—you have proven your worth," she continued. "But know this, Murkor: I do not hold back for anyone, least of all a lesser being."

He stiffened at her final words. She smiled cruelly, pleased she'd managed to elicit a response from him. The status of his people seemed to be a sore spot for him, one she meant to exploit.

"I will prove my worth," he replied, his voice tight. "We are not a lesser people."

"That will be determined by Garin." She turned from him and inserted the iron key into the door. "You will be given ten seconds to prepare yourself once the doors close."

She pushed open the doors and cackled as the Murkor strode past her brusquely. His long strides were clipped, and his fists were clenched at his sides in anger. It amused her that she'd finally wormed her way beneath his tattooed, midnight blue skin.

The room was a long rectangle, with two wide circles painted on the obsidian floor. The circle opposite the door was yellow, to signify the initiate; the other was red, meant for the Enlightened examiner. A span of fifty paces stretched between the circles. A broad balcony hung high above the floor; from it, one could watch the duel unfold in its entirety and monitor the outcome. A ring of torches surrounded the chamber, each lit by a magical, red-purple flame.

The Murkor took up his position in the initiate's circle while she closed the doors. As she made her way to the examiner's circle, she began to count the seconds. She stepped into position at seven, glanced at the balcony, and noted Garin stood at the balustrade. He picked at his fingernails in a display of boredom. She shifted her gaze to the Murkor at the count of nine, and at ten, she seized her power. The Murkor did the same.

She formed an invisible shield around her person while he erected a shimmering barrier of his own. She arched an eyebrow, impressed and surprised that he possessed the power required to create the barrier with such apparent ease. Perhaps Kama and Alyra weren't merely attempting to throw her off with their insinuations of the Murkor's Ability.

He conjured a volley of fire to rain from the ceiling above her location while she pondered his strength. Her shield vibrated with the assault, but its integrity held. She struck with vortex of swirling energy and followed immediately with an arcing bolt of lightning that struck the barrier directly above the Murkor's hood. Rather than winking out at the dual assault, the barrier became denser, more substantial. He'd anticipated her attack.

"The abomination does the impossible," she muttered angrily and struck again.

The barrier held and grew opaque, absorbing her magical energy. The Murkor moved swiftly, his hands a whirl of blue and silver as he summoned a more powerful magic. She narrowed her eyes and poured additional energy into her shield while striking at his barrier a fourth time.

As her last attack made contact, the Murkor knelt and placed both of his hands, fingers splayed, against the floor. A rumble coursed through the room as a violent shockwave of energy thundered through the air. When it collided with her shield, her defenses faltered and vanished.

Rage suffused her; she would not be outdone by this initiate as she'd been outmatched by Kama. One humiliating defeat was enough. She reformed her shield as he buffeted her position with an unnatural wind. She leaned into the attack in order to keep her footing, then unleashed a series of purple-blue bolts of crackling energy, one after another, relentlessly.

She watched as his barrier thickened and grew. Its continued presence fueled her fury. Bolt after bolt flew through the air, each striking precisely where she commanded. Suddenly the barrier exploded outward in a magical tidal wave that rushed toward her.

She ceased her assault on the Murkor in order to fortify her shield; the energy would consume her if she did not focus on defense. The wash of magic knocked her from her feet and swept her toward the door, but her shield held. As the assault abated, she scrambled to her feet, prepared to strike the Murkor down for his insolence.

"That is enough, Dranamir." Garin's voice reverberated through the room, magically enhanced to fill the space. "You are no longer in position. The Murkor—Sal'zar—has proven himself."

She glared at the balcony and the deceptively frail man who occupied it. She'd intended to make an example of the Murkor, to hear his screams of agony as she overwhelmed and defeated him. Instead, he'd bested her with a flashy display of magic that forced her from the assigned position and into a forfeiture of the duel.

"Murkor trickery will not save you in a true battle," she sneered at the hooded figure.

"I studied the rules of the initiation rite and formed a plan." He shrugged indifferently. "I have broken none of your rules."

Garin floated to the floor from the balcony and landed lightly between them. "That is true. Our master has deemed you worthy of his brand." He glanced at Dranamir. "As this initiate's examiner, it is your right to perform the branding, if you wish to do so."

Dranamir frowned, nonplussed. Garin did not want to dirty his pallid hands by placing them in contact with the Murkor. "And if I don't?" she challenged.

Garin sighed in exasperation, his crimson eyes glinting dangerously. "I will not be pleased, Dranamir."

She smirked. "I will perform the branding. It's always a pleasure to see a powerful initiate squirm a final time."

She crossed the room, aware that Garin followed a few steps behind. The Murkor stood stiffly; once more, she wished she could peer beneath his green hood to gauge his reaction. With Garin present, she would not be allowed the luxury of sating her curiosity.

"Show me your hands," she ordered once she stood within arm's reach of the Murkor.

He extended them toward her, palm up. It seemed the palms were the only portion of his midnight skin that were not marked by a swirl of silvery tattoos. If not for the coloration, the hands could have belonged to a human. She noted the callouses that roughened several of his fingertips, likely from his work as an alchemist.

"The branding requires skin contact."

She gripped his hands firmly in her own. She was unsurprised when he jerked backward; the Murkor were strangely affronted by physical contact from those they deemed outsiders. Dranamir increased the pressure of her grip and glared at him. The Murkor relaxed after a moment, though she could sense his reluctance.

"This will only take a moment."

She closed her eyes as she channeled the magic the Nameless god had taught her long ago. It served to bind the Enlightened to his will. The Murkor would be compelled to obey the god's orders and those of his chosen—the Soulless.

Dranamir forced the magic to flow into the Murkor but was met with resistance that went beyond a mere shield. She sensed no magic flowing within the Murkor; he was not responsible for the interference, though she would make him suffer for it. When she opened her eyes to examine his palms, she became further enraged. Where the mark of the Nameless god should have appeared on the Murkor's flesh, there was nothing.

"What manner of treachery is this?" she hissed. She lifted her arm in preparation to strike but was swiftly interrupted.

Garin grasped her wrist in an iron grip, and she was grudgingly reminded of the unusual strength the small man possessed. "He is not responsible for this anomaly, Dranamir."

"I'm aware that he did not shield himself, Garin," she snapped. She wrenched her arm free and spun to face him. "What happened, Garin?"

Garin shook his head. "I don't know. It seems he is immune to branding. Perhaps it is a Murkor trait, or perhaps something else has occurred here. I must confer with our master."

"Immunity is impossible."

Garin chuckled darkly. "Hold your temper, Dranamir. The brand is not infallible, as Ravin proved so long ago. Our master knows this."

"What are we to do with this abomination?" She gestured vaguely at the Murkor, who stiffened further at her words. "By rights, I should kill him. He is a threat—"

"You will not," Garin stated forcefully. "The master has a plan for Sal'zar, and this is but a minor setback. He has proven himself worthy of the title Enlightened, though he will not bear the brand."

"One day I will find a means to part you from your own brand, Garin," she promised through clenched teeth. "When that day comes, I will see you suffer as no other has."

Garin shrugged indifferently. "The master will never allow that, Dranamir, but you may continue to delude yourself if you wish." He glanced at the Murkor. "We are finished here. I will summon you tomorrow to discuss your new role within our council, Sal'zar."

Dranamir bristled at the dismissal and stalked away. She ignored Garin's parting words and stormed through the double doors. Her rage would not abate without bloodshed.

She created a portal and stepped into the Aethereum. She traveled to a remote farming village in the southern reaches of Masmoone Kingdom, the same village Garin claimed his captive wench had come from. He seemed determined to keep her alive, though he tortured and maimed her at every opportunity. He was a vicious creature, but so was Dranamir.

She exited the Aethereum in the cloying darkness of early morning. The village was silent, its inhabitants peacefully asleep in their beds. As fire began to rain from the sky and pummel the homes, the night erupted into a symphony of shrieks.

Dranamir tipped her head back and laughed as the village was consumed by her magical fire, its citizens reduced to cinders in her wake.

CHAPTER THIRTY-EIGHT

THE RIDDLE'S ANSWER

"Gods, this is frustrating." Ravin pushed away from the table and began to pace along the nearest bookshelf while he tried to order his thoughts.

"Give it time, Ravin," Adalin said gently. She remained hunched over the latest book they'd been scouring while her eyes scanned the text rapidly.

"It's been ten days," he growled. "Ten gods-damned days with nothing to show for our efforts but a series of headaches."

"Ravin."

The sharpness in her tone caused him to pause mid-stride. She fixed him with a pointed glare and placed her hands on her hips.

"I understand your frustration well enough, but your moaning does nothing but give *me* a headache. It's counter-productive." She sighed and looked away. "It's clear we're missing a key piece to the final puzzle, but we *will* find it. Patience and perseverance, Ravin."

He scowled. "Patience does us little good, Adalin. The Murkor army is on its way here. Jadosin's scouts informed us this morning it will be upon the city within two days, three at most." He sighed heavily, the weight of his burden threatening to consume him. "I must have the talisman before they reach the city, or all is lost."

The final barrier was impenetrable. The day after he ventured into the catacombs alone, he returned with Adalin to the room where he'd encountered the specters. A short distance beyond the chamber, they'd come to a semi-transparent magical barrier the like of which he was wholly unfamiliar with. Its surface was smooth, a shimmering, pale yellow dome. At the dome's center stood a solitary stone pedestal, and upon it, the relic he sought.

The Eshmere Stone, the wraiths had called it; the Peace Talisman of Delucha. It was fashioned to resemble an eagle with wings spread wide as if in flight. It was constructed of a golden, jewel-like stone reminiscent of topaz, and was small enough to fit in the palm of his hand.

The pair had spent hours searching the exterior of the dome for a clue to its mechanism, but it yielded nothing. When Ravin had attempted to step through it, he'd been repelled with such force he stumbled and fell.

During the intervening days, he'd spent every spare moment in the palace's library, searching for additional information. Adalin had pored through countless tomes; she often was within the library when he arrived in the morning and remained when he was called away to his duties as royal advisor. Between them, Ravin guessed they'd scoured half the collection. He believed his present frustration was warranted.

A tap on the door to the corridor drew his attention. He peered around the corner of the bookshelf to find one of the palace's many pages framed in the doorway. "Yes?"

"Sir, there is a…man here to speak with you." The boy appeared nervous. "He's in the great hall."

Ravin frowned; he wasn't expecting any outside visitors. "I'm busy. Ask him to come back tomorrow. I'll speak with him then."

The page fidgeted. "Sir, I don't think he's willing to wait. He's one of the Scorpion Men."

Ravin tilted his head, his curiosity piqued. "Go on."

"He, ah, he said he has an important message for you. From *Flariel*." The boy blanched as he spoke the goddess' name.

Ravin glanced at Adalin and beckoned to her. The timing of this visit was too strange to be mere coincidence, and he wanted the duchess present to hear whatever was said. His instincts told him his search for the talisman was related to the message, and its bearer intrigued him. During their many hours of research, he'd skimmed several passages that told the sad tale of the Scorpion Men. He was keen to meet one of their number.

"We'll see this visitor," Ravin told the page as he offered his arm to Adalin.

"Are you certain you require my presence?" she asked quietly once the boy had disappeared into the hall.

"Yes."

"I suppose a better question is, why is one of the Scorpion Men in Delucha with a message from the fire goddess?" she mused. "I'd be more grateful if he came with news from Blademon."

Ravin shook his head and chuckled softly. "Seeking the interference of the gods is a dangerous game, Adalin."

"You sound like the priests."

"I speak from experience."

He hadn't yet found the courage to share his tale with her, and he was beginning to run out of excuses. He'd also put off the task of contacting his mother. It was a confrontation he would rather not endure.

Adalin froze as they entered the great hall. There was not one, but two armored Scorpion Men, along with a tall woman in full plate mail befitting a Balotican knight. Ravin could sense the Ability within the woman like a beacon in a storm. She was powerful, though he sensed no malice in her expression. Her cool gray eyes studied their approach, while the taller of the two Scorpion Men whispered to the other. Siblings, Ravin believed. They sported the same light blond hair and piercing blue eyes.

Setting his curiosity aside, he donned his diplomatic guise. "Welcome to the palace. I am Ravin, the queen's advisor in matters of magic." He nodded to Adalin. "This is the Duchess of the Mers, Lady Adalin."

The woman stepped forward, clearly the leader of the trio. "Emra Castledowns, knight of Balotica."

She tugged at the hilt of her sword to reveal several inches of steel limned with magical flames. Adalin gasped, one hand fluttering to cover her mouth to conceal her surprise. Ravin understood a magical relic when he saw one, and he'd learned enough of history from his perusal of the library to recognize hers.

He lifted his eyebrows, impressed. "The Fireblade. So, the legends are true."

"I find it easier to demonstrate who I am than explain and be called into question." Emra smiled ruefully. "This is Vardak, general of my army, and his brother, Patak."

The marginally shorter of the pair, Vardak, stepped forward. "You are the mage Flariel tasked me to locate." He withdrew a silver cylinder from his belt and handed it to Ravin. "She ordered me to give you this."

"I find the Fire Maiden's involvement strange," Ravin replied while he examined the cylinder and turned it over in his hands.

"It's a very long story. Let it suffice that she believes I owe her this favor."

The cylinder was sealed at one end with a magical ward. The energy that wove through the cylinder was intimately familiar to him, and he sighed heavily. The thing may have come to Vardak through Flariel, but Ravin knew the contents were from his mother.

"Ravin?" Adalin asked softly, sensing the change in his mood.

"It comes from Solsticia," he said as he dissolved the ward and the cylinder sprang open.

"How do you know that?" Patak blurted. He received a sharp look from Emra and glanced away, chagrined.

Ravin ignored the question and pulled the rolled slip of parchment contained within the cylinder free. He unfurled it and scanned the contents, a smile forming on his lips. Perhaps the correspondence from his mother wasn't unfortunate, after all.

The answer you seek has been beside you all along, dear Ravin. The final barrier cannot be breached by anyone marked with the Ability, but the lovely duchess can pass safely through.

It was signed in her typical, flowery script, the edges of the parchment decorated in a series of stars and celestial symbols.

"She refers to you as 'dear'? Ravin, I believe you owe me an explanation." Adalin's tone was amused, and he felt heat rise into his cheeks.

"Yes, an explanation would be welcome," Emra agreed. "You are more powerful than any mage I've met, and the wizards did not know of your existence. Yet you are not branded as a member of the Shadow Council. An *unaffiliated* mage is a rarity."

When she crossed her arms, he knew he'd be forced to divulge his story. It wasn't a tale he wished to tell, and he feared the outcome.

A commotion near the palace entrance spared him further awkwardness. A Drakkon strode inside, two humans in her wake. The arrival had drawn the notice of palace staff and nobility alike; the noise had come from a maid who had dropped the stack of tin plates she'd been carrying. The Drakkon and her escorts ignored the mess and the stares as they made their way into the great hall. All three were powerful wielders of magic, Ravin noted. He stiffened with unease.

"They are with us," Emra said softly.

Ravin nodded as his gaze swept past the Drakkon to take in the two humans. One was a middle-aged man with a pale scar along one side of his face. The other was a boy. Recognition shot through him as the boy's blue eyes met his. It was the child he'd spared from Garin's brutality in the Aethereum, the child with magical strength to rival the Soulless.

"It's you," the boy said, eyes wide.

"Yes."

The Drakkon turned to peer at her young companion, concern etched across her scaly features. "Tavesin?"

"Aziarah, he saved me. He's the one that sent the Soulless away that night when I..." Tavesin looked down, helplessness and shame in his expression.

"You told me you escaped," the Drakkon replied warily.

Tavesin met her gaze with a terrified one of his own. "I did. With help." He looked beyond her to Ravin and chewed his lower lip uncertainly.

"I sent the Soulless away to lick his wounds," Ravin replied evenly. "I will not abide the abuse of a child."

Tavesin broke away from the others and sprinted the remaining distance to Ravin. He stopped abruptly and extended his hand. "I never properly thanked you, sir."

"No thanks are necessary. Tavesin, was it?" When the boy nodded, he said, "I believe you and I both have some explaining to do."

CHAPTER THIRTY-NINE

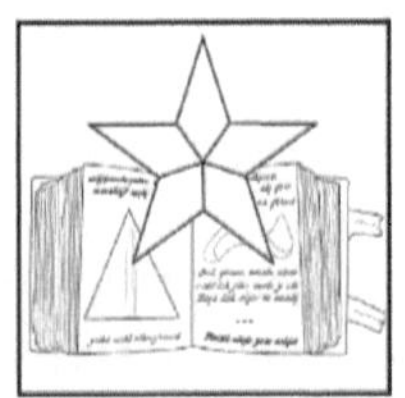

RAVIN'S TALE

Formal introductions were made, and the group was taken to a private meeting chamber some distance from the palace's great hall. Tavesin stared at the tapestries that lined the walls, the thick velvet draperies that hung from the crystalline windows, the plush carpets on the polished stone floors, unable to conceal his wonder at his resplendent surroundings. He was Deluchan, but it was his first exposure to the royal palace. Where the Shining Tower was a wonder of magic, the palace was a testament to the queen's extravagance and boundless wealth.

The chamber contained a long oak table, its surface polished to a bright sheen. A dozen chairs surrounded it, each furnished with a plush velvet cushion stitched with the eagle emblem of the royal house. Vardak and Patak moved several chairs to the perimeter of the room to make room for themselves while the remainder of the group was seated. Tavesin found himself perched on a chair, which he found surprisingly uncomfortable, between Aziarah and the kindly Duchess of the Mers.

Tavesin clasped his hands tightly together, fearful he might unknowingly breach some unspoken etiquette and offend the noble lady. She was beautiful in her silken gown, her dark hair piled atop her head. Her blue eyes were kind, and he found himself comparing her in many ways to his mother. He had been unable to visit his family since he'd been sent off to the Shining Tower months ago; he was homesick, but there were more important matters he must focus on.

A pair of women in servant garb entered the room bearing trays filled with tiny cakes, mounds of fresh blueberries, honey, and butter. Another followed with goblets and pitchers of a golden liquid. When a plate of the dainty food and a goblet was placed in front of Tavesin, he stared first at Aziarah, then at Emra across the table. What was the proper protocol for dining in such an extravagant setting?

It was the duchess who noted his terror and confusion. She patted his hand and bent her head toward his ear. "Follow my lead, dear. We'll wait until the servants depart."

He risked a glance at her and was relieved to find a patient smile on her lips. "Thank you," he mumbled. "I've never been in a place like this."

"I know, Tavesin. Be at ease. You are a guest."

He settled back in his chair to observe the others while he waited for the duchess' cue. Ravin stood at the head of the table, bronze hands clasped behind his back, his golden eyes taking a moment to study each of those gathered in turn. On Ravin's right sat the duchess, Tavesin, and Aziarah. On his left were the pair of Scorpion Men and Emra. Radosan occupied the seat at the opposite end.

As the servants departed and the door was closed softly behind them, Ravin began to pace. Tavesin watched him with wide eyes, in awe of the other's magical power. Tavesin had never encountered anyone with such strength, but rather than feel intimidated, he was undeniably grateful. Ravin had spared him from Garin's wrath and likely saved his life.

The duchess gestured at the food before her. "Please, enjoy the refreshments courtesy of our good queen."

Ravin paused mid-stride, eyebrows raised in question at her words. She ignored him and turned to Tavesin. "I think you'll like the cakes, Tavesin. They happen to be my favorite."

Tavesin smiled timidly and reached for a cake. He took a bite and chewed slowly, savoring its slightly sweet flavor.

"Why don't we begin with your tale, Ravin? I believe we'd all like to know why Solsticia holds such a keen interest in you," Aziarah stated.

Ravin glowered at the floor but managed a reluctant nod. "I've promised Adalin I would share my story with her on numerous occasions, and I've been avoiding this moment. My past was…difficult."

"Be that as it may, I am keen to learn why the goddess referred to you as *dear*," the duchess replied with a knowing smirk. "I'm grateful for her guidance, but the familiarity you seem to share is fascinating."

Ravin sighed heavily and his shoulders slumped in defeat. "Solsticia is my mother."

The room fell silent at his revelation, and Ravin began to pace once more. Tavesin could see the mage's discomfort inherent in his every movement. He thought back to his lessons and recalled the legends claimed the Aethereum had been created by Solsticia in honor of her only child, but that had been centuries ago. Millennia…

"Gods, Ravin," the duchess breathed, "I cannot believe I didn't piece it together sooner. You've hinted at it enough. You have her eyes."

Ravin scowled but didn't look up. "Our relationship is tumultuous at the best of times, and I'd rather not be drawn into her schemes. Some of what I discovered in the catacombs leads me to believe she's been driving my destiny without my knowledge for centuries—" His eyes widened and he peered at the group uneasily.

Emra folded her arms and sat back in her chair, her gaze unreadable. "I've begun to wonder about your age, Ravin. The histories state Solsticia constructed the Aethereum for her *only* child, and its existence has been known to the world's mages for nearly a thousand years."

Ravin shook his head, his jaw clenched in frustration. "A lapse, a gods-damned lapse." He sighed and squeezed his eyes shut, one hand rising to pinch the bridge of his nose. "I am not centuries old, not truly. Do any of you know what a soul-stone is?"

Emra's eyebrows rose. "A relic that can grant its creator a second chance at life. They are purportedly impossible to forge."

Ravin shrugged. "Yes, and they are not an impossibility. I once created a soul-stone."

"Aeon must have been livid," Emra remarked.

"Why would you seek the creation of such a thing?" Aziarah demanded. "It's a subversion of Aeon's will—even for the child of a god."

"In order for the magic to work properly, I was forced to seek Aeon's blessing directly," Ravin replied sullenly. "My situation was spiraling into untoward destruction, my freedom had been stolen, I'd been tortured for weeks on end, and I knew my captor planned to kill me. I wasn't prepared to allow it. I believed Aeon took pity on me and granted his blessing. I now know I was wrong."

Ravin paused to run a hand through his dark hair. Tavesin watched him, enrapt, his half-eaten cake forgotten.

"While we were investigating the catacombs beneath the palace, I learned several important details that have forced me to question my mother's motives," Ravin continued after a time. "I believe she knew I would come into her life at a future date, and I also believe she knew much of the path my life would take. There have been too many signs for my recent arrival in Delucha to be mere coincidence. I loathe the notion that my destiny was dictated by my mother long ago, but it is the only logical conclusion."

"You have not answered my question," Aziarah stated. Her leathery wings twitched in agitation.

"You fear to do so," the duchess said, compassion in her gaze. "Oh, Ravin, how bad can it be?"

He peered at her with wounded eyes. "I'm not certain any of you will wish to trust me if I reveal the truth about my past. I've always believed my actions carried great weight, that I must prove to others my intentions are pure." He drew an unsteady breath and turned to face Emra. "Upon our first moments together, you stated I did not bear the brand. I want nothing more than to see the Soulless destroyed, even if I am not a part of the Shining Tower. It's why I created the soul-stone. I wished to return to correct my mistakes, to see the Soulless ended, to wound the Nameless god in the only manner I know how."

Ravin's voice had taken on a pleading tone as he sought the understanding of the others.

"You saved me from Garin," Tavesin pointed out and received a grateful smile from Ravin in return. Tavesin beamed at the silent acknowledgment.

"And by all accounts, you saved the queen from their grasp," the duchess added. "Ravin…however terrible your past is, I think we deserve to hear it. You've become my dearest friend. I will not abandon you."

Vardak shifted slightly and crossed his arms. "Flariel sent me to seek your aid, Ravin. The gods do not act without good reason and will not interfere in mortal wars—unless larger forces than our own are at play."

Patak snorted. "I believe what my brother is trying to say is we need your help. Your past is irrelevant."

"Still, it raises many questions," Aziarah replied. "Perhaps the telling of your tale will provide answers. I do not know you as the others seem to, but if you are responsible for rescuing Tavesin, I'm willing to believe your actions speak to your true character."

Ravin drew a breath. "It seems I've no choice. I'll pray the lot of you don't call for my head before its conclusion."

The duchess appeared amused. "Ravin, you're stalling."

"With good reason." He stopped pacing and turned to face them. "I've told you about my mother. My father raised me—he was Santinian, as I'm sure you've gathered—and we understood before I was ten summers old the sort of power I was capable of harnessing. He never mentioned my mother, and I didn't know her identity until my twentieth birthday. The gods have a rule about that, it seems."

He paused to gather his thoughts. "I was very young when my power began to manifest. Given our location, we were equidistant between the Shining Tower and its wizards, and the…other Council of Magic."

Emra narrowed her eyes. "How long ago was this, Ravin?"

He shifted uncomfortably. "Perhaps thirty-five years prior to the onset of the First Great War."

She nodded knowingly. "It was before the Soulless. Before that council was corrupted by the Nameless god."

Relief flooded Ravin's features. "Yes! Thank the gods you're here, because I don't believe anyone else would understand the importance of the timing."

Emra cracked a wry grin. "Rarely does anyone thank me for my presence. My arrival is usually considered a harbinger of destruction."

Ravin managed a weary chuckle. "I suppose that's true enough."

"You were once a part of the Council of Enlightened," Radosan stated quietly. Tavesin turned to look at the Green Sect Master, who had remained silent throughout the previous conversation.

Ravin looked down. "Yes. Because I was so young, my father made the decision for me. He was a merchant and traveled into the lands east of the Gray Mountains to trade with the tower and the Murkor. It was convenient." He lifted his gaze to meet Tavesin's. "I was fully trained in the Ability before I reached your age, Tavesin. I understand all too well what you must be feeling, thrust into an adult's role when you are merely a child."

Tavesin nodded but made no reply. Ravin was the first to acknowledge his struggle with the demands of the Radiant and the larger council. A part of him felt vindicated; he was not alone, not any longer. Ravin had become his unspoken ally.

"Then you were trained years before your mother revealed herself," the duchess said.

Ravin nodded. "When I was twenty, I was summoned to the nearest shrine. It was deep within the Underground Caverns—the Murkor homeland. Traveling through the caverns is uncomfortable for any mage. The area is sealed, and I was cut off from the Ability. The Murkor were a peaceful people then, and they showed no malice toward me. At the shrine dedicated to their patron, Ukase, I was met by Solsticia. I understood our connection immediately." His gaze met the duchess'. "As I once told you, I inherited many of her outward traits."

"Is that when she created the Aethereum?" Tavesin asked eagerly.

Ravin smiled wearily. "No. She created it before that date, but it was then that she introduced me to it. She…imparted the knowledge of its magic to me. I'm not certain how to describe the sensation. When a god deigns to pour information into your skull, it's not a pleasant process."

Vardak chuckled dryly. "I've experienced it, and you're right."

Ravin's eyebrows rose in silent question, but Vardak did not elaborate.

"She informed me the realm had been created for my use. If I wished to share its secrets with others, there were a handful of other mages graced with the ability to access it. I was young and elated by my lineage, and enamored with what she'd created for me. I kept the Aethereum's existence a secret for many years." He glanced at Aziarah. "One day, while I was traversing my realm, I encountered one of your ancestors. He'd inadvertently entered while asleep. He was lost and confused. I realized then that I must teach him the basics of the Aethereum, simply so he could return home."

"My people are gifted with Aethereal magic more often than present-day humans," Aziarah replied. "I suppose I ought to thank you for the kindness you showed him."

Ravin shrugged. "It was the right thing to do, and in spite of what the Shadow Council attempted to do to me, I am not a monstrous person."

"What happened, Ravin?" the duchess asked, her tone compassionate.

"Several new recruits entered the tower at approximately the same time. They learned and trained together. Most harbored a streak of cruelty that was beyond reason. The Enlightened's leader at the time feared what would happen if they were granted status within the council. Rightly so, it turned out."

Ravin shook his head at the memory. "They staged a coup. I believe it was planned before their arrival at the tower. All of them were followers of the Nameless god, zealots willing to go to any length to see him restored. During the course of a single night, they killed all of the council's leaders, and would have killed me as well if I'd been present. As it happened, I was with the Drakkon."

He sighed and began to pace once more. "Word came to me the following day. It was then that I determined I must put a stop to the uprising. I spent several weeks among the Drakkon, preparing myself for the greatest confrontation of my life. I prepared the soul-stone in case my strength in magic proved insufficient. It was fortunate that I did. I wouldn't be standing here today, otherwise."

"Ravin, you said you were tortured…" The duchess' voice broke with emotion, and she trailed off.

"Yes. They awaited my return, and when I arrived at the tower, I fell victim to their trap." He looked down. "These are memories I don't like to recall."

After a moment, he drew a breath, released it forcefully, then continued. "They were led by a woman without conscience. Her name is Dranamir, and she became the first of the Soulless. The trap they devised for me was triggered the moment I entered the tower. I was simultaneously cut from the source of my Ability, frozen in place, and assaulted by excruciating pain of a magnitude I hope to never endure again. They left me in that state for two days, but it felt like a lifetime."

"I know of Dranamir," Emra said quietly. "She is the only Soulless I have not battled personally, but her reputation aligns with your account."

Ravin sighed. "The trap wasn't enough to sate her desire for torture. When she finally grew tired of my screams, she disabled the portion of the trap that caused my pain, but left me unable to defend myself. She progressed to physical torture, demanding to know my secret to instantaneous travel. I resisted for another three days. She was unworthy of the Aethereum."

He stopped pacing and hung his head. "When her frustration grew too much, she forced the brand onto my flesh. It was a violation of my person, my *mind*, so absolute I wished for death. Once branded, I could not resist the Nameless' will any longer. I told her everything."

The duchess rose to her feet and pulled him into her embrace. "Ravin, gods…"

When he looked up, his golden eyes were haunted. "I suppose it's fortunate her temper was spent by the time I finally divulged my knowledge. Dranamir is merciless and driven by her lust for blood. She killed me the next day." He managed a strained smile. "She never asked of the soul-stone, or what I'd been doing amongst the Drakkon. I spent centuries with my spirit trapped within a lightless void. Aeon didn't tell me I'd be aware of my circumstances for the duration of the time I was trapped within the stone."

Emra eyed him with horror. "I can't imagine what that must have been like."

Ravin shrugged and disentangled himself from the duchess. "I believe it's why Aeon doesn't grant soul-stones without good reason. There is a high likelihood the creator will emerge from the ordeal mindless or insane."

Tavesin sat forward and studied Ravin, a question forming in his mind. "Who used your stone, Ravin?"

Ravin stiffened. "The words to perform the resurrection were etched upon the stone's surface. Anyone could have used the stone if they spoke the words aloud. It was my unfortunate luck that the Nameless learned of it at some time during the intervening centuries." He met Tavesin's curious gaze with a hesitant one of his own. "It was Garin. He was a fool and underestimated my power. I managed to take him by surprise. Then I fled."

He turned to the duchess standing at his side. "I came to Delucha and stayed at an inn for a while. One of the perks of being a mage is the ability to conjure coin when it's needed."

"That's unethical," Radosan said, not unkindly, "but you had good reason for it."

Ravin chuckled. "What other choice did I have? I found myself drawn to the palace one day when I sensed powerful magic in use." He glanced at the others warily. "I'm not certain I can share the rest without angering the queen. I became her advisor in magical affairs and have remained here since."

"And this business between you and Flariel?" Vardak asked. "Or rather, your mother?"

"You've come here to drive the Soulless' army back," Ravin replied. "They will arrive any day. I was unaware of your journey here and have made my own preparations for the defense of this city. The message from my mother was the final piece to the puzzle we've been grappling with."

"Which is?" Emra prompted.

Ravin grinned. "I've uncovered a relic more powerful than your sword. It's simply a matter of extracting it."

CHAPTER FORTY

SECURING THE STONE

"Ravin, you could have told me," Adalin said quietly after the others had departed.

He looked away, unable to meet her gaze. "I've met very few people I consider true friends in my life. I didn't want to risk losing what we've built."

Adalin laughed softly. "You silly, silly man. I'm still here, aren't I?"

He risked a glance in her direction and was relieved to see she smiled. "Gods, I'd hoped to never retell that damned tale."

He glanced at the table, his untouched plate of food, the full goblet of mead. Ignoring the cake and berries, he grasped the goblet and downed half its contents, hoping to drown his misery in the honeyed elixir. Adalin gently took the cup from him and set it carefully on the table beyond his immediate reach.

"Ravin, sit down."

He obeyed without question. He collapsed into his chair and stared forlornly at the tabletop; the afternoon had not gone according to plan. He'd learned the answer to the catacombs' final riddle, but the cost had been the baring of his soul, his secrets made public to some of the greatest figures the era would produce. If the queen learned of his past, his post as advisor would be rescinded, his position in the palace ruined. He would lose Adalin to the whims of the court while he was cut adrift to fend for himself once more.

"Mead isn't the answer, Ravin. We both know what it does to your beautiful mind." Adalin pulled the nearest chair toward him and sat down at his side. "Although I must admit, I found it amusing when you became so formal that day in the catacombs."

He tried to muster a smile and failed. "You're right, lady duchess." Melancholy infused his tone, though he'd tried to impart cheer.

Adalin took his hand in hers. "Take all the time you need, Ravin. I'm here as I promised I would be."

"She can't know of this, Adalin. I'll lose everything."

"She? Oh, you mean Tamarin." Her tone took on a note of disapproval. "I will not tell her, and the others will be busy with their army. They won't have the time—and I doubt our queen will bother summoning them. She'll expect them to come to her."

Ravin pulled his gaze away from the tabletop to meet Adalin's. "Do you truly believe that?" He hated the pleading note in his tone, but he needed her validation.

She smiled, understanding. "I do, Ravin." She squeezed his hand gently. "Perhaps we ought to see about the talisman, now that we've received the key to its final defense."

He nodded. She was right; stewing about what might be was counter-productive. The Murkor were nearing the city, and he needed to clear his mind, to focus his energy on the brewing storm. He would not find himself mired in another of the Soulless' traps, and he would not allow Delucha to fall. The talisman must be secured.

He rose to his feet and offered the duchess his arm before creating a portal into the Aethereum. They returned to the darkened chamber where he'd encountered the wraiths, and after he closed the second portal, he produced a magical light. Adalin clutched his arm firmly, her eyes alight with the promise of achieving their goal.

"I cannot believe the answer is so simple," Adalin said quietly as they began to wend their way along the final stretch of stone corridor. "If I'd merely thought to touch the barrier—"

"I warned you away from that course," Ravin replied firmly, cutting her off. "Ancient magic is often dangerous and I could sense nothing of its nature."

"It seems it was designed that way." She smiled up at him, mischief in her eyes. "Your mother didn't wish to see the talisman fall to a single, all-powerful mage, Ravin. This last barrier requires great trust on your part, and a mastery of fear on mine."

"I'm not all-powerful, Adalin, and you have nothing to fear."

"Given the way the wizard gaped at you and the boy idolized you, I must disagree on the first point." Her smile faltered, and she gripped his arm more tightly. "Ravin, do you trust your mother in this matter?"

Startled by the question, he peered down at her with concern. "We've had our disagreements, but I don't believe she'd set us up for failure."

"I won't be harmed by this venture?" she pressed, fear clouding her eyes.

"Gods, Adalin, I hadn't thought of that," he admitted. "But no, I don't believe you will. Solsticia is the patron goddess of the human species—to my knowledge, she has never sent one of us on a dangerous errand without directly informing us of the risks first. In that regard, I trust her implicitly."

She nodded thoughtfully. "Then I will trust you in this matter, Ravin, just as you must trust me. Gods, I didn't think I'd be so terrified of this, but now that we're here…"

He stopped abruptly and spun her around to face him. "I will not allow anything to happen to you, Adalin. You have my word."

A tremulous smile crossed her lips. "Thank you, Ravin. I'll be fine. Let's continue."

They fell into silence as they traversed the final bend in the corridor. Despite his words to the contrary, he worried for the duchess' safety now that the subject had been broached. He wanted to believe his mother wouldn't send Adalin into harm's way, but she was a goddess; the gods often failed to recognize the dangers presented to the mortals ensnared in their schemes.

A faint golden glow announced their proximity to the final barrier and the talisman enshrouded at its heart. Adalin's fingers dug into his forearm as her anxiety increased, but he did not voice his discomfort. He must act as her support in this endeavor, for it was her life potentially at risk. If he lost her to this scheme, he would never forgive Solsticia for her role in the affair—or himself.

They halted after rounding the final bend, and the barrier came into view. Ravin gazed at its shimmering surface and tried to ignore the anxiety that gnawed at his gut by focusing his attention on the stone pedestal within. The delicately carved jewel perched atop the stone, a tiny eagle with wings spread as if it were in mid-flight. The talisman gleamed in the light from the magical dome, its facets twinkling.

Adalin released his arm and drew a breath, her eyes fixed on the stone. "Whatever transpires, Ravin, know that I spoke the truth when I said you are my greatest friend."

"Adalin…"

He reached out to grasp her hand once more, but she stepped forward and eluded his touch. Terror rooted him in place—terror that she might not survive his mother's game. She walked steadily toward the barrier without looking back.

She paused as she came abreast of it and studied its surface for a time. Ravin watched as she straightened and braced herself, then stepped through the magical construct that had denied him. She visibly relaxed once inside, as though the act of crossing had been the greatest source of her anxiety.

She paused again at the pedestal and raised her hands tentatively, slowly reaching for the relic. Ravin's pulse accelerated; this was the moment he was most concerned with, the moment that would prove his earlier words of encouragement—or would see them rent asunder to leave him wracked with guilt. As her hands neared the talisman, Ravin did something he'd refused to do for years—he closed his eyes and prayed silently to his mother.

He heard Adalin's rapid footfalls a moment later and opened his eyes. Breathless, she strode toward him, safely beyond the barrier once more. She smiled up at him as she pressed the talisman into his palm. He grinned, the tension he'd been holding melting away in an instant.

"You're safe."

"You promised I would be. I trusted in your words."

He waved a portal into existence and took her arm. "I'd like to examine it further, but not here. Somewhere private, but with ample daylight. I'm weary of the dark."

They returned to his quarters and sat across from one another near the room's only window. He examined the stone carefully; in the light of the afternoon sun, it gleamed almost as brilliantly as it had in the depths beneath the palace. Without using his power to probe its abilities, he could sense nothing of its nature, and their long days of research had yielded nothing. That the Soulless wanted the relic for themselves had been reason enough to acquire it, but now that he held it in his palm, he was uncertain of its purpose.

"I need to link my power with the talisman's in order to understand its uses." He looked up at the duchess pensively. "I don't know what might happen."

"Should I wait outside?" she asked.

"No." He sighed. "I don't believe you're in danger. I was referring to myself. Sometimes relics—particularly the powerful ones—can cause…adverse reactions in their user."

She leaned toward him and placed her hands over his. "Ravin, I'm going to turn the tables on you. Your mother gave you the means to acquire the talisman. If I was unharmed retrieving it for you, there is no doubt you will be safe in this process, too. Out of all humanity, she would protect you first, without question. She may be a goddess, but even her kind possesses maternal instinct."

He wanted to argue, but understood on a subconscious level that Adalin was right. Solsticia had created the Aethereum for him, as a refuge, she'd said. She would not have led him to Delucha's talisman if she meant him harm. She cared for his well-being insofar as furthering her own schemes were concerned.

He nodded. "You're likely right, and I'm being a fool. Nevertheless, should anything happen, send word to Emra or the Drakkon. There is no one within the palace who can help me."

She released his hands and sat back. "I promise, Ravin."

"Thank you."

He closed his hand over the stone, shut his eyes to better concentrate, then tapped into his power. He sent a tentative tendril of magic into the heart of the talisman and was immediately glad he'd taken the cautious approach. The relic's power was immense, unlike anything he'd encountered previously. He felt it enhance his own offensive magics and strengthen his shields to a level the Soulless could never hope to match with any of the trinkets they possessed.

As he continued to probe, he sensed another purpose within the relic, one that was strictly forbidden by the code of the Shining Tower. His skin crawled in revulsion as he made the realization—the Eshmere Stone harbored the power of mind-control. The relic's power was so vast he believed even the most powerful wielders of magic would succumb to its influence.

His stomach soured at the thought. Dranamir had once branded him. Garin had attempted to recruit him. Jannyn had come to Delucha in search of this stone. Once the Nameless had become aware of Ravin's power, the fallen god had lusted for the opportunity to exert his will over him. He was certain the Soulless had been sent to obtain this relic specifically to subdue him.

He relinquished his power and the intoxicating bond with the talisman, then opened his eyes to study Adalin. Questions filled her eyes, but she did not speak.

"With this, I can defend the city alone, if need be." He shook his head in wonder and disgust. "It also harbors another, rather sinister power."

As he formed the words, an idea came to him. Mind-control was the worst sort of magic, but perhaps it would indeed serve a purpose in the city's defense. Jannyn had controlled Jasom. Perhaps it was time the Soulless met the same fate and used his powers in the fight against his own.

"Ravin?"

He smiled. "I know exactly what I will use this for. I need to speak with the queen, and I believe she'll be pleased with what I plan to accomplish."

CHAPTER FORTY-ONE

PREPARING THE STRIKE

Dranamir studied the gathered Enlightened, a haughty frown of disapproval etched upon her face. They were a meager bunch, less than thirty in number, and many possessed a pitifully diminutive amount of magical Ability. She assumed Alyra had tested those; the soft-hearted bitch rarely failed anyone. It was fortuitous that Dranamir had been assigned the task of selecting those who would accompany the Murkor army on the field of battle.

Of the group, only Sal'zar was not human. His tall, wiry, hood-enshrouded form stood apart from the others like a beacon of trouble. He remained unbranded, much to her chagrin. Garin had informed her hours after his initiation that the Nameless had failed to account for the Murkor people when the magic of branding had been bestowed upon the Enlightened, and it was now too late to correct his mistake. It seemed the other gods had conspired to protect them from the Nameless' influence by subverting that aspect of his power.

Sal'zar had proven obedient and willing to listen, and his power was astounding. Grudgingly, she knew his presence would prove a boon to them on the field. Ravin would never anticipate a Murkor mage, and she planned to confound her nemesis at every turn.

The rest were a motley assortment of men and women from throughout the Five Kingdoms. Most were fervent in their desire to see the Nameless restored to his former glory and obeyed the Soulless' commands easily. There were several whose true allegiance was questionable, however. She would not select them for the battle; in the inevitable chaos, she could not trust them to remain loyal.

Kama had asked for ten of their best and most powerful. She paced across the room as she studied each Enlightened carefully. Some met her gaze, while others looked away, uncomfortable or terrified. The room remained silent, her footfalls on the tiled floor the only sound for some minutes.

Dranamir's reputation was known to each of them, and she had no intention of correcting any preconceptions they might have. They were wise not to provoke her, wise to keep their thoughts to themselves.

Finally, she shook her head in a show of disdain. "You are the Enlightened. I'd hoped for a better array of talent, but I must make do with what is presented."

A few individuals stiffened, affronted by her words. Others looked down with disappointment or frustration in their expressions. Some met her gaze stoically. None spoke.

She ignored their reactions and continued to pace, sizing them up. Their anxiety was palpable, a delicious undercurrent to the scene that fueled her desire to debase them further. There were far too many anemic mages amongst those gathered, far too many potential liabilities, and she did not possess the patience to chaperone them in the heat of battle. It was a disgrace, a testament to Alyra's poor standards and their collective lack of resources.

She ceased pacing and turned to face the gathered Enlightened, her hands clasped behind her. "If I state your name, step forward. You will join the Soulless in battle as we crush Delucha under our heel."

She spoke the names of the nine humans she deemed adequate first. None could boast the same magnitude of power the Murkor possessed, but they would serve their purpose well enough. She reserved Sal'zar's name for last, both as a reminder to him that he was an aberration and as a statement to the others that he was one of them, even if he lacked their master's brand. For his part, Sal'zar nodded imperceptibly and stepped forward to join the other chosen.

She could sense his pale eyes on her as she issued terse instructions to the remainder of the Enlightened. They were to remain in the tower and prepare the newest arrivals to join their ranks while they awaited the army's return for the winter. They would report to Garin in the absence of the other Soulless. Several shuddered visibly at the order; Garin lacked her reputation for bloodshed, but his unique bond with the Nameless had become a topic of great debate—and the source of countless nightmares. It was also no secret that Garin preferred to dole out punishment with his fists before sending a recruit to Alyra for healing. They would be without Alyra's tempering presence during the battle; she had been ordered to fight alongside the other Soulless in spite of her lengthy protests.

As the weak and unimpressive were dismissed, Dranamir took the time to scrutinize the ten she had chosen, her expression impassive. She did not speak until the others were gone.

"Each of you will be permitted the use of one of the tower's relics," she stated. "Report to the top floor at sundown. I will be present to oversee the selections. In the meantime, pack the belongings you require for the journey. One of us will transport you to the army's camp directly once Kama returns from the field. The army is nearly in place, so be prepared for the summons at any time. If you fail to report as directed, you will not share in the glory of watching Delucha crumble to dust, and I will deal with you personally when I return."

She eyed them each in turn, her icy glare impressing upon them the importance of obedience. Failure would result in death.

When no one spoke, she nodded in satisfaction. "You are dismissed."

As they began to exit, she drew the Murkor aside. "We risk a great deal sending you to this battle," she told him in a low tone. "Consider this your final rite of initiation. If you fail to impress me, you will not survive to return with the others."

"I understand."

"Good. Make certain you choose your relic wisely."

"I will."

Her threat was not lost upon him, and she appraised him for another moment. "You continue to surprise me, Sal'zar. Go. You have much to do before nightfall."

Hours later, Dranamir leaned against one of the glass cases on the tower's top floor, her eyes trailing the last of the chosen Enlightened as they departed. Garin paced before the smoked-glass mirror that hung on the adjacent wall, the conduit to their master glaring like a serpent's eye as it reflected the room's light. The small man was agitated, though not at the tedium he'd borne witness to as Dranamir doled out the relics.

He stopped to peer at her as the room quieted. "Kama should have returned by now."

"I'm aware," she replied indifferently. "Perhaps the army met with a delay."

A part of her hoped that delay was in the form of a tall, dark-skinned man with golden eyes. Kama had remained a skeptic of Ravin's purported power, and she no longer cared for the Kamshati's fate. The Soulless would be stronger without him and his constant desire to assert his dominance. Perhaps Ravin would save her the trouble of killing Kama herself. The memory of her humiliation at his hands continued to sting.

"Perhaps." Garin was unconvinced, and he resumed pacing.

"Has our master located Jannyn?" she asked, feigning boredom, though the man's abrupt disappearance had alarmed her. She would not allow Garin to uncover her weakness by putting voice to the idea that Ravin likely had something to do with it.

Garin eyed her suspiciously. "No. He is not dead. He's vanished."

"Perhaps it's for the best." She crossed her arms and smirked. "Jannyn was useless, as I proved on our first meeting."

Garin's scowl deepened, but he did not respond. In that moment, a portal opened in the air between them, revealing Kama's lanky form seconds later. Dranamir sneered at the tall Kamshati, disappointed that he'd returned unscathed from Delucha's outskirts.

He closed the portal and turned to address Garin directly, pointedly ignoring Dranamir. "The army is in position. We plan to attack before dawn."

"Good." Garin smiled coldly. "I will summon the others."

She found herself alone with Kama for the first time in many weeks. He watched her silently, his eyes tracing her every movement in the manner of a hungry predator as she made her way along the glass case. Her avoidance of him had seemed to stoke his appetite, though she had no desire to reciprocate his unspoken lust. What little trust she'd placed in him had been shattered when he'd chosen the Murkor commander's life over her authority.

"Dranamir."

She ignored him and continued to glide alongside the case, inspecting the relics within for the hundredth time.

He growled and muttered a string of curses under his breath. "Gods-damn it, we need to talk. This has gone on long enough."

She whirled to face him, eyes ablaze with unmitigated rage. "There is nothing left to say, Kama. You made your allegiance painfully clear."

He snorted. "You attempted to usurp my authority. What did you fucking expect? You'd have reacted the same if I'd arrived to declare your teaching methods faulty." He shook his head, exasperated. "The Murkor army requires a leader, and Aran'daj is the best they have to offer. I will *not* see him murdered on a whim. *Do you fucking understand?*"

She smirked; she'd finally needled her way beneath his gray, corrupted skin. "Fine. The commander is off limits."

"As is the Arms Master, his second."

She arched an eyebrow. "That was not part of the initial agreement, Kama."

He snarled in frustration. "It's part of the agreement *now.*"

She resisted the urge to laugh. "Very well."

"You play with fire, Dranamir."

"An element I rather enjoy toying with."

Kama opened his mouth to make a final retort, but another portal opened at the room's center. Alyra exited, followed by the ten chosen Enlightened, while Garin brought up the rear. Dranamir assessed the group coldly, mildly disappointed that none of the chosen had failed to heed the summons. After her conversation with Kama, she craved the spilling of blood.

"It seems everything is in order," Alyra said, heedless of the tension within the room.

"About time," Kama growled. "Let's be off. There is still much to do before morning."

CHAPTER FORTY-TWO

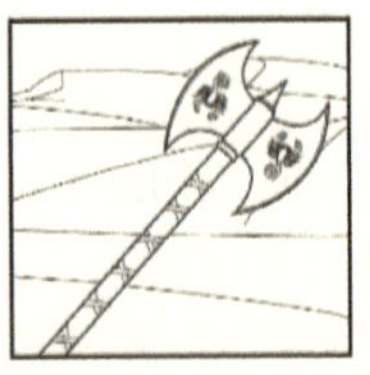

WAR COUNCIL

"The last of our forces are within the city, sir. With the assistance of the queen's advisors, accommodations have been made for everyone." Maryn shook his head, an impressed grin on his feline features. "The city watch and many of our own will guard the walls. I think we'll sleep peacefully enough tonight."

Vardak nodded absently as he studied the map spread on the table before him. "I've told you many times, you don't need to call me 'sir'. You're a friend."

The map depicted the city of Delucha in minute detail, its defenses, its structures, its maze of cobblestone streets. At its heart was the palace complex, ringed by its own wall. Watchtowers adorned the city's walls at intervals. Copious notes were scrawled along the map's margins, hastily written by the queen's military advisor, Jadosin, when he'd stopped to deliver the document in the late afternoon. The notes outlined the locations of the city's defenders, its weapon stores, and its weak points.

Ravin had wasted little time in informing Her Majesty of Emra's arrival, and she'd ordered her advisors to assist Fireblade's wielder in every capacity. Jadosin had been unable to remain at the inn that had become Emra's makeshift headquarters but a few minutes, time enough to share the most critical information with Vardak and no longer. He had his own forces to oversee.

Maryn snickered. "I must set an example for the others, Vardak, *sir*."

Vardak looked up from the map then, unable to hide his amused smile. "You've spent entirely too much time with my brother."

"Ah, that reminds me," Maryn replied in a more serious tone, "Patak asked me to mention that he was escorting Emra to the palace. She has business there."

"It's late for such business, Maryn."

The Felene shrugged. "I know only what Patak told me. Perhaps she had further questions for Ravin."

Vardak nodded. It was plausible, though he wondered if his brother had simply manufactured an excuse to steal away with her for a time. However, Emra might have gone to meet with Ravin a second time, as Maryn indicated. He assumed she had much to discuss with the advisor.

The enigmatic mage may have told them his tale, but he'd sensed Ravin had withheld even more. His apparent desire to protect the city aside, Vardak found it difficult to trust the golden-eyed man. He'd expressed his concerns to Emra on their return from the palace, and she'd shared his sentiments. It was clear Ravin operated according to his own agenda.

"Are the scouts settled in?" he asked of Maryn.

Maryn grinned. "As settled as they will be. Many volunteered for the night watch to keep busy." His gaze flickered to the map. "And what of you, Vardak? Since leaving Dar Daelad, you've scarcely taken a moment for yourself."

"My time is better spent in preparation." He shrugged and pointed at a location along the city's eastern wall. "There's a weak spot here, in the foundation. Jadosin indicated it's been scheduled for repair, but the work hasn't been started yet. If it were elsewhere along the wall, I'd be less concerned. By all accounts, the Murkor—"

He stopped as movement caught his eye. He looked up to find a boy of perhaps ten, dressed in palace livery, crossing the otherwise empty room. He carried a scroll and nervously placed it on the table. He gazed up at Vardak with wide, terrified eyes.

"Who sent you?" Vardak asked quietly as he took up the scroll.

"Advisor Ravin, sir. He said it was urgent, and I should wake you if you were abed." The boy bit his lower lip and clasped his hands together nervously.

"Thank you." Vardak unfurled the message and scanned it quickly.

Murkor have been sighted on the plains less than a mile from the city's eastern flank. Meet me in the palace courtyard as soon as you are able. I have summoned Jadosin and others critical to the city's defense. We have little time to finalize our plans.

He peered up at Maryn and passed him the note. "Rouse the others and await my command."

Maryn glanced at the message and nodded. "Yes, sir."

Vardak turned his attention on the boy as Maryn quickly departed. "I'll accompany you back to the palace. Come."

By the time he reached the palace courtyard, another page was waiting to inform him Ravin and the others were within. He was led to the same chamber where they had spoken at length with the mage earlier in the day. Ravin and Jadosin stood just inside the door, speaking quietly with one another. Radosan sat at the table, his expression circumspect. Seated at the opposite end was a young woman in a resplendent gown of gold silks and ivory lace. She observed the others with a cool, unreadable gaze.

Vardak pushed one of the cushioned chairs aside and settled himself next to Radosan. "Has Emra been summoned?" he asked.

Radosan shrugged. "I'm not certain, though since Ravin sent for you, perhaps he believed her presence wasn't necessary. He mentioned the Drakkon, however. I imagine Aziarah will be arriving soon."

As if on cue, the garnet-scaled countenance of the Drakkon mage appeared in the door. Ravin nodded to her in greeting, and as she seated herself across from Vardak, the golden-eyed mage closed the door. He introduced the aloof young woman seated at the table's head as the queen, Tamarin Serales.

Uncertain of the proper protocol when meeting a human monarch, Vardak made an awkward half-bow in her direction. Her green-eyed gaze swept past him, and she made no effort at welcoming him or the others from Emra's army into the palace. Her behavior puzzled him; Sevic would have acknowledged the visitors and spoken with them directly. He pushed his misgivings aside and decided it wasn't worth troubling himself over. There were more important matters that demanded his attention.

"I summoned you here as soon as I learned our scouts had sighted the Murkor," Ravin stated as he took the open seat between Radosan and the queen. "We must finalize our plans while we can. I suspect they won't wait long to begin the assault."

"I have already ordered the gates to the city be closed and barred," Jadosin added gruffly. "I sent word to the barracks that more soldiers are required on the walls. It's a pity our forces dispatched to Daesan haven't sent word—they've been in pursuit of the Murkor for some time but are several days behind, from what I understand. We could certainly use them tonight."

"And the weak point on the eastern wall?" Vardak asked.

"I've instructed additional soldiers be routed there," Jadosin replied with a faint smile. "I see you've taken some time to study the map."

Vardak nodded. "I have several ideas for how we might go about the military defense, but I must know what the wizards and Ravin have planned."

"We were discussing that before the scout returned," Radosan said quietly. "I will remain with Coreyaless and the other healers, where my skills are best put to use. We plan to set up our base of operations in the palace's outer courtyard. I spoke to the other wizards several hours ago, and they have agreed to follow Ravin's lead during the assault. After all, he is familiar with this city and has greater knowledge of our enemy than we do."

Vardak shifted his gaze to Ravin. "And what do you plan?"

"The Grays will march with your soldiers, as it seems their preference is wielding magic alongside a blade." Ravin shook his head, baffled. "The others will go to the eastern gate with me. We can attack from afar."

Vardak nodded thoughtfully. "I must ask you to look out for Tavesin. He is young, but he will not stand idly by."

"Of course. I'll make certain he remains at my side."

Vardak considered broaching the subject of the Moon's Eye but decided against it. He would relinquish it to Tavesin for use in the battle, if indeed that was the stone's purpose. Vardak believed Tavesin was the more trustworthy mage, despite Flariel's insistence that Ravin become involved.

"I certainly hope you plan to keep the prisoner on your *other* side, Ravin." The queen's tone was cold, unyielding.

"Prisoner?" Radosan echoed, his gaze shifting between the two.

Ravin glared at the tabletop, his jaw clenched in anger. Before he could respond, the queen laughed darkly.

"Oh, yes. Ravin has captured one of the enemy." She smiled coldly. "I don't fully understand how he's done it, but he's...*convinced* that enemy to fight for our side."

"I was coming to that," Ravin growled, his gaze still fixed on the tabletop. "After we met earlier, I returned to the catacombs and retrieved the relic I'd uncovered, thanks to the message you delivered from Solsticia. With it, I can persuade the prisoner to act as an ally."

Radosan stiffed in his seat. "Gods! You cannot mean—"

Ravin looked up, his expression steely. "I do, but perhaps the prisoner's nature will sway your opinion of me. He is one of the Soulless. My treatment of him is no less than he deserves."

Vardak stared at the mage, cold fingers of dread wrapping around his spine. "You keep one of the Soulless *here?*"

"Have no fear, general," Ravin replied, a dangerous light in his golden eyes. "Our prisoner will be fully under my control, and I mean to utilize his power."

Vardak nodded tersely, convinced his previous assessment of Ravin was correct. It was fortunate he'd hesitated to mention the Moon's Eye; Ravin was dangerous, and Vardak trusted him less the more he learned of the man.

"Very well, but I don't like it." Vardak met Ravin's gaze unflinchingly.

"You don't have to like it, general," the queen replied icily. "He acts under my authority. Do not question him."

Vardak raised his eyebrows, unsettled by her words, but he said nothing. Engaging in a pointless argument would do nothing to bolster the city's defense.

"You stated you had an idea." Jadosin's voice cut through the tense silence and forced Vardak to refocus on the task at hand.

"I do." Vardak paused to gather his thoughts. "We will allow the Murkor to engage first. The walls will slow their progress, even if they have the might of the Soulless behind them. We have archers stationed on the walls at present, and the wizards will soon join them. Between them, we should be able to hold the Murkor at bay for some time." He glanced at Aziarah. "I believe your people will be of most use on the walls, as well."

"Of course."

"At an appointed time, we will open the eastern gates," Vardak continued. "Our foot soldiers will be stationed there, and will engage the enemy from that location. At the same time, the cavalry will exit the northern gate and circle around to flank the Murkor. I will accompany them. I can keep pace with the horses."

Jadosin nodded in approval. "Yes, this may work."

"There is one more piece to my plan," Vardak replied evenly. "Emra and her personal guard will leave through the southern gate and circle around from the other direction. She indicated that it's best she work separately. From my understanding, the sword's power can be unpredictable and difficult to control."

Ravin crossed his arms and sat back in his chair. "Then my proposal of reinforcing the eastern wall is in accordance with your own strategy."

Vardak frowned at the mage. "Yes."

"Good. I ought to—"

Ravin was interrupted as the door burst open and crashed against the wall. Patak skittered inside, his expression distraught, as Emra lay unconscious in his arms. Her lips moved, forming muted whispers that Vardak could not hear. Patak ignored most of those gathered and made his way toward Radosan.

"They said you'd be here," he explained breathlessly as he lay her carefully on the floor. "I don't know what happened. One moment we were walking, the next, she stumbled and began to convulse. I went to the inn, but Maryn indicated you were here."

Radosan rose swiftly and motioned Patak to stand aside. Ravin and Aziarah quickly joined the healer, though Ravin kept a respectful distance. Radosan leaned over her, his eyes scanning her features in concern. After a moment, he met Aziarah's gaze, and the two nodded.

"She is not ill, Patak," Radosan said quietly. "She has fallen into a trance."

Patak shook his head, bewildered. "I don't understand."

Ravin moved forward, his gaze flicking between the others. "I've seen this condition before. There is a way to awaken her quickly."

Radosan sighed. "Yes, but I lack the skill to do so. The last wizard capable of reading the past in the form of a trance departed for Aeon's realm decades ago. The council deemed it unnecessary that Greens maintain the ability."

"Luckily for you, I was never bound by the convoluted laws of your council," Ravin replied. "May I?"

Vardak met his brother's terrified gaze and wished there were something he could do to assist, but it seemed Emra's sudden collapse was a matter of magic alone. Patak swallowed hard and looked away.

"Do what you must," he said quietly. "Will she be alright?"

"The trance cannot be controlled," Ravin replied. "It's likely this will happen again when she least expects it. She will awaken with no memory of this, or of what she may say once I induce her to conclude her vision."

Ravin knelt beside Emra and held his hands a short distance above her face. He closed his eyes, and as Vardak watched, a faint glow suffused his palms. Beneath him, Emra gasped and her back arched as though she were in great pain. Her eyes fluttered open to reveal the sclera alone; the gray irises had rolled back into her skull. When her lips next moved, she began to speak aloud.

"Lukin was innocent, murdered for the crimes of his kin. An usurper sits upon the eagle's throne with the blood of the rightful heir staining—"

Emra's words were drowned out by an angry snarl from the queen. "What is the meaning of this madness?" she demanded, her voice growing in volume as Emra continued to speak. "I will not have this blasphemy spewed in my hall!"

Vardak looked between her and Ravin, whose bronze skin had grown ashen. His haunted gaze was fixed on the queen's, horror and shock in the depths of his eyes. The queen glared at him in furious challenge as Emra's voice faded.

"I've been a gods-damned fool," he whispered into the sudden silence. He stumbled to his feet and shook his head. "You're no better than Dranamir. You killed them to secure your crown."

She crossed her arms and frowned in icy disdain. "It was the only way, Ravin."

"No." Ravin's voice was hoarse. "No, it wasn't. I will ensure this city's defense, Your Majesty, but consider this my resignation. I'll have nothing to do with a gods-damned murderer."

Vardak watched as Ravin turned on his heel and fled the room. He didn't fully understand what had just transpired, but it was clear Emra's trance-induced words had shaken the mage to his core. He glanced toward the queen who sneered at him, then gathered her skirts and stormed out of the room in a swish of silks. He looked helplessly at Jadosin, hoping the military advisor could provide some insight into the affair.

"I cannot claim to understand the workings of magic, but from Ravin's reaction, I believe the wrong man was hung for the death of our late king and queen." Jadosin's countenance was drawn, his eyes a mirror of the abject horror Vardak had spied in Ravin's. "I believe the queen will have more than one advisor to replace in the coming days, should we survive this battle."

Emra moaned, and Vardak turned his attention to her once more. She was paramount to the success of his plans, and he prayed she had suffered no lasting damage from her strange malady.

Emra coughed weakly and sat up, blinking her gray eyes in confusion as Patak rushed to her side. She rubbed her temples and grimaced. "Gods, I have a headache. What happened?"

CHAPTER FORTY-THREE

SHATTERED TRUST AND HIDDEN RELICS

He'd been a damned fool, and it was no one's fault but his own. He'd trusted the queen blindly, believing the girl a victim of her unfortunate circumstances. He knew her parents had been killed and learned after entering her employ that her older brother, Lukin, had hanged for the crime. In her state of vulnerability and grief, Ravin had mistakenly believed the Soulless had taken advantage of her. When he routed them from the palace, he'd believed he had saved an innocent from their clutches.

His belief meant nothing. His trust was shattered, and he knew he would never be welcome in the palace again once the battle had been won. He knew her secret, a secret he was certain would drive her to murder again to maintain. Rather than travel immediately to the dungeon in order to secure Jannyn, Ravin went first to Adalin's quarters.

It was past midnight, and though he was loathe to wake her, she was the only person who would fully understand his plight. He also feared the queen would strike at the duchess simply because she'd become close to Ravin. It was no longer safe for either of them to remain in the palace.

He rapped loudly on her door, and only then took the time to survey his surroundings. The corridor was lit by a single torch some distance away from the duchess' chamber. In spite of the darkness, he believed no one else was present to take note of his late-night visit. He feared the repercussions should word find its way to the queen and chastised himself for his lapse in focus.

It was several moments before Adalin cracked the door open and peered at him through bleary eyes. "Ravin? Gods, what time is it?"

"It doesn't matter, and I can't stay long." He glanced along the hallway again. "May I come in? I don't want to risk being overheard."

A troubled frown creased her brow. "Ravin, I'm in my nightclothes."

"This is important, Adalin. I wouldn't have come otherwise."

With a sigh, she relented and stepped back to open the door further. "If anyone *has* seen you here, I suppose we can use it to bolster our ruse."

Ravin shrugged and began to pace, his agitation propelling him forward. "Our ruse…I suppose that's why I've come."

She began to rummage in the wardrobe, but he paid her no mind.

"Adalin, I've resigned my post. My conscience would not allow me to remain in the employ of a…of the queen." He grimaced; he wasn't certain he should reveal the entire scenario to the duchess, and he'd nearly made another lapse. His shock at the news ran deep, rattling his core at a time when he required crystalline focus.

"Why, Ravin? What happened?"

He continued to pace the length of her room while he pondered the best course of action. Time was running short, the Murkor were at their door, and he must secure Jannyn before the assault began. This business with the queen's ascension had arrived at the worst possible moment. Silently, he cursed Minora for the poor timing, though he knew it was unlikely the goddess had played a hand in the event.

"Some news came to light regarding the queen. I cannot remain at her side, Adalin. She's…she's not the innocent I've believed she was." Ravin sighed. "What I overheard puts us both at risk. Even if you do not know the details, she will seek revenge on you for your perceived attachment to me."

"You're telling me that I must leave."

He looked up at the hollow tone in her voice. She had donned her riding attire, but was now perched on the end of the wide, canopied bed, staring at the pair of boots she held in her hands.

"Yes. I'm sorry."

"I have nowhere to go, Ravin. You know this."

His heart ached at her words. "I know." He reached into a pocket to withdraw his coin purse; it would be enough to see her lodged in the best of Delucha's inns for several months. He strode toward her and pressed it into her palm. "Take it. It was my monthly stipend. I haven't spent any of it."

"Ravin, I can't take this. What will you do?"

He managed a half-hearted grin. "I'm a mage, Adalin. I'll conjure more coin if I need to."

She laughed softly. "But that's unethical."

"What choice do I have?"

She drew him into a brief embrace. When she stepped back, tears glistened in her eyes. "Ravin, I sincerely hope this is not our last goodbye."

He nodded. "As do I. If you go to the Three Roses Inn, tell them I've sent you…but perhaps you ought to use an assumed name. They'll make arrangements. Emra and her guard are staying there as well. You'll be safe."

"If I must leave and go into hiding, please tell me the full story. I deserve to know."

He drew a breath and conceded to her request. He told her of the Murkor sighting, the meeting, his plans for the battle, and the panicked interruption by Patak. He recited the words Emra had spoken, the words that continued to batter at the brittle foundations of his trust. The queen had committed murder to secure her throne, an act he could not condone nor abide.

Adalin was silent for several moments as she processed his tale. "There have been rumors that Lukin was innocent, but no one could prove them. You're right, Ravin. We both must leave."

"I will seek you after the battle is done," he promised.

"You'd best keep your word," she replied through a threatening veil of tears. "Go, Ravin. You have much to do before the attack begins."

Ravin made his way into the dungeons beneath the castle, alone in the Aethereum. He was dimly aware that none of his traps or alarms had been triggered, but it brought him cold comfort. He vowed when the battle was done, he would unravel all of his work. The queen was unworthy of his continued protection.

He withdrew the talisman from within his pocket and grasped it tightly before he exited the Aethereum once more. He found himself in the dank corridor, steps away from Jannyn's cell. It was lightless; the guards had either forgone their evening ritual of lighting torches, or they'd been called away to assist in the city's defense. Ravin created a magical light, then cautiously connected his power with the talisman's for the second time.

Jannyn stirred on the moldering straw mat he'd been given for use as a bed. The Soulless grumbled unintelligibly and turned onto his side, his gray features seeming to shun the faint illumination.

Ravin was thankful the man was asleep. Even with the talisman's remarkable power, he feared the Soulless would struggle to maintain his freedom from Ravin's control. It would have been an expenditure of energy better saved for the battle, but one he no longer needed to concern himself with. Asleep, Jannyn was vulnerable.

Ravin funneled the talisman's power into the slumbering form on the opposite side of the iron bars. Jannyn inhaled sharply as Ravin took hold of his mind. His eyes snapped open and rolled upward, the crimson irises invisible within their sockets.

Ravin shuddered and stumbled against the nearby wall as he grappled with the depravity contained within Jannyn's twisted mind. He was the orchestrator of countless atrocities, the least of which was his own mind-control over Jasom Riversend. His cruelty was a match for Dranamir's, though his strength in magic would never compare to hers. Jannyn was responsible for the deaths of thousands and the torture of thousands more.

His stomach slithering in oily knots, Ravin forced himself to ignore the Soulless' perversity and instead instructed the man to rise and move to the cell door. Jannyn's movements were erratic and his limbs jerked as though he were a poorly operated marionette. Ravin lacked the time required to understand the full mechanics at work in the mind-control magic; the man's unsteady gait would simply remain a symptom of his possession.

Ravin swallowed his distaste and unlocked the cell door. He ordered Jannyn to follow him as he made his way through the darkened corridors toward the stairs that would lead them up to the palace proper. He could not risk transporting Jannyn through the Aethereum; his grasp on the mind-control magic was limited, and he couldn't be certain the rules of the magical realm would not interfere with the process. Even subdued as he was, Jannyn's magical abilities outshone most of the wizards gathered in the city. He was a valuable weapon in Ravin's arsenal.

As they reached the main level of the palace, they encountered a number of servants scurrying about on errands as they prepared for the coming assault. Most were too consumed in their work to give the pair more than a passing glance, though several paused to openly gape at Jannyn's corrupted form.

Ravin ignored the stares and the few stammered questions he received and pressed on. He could sense the passage of time and the dwindling number of minutes left to him before the Murkor struck. He must lead the staggering Soulless to the eastern gates and find Tavesin prior to the onslaught. He'd given Vardak his word to watch over the boy, but he also felt a strange kinship with the young wizard in spite of their age difference. He saw much of his younger self reflected in Tavesin.

The city's streets were devoid of townspeople, but a steady stream of armored soldiers walked the streets as they rallied to their assigned positions. Ravin led Jannyn toward the eastern wall, where the greatest number of foot soldiers had gathered. Jadosin and several of his trusted officers paced through the ranks, issuing orders and offering encouragement as needed. Two dozen wizards clustered to one side, each armored in their own fashion, at ease amongst the other soldiers. Ravin suspected they were the Grays Radosan had mentioned.

Atop the wall, Ravin spied pairs of archers spaced at intervals, and between them, the handful of wizards that would engage the enemy from afar. He led Jannyn to the nearest watchtower and up the narrow flight of steps that would take them to the wall's apex. Once there, he made his way to the nearest wizard, who seemed to recognize him though they'd never met.

"Where is Tavesin?"

The woman pointed north. "Just there, sir. Radosan informed us of your plan. We're ready."

He nodded. "Good. I must remain with the boy. If the world were less cruel, he would be miles away from this fight."

"He's been expecting you, sir." She offered a tentative smile. "I'm pleased someone here can watch over him."

It was several moments before Tavesin's silhouette coalesced out of the gloom. He stood at the wall's edge, gripping the ledge of stone before him as he peered eastward. A sea of twinkling lights filled the plains, the fires of the enemy camp marking the Murkors' location. Tavesin's young face was drawn, but Ravin detected no fear within him, only determination.

"Tavesin," he called at their approach.

The boy turned at the sound, and a relieved grin spread across his face. "Ravin! I was hoping you'd arrive soon. I…I need your help." He bit his lower lip and looked down uncertainly.

Ravin positioned Jannyn on his right and lifted his eyebrows in question at Tavesin. "What is it?"

"Well, sir, you know some of Vardak's business with Flariel, but not the whole of his story." Tavesin glanced up at Ravin sheepishly. "He was sent to retrieve a relic, sir. Flariel told him there were only two people capable of using it…Me, and you."

Ravin scowled, angered that the relic had not been mentioned in their previous discussions. "What manner of relic is it? And why did no one inform me of this?"

Tavesin chewed his lip before he made his response. "Vardak doesn't trust you," he admitted finally. "But I don't care. He gave it to me, but I don't know how to use it. None of my lessons covered how to use such things, and Badolo only *creates* them. He was no help."

Ravin pushed aside his questions regarding Badolo and studied Tavesin carefully. "I can explain what you must do, but I cannot demonstrate it for you. Linking with two relics is dangerous, and I will not risk losing control of our captive."

Tavesin nodded. "I understand." He pulled at a cord hanging from his neck and pulled a green-white, teardrop-shaped stone from beneath his tunic. It emanated a soft light. "It's called the Moon's Eye, sir."

Ravin was familiar with the name and its associated story. His mother had been the relic's keeper for centuries. "I didn't believe I'd ever see that relic in the hands of a mage," he whispered. "The cost of obtaining it was too great…"

Again, Tavesin nodded. "I know, sir. Vardak would not pass the stone to just anyone. He said it would be an 'affront to Janna's memory' if he gave it to you." He looked down at the stone helplessly. "What must I do?"

"The Moon's Eye is as powerful as the relic I possess, Tavesin. You must be very cautious when linking with it. If you are not, its energy will consume you."

"I understand, sir."

Ravin wished fate had granted the boy a life of normalcy, where he would be leagues away from Delucha, safe in his home without one of the greatest magical artifacts clutched in his hand. His obvious strength in magic had trumped his youth, and the wizards had sent him to the front lines of a war that would destroy many. He prayed Tavesin would not be among the fallen by the war's end. He deserved a chance at life, at peace.

Reluctantly, Ravin began to instruct the young wizard on the process of linking as the first cadence of the Murkor drums began to echo across the plain.

CHAPTER FORTY-FOUR

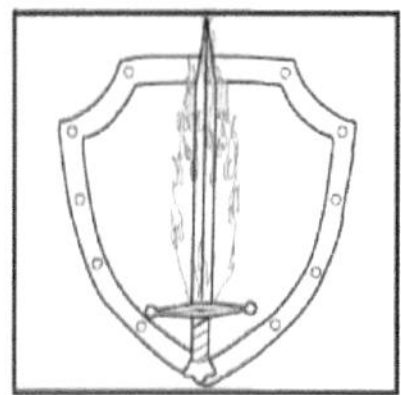

THE BLADE ERUPTS

Drums pounded a rhythmic cadence in the distance as they reached the southern gate. Emra glanced at Patak warily, though she needed no confirmation of what the noise signified. The Murkor were in formation, the order to charge had been issued, and the assault would soon begin. Patak glared in the direction of the sound as he unsheathed his mace and adjusted the shield strapped to his left arm.

"I hope your brother's signal is visible," one of the guards said from behind them.

Patak smirked. "Vardak is nothing if not thorough. We'll see it, when the time comes."

"Waiting is the most difficult part of any battle," Emra added without turning to face the soldier who had addressed Patak. "But we must, if this plan is to work."

Emra sensed the barrage of magical energy before it became visible above the rooftops in the east. She tensed, and her hand strayed to Fireblade's hilt as fire and lightning rained from the sky. Just as she feared the eastern wall would be lost to the Soulless' assault, a dazzling wall of shimmering blue sprang to life and deflected much of the attack. She smiled sadly; Tavesin was young, but he was proving himself capable.

"How are we to differentiate the general's signal from that blasted magical rubbish?" a woman snarled behind her.

"Vardak is at the northern gate," Patak reminded them with a grin. "The signal will come from his position. Focus there."

Emra was impressed at the deftness with which Patak handled those under his command. Unlike the others, she'd given him the post simply because she knew he would protect her with his life. He was often excitable and impatient, but he was beginning to prove himself a leader as well. Perhaps it was due to the fact his youngest brother was in command of the army, and Patak desired to compete with him, or perhaps he acted as he did in order to impress Emra. Regardless of his reason, Emra was pleased with the change. There was no one else she trusted as implicitly as she did Patak with the exception of Lucas, but Lucas' talents were better utilized elsewhere.

She watched as a return volley of flaming arrows and magical missiles issued from the eastern wall to bombard the foes hidden beyond, much of the arcane counterattack concentrated from a single location. She had no doubt it was Ravin and his prisoner leading the assault.

She frowned, troubled by the mage's secretive behavior, though she understood some of his reasoning. His unfortunate history undoubtedly made it difficult for him to place his trust in anyone, but she wished he'd informed them of his prisoner upon their first meeting. She could have provided further insight about the man, having dealt with most of the Soulless personally in her previous lives. She shook her head in frustration; dwelling on the matter would solve nothing. Ravin's decision had been made, and he was carrying out his schemes at present—though she grudgingly admitted she rather enjoyed the notion of forcing one of the Soulless to fight against his own.

"Are you feeling well, Em?" Patak asked quietly, drawing her from the mire of her thoughts.

She looked up at him and nodded. "Yes, the headache has gone. I was merely thinking."

"Judging from your expression, I'd say you weren't pleased with those thoughts." He smiled though she could see concern in his eyes.

"It's a matter to discuss later."

"There's our signal!" One of the guards called.

Emra turned to face north and watched the brilliant orange flare they'd been watching for arc high into the predawn sky. She unsheathed Fireblade and felt the weapon respond to her touch. She held it aloft, a signal to her small group to follow her lead. As they began to surge toward the southern gate, the soldiers atop the wall worked the winches to pull it open.

It would take a half-hour to reach a suitable location in which to strike the Murkor army on foot. Emra had briefly considered acquiring mounts for the others, but Fyrmane had proven skittish each time she'd wielded Fireblade in his presence. It was best to leave the animals behind for the sake of everyone's safety. Fireblade's power was immense and difficult to control, a relic designed for devastation.

"Vardak and the cavalry will reach the northern flank long before we'll be in position." Patak rolled his shoulders and grinned. "I hope my brother saves some action for our group."

"There will be plenty left to do," she replied quietly as they passed through the gate. "Even if the Murkor have been routed by the time we reach our destination, there will be much to do."

Patak's grin faltered and was replaced by a grim expression. "Indeed."

They followed the city's wall as it curved gently eastward. Once off the southern road, they were forced to wade through knee-high grasses, the stalks brown and brittle as winter approached. Several guards stationed upon the wall called to them as they passed, wishing them Blademon's favor and Karmada's blessing in their endeavor.

"I'd rather not garner Karmada's notice," Patak grumbled beside her.

"Nor would I," she agreed with a wry smile, "though I'm not certain I'd be comfortable with your patron's interference, either."

The cacophony of battle gradually grew louder as they pressed on. Shouts and curses filled the air, both in the common tongue and the fluid, musical language of the Murkor. Steel crashed, energy crackled through the air, bowstrings sang and snapped, soldiers and horses screamed, but from their position along the wall, Emra could see little of the goings-on. She knew enough of battle to anticipate chaos amidst the ranks on both sides, and her entrance on the field with Fireblade would only serve to enhance it.

"When we reach our position, you must all remain behind me and follow my lead," she instructed with a glance over her shoulder.

Her guards acknowledged the words, though she sensed they didn't fully understand the importance of them. They would learn soon; anyone unfortunate enough to be caught in Fireblade's path would not survive the encounter. It was a weapon forged in the last days of the Time of Chaos, meant to put an end to the centuries-long bloodshed in the most dramatic and terrible of fashions.

As its creator, she'd tied her soul to the weapon, fearing its power would be used to destroy entire civilizations if it fell into the wrong hands. Only she could wield its power, and when Aeon finally deigned to put a stop to the cycle of her rebirth, the Fireblade would become nothing more than a decorative sword. Aeon had informed her, in his typical, evasive style, that the cycle would continue until the Nameless was no longer a threat. She was tethered to her fate until that time came to pass, but how many lives would be snuffed out in the interim?

She'd paid a dire price to forge the blade, and each use weighed more heavily upon her heart than the last. How many thousands had been killed over the centuries by her hand? How many more must perish before the servants of the Nameless god were finally vanquished?

She was roused from her grim thoughts as they neared a watchtower and a sharp bend in the city's wall. The clash of combatants on the field rang through the cool autumn air, individual voices becoming more distinct as their destination drew closer. On the wall above, a gruff tone shouted commands to the archers, and moments later a volley of arrows flew across the bloodied plain.

She glanced at Patak. "Whatever transpires, make certain they stay to the rear. I don't wish to bring harm to anyone who doesn't deserve it."

"Em—" he began to protest, but she shook her head firmly.

"This relic is dangerous. It is my burden to bear it, and it is yours to ensure my safety while I wield it. You cannot fulfill your duty if you're maimed, or worse." She sighed heavily. "I am weary of this role, Patak, but there is no other who can take up the mantle. The Fireblade is my creation, and so I must suffer the consequences of its existence. In each life, I return for the sole purpose of defeating the Soulless and weakening the Nameless god. My relic was designed for death. Please do not stand in its path, and make certain the others do not, either. I cannot abide losing you…Any of you.”

“We’re not going anywhere, Em. Least of all, me.” Patak grinned roguishly. “I believe we’re all aware of the risks. Do what you came to do—we’re here to watch your back.”

She smiled in spite of herself. Patak had that effect on her, and she hoped it would never fade. “Thank you.”

He nodded and gestured to the bend in the wall, paces away. “Tell us where to stand, Em. We’ll hold that position. We’ve all come here because we believe in you, because we trust you, and I will do my damnedest to make certain you walk away from this battle to fight another day.”

Bolstered by his words, she straightened and strode to the corner of the wall. She peered around its stony circumference to assess the scene before them. Hooded Murkor stretched across the eastern plain, weapons forged of poisoned black metal clutched in their tattooed blue hands. An arc of fiery energy burst through the air from a position at the rear of the Murkor ranks to explode ineffectively against a shimmering shield that appeared over the wall moments later. She traced the fire’s source to a cluster of figures.

Even from a distance, she recognized the long, angular features of Kama and the diminutive form of the dark-haired Alyra. There were others with them, though only one possessed the graying features and crimson eyes that marked her as Soulless. Emra had never battled Dranamir, but she was familiar with the woman’s handiwork and had seen the aftermath she’d left in her wake. Of the three Soulless in her field of view, Emra feared Dranamir the most.

She pointed Fireblade’s tip in the direction of the Soulless. “They are my target. Anything standing in the path between myself and the Soulless will rue their current position.” She turned to look at the others. “Guard my flank, but do not cross my path. We will cut our way through and pray that Ravin holds their attention for a while longer.”

As the others took up their positions, she linked her magic with the blade’s. Flames coursed along its cutting edges in response, a meager precursor to the firestorm she was preparing to unleash.

"We move on your signal," Patak stated, his eyes narrowed as he surveilled the Murkor in their path.

The Murkor hadn't taken notice of them yet, but they would soon. Emra gripped the Fireblade, and resolved once more to do what the gods had deemed necessary. "It is time."

A curtain of flame erupted from the sword, carving a gash through the battlefield and incinerating the nearest Murkor. Fireblade's entrance into the fray was met with screams of terror and agony from both sides, screams that Emra strove to ignore. Friend or foe, the weapon was indiscriminate in its destruction. She channeled the flames along a path toward the Soulless as the dried grasses began to ignite around the Murkor army. Those too slow to evade the fire were burned to ash in seconds, but their screams would haunt her for eternity, just as those of their unfortunate predecessors did.

She relinquished the flames, sickened once more by the act that had won her renown in ages past. The earth was scorched in the wake of Fireblade's blazing discharge, the grasses on the edge of the devastation charred to mere cinders. A channel of devastation led from her location into the heart of the fray. The nearby Murkor who had managed to avoid a direct strike suffered blistering burns and severed limbs.

She would be forced to press forward if she intended the inferno to reach the Soulless, but at what cost?

Patak's horrorstruck tone greeted her ears over the sound of the Murkors' agonized cries. Her heart wrenched, and sudden tears of shame pricked her eyes as he spoke.

"Fucking gods. I'd never wish this fate on anyone."

CHAPTER FORTY-FIVE

JANNYN'S FATE

She sensed Ravin's presence as soon as he arrived atop the city's walls. From her position at the rear of the Murkor army, Dranamir could not see his figure, but his telltale energy signature was unmistakable. There were others along the walls and some within—wizards, she suspected. None would pose a threat to her singly apart from one who stood very near Ravin. As she scanned the area, she sensed yet another presence with Ravin, one that she hadn't accounted for previously. Jannyn was atop Delucha's wall, assisting with her enemy's schemes.

Fury suffused her and she nearly lashed out to strike the traitor down. Kama loomed at her side, the only factor that staid her hand. His plan relied on precise timing, and a premature strike on her part would undo much of his work. She would risk a reprimand by their master and the possibility of finding herself collared. It was a fate she would not accept.

She turned to face the tall Kamshati, fists clenched at her side. "Jannyn has betrayed us."

Kama closed his eyes briefly. She watched as his mouth twisted into a sneer. When he opened his eyes once more, they glowed balefully. "I suppose that explains his lengthy disappearance. I'll kill the worthless shit."

"Not if I do it first." Dranamir smirked. "You have the Murkor to oversee. I'll make certain his end is painful."

Kama nodded stiffly. "Once I signal the attack, strike that bastard down. End him."

"Gladly."

She fingered the relic she'd chosen for herself, a palm-sized ebony disk carved with a likeness of the wind god, Cirrus. The relic did not enhance her power but merely extended its range. She would not be forced to draw any nearer to the wall or the physical fighting than her present location. If Ravin were to locate her amongst the throng, she had no doubt he would rain his terrible power upon her. Garin had relayed the man's desire for revenge, and with Ravin no longer bound to the Nameless' will, he was a greater threat than the whole of Delucha's army.

What had he done to convince Jannyn to turn upon the Soulless, to shun the orders of their master? Ravin's power was unrivaled, but even *he* could not force one of the Soulless to bend to his will. The bond they shared with their master did not allow it, which left only one motive for Jannyn's betrayal—Ravin had promised him something greater, something Jannyn coveted beyond the glory of the Nameless' return.

She scowled at the realization that only Alyra might understand what had driven Jannyn's deception. The other woman was positioned some distance away, near the southern fringe of the army's ranks, too distant to reach before the assault began. Dranamir would not risk entering the Aethereum with Ravin so near, and Alyra could be interrogated later. She hoped Alyra was complicit in Jannyn's schemes; she desired to see the other woman ruined beyond redemption in the Nameless' eyes.

"Be ready." Kama's voice cut through her reverie.

She watched as he strode ahead to confer with the Murkor commander. Moments later, the commander lifted his black saber skyward and the drummers arrayed at the rear of the army began to pound a threatening cadence. The black-clad soldiers surged forward at the sound, their heavy boots stomping in time to the beat. It was the signal Dranamir had been awaiting.

She grasped the disc in her hand and harnessed her power. She sent a volley of charged energy bolts in Jannyn's direction while some of the nearby Enlightened moved forward in the army's wake, seeking a better location for their own attacks. Dranamir watched as her first offensive neared the wall, then was summarily deflected as an impressive shield erupted an instant before her magic would have hit its mark.

She narrowed her eyes, enraged. Defensive shields of that magnitude were not Ravin's style, nor were they Jannyn's. That left only the powerful stranger she'd sensed earlier—a Blue wizard if she was not mistaken. Blues had always proven a thorn in her side, and this one was the strongest she'd ever encountered. She must alter her tactic with the wizard's ability revealed.

In order to destroy Jannyn and deal with Ravin, the wizard must be removed from the equation first.

Before she had the opportunity to consider her next move, a counterstrike from the wall was launched. Magical attacks in an array of forms streamed through the predawn sky to land amongst the Murkor, while archers began to fire arrows tipped with flame upon those in the front lines. Several of the Enlightened used their skills to deflect some of the attacks, but dozens of Murkor fell victim to the onslaught.

Moments later, a brilliant orange flare burst above the city. She narrowed her eyes with renewed suspicion; flares were the work of alchemists. Unless Delucha had arranged trade with the Murkor prior to the Soulless' return, the humans should not have such items in their arsenal. An equally unlikely scenario was the presence of Scorpion Men in the city. No, it was undoubtedly the work of Jannyn, the flares stolen from the army before he offered himself to Ravin in betrayal.

She noted the commander shifted his position as he signaled the drummers. The beat changed subtly, and the army responded to the unspoken order. He understood the significance of the flare; the city's defenders were preparing to mount their own offensive.

Dranamir struck at Ravin's location a second time, mustering a more powerful attack that would prove difficult for even the most skilled of Blue wizards to deflect. She would make good on her promise to Kama before the battle was won; Jannyn would lie writhing at her feet, screaming for a mercy that she would never give.

Rage was supplanted by astonishment as another, more powerful shield shimmered into existence and her magic was absorbed. Ravin had recruited an impressive ally, but like all wielders of magic, the wizard would eventually reveal a source of weakness that could be exploited. She resolved to continue her assaults, probing for a chink in the wizard's defense as she did so. Eventually the wizard would falter, and in that instant Dranamir would pounce.

Kama reappeared at her side, though she was dimly aware of his presence as she struck time and again at Ravin's location. Her concentration was shattered, however, with the entrance of a new threat upon the field. A sinuous curtain of flame slashed across the battlefield from the south. It incinerated everything in its path and left those on the fringes maimed or burned. Their agonized screams tore through the early morning air as a momentary stillness settled over the scene.

Kama froze, his eyes riveted to the magical fire. "Fuck."

Dranamir felt the icy grip of dread on her spine as she gauged his reaction. Kama had never shown fear, but his eyes were wide with terror as he watched the flames consume dozens of Murkor before suddenly winking from existence.

"You know something, Kama. Tell me."

"The Fireblade. There were no indications its wielder had been reborn, nothing to convince me that weapon would make its appearance today." He shook his head, his expression haunted. "I failed to account for this."

Dranamir knew of the relic in passing, though she'd never experienced its fury firsthand. The other Soulless had, and if Kama's reaction were proof of its power, its presence could change the course of the battle in Ravin's favor.

"Then we must adapt," she snapped. "Is this blade a greater threat than Ravin? I will concentrate my efforts elsewhere, if need be."

Kama shook his head, helpless in the face of the latest development. "We cannot hope to overcome them both, Dranamir. We lack the forces. The Enlightened are too few."

"Do you suggest retreat, then?"

He tore his gaze away from the spectacle and nodded imperceptibly. "It may be the only way. If we retreat and return to the tower, it will be spring before the mountains are passable again. This was to be our final strike before winter." He ran one hand through his dark hair as his eyes darted across the battlefield. "Gods-damn it, this changes everything for the worse. I'd hoped to never witness that fucking sword in action again."

Dranamir crossed her arms. "You're afraid."

"You should be, too," he snarled. "That blade and its wielder were responsible for the downfall of every last one of us, Dranamir. You're the exception."

She shrugged indifferently. "Surely the four of us together can overwhelm this—"

"Don't delude yourself, Dranamir. You are ignorant of what that blade is capable of. I say we must retreat. We can use the winter months to grow our numbers, and when spring arrives, perhaps we'll have the numbers required to deal with the Fireblade and your nemesis both."

"It is *your* decision, Kama. As you made it abundantly clear, I am not to interfere in your militaristic decisions."

"Fucking gods, Dranamir! Now is not the time to devolve into petty arguments. I must—"

His words were cut short by the appearance of a portal steps in front of them. Jannyn stumbled out, his eyes wild and face more ashen than was its norm. He glanced behind him as the portal swiftly closed, but Dranamir had sensed Ravin on the other side.

While Jannyn attempted to recover his faculties, she cut him from the source of his power and created a razor-sharp tendril of air. She slashed it across his collarbones, only deep enough to penetrate the outer layers of his skin. The dingy shirt he wore was rent and fell away in tatters.

"You have some gall returning here," she hissed at him as he cried out in surprise and terror.

"Dranamir, I can explain—"

She rent another gash in his flesh, perpendicular to the first. "There's no need, Jannyn. It's clear where your allegiance lies."

"I wasn't myself!" He bellowed as she used her magic and began to peel the flesh away from her incisions, revealing the bloody muscle and sinew beneath.

"Lies will not save you."

Jannyn screamed and fell to his knees as tears began to leak from his eyes. "D-Dranamir, p-please listen…"

"Your actions today spoke volumes."

As she forced the magical incisions to strip the flesh from his abdomen, Jannyn shrieked wordlessly. A foul stench wafted from him as he defecated, the intensity of his agony overwhelming his bodily functions. Dranamir fixed him in an icy gaze and continued with the surgical removal of his corrupted, gray flesh. She'd promised Kama that she would ensure Jannyn suffered for every ounce of his treachery, after all.

"Dranamir!" Alyra's breathless voice cried.

Dranamir shifted her gaze to take in the other woman's horrified countenance. "Traitors must be punished."

"Shouldn't we allow our master to decide his fate?" Alyra demanded in a tremulous tone. "Oh, gods, Jannyn…"

Dranamir ignored the protest and continued her work mercilessly. Jannyn began to retch as the flesh was pared away from his arms and the more sensitive region of his groin in tandem. His eyes rolled wildly as he sought interference from one of the others that did not come.

"D-Dranamir…" he wheezed. "R-ravin…He…" Jannyn shrieked as her assault reached his wrists and the cluster of nerve endings near his hands. "Mind-c-c-control…"

Dranamir snorted. "Even Ravin does not possess that power, nor would he engage in such behavior. I believe he once told me it was 'distasteful'." Her lips curled in disgust at the grotesque, bleeding heap of rubbish that called himself Jannyn. "Try again."

"Dranamir, what if he speaks true?" Alyra demanded. "If Ravin *has*—"

Dranamir sneered at the other woman. "We both know that's an impossibility. I've long believed you inept, but even you must admit the reality we face. Jannyn has betrayed us and our master."

"I'm not willing to allow him to throw my plans into further disarray," Kama growled. "Kill him, Dranamir, and be done with it. I must speak with the commander."

Alyra released a strangled moan, then turned on her heel and fled, leaving Jannyn alone with his tormentor. Dranamir smiled maliciously.

"P-please," Jannyn begged. "See reason…"

"I already have."

She maneuvered the sharp tendril of air to the side of Jannyn's neck and pressed its tip against the bulging artery just far enough to release a trickle of blood with each panicked beat of his heart. His crimson eyes pled silently, a wild hope in their depths as he prayed for salvation. She would provide him with the release he sought, though his pain would be eternal once his soul was banished to the Nameless god's realm. Their master did not suffer failure and would not allow Jannyn's treachery to go unpunished.

"You have disgraced our master for the last time."

Jannyn opened his mouth to scream as Dranamir slashed the magical blade viciously across his neck, severing the artery, spinal cord, and esophagus in an instant. Jannyn's head bounced to the ground with a sickening thud while his maimed body fell forward to land at her feet.

"I do not abide traitors."

CHAPTER FORTY-SIX

BLADEMON'S CHOSEN

Murkor drums beat rhythmically in the distance, a cadence meant to signal their forces to begin moving toward the wall. Vardak analyzed the nuances of the sound in the darkness before dawn from his position near Delucha's northern gate. Lucas and the cavalry, most of them soldiers from Santine, began to mount up and unsheathe their weapons.

Vardak glanced at Lucas. "We wait for Jadosin's word, then I'll send the signal to Emra's party. We do not move until then."

Lucas smiled grimly. "And when we do, we give the bastards hell."

"Are you sure you'll keep up, general?" one of the Santinians and Lucas' recently named second, Danian, asked from his other side. He flashed a lopsided grin, his dark eyes gleaming with mischief.

Vardak chuckled. "My people don't require horses to grant us speed on the battlefield. You'll see."

"A race, then." Danian's grin widened. "We'll see who draws first blood this day."

Vardak counted the minutes from the onset of the drums while they awaited word from the eastern gate. The sky above Delucha began to erupt into a dazzling display of magical energy as Ravin and the wizards engaged in battle with the Soulless.

He prayed the scheming mage would keep his word and watch over Tavesin; the boy needed guidance, and despite Vardak's misgivings, Tavesin was star-struck by Ravin. He'd insisted upon a position near the eastern gate where the Murkor assault would be the most concentrated, simply to ensure he'd be at Ravin's side. Vardak had attempted to reason with him briefly, but Tavesin's mind was set.

"This business with magic makes my skin crawl," Lucas remarked quietly, his eyes fixed on the sky as a shimmering dome of blue energy formed above the eastern wall.

"How long before we receive word?" Danian asked, eager to begin the charge.

"Jadosin was to send word once our forces at the eastern gate were prepared to charge," Vardak replied. "He will open the gates one hour after my signal is sent. By then, we should have the Murkors' attention split to the north and south, freeing those at the eastern gate to engage without risk of the city being overrun."

It was at least the third time he'd explained their plan, but he hoped the repetition would solidify their role in the minds of the soldiers. There would be less risk of confusion when they reached the Murkor on the plains.

"Deluchans are known to move at their own speed," Danian grumbled. "If we were fighting this battle in Santine, our forces in the east would have been prepared hours ago."

Vardak chuckled. "Jadosin's word will come. For this plan to work, we must be patient."

"This is why I'll never be general," Danian replied with another grin. "Patience. Bah!"

"Remind me to never pair you with Patak." Vardak shook his head in amusement. "It would be a disaster in the making."

"Your brother had best keep her safe," Lucas stated darkly.

Vardak studied the other man as he scowled toward the gate, his jaw set in frustration or anger. Lucas cared deeply for Emra, and the burgeoning relationship between she and Patak had become a source of contention. Vardak wasn't certain Lucas' feelings toward Emra were as brotherly as he claimed; of late, his interactions with Patak had become terse and at times confrontational. Vardak did not have experience with romantic relationships, but he wasn't blind to the jealousy that Lucas displayed. It was a source of conflict none of them could afford at present.

Danian spoke up, saving Vardak the chore of diffusing Lucas' temper. "I'm fairly certain Emra can take care of herself, Luke. More than likely, *she'll* be busy saving *him*."

Lucas snorted derisively but made no reply.

Danian shrugged helplessly and turned his attention to settling his mount. Vardak grudgingly vowed to speak with both Lucas and his brother once the battle was done. The two needed to settle their differences before things became too heated. They had more important matters to dwell on than a squabble over a woman who had made her decision clear to everyone.

"General, sir!"

Vardak turned toward the voice and smiled grimly as he noted the foot soldier that approached his group.

"Is Jadosin ready?" he asked.

The man smiled uneasily. "Yes, sir. It's time."

Vardak nodded his thanks and turned to the cavalry. "Once the gates open, we move east."

He pulled off his gauntlets and withdrew a slender, brown tube the length of his hand from beneath his left armguard. Before leaving the Stronghold, Patak had teased him for purchasing the handful of light-signals at the marketplace, but he was glad to have them now. They were crafted by Murkor alchemists and often used by their army to issue commands when the drums proved unreliable.

A cord hung from the base of the tube. He pulled it roughly, then planted the cylinder carefully in a chink of the roadway and stepped back. He replaced his gauntlets and watched as the cylinder began to glow orange and shot suddenly skyward in a high arc, a trail of orange embers following in its wake.

"What magic is that?" Danian asked in awe.

Vardak chuckled as he unsheathed his axe and waited for the gates to swing open. "It's not magic, it's Murkor alchemy. Prior to this war, our peoples often engaged in trade."

The gate began to swing open, and Vardak motioned to the others.

"We ride!" Lucas shouted, brandishing his sword.

They spilled from the gate, then wheeled toward the east and the lightening horizon. Vardak kept pace with the horses, but only just. He was immensely grateful to Travin's smithing skill as he raced across the grassland; if he were wearing standard steel plate and not the lighter-weight variety his brother had crafted, he would have been winded long before they reached the enemy's flank.

It took them less than a quarter-hour to reach the bend in the wall. As they rounded it, the expanse of the Murkor army came into view, hundreds of hooded figures spread across the plains. The Murkor were focused on the wall and did not immediately take note of the horsemen bearing down on them. Energy crackled overhead and through the ranks of both sides as the wizards and the Soulless continued to battle. Arrows rained from the wall at intervals to strike amongst the Murkor nearest its base. Several clusters of Murkor carried ladders, while others surrounded green-hooded figures that Vardak recognized as alchemists. He was certain they'd concocted a means to damage the wall; it was only a matter of drawing near enough to deploy their creation.

When he and the cavalry collided with the nearest Murkor, there was a deafening crash as steel met steel. Soldiers shouted and cursed, horses screamed, and the carefully formed line they'd maintained throughout their journey dissolved into a chaotic tangle.

Vardak found himself facing a pair of Murkor, one armed with a mace, the other with a short-hafted axe in each hand. Their weapons were forged of the black metal the Murkor coveted; it was infused with venom, and its creation had prompted the capture of Travin and the others. Vardak channeled his anger and indignation into the haft of his axe, and the weapon became a deadly blur in his hands.

He blocked a strike from the mace, then spun his weapon in a low arc toward the axe-wielding Murkor, who was taken by surprise at the maneuver. Vardak's blade buried itself in the Murkor's side. As he wrenched it free, he turned to face the mace-wielder in time to block another blow with the end of its haft. In the same moment, he struck the Murkor's shoulder with his tail. The stinger buried itself in the Murkor's flesh, and he felt the release of poison as it was injected into his opponent's body. The Murkor stumbled backward as Vardak yanked the stinger free, the venom already taking its toll on his body. Without rapid treatment, the Murkor would die as the venom worked its way through his veins and into his heart.

Vardak spun to face the axe-wielder again, but the injured Murkor had fallen, the shaft of an arrow protruding from the side of his neck. Another Murkor charged toward him, his shield raised as he brandished a spear. Vardak braced himself for the assault while risking a glance at the cavalry. Lucas was some distance ahead of him, surrounded by dark hoods and cut off from the others. Vardak swore.

He blocked a strike from the spear with the blade of his axe and shoved the Murkor backwards. While the soldier regained his footing, Vardak struck again with his tail, but it met with the Murkor's shield. A trail of venom splattered across its surface, wasted in Vardak's haste to reach Lucas' position. The Murkor shifted slightly and jabbed at Vardak's midsection with his spear. Vardak sidestepped the attack, quicker on his feet than the Murkor, and swung his axe at the Murkor's vulnerable side. As blade met flesh, the Murkor screamed and released his hold on the spear.

He scanned the field for Lucas again, but couldn't locate the Balotican before the next Murkor was upon him. This Murkor strode toward him purposefully, a steel broadsword of excellent craftsmanship gripped in his hands. At his belt hung a curved, black saber that Vardak recognized as the weapon reserved for the army's officers. The Murkor paused briefly to study him, just beyond the range of Vardak's axe. It was then that Vardak spied the sigil etched into the broadsword's blade—an ornate scorpion with its tail curled over its back.

He lifted his gaze to peer into the Murkor's hood, though he could not make out his opponent's eyes. The sword was the work of Blademon, a gift the war god bestowed only upon his chosen; his axe bore the same sigil. Vardak had finally met his destined adversary, in the form of a Murkor soldier.

They began to circle one another as the battle raged around them, an eddy of their own making amidst the tide. Vardak watched the Murkor warily, but the other gave no indication of his intent. Vardak would wait for him to make the first move, to gauge his opponent's strength and assess any apparent weaknesses. He adjusted the grip on the axe's haft, his eyes fixed on the hooded figure before him.

Without warning, the Murkor darted forward, his blade a silver arc aimed toward Vardak's midsection. Vardak brought his axe blade down to meet the sword with a clash of steel.

"Blademon said we'd meet one day," the Murkor stated in the common tongue through gritted teeth. He slid his blade from the axe's and swung it deftly toward Vardak's shoulder.

Vardak managed to parry the second strike, but it had proven a near thing. He narrowed his eyes in concentration; he could afford no mistakes with this foe. He shoved the Murkor away with as much strength as he could muster, but the Murkor nimbly kept his footing.

"That he did," Vardak agreed, blinking sweat from his eyes.

The Murkor sprang forward once more, grim laughter spilling from within his hood. His blade slashed toward Vardak's skull, its length reflecting the first light of the morning sun. Vardak sidestepped, and the sword whirled a hair's breadth away from him with such force its tip lodged itself into the earth before the Murkor could forestall its progress.

Vardak took the opportunity to take the offensive. He closed the distance between them and swung his axe toward the Murkor's midsection. The Murkor anticipated his move and managed to evade a direct blow as he pulled his sword free of the cloying earth. The axe struck a glancing blow to the Murkor's shoulder.

The Murkor snarled and backed away. He glanced over his wounded shoulder toward the rear of the army and shook his head. "We'll meet again," he promised before he loped away to disappear amongst the sea of dark hoods.

Vardak realized belatedly that the cadence of the Murkor drums had altered. A retreat was being sounded, and scores of Murkor were disengaging from the battle to return as commanded. Vardak scanned the field in search of Lucas and located him amongst a pile of black-clad Murkor bodies not far away.

"Shit."

The other members of the cavalry were some distance ahead, trailing the Murkor as they retreated farther from Delucha's walls. He called to Danian, who reined his steed to a halt and peered in Vardak's direction. He beckoned to the Santinian as he made his way toward

Lucas' location. He feared he knew what he would find before he reached his fallen friend.

Danian arrived at the site as Vardak peered down at Lucas' still form. "Ah, gods, not Luke."

Vardak nodded solemnly. Lucas had taken a Murkor blade to his gut, the instrument of his death still lodged firmly in place.

"Signal the others," he told Danian. "The Murkor are retreating. We ought to return to the city, to regroup."

Danian saluted. "Yes, sir."

A burst of fiery magic collided overhead as Vardak carefully collected Lucas' body. The mages were still at war even though the Murkor were beginning to withdraw.

He began the trek back toward the city, his thoughts upon what he must say to Emra when the battle was done. They would all mourn Lucas' loss, but it would cut her far more deeply than any other.

CHAPTER FORTY-SEVEN

RAVIN'S PATH

Even with the talisman to augment his power, the mental strain of his attacks, coupled with the oversight of Tavesin and the manipulation of Jannyn began to take their toll on Ravin before Emra presented her fiery spectacle on the battlefield below. He could not maintain the triple effort for much longer without draining himself dry. It was an outcome he could not afford; Tavesin needed his guidance and protection, and allowing Jannyn to break free was unthinkable.

Ravin paused in his attacks to assess the roil of bodies on the plains below. The Murkor continued to press toward the wall, despite the devastation Fireblade had wrought through their ranks toward the south. In the north, the Murkor were pushed back by the cavalry; he could just make out the mass of horsemen stampeding through the ranks of hooded foot soldiers. Before him, Murkor were engaged with the Deluchan soldiers under Jadosin's command, while the Drakkon and Gray wizards antagonized them from one side.

Ravin lifted his gaze to take in the cluster of Soulless and Enlightened near the rear of their army. Between himself and the wizards, a number of their weaker members had been killed or wounded significantly, but the Soulless remained untouched. Ravin spied a pair of them near the center of the line and was certain the shorter form belonged to Dranamir. Her energy signature was unmistakable, and the fury with which she launched attacks in his direction solidified his assumption.

He pinched the bridge of his nose in an attempt to stave off the fatigue that threatened to overwhelm him. He could not continue to manipulate Jannyn and maintain the reserves necessary to see the fight to its conclusion. His mother had granted him power beyond the norm, but even Ravin had his limits.

An energy shield bloomed in front of them as Tavesin deflected another deadly barrage of magical fire. Ravin had lost count of the number of times the boy had deployed his impressive defensive abilities, sparing himself and much of the eastern wall from damage. He worried Tavesin's energy was waning, yet the boy showed no sign of fatigue. As the shield dissipated, Ravin formulated a plan.

He glanced at Tavesin, praying the boy was amenable to the idea. "There is something I must do. I'll be away from the wall for a short time, but I won't leave you to defend yourself for long. I promise I'll return as swiftly as I'm able." He was shocked at the weariness he heard in his own tone.

Tavesin chewed his lower lip as his eyes scanned the air for the next attack. "Where will you go?"

Ravin sighed. "I must…divest myself of the prisoner. I'm growing tired, Tavesin."

Tavesin's gaze flicked to meet his for a brief moment. Ravin detected no fear in his expression, only analytical calculation. "I understand."

"Thank you. I won't be long."

He meant to take advantage of Dranamir's unbridled rage and prayed his gamble with Jannyn would bear fruit. He focused his waning energy on the Soulless and created a portal into the Aethereum, his previous reservations about transporting the man through the realm gone. If Jannyn broke free of his hold while within, Ravin should still be afforded a few moments to escape while the Soulless regained his faculties.

He ushered Jannyn through the glowing oval, his hand clamped firmly around the other's elbow. To his relief, his control over the Soulless held. He transported them to the location where he'd last glimpsed Dranamir, then took a moment to prepare and shake off some of his exhaustion. He'd overextended himself, yet there was still much to be done.

He drew a breath, braced himself, then simultaneously opened a portal and released his grip on Jannyn's mind. He shoved the Soulless through the opening and into the physical realm before the man was fully aware of what he'd done. He glimpsed Dranamir through the portal alongside a tall, angular man with the graying skin and crimson eyes that marked him as Soulless. He swiftly closed the portal and made his way back to the eastern wall. He prayed Dranamir's temper remained as fierce as he remembered, otherwise he'd just made a dire mistake.

As he reemerged beside Tavesin, the boy flashed him a weary grin. "You're back!"

Ravin nodded. "I gave you my word."

Ravin stepped forward to grasp the ledge of the wall as he peered across the battlefield once more. Without the strain of maintaining his domination of Jannyn's mind, he could feel some of his energy begin to return. He decided he would observe while he gathered his strength for a second assault. In the meantime, he could provide Tavesin with any advice he might require, though the boy had proven himself capable. He was once more reminded of his younger self, thrust into a position meant for an adult due to the magnitude of his magical prowess. He prayed Tavesin's life would follow a happier path than his own.

He scanned the dwindling ranks of the Enlightened and located Dranamir once more. She and the tall man were still together, and a third—another woman—had joined them. Ravin was uncertain of her identity, though her energy signature was familiar to him. Jannyn knelt before them, and as he watched, his corrupted, gray skin began to peel away like the rind of an overripe citron. Ravin grimaced and prayed Tavesin's focus was locked elsewhere. The boy did not need to observe Dranamir's handiwork unfold.

At least, he consoled himself, his gamble had paid off. Dranamir's rage would end Jannyn's life, and he doubted the other Soulless would stand in the way of her perverse sense of vengeance. It was one less of the Nameless god's chosen left to plague the world.

Beside him, Tavesin brought another shield to life as a green flare of energy burst overhead. Ravin shook himself and pushed away from the wall. He'd loitered, inactive, too long; he should not have left Tavesin to defend their portion of the wall alone as he'd done.

He spied one of the Soulless on the field below, running full-tilt away from the scene unfolding between Dranamir and Jannyn. The sense she was familiar continued to tug at the back of his mind, but he pushed his curiosity aside. The woman had chosen the path of the Soulless, and he had an opportunity to strike at her while she was somewhat vulnerable. He would capitalize on the brief moment chance provided.

Drawing on the last vestiges of his energy, Ravin sent a barrage of lightning bolts in her direction. He watched intently as she became aware of the deadly magic and flung a meager shield about her person, though the act came too late. One of the bolts struck the ground at her heels, while a second hit her shoulder with such force she spun a full circle and fell into a heap, her form disappearing behind the ranks of Murkor.

He wasn't certain the woman was dead, but she was undoubtedly injured. He was too drained to pursue her any further.

Belatedly, he realized the hooded soldiers had begun to retreat. He stumbled forward and caught himself against the wall, limbs weakened from exertion. He peered over its ledge once more, his lips forming a weary smile. Dawn was breaking in the east, and with it, the hours-long battle seemed to be won. He was certain the Soulless would return, but they were given a respite from the fighting at present.

"Ravin?" Tavesin asked cautiously from his left.

He turned to study the boy while his eyelids struggled to remain open. "Hmm?"

"Are you well?"

Ravin laughed. "Well enough, but I need to rest." He gazed across the plain, taking in the sight of the Murkor army in full retreat with Jadosin's soldiers in pursuit. "We've won the night, but they'll return."

"Even with the talisman, it was too much, wasn't it?" Tavesin leaned on the wall next to him, and in the first rays of daylight, Ravin noted his appearance was haggard.

"Yes, and I detest mind-control magic. Yet in this case, I suppose it was justified." He thought of Jasom and wondered if he'd be granted an opportunity to tell him Jannyn had finally been forced to pay for his crimes.

Tavesin shrugged. "He paid with his life, in the end. The Soulless don't give their people second chances, do they?"

Ravin grimaced. "Gods, I'd hoped you were too busy to witness that, Tavesin. Dranamir is…vicious."

"I'd hoped Garin would be here," Tavesin remarked with a frown. "I'd like to see him meet the same fate after all he's done to Arra."

"I was aware Garin had harmed you, but who is Arra?"

"She's my friend." Tavesin looked away, blinking tears from his eyes. In that moment, he looked far younger than his fourteen years. Ravin's heart ached for the boy's plight; unlike the queen, Tavesin truly was an innocent soul.

"I'm sorry," Ravin offered. "Whatever Garin has done, we will make it right."

Hope suffused his expression. "You would help me, Ravin? The wizards cannot, and Aziarah has tried, but…Garin took her to the black tower. She's a prisoner. He's…he's hurt her."

For the first time since he'd arrived in Delucha, Ravin understood the path he must take clearly. He no longer needed the post as advisor, no longer wished to have anything to do with Tamarin Serales, murderer and usurper. His place was with Emra's growing army— Tavesin required a mentor, and there was no one else qualified to teach him. If the boy went with her, then so would he.

"Yes, Tavesin, I'll help you. Garin is nearly as appalling as Dranamir, and you cannot fight the Soulless alone."

Tavesin brightened. "When I see her next, I'll finally be able to tell her help is coming."

"You still see her, Tavesin?" Ravin asked warily.

"Sometimes she's able to enter the Aethereum if he's away. It was Arra who warned us they were planning to strike Delucha." Tavesin shrugged. "I suppose Flariel also told Vardak to come here."

"She may be your friend, but you must remain cautious with her, Tavesin. You saw what I did with Jannyn today—the Soulless often do the same." Ravin suppressed a shudder and looked away. "Unlike me, they have no qualms in doing so, either."

"I understand, sir." Tavesin seemed to deflate and rested his head against the wall.

"We ought to find our way to the inn. It won't be long before Emra returns, and we'll need to report." He pushed himself upright as Tavesin did the same. "It looks as though I'm not the only one who needs rest. Come."

He made certain Tavesin was settled in the common room of The Three Roses Inn with another pair of young wizards whom he seemed to be on friendly terms with, before he flagged down the innkeeper. Emra and her guard had not yet returned from the field, but he believed the boy was safe enough while he left to speak with Adalin. When the innkeeper bustled toward him, a bright smile on her plump features, Ravin knew he'd made the right choice in sending the duchess there.

"Ravin, isn't it?" she inquired with an appraising eye. "Advisor to the queen, or so the rumors state. A lady came in several hours ago, just before the attack. Said you sent her."

"I did." Relief flooded his veins at the news; Adalin was safely outside of the palace. "I'd like to speak with her. Which room is she in?"

"She asked for a room on the top floor, though I can't imagine why a noble lady would seek a commoner's room." The innkeeper shrugged. "Not my business, I suppose. As I said, she's on the top floor. First door on the left."

"Thank you."

He took the stairs two at a time and was breathless by the time he reached her door. He'd promised to speak with her once the battle was done, though at the time, he wasn't certain what he planned to say. He knew now that he was committed to Emra's cause for Tavesin's sake, and when the army moved on from Delucha, he'd be traveling with it. He hesitated in the corridor, his knuckles poised to knock. He wasn't sure how she'd take the news of his pending departure.

He drew a breath, confused by his sudden bout of nerves, and rapped on the door. She opened it moments later. She studied him quietly for a time, relief and joy in her expression. Finally, she pulled the door open and gestured that he should enter.

"I'm afraid my quarters are in disarray," she said as she closed the door firmly behind them. "I had more belongings crammed into my rooms in the palace than I realized."

"I'm glad you made it out of the palace safely."

She laughed softly. "It was after midnight, Ravin. Who would have been awake to stop me?" Her smile faltered and she looked down. "Gods, I never believed I'd be forced to flee from the queen."

"Adalin, I—"

"Don't apologize, Ravin. You likely saved my life—or at the very least, spared me from exile." She sighed. "The innkeeper is kind enough, though she seems keen to know why I arrived in the dead of night moments prior to the battle. And when I mentioned your name, I'm certain she believed we're involved in a scandalous affair."

"I suppose we are, just not the sort she'd like the details of."

He ran one hand through his hair. Now that the moment was upon him, he didn't know how to begin breaking the next wave of unfortunate news to her.

"Ravin, what else has gone wrong?" she asked quietly. "You're clearly troubled."

He nodded. "Adalin, I must go with Emra's army when the time comes."

A knowing smile touched her lips. "I assumed you would. They need your skills." She studied him for a moment, amusement in her eyes. "You didn't make the decision yourself until sometime during the battle. What changed?"

"Tavesin needs a mentor, and I don't believe any of the wizards can appropriately teach him what he needs to learn." Ravin shook his head, bewildered by his own response.

"From our brief meeting in the palace, I could see he idolized you. And if I'm not mistaken, you see something of yourself in him."

"I…Yes."

She took his hands in her own. "Before your business with the soul-stone, did you never have children, Ravin?"

He snorted. "No. I rarely allowed myself to become close enough to anyone to…start a family. Why do you ask?"

She arched her eyebrows in mock surprise. "It seems to me you're taking on the role of a father to this boy. And willingly."

Ravin flushed at the realization; he hadn't seen it himself. "I don't want his life to become like mine… He deserves better."

"Then show him what's possible, Ravin." She smiled and touched the side of his face. "You may not have been expecting to leave Delucha a few hours ago, but in my heart, I knew you would be going. If we both survive to see the conclusion of this war, I will await you here—should you wish to see me, that is."

"Gods, Adalin, you're the only person I believe I can trust in all the world. Why *wouldn't* I return?"

She beamed at him. "It seems I have redeemed myself, then."

He chuckled. "Of course, you have. Without you, I'd never have reached the talisman, and this city would likely be overrun by now. I owe you a debt I doubt I'll be able to repay. The *world* owes you a debt."

"The queen will not see it that way, but I believe I'm safe enough here." She dropped her hand to her side and eyed him wistfully. "No matter what comes to pass, I will always remember you fondly, Ravin."

"Likewise, lady duchess."

She laughed softly. "There will be time enough for a proper goodbye later. Visit me when you can, Ravin. I enjoy these conversations."

He returned her smile. "As do I. When we first met, I would never have admitted such a thing was possible."

"Yet here we are, the unlikeliest pair of friends imaginable."

CHAPTER FORTY-EIGHT

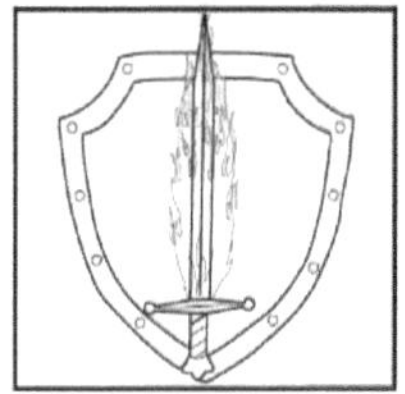

LOSS

The others chatted amiably as they reentered Delucha's walls from the eastern side, but Emra was silent, brooding over the destruction she'd wrought. The burns from Fireblade seared across the brittle grasses behind them like dark scars on the landscape, a reminder of the power she alone could wield. It was a power she'd regretted forging centuries ago when she'd realized the truth of her rebirth for the first time. Too many lives had been extinguished in the flames, yet Aeon seemed content to allow the cycle to repeat time and again.

A part of her wished she could rail at the Underworld's keeper, but it would solve nothing. Fireblade's creation had been her doing, the binding of her soul to the blade her decision. The gods were not at fault for the weapon's existence, though they were complicit. She had no one to blame but her past self. That she'd acted with good intent no longer mattered—her soul was steeped in death beyond reckoning.

Patak kept pace with her and said little to the other guards. She sensed his eyes upon her, his concern like a smothering blanket. She wanted to share with him her dark thoughts, but not with the others nearby. They did not need to know the burden she bore, nor understand the depth of her despair. She was their leader, an icon meant to give hope. Her pain must not be allowed to affect them, or the Soulless would have already won.

Few people roamed the streets who weren't attired for battle. Those that did shuffled by with their heads down, their eyes darting furtively at passersby. They were in shock, a reaction she'd witnessed a hundred times and more. For the people of Delucha, life would never again be the same, even though there was little to remind them of the battle that had been waged just beyond their gates.

Vardak's plan had worked remarkably well, but she knew their victory was only temporary. The war would not be finished until the Soulless lay dead, or until they finally achieved the domination their god craved. There would be no negotiations, no bids for peace between the Five Kingdoms and the Shadow Council. The Nameless did not entertain such notions, nor did his most powerful minions.

"It seems Radosan has arrived ahead of us," Patak stated as they approached The Three Roses. He gestured toward the stable yard, where several of the younger wizards were gathered. Each wore a green cloak to indicate their Sect.

"He and his people will be very busy as more of the soldiers return," she replied. "I wasn't expecting him to meet us here. The healers were staged in the palace courtyard."

Patak shrugged. "Perhaps he brings news."

"Perhaps."

"Em, do we need to talk?" Concern etched his features and laced his tone.

She felt the tenuous threads holding her composure begin to unravel, and she hurriedly looked away. "We do, but not now, Patak. Not with…" She gestured vaguely in the direction of the others. "They don't need to watch their leader fall to pieces."

He nodded and reached one hand toward her, thought better of it, and let the limb fall to his side once more. "Whatever you need of me, I'm here, Em. I always will be."

She managed a smile through a curtain of threatening tears, grateful beyond measure for his support. In all her lives, it had been a rarity to find anyone as genuine as Patak, who placed her welfare above all else. She cherished each moment she shared with him.

Despite his brothers' protestations, she'd fallen in love with him, and her heart yearned for more than their current arrangement could offer. The last thing she wanted was to hurt him or drive him away from his people and family, yet his every smile tempted her further from the path of propriety. Eventually his charm would erode her defenses entirely, and taboo or not, she would succumb.

She paused at the inn's threshold. "I'll hear what the wizards have to say. See that the others are settled, then join me. We'll talk privately later."

"Of course."

As she turned away, Patak began calling orders to the others. She could hear the grin in his tone; he was enjoying himself and his role as captain of her guard.

The inn's common room was crammed with locals seeking news or gossip from their neighbors. She scanned the room with a sigh but located no one from her army nor any of the wizards. At her entrance, several of the nearest locals ceased their conversations to gawp in her direction, and within moments, much of the room fell silent with anticipation. She swallowed a wave of sudden irritation, but knew she must say something in order to appease them and learn where Radosan might be.

"The Murkor have been routed—for now."

The room erupted into an explosion of sound as those gathered cheered, shouted, and began calling for rounds of drinks. She spied the innkeeper on the far side of the room as she exited the kitchen to assess the source of the sudden noise. Emra waved to her and remained near the door as the innkeeper threaded her way through the bustling room.

"You certainly know how to drum up business," the innkeeper informed her with a wry grin. "I'll be out of ale by mid-afternoon at this rate."

"I was obligated to say something." Emra glanced across the room once more but still saw no sign of Radosan or any of the others. "Where are the wizards? I saw—"

"Ah, yes. I put them up in the private room at the back. Less chance of interruption that way." She motioned to Emra. "Come."

Emra followed her across the crowded room to a door adjacent to the kitchen's. The corridor beyond was blissfully quiet and considerably cooler, the aroma of baking bread a pleasant change from the sour odor of unwashed bodies and ale that permeated the common room. They went to another door a short distance along the corridor.

"The wizards are inside. Should I send anyone else this way once they arrive?"

"Yes, Patak will wish to know where I've gone. He's outside."

The innkeeper smiled knowingly. "Of course. Hard to dismiss, that one is. I'll make certain he knows you're here."

She winked and turned away, leaving Emra to blush furiously in her wake. She and Patak hadn't attempted to hide their attraction to one another, but she was flustered by the remarks all the same. The innkeeper was a relative stranger; Emra wasn't certain she could recall the woman's name if she tried. Yet the woman was brazen enough to insinuate a greater attachment than they truly shared.

Emra shook her head and waited for the heat to fade from her cheeks before she entered the room. She pushed thoughts of Patak aside to focus on the group that had clearly been awaiting her return. Radosan was speaking quietly with Ravin at one end of the room, while Tavesin and the two apprentices he'd left Dar Daelad with huddled around the table at the other end. A half-empty tray of fruit and bread sat between the trio of boys. Tavesin was slumped in his chair, his eyes closed, his face pale with exhaustion. Emra was relieved to see he had emerged from the battle unscathed.

She joined the two men where they stood. Radosan smiled in greeting, while Ravin merely studied her with his strange, golden eyes. He seemed wary, though she did not understand why.

"I was hoping to speak with you before I left for the palace," Radosan said. "I spoke with Aziarah not long ago. She came to the palace to inform us the Murkor were retreating, then left with several other Drakkon. She planned to follow the enemy, to learn where they've gone. I told her I'd send word to you, but since the casualties haven't begun to arrive yet, I came in person."

"Thank you, but you shouldn't have," she replied. "Your work with the wounded should come first."

Radosan shrugged uncomfortably and glanced at the boys. "In truth, I wanted to make certain Tavesin was well. Rostin and Badolo remained here during the fight—they are still apprentices, after all. But Tavesin…"

"I gave my word that I'd watch over him," Ravin stated defensively. "Much of his energy is spent, but after a few hours' rest, he'll be fine." He leaned against the wall, his arms crossed. "I could do with a nap, myself."

Radosan frowned uncertainly. "Yes. Well, it seems that perhaps I was wrong about you, Ravin. As I said, I must return to the palace."

Emra raised her eyebrows in question as the Sect Master strode from the room.

Ravin smirked. "I expect that's the extent of the apology I'll receive from him—or the other wizards." He pushed himself upright once more and sighed. "I'm well aware your general doesn't trust me, either."

"Vardak will come around," she replied. "We witnessed what you did today for Delucha. Your actions account for much."

He chuckled dryly. "I'm grateful to hear you say that. I've decided I must accompany you. And before you begin to thank me, it's not for the reasons you might believe. I didn't make this decision for power or glory, or simply to cut my remaining ties with the queen." His gaze drifted to the table across the room and his expression became circumspect. "Tavesin may be considered fully trained by his council's standards, but he could do with some additional education. He is…"

"He needs you," Emra agreed quietly. "And I would welcome your help, as well."

"I'll see him to his room. I thought he could use something to eat first, but it seems he requires sleep more." Ravin managed a weary smile. "He reminds me of myself, when I was young. And, as Adalin pointed out to me earlier, I suppose I've unwittingly taken on the role of guardian over him. My reason for joining you is simple, Emra. Tavesin deserves to make a life for himself after this war is ended, but for all his power, he is only a child. He needs someone to look after him, to make certain he lives to be given that chance."

"And you are uniquely suited to teach him advanced magics," she added. "No matter what some of the others might believe, you're a good man, Ravin."

He laughed. "I don't—"

The door to the corridor crashed open, cutting off his remaining words. Emra spun around to find Patak framed in the doorway, his expression strained, his eyes haunted. She knew without asking that something was terribly wrong. He ducked into the room and made his way toward her, while Ravin crossed the room to speak with the boys. Within moments, he'd roused Tavesin and was busy ushering the trio into the corridor. His parting glance told her he'd seek her out later. She was grateful he'd intuited their need for privacy.

"Patak, what is it?"

"Vardak has returned from the field," he said, his voice roughened by emotion. "Em, he…"

"Is he well?" she pressed.

Patak grimaced but nodded. "Vardak's fine. He returned with…Luke. Lucas is dead, Em. I'm so sorry."

It was as though her breath had been stolen, and she gasped for air. The sound that emerged from her throat was an anguished sob, wrenched from the center of her being. She would have collapsed to her knees, if not for Patak; his arms wrapped around her protectively, and he held her as she grieved.

Lucas was her oldest friend in this life, the closest to a brother she'd ever known. Every battle came with its losses, but when it was those dearest to her heart, the agony was unparalleled. She'd expected to see Lucas swagger inside, a cheeky grin plastered across his face as he informed her of the cavalry's success. She'd never imagined he would fall during their first fight, that when they'd departed for their posts earlier, it would be the last time she'd see him alive.

She wasn't certain how long she spent bawling in Patak's embrace. It could have been minutes or hours. Her throat was raw, her eyes were sore and puffy, and the side of her face ached from where she'd pressed it against his armored shoulder. She hoped none of the others had stopped to deliver news; she'd unraveled in an instant and lost herself in a riptide of grief.

Slowly, she straightened and wiped at her face. Patak's blue eyes searched hers with concern, but she had nothing to say. In the wake of her sorrow, she felt hollow, a mere shell.

"You said Vardak returned with him?" she whispered.

"Yes. We weren't certain what the proper custom was for your people, but Vardak didn't believe it was right to leave him in the field." He touched the side of her face gently. "Em, if there is anything I can do, name it. I'll see it done."

"He deserves a proper burial. I'm in no state to make the arrangements. Perhaps Ravin can assist—he has connections in the city." She blinked away a fresh wave of tears. "Gods, Patak, you'd think

I'd be used to loss by now. There have been so many deaths, but every time, it hurts just as badly as the first."

His arms tightened around her. "You care about your people, Em. I hope that never changes."

"I'm glad you're here."

"I promised I would be. Tell me what you need, and I'll make certain it's done."

CHAPTER FORTY-NINE

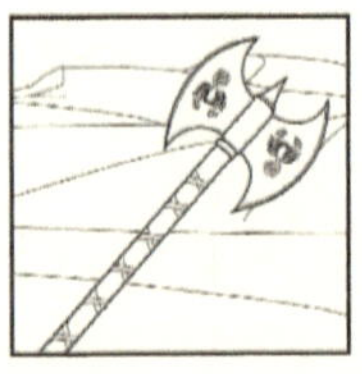

LOOKING EAST

It was evening before Vardak managed to escape his duties and retire to his quarters. He and Patak had been forced to take rooms at an inn some distance away from The Three Roses, the only establishment nearby with accommodations on the ground floor. Vardak had returned alone; his brother was reluctant to leave Emra, though Vardak was uncertain how Patak intended to navigate the stairs. Perhaps he would return once she retired for the night, but Vardak doubted it.

Vardak was exhausted but knew it would be some time before he drifted to sleep. His mind continued to work, to mull over the day's events relentlessly, though his body screamed for a respite. He'd failed to sleep the previous night, as he'd been busy poring over the city's maps before Ravin's summons arrived. There were too many items demanding his attention and too few hours in which to address them all.

As he closed the door to his cramped room, he noted his armor had been cleaned and polished, though he couldn't recall asking anyone to complete the chore. He'd intended to do it himself once he had an hour to spare, but the hour had never come.

He pulled off his shirt and winced at the movement. His arms and torso were a mottle of bruises, his muscles were sore, and his fatigue exacerbated the discomfort. His injuries were minor compared to many of the others'; he'd forgone Radosan's offer of healing multiple times throughout the day. The wizards had scores of others to attend; he would not add to their burden when his bruises would heal on their own.

He extinguished the candle that had been left on the room's only chair, then laid down on the sleeping mat the room was furnished with and closed his eyes. Images of the battle played behind his lids; the faces of the fallen, the hooded countenances of his foes, and the fight with Blademon's other protégé. His plan for defending Delucha had worked well enough, but he wondered if the outcome would have been different if he'd adjusted some of the minor details of his strategy. Perhaps Lucas might have survived, but who would have been lost in his stead? The fate of countless lives had ridden on his decisions, and no one had questioned his judgment. He found the notion unsettling.

An urgent knock on his door roused him from his troubled thoughts. Wearily, he pushed himself upright and fumbled for his shirt in the darkness. He tugged the garment on as he opened the door to the hall.

Aziarah greeted him with an agitated flutter of her wings. "Patak told me you'd be here. My apologies for waking you, but it's important."

He shrugged indifferently. "I wasn't asleep. What did you learn?" He knew she and several other Drakkon had pursued the Murkor as they retreated to the east. He prayed she'd learned the location of their camp and perhaps the scope of their army as well.

"The Murkor are gone, Vardak."

He frowned in confusion. "Gone?"

"Yes, gone." She crossed her arms. "Ravin was with your brother when I inquired after you. He suspects they've retreated back to the Wasted Land, perhaps to recover and gather more forces during the winter."

Vardak rubbed his forehead. Between his exhaustion and Aziarah's news, he was developing a headache. "I ought to speak with him."

"In the morning," she said firmly. "Ravin left to see for himself. He is…better suited to the task than any of my people are. The Aethereum is *his* domain, after all." Her tone was bitter.

"I don't know if we should trust him, but I know little of magic." He sighed. "His theory is sound, however. The Murkor wouldn't risk trapping themselves on this side of the mountains during winter, though I'm not certain they're the ones deciding the army's path."

"Likely they aren't," she agreed. "Did your mentor provide any insight into the Soulless' histories when he imparted his knowledge to you?"

Vardak groaned. "Coreyaless told you?"

"It isn't something you should keep to yourself, nor be ashamed of. You were blessed by one of the gods. It was an honor, Vardak."

He snorted, incredulous. "What Blademon gave me included strategy, the lay of the lands, and a means to navigate Stonewall Hall. Yes, it has been useful, and I'm grateful for that, but I know nothing more of the Soulless than anyone else. We ought to ask Emra for her opinion on the matter."

"Tomorrow, then." Aziarah sighed. "Patak said she was asleep, and he would not disturb her for all the gold in the palace. He sent me to speak with you instead."

"I should have anticipated Patak would put her welfare above my own," he grumbled, though he wasn't truly angered by his brother's thoughtlessness. It was typical of Patak. "If you speak with my brother again, please tell him I *also* require rest. We can discuss this in the morning, Aziarah, and perhaps Ravin will have news for us by then."

He didn't recall falling asleep, but he was awakened well after dawn when Patak barged into the room. Disoriented, Vardak peered up at his elder brother and rubbed his eyes while Patak grinned at him.

"Everyone's been waiting for the general to make an appearance this morning. It seems he needs his beauty rest. Not that's it's helped you any, little brother." Patak tossed a clean shirt toward him and continued to grin while Vardak pulled it over his head.

"Gods-damn it, Patak, what has you so pleased this morning?" Vardak growled.

"Ravin's as good as his word, believe it or not. You might have the break you were looking for in Dar Daelad." Patak crossed his arms and studied Vardak for a few moments, his expression growing serious. "He also came through for Em. Or rather, his duchess friend did. Lucas' burial will be this afternoon."

Vardak nodded thoughtfully. "I'm glad to hear they've arranged something for him. He was a good man." He paused to reflect on

Lucas' brief time spent traveling with them. "I spoke with Aziarah last night."

"She told us as much. Let's go, little brother. They'll have breakfast waiting for you at The Three Roses when we arrive." Patak smirked. "Well, perhaps it'll be lunch at this rate."

Vardak rolled his eyes and gestured toward the door. "We should go."

As soon as they stepped outside, Vardak realized his brother hadn't been jesting—the sun had nearly reached its zenith and midday would soon be upon them. The city's streets were quiet as Delucha's residents largely remained indoors until word spread that the attack was truly over.

"You should have come for me sooner, Patak. I've a thousand things to do, and—"

"And Em ordered us all to let you rest," Patak cut him off with a grin. "You've been working without end since we crossed the mountains. Besides, with the news Ravin brought, a few hours' sleep was warranted, Vardak. You cannot take care of the soldiers under your command if you fail to tend your own needs."

Vardak frowned at him. "Wise words, though I can hardly believe they've come from you."

Patak reddened. "It was Em."

"I should have known." He studied Patak for a moment while he gathered the courage to ask the question that had been nagging him since he'd awakened. "Did you return to your room last night?"

Patak's good humor fled as he clenched his jaw. "Now isn't the time, Vardak, and it's none of your gods-damned business."

Vardak sighed. "I've given up attempting to change your mind, brother. I asked out of curiosity, nothing more."

Patak scowled at the street before them for several moments. "Catalin, the innkeeper, set up one of the private dining rooms as...sleeping quarters for me. I wasn't about to leave her alone, Vardak. Luke's death has affected her more than she'll let anyone else know, and I..." He shook his head with a sigh. "I promised I'd be there for her. I won't break my word."

"I believe this is the first time you've made a vow of that sort to any woman." Vardak watched as Patak's expression shifted to one of sadness and longing. "You love her, don't you?"

Patak nodded. "I confessed some of my history with women to Em some time ago. She laughed and told me none of it mattered. She's different from the rest, Vardak. Special. I'd do anything she asked of me, and I'd give up my life if it meant saving hers. I've never felt so strongly about…anyone."

"Perhaps our people will understand. Mother certainly will—if you tell her what you've just told me."

Patak glanced at him hopefully. "I pray you're right. She won't be pleased that I'll never have children, but Travin's good for that. And you, one day, if you allow yourself to settle down and take the time to *meet* someone."

Vardak chuckled. "I have time, Patak."

They ducked inside the narrow door of The Three Roses. The common room was beginning to fill with locals, and several faces turned eagerly in their direction, seeking news. Vardak fixed his eyes on the door that would lead them to the inn's private dining rooms and ignored the volley of calls and questions hurled in their direction. There would be time enough to address the townsfolk later.

Inside the private room, Emra sat across the table from Radosan and Ravin, while Aziarah stood to one side conversing with Danian. Emra's face was drawn. It was immediately clear she'd managed less sleep than Vardak. A pang of guilt shot through him; he should have awakened sooner, should have been there to do his part for the soldiers under their command.

They joined those gathered around the table while Aziarah and Danian did the same. Emra motioned for Ravin to begin.

"As most of you know, the Drakkon followed the Murkor into the plains after we routed them yesterday," Ravin began. "Their trail led several miles east, then abruptly vanished. When I learned of this, I suspected they'd returned to the Wasted Land. I entered the Aethereum to learn for myself. The Murkor army has reestablished itself near the black tower."

"We believe they'll overwinter in that location," Emra added. "Based on what we know of the Murkor, and what I know of the Soulless, it makes sense."

"From my vantage on the field yesterday, I did not question the reason for their retreat," Vardak said slowly. "As I read through reports and received word from our various units afterward, I believe they called the retreat prematurely. Something happened that they did not expect." He eyed Emra and Ravin in turn. "I'm certain it had to do with one of you."

Emra sighed, but it was Ravin who spoke. "We were discussing this very matter an hour ago. The Soulless were aware of my presence here, though they could not have known about the talisman. They did not know of Emra—or that the Fireblade had been reclaimed. I'm afraid I've missed much of that portion of our history, but Adalin will fill me in later."

"I recognized two of the Soulless from afar," Emra replied quietly. "Alyra, who never had a mind for tactics, and Kama who certainly *did*. If the Soulless are as organized as we believe, it must be Kama behind the army's movements. Dranamir would never have called a retreat, from what I understand."

Ravin snorted. "She would have been more likely to slaughter her followers for insubordination if they questioned her for pressing the attack." He crossed his arms with a troubled frown. "And Alyra... I *knew* I sensed something familiar about the other woman."

"You knew her as well?" Emra asked, her eyebrows raised.

"Yes. She was not one of the Nameless' followers when Dranamir overthrew the Council of Enlightened, but it seems she converted. She was always ambitious, though her magical ability is relatively weak." Ravin sighed and shook his head. "Alyra was...interested in me for a number of years. I never returned the sentiment—I'd rather be with an intellectual equal, and she is...not. It infuriated her. Alyra's primary talent is seduction, and I was the only man to resist her charms. That she came to Delucha tells me one of two things. She was either compelled to engage in the fight by the Nameless, or she is seeking revenge. As I said, they were aware of my presence here."

"Does every human woman fall over herself in your presence, Ravin?" Aziarah demanded, nonplussed.

Ravin shrugged helplessly and flushed. "If you're referring to the duchess, I…It's not like that."

Patak snickered, and Ravin's features reddened further. "Unlikely. You ought to share some pointers with my brother."

Vardak groaned and felt his own face begin to heat. He should have expected Patak to draw him into the conversation against his will.

"That's enough," Emra cut in with a laugh. "We've more important matters to discuss than matchmaking. If we're in agreement that the Murkor will likely remain east of the mountains for the winter, then we can prepare our next move." She glanced at Ravin knowingly. "I expect you'll keep watch on their location, Ravin? Few others can walk the Aethereum with impunity as you do."

"Of course. I've arranged advanced lessons with Tavesin, so we will be roaming the magical realm regardless. It will be a simple matter to add spying to my list of objectives while there."

"You will keep him safe?" Aziarah demanded. "He is a child, and a naïve one at that. I will tear you limb from limb with my own claws if he is hurt, Ravin."

Ravin chuckled, though Vardak detected unease in the depths of his golden eyes. "I'll not let any harm come to him. You have my word."

"Perhaps you can spare a few hours to accompany him to Dar Daelad?" Radosan asked. "The Grays here have deemed Rostin worthy of his challenge, and I was planning to ask Tavesin to escort him to the tower. Given Tavesin's history in the Aethereum, I am wary of asking him to travel alone."

"With good reason," Ravin replied. "He knows enough to defend himself now, but he has a habit of crossing paths with Garin. I'll make certain both boys make the journey safely."

Emra's gaze shifted to meet Vardak's. "I believe we ought to remain in Delucha for a few weeks. It will give our wounded time to recover and provide us with an opportunity to resupply and plan for the next stage of our journey. What are your thoughts, Vardak?"

"It's a good plan. And as word of our victory here spreads, I'm certain more soldiers will arrive to join you." Vardak sighed. "I'll make a list of what we might need and speak with Danness about acquiring them."

"He's proven himself adept at the role of quartermaster," Emra replied. "The same goes for your people, Radosan. If there are any goods you require, speak with Danness." She glanced up as the door opened, then grinned. "Lunch has arrived. We can speak more of strategy later."

CHAPTER FIFTY

ALCHEMY AND STEEL

Aran'daj was thankful to be in the barren wasteland that was his people's ancestral home once more, though his happiness was tempered by the army's proximity to the black tower. The Soulless' beacon loomed over the landscape, casting its inky shadow across its face like a dark scar. At least they had received a few months' peace before they were forced to renew the fight. His people were once again safe, if only for a short time.

He strode through the camp as evening fell, slowly making his way toward the alchemists' busy area. He stopped to speak with several soldiers on his way, in part to assess their morale and in part to ensure they were well. Like himself, most were pleased to be home, away from the foul weather and biting cold of the lands to the west.

Not all were content with the terms of their retreat. Aran'daj had called it at Kama's behest, though he still had not puzzled out the reason behind it. It had come prematurely. He'd never believed the Soulless capable of fear, but he'd witnessed sheer terror in the corrupted man's eyes. Something had occurred that the Soulless weren't expecting, yet Kama had been close-mouthed when Aran'daj inquired.

As he reached the alchemists' section of camp, he was surrounded by a flurry of activity. The alchemists had put their fiery and explosive weapons aside in favor of healing salves and elixirs. The injured Murkor were attended to here, amidst the careful ministrations of the green-robed alchemists. Aran'daj made his way to Sal'zar's tent, where he believed Jal'den had gone. The Arms Master had suffered a shoulder injury during the battle, and despite his protests, Aran'daj had insisted he seek treatment. He doubted Jal'den would have sought the aid of anyone other than Sal'zar.

At the entrance of Sal'zar's tent, a trio of black-clad soldiers stood guard. They saluted at his approach, and Aran'daj knew he'd come to the right location.

"Is the Arms Master here?"

One of the guards nodded and turned to whisper through the tent's flap. He did not disturb its location, out of respect for Jal'den's privacy, merely spoke through the hairline crack at the opening. Moments later, Sal'zar emerged.

"Ah, Commander. How might I help you?"

"The Arms Master and I have a matter to discuss. You are welcome to join, of course." Aran'daj smiled beneath his hood while Sal'zar hesitated. With the Soulless busy in their tower, he'd hoped to speak with the pair regarding the Kal's nebulous plans.

"Jal'den told me he's informed you of our…situation, Commander," Sal'zar replied quietly. He cast a furtive glance toward the guards, who appeared to be uninterested in the conversation. "I was changing the bandage on his shoulder. He is unmasked. I'll ask if he is willing to speak now, or if you must wait."

Aran'daj nodded. "I will wait, if that's his wish."

"Thank you. You aren't truly family, though he's mentioned your…ties to his uncle. It may be enough."

As Sal'zar disappeared into the tent once more, Aran'daj began to pace. Beyond the Kal's plans, he needed to discuss the battle with Jal'den. It was unexpected for the Arms Master to sustain an injury during the fight; Aran'daj had watched him spar often enough to understand Jal'den's prowess exceeded all others. That he'd been bested by a human foe was troubling.

Sal'zar returned moments later. "He will see you, Commander."

Aran'daj followed the alchemist into the tent. Jal'den was propped against a mound of cushions, shirtless and without hood. The silver tattoos that covered his body depicted his life's story and family ties, a glimpse into Jal'den's past that few were privy to. Propriety and his respect for Jal'den compelled him to reply in kind; Aran'daj tugged his hood down and allowed the Arms Master and his partner to look upon his face for the first time.

Jal'den smiled weakly at the gesture as Sal'zar knelt at his side and resumed the bandaging of Jal'den's right shoulder.

"Commander, I'm glad you've come." Jal'den winced as Sal'zar drew the cloth strips tight and began to bind the ends.

"How is your arm?" Aran'daj sat down facing the pair, his back to the tent flap.

"It looks worse than it is," Jal'den replied.

Sal'zar snorted. "Do not let him mislead you, Commander. He will bear a deep scar. If I were not trained as I am, he may have lost the arm to infection. I am grateful you talked sense into his thick skull."

"What Sal'zar means is, without his magic to heal me, I'd not be as well as I am today." Jal'den eyed the alchemist with amusement.

Aran'daj nodded thoughtfully. "I'm glad that you were chosen for the tower for this reason alone, Sal'zar. Jal'den is an invaluable part of this army."

Sal'zar shrugged uncomfortably. "If we are to speak of that place, I must protect our conversation from prying ears."

Aran'daj watched as the green-hooded alchemist rose to his feet and made a sweeping gesture with his hands. A faint illumination began to permeate the tent, as though the canvas walls themselves produced light. Aran'daj waited silently, uncertain what Sal'zar had done. Other than the dim light, he sensed no change in their surroundings.

Sal'zar resumed his place at Jal'den's side and nodded. "No one outside can overhear us, Commander. We may speak freely."

"Is this magic, Sal'zar? Or some new method of alchemy?" Aran'daj asked.

Jal'den chuckled while the alchemist adjusted his hood and considered his answer. "It is magic, sir, though I wish I could form a means for the alchemists to replicate the result. It is a useful trick."

"If anyone can find a way to do so, it is you," Jal'den replied with a smile.

"I am less confident in my abilities than he is," Sal'zar said to Aran'daj. "Jal'den seems to believe I am capable of many things which are simply impossible."

Jal'den grinned. "In all our long history, Sal'zar is the only Murkor favored by Solsticia with the gift of magic. Combined with his alchemical training, he's a force unto himself."

Sal'zar crossed his arms and tilted his head away, flustered by Jal'den's words. "Do not mistake his words for truth, Commander. Jal'den has spent far too much time in conversation with the Kal regarding abilities I may or may not possess."

Aran'daj chuckled. The pair's banter was a poignant reminder of why he'd come, why their work to carry out the Kal's plot was imperative. They and their generation were the future of the Murkor people. Aran'daj hoped to secure a world for them in which there was no longer a threat of annihilation or domination by the Soulless, a world where they might lay down their weapons and enjoy a peaceful existence.

"It is this business with the Kal that brought me here," Aran'daj confessed. "Jal'den and I have played our parts as well as we are able, but we must know what he plans—and what your role is, Sal'zar. The last communication we received indicated you were awaiting the army's return to the tower before you made your next move. If we are to help you, we must know more."

Sal'zar sighed heavily and seemed to deflate. A look of concern crossed Jal'den's face, and he moved as though to draw his arm around the alchemist protectively, but grimaced at the motion. He scowled at his bandaged shoulder instead and leaned further into the cushions behind him.

"He's right, Sal'zar," Jal'den said.

Sal'zar turned to study Jal'den, his rigid posture a sign of his discomfort. "You will not like what I have to say, *ama*."

Jal'den frowned and peered into Sal'zar's hood, jaw set in determination. "We need to know."

Sal'zar sighed again and looked away. It was several moments before he next spoke. "The Kal has convinced many families to send word to their soldiers in the camp. It will not draw the suspicion of the Soulless, as this is typical of our people. The letters will contain a message from the Kal, hidden within. They are instructed to destroy the letter upon reading and await a prescribed date and time in which to act. I am…I am to lead them away from this place, Jal'den. The soldiers chosen are those sympathetic to our people's plight, those who will act no matter the potential repercussions we may face, but the Kal will not have messages sent to those in…positions of authority."

Jal'den lay back and glared at the ceiling, hurt and fury warring within his pale eyes. "You both know I will do everything in my power to see you safe, Sal'zar, and yet you cut me out of this plot."

"It was not my decision, Jal'den."

"Jal'den," Aran'daj said firmly before the Arms Master could form his next argument, "I know this is difficult for you, but I believe I understand the Kal's reasoning."

"I suppose you would. He is your kin." Jal'den continued to stare upward as his temper raged.

"If too many of our soldiers disappear during the night, the Soulless will not only seek to hunt them down, they will systematically exterminate our people. It won't matter if they were privy to this scheme or not." Aran'daj shook his head. "If the Kal has determined we must remain here, we will do so, Jal'den. And the army may need you more than ever in the wake of Sal'zar's departure."

Jal'den peered at him suspiciously. "What do you mean, Commander? I'm your second—and as I've explained previously, strategy is not one of my strengths. The army will need both of us."

Aran'daj shrugged, unwilling to detail the inevitable future he saw for himself.

"The Soulless will demand someone pays for our actions," Sal'zar said quietly. "If the Kal's plan succeeds, a third of our soldiers will be safe, though we cannot return to the caverns. A third of their army will vanish into the night, Jal'den. I believe the commander understands what the Kal demands of him."

"I do." Aran'daj had sealed his own fate when he'd asked Jal'den to have his message delivered to Rej'amin. The Kal realized Aran'daj believed his days were limited and decided the commander must be sacrificed in order to spare the rest of their people from the Soulless' wrath. He prayed when the day came, he would face Kama and receive a swift end rather than one of the others.

"No," Jal'den stated forcefully. "This is madness, Sal'zar! They will hunt you like an animal and show no mercy once they find you. I won't let you do this."

"You must, *ama*. It is the only way."

"And I'll be left behind, left *here*, under their command to…to…" Jal'den's voice cracked, and he turned away.

"We have always dreamed of the day when we can finally be together," Sal'zar replied, his voice laden with sorrow. "The time will come, but only if we continue to play the parts the Kal has assigned. I believe his plan is our only hope for freedom, and so I must do this, Jal'den. When the war is ended and our people are safe once more, I will make it up to you."

"I will hold you to that promise," Jal'den replied gruffly.

Aran'daj sensed it was past time he left the pair to work out their disagreement alone. He pulled up his hood and nodded to Sal'zar. "Thank you. I'll make certain the Kal's plan succeeds."

"Commander, wait." Jal'den turned to face him with haunted eyes. "I thought you ought to know this, and given *his* news, I've nearly forgotten. I encountered the other man chosen by Blademon outside of Delucha."

"The Master of War has chosen a human?" Aran'daj asked incredulously.

"No, sir. He is one of the Scorpion Men. He was with the horsemen during the attack. He is the reason I received this." Jal'den pointed to the bandages that adorned his shoulder.

"You're certain he was trained by Blademon?" Aran'daj pressed. The news unnerved him.

"Yes. He'd stung several others before I faced him, else I may not have returned from that fight alive. He wields an axe, commander, and his weapon bore Blademon's mark just as my sword does." Jal'den frowned in determination. "I won't be bested by him a second time."

CHAPTER FIFTY-ONE

PROMISES

Restlessness drove him to walk the streets, empty as they were after the battle two days prior. His feet led him through a maze of alleys interspersed with wide boulevards. The city was quiet, mourning its losses while celebrating its unexpected victory.

The relative silence suited Tavesin's mood; he was troubled by what he'd witnessed atop the walls, and neither Rostin nor Badolo seemed to understand the source of his melancholy. They'd remained within The Three Roses, under strict orders not to engage unless one of the wizards demanded otherwise. They'd been sheltered from the horrors of death, from the attacks that Tavesin knew had targeted him. His shields had drawn the attention of the Soulless, or at the very least, their followers. When he'd questioned Ravin about his theory, the mage had merely nodded. It was all the affirmation Tavesin required.

The morning was overcast and cold, but rather than deter him from his wandering, it pushed him to continue. The thought of returning to the inn and his friends' carefree laughter caused his stomach to twist in knots. Rostin's attempt to cheer him the previous day had failed, spurring his friend to persevere and try even harder. Tavesin simply wished to be left alone, to sort out his thoughts without the distraction of others, a concept Rostin struggled to grasp.

His feet led him from the city's heart to its eastern outskirts. He paused in the street to study the gate, the wall upon which he'd stood alongside Ravin as the battle raged in the grassy plain beyond. Though his attention had been focused on deflecting the magical attacks of the Soulless, he'd been aware of the casualties both sides had taken. Prior to the battle, he'd never witnessed a death firsthand, and the bloody fight between soldiers on the field had been filled with them. He was overwhelmed by the loss, uncertain of how he ought to react.

Tavesin shook his head and continued his journey toward the watchtower and the steps within that would lead him atop the wall. He wasn't certain why he'd returned to the place, but was compelled to look upon the plains without the presence of warring armies to obscure its natural state.

A light breeze rippled through the dry, golden stalks as he peered over the edge. Teams of soldiers moved across the plains, gathering the remains of the fallen from both sides. Others busied themselves digging graves a short distance away from the city's wall. Tavesin's heart grew heavy at the sight, and he wished he'd never come. In his foolish fantasy, he'd returned to the wall to look out upon an untouched grassland, but the presence of the soldiers clearing away the aftermath of the fight was a harsh reminder of reality.

He turned away from the sight and slumped against the wall, unable to contain his grief any longer. He'd been thrilled at the prospect of joining Emra in the fight, the stories from his childhood guiding his steps along the road to Delucha. The battle had broken something deep within his soul, and he believed he'd never be the same. He drew his knees into his chest and began to sob, alone atop the wall. He wanted nothing more than to leave Delucha and the war behind, to return not to the Shining Tower, but to Rican Mer. He longed for his home, its familiarity, his family.

Sometime later, he heard the scuff of boots against the stone nearby, but he did not look up to see who they belonged to. The footsteps grew louder and stopped at his side, then moments later his visitor sat down an arm's length away. Tavesin buried his tear-stained face behind his knees. His throat was sore and constricted; he wasn't certain he'd be able to speak if he tried.

"I've been searching for you," Ravin's voice said quietly. "I'm surprised to find you here."

Hot tears spilled from his eyes as he shook his head. "I'm not…not sure why I came."

"The battle was difficult for all of us, Tavesin. There is no shame in grief."

Tavesin wiped at his eyes and peered at Ravin. "Rostin doesn't understand. None of them seem to understand. Do you?"

Deep compassion shone in the mage's eyes as he nodded. "Yes. I was made Enlightened by the age of eleven. I was expected to carry out all the duties required of an adult. I was fortunate that the civil wars had ended a few years prior to my birth, but the world remained on edge, wary of what each day might bring. We were constantly assessing the new monarchs of the Five Kingdoms for threats to the newfound peace." He sighed. "The wizards should not have forced you to come here, no matter your power. They have murdered your childhood."

"When Emra came to Dar Daelad, she spoke to the Radiant. She needed the tower's help. Even if Vardak didn't have the Moon's Eye, I would have volunteered." He hung his head. "The wizards allowed me to choose, and Aziarah supported my decision. Rostin's and Badolo's, as well. I was wrong, and now I just want to go home."

"No one is keeping you here, Tavesin," Ravin replied gently. "If you wish to leave, you may. Radosan will understand—we've spoken at length, and he is more sympathetic to your situation than you may believe."

Tavesin shook his head miserably. "I promised to obey the council when I became a wizard. The Radiant expects me to follow through. I can't go home, not yet."

"I understand."

"Why were you looking for me, sir?"

Ravin chuckled sadly. "I came on business for your wizards, but it seems to me that it can wait."

Tavesin shrugged. "Perhaps I need the distraction. What did Radosan want of me?"

"Your friend Rostin is scheduled for his challenge. I promised your Sect Master that I'd escort you both through the Aethereum, though I'll remain within my realm while you're in the tower." Ravin offered a tired grin. "I may be working with Emra, but your council will never fully trust me."

"Radosan isn't *my* Sect Master, but I must do as he asks." Tavesin pushed himself to his feet. He was looking forward to spending time away from Delucha, however brief it might be.

"Perhaps while I teach you more of the Aethereum, you can share the hierarchy of your council," Ravin replied as he stood. "This business with Sect Masters and the like seems an inefficient system, one that does not make sense to me."

Tavesin managed a smile, grateful for Ravin's offer and his aid. "Thank you, but there is one other thing I need to do while in the Aethereum. If you don't mind, that is? I need to…I want to search for Arra."

Ravin's eyes were guarded, but he nodded. "We can seek her out, if she's there. I hope you will heed my warning, Tavesin. She is their prisoner, and you've seen what mind-control can do."

"I know, sir. Is there a way to sense if she is not…herself?"

"There are signs. I will explain them to you once we've finished with our errand."

Tavesin left Rostin with the Gray Sect Master in the tower's library. He wished his friend well before he departed to rejoin Ravin in the Aethereum. They agreed Tavesin would return the next morning— neither boy mentioned Ravin in the presence of the other wizards, for both held the unaffiliated mage in high esteem.

Rostin was characteristically buoyant, elated at the opportunity to prove himself to the council. Tavesin was certain he'd complete his challenge and be eager to return to Delucha afterwards. Tavesin prayed his friend's demeanor would remain unchanged after he was thrust into his first true battle.

When he reentered the Aethereum, Ravin was in the tower's garden as they'd arranged. The golden-eyed man strolled amongst the trees, inspecting the wizards' handiwork with the flourishing foliage with an appraising eye.

"The flowers bloom year-round," Tavesin said as he approached.

"Yes. I never took the time to learn such frivolous magics, though I can appreciate the beauty of them." He turned to smile over his shoulder. "I've often wondered how my life might have been different if my father brought me here as a child."

"Instead of the…other tower?"

Ravin shrugged. "Call it what you like, Tavesin. I care not."

Tavesin came to stand at Ravin's side. "May we go to Rican Mer?"

"Of course. I gave you my word. Your friend arrived there some time ago."

Tavesin gaped at him. "You can sense her from *here*?"

Ravin grinned. "This is my realm, Tavesin. My mother made certain my abilities were greatly enhanced while here. Recall what you felt while linked with your relic, then double its power. That is what the Aethereum is like for me."

"Sir, that's…amazing. What would happen if you linked with the talisman here?"

Tavesin wished to learn everything he could from Ravin, and his wonder replaced the sorrow he'd been feeling for a time. A distraction from the horrors of battle was precisely what he'd needed.

"I don't know, Tavesin, and a part of me is terrified at the prospect. I'm not certain I would survive wielding so much power, even here. As a wizard, you must recognize your limits. It's equally important as learning your strengths. I knew a mage who drew upon two relics at once—he was a damned fool and attempted the stunt merely to impress a woman. It didn't end as he'd hoped."

"What happened?" Tavesin pressed.

"His power ignited, and he was reduced to a pile of ash in the process. The woman was not impressed." Ravin shrugged. "We ought to discuss this later. You wished to speak with your friend."

"Yes, I…" he sighed, Ravin's previous warning forefront in his mind. "Do you also know if she is controlled, sir?"

"I must look at her first. Mind-control magic is subtle. I don't know of another mage who has been able to sense its effects on another's mind, but the victim will display certain physical signs." He motioned for Tavesin to follow him. "I'll meet you in the village."

Tavesin nodded and transported himself to the riverbank that he often used to meet Arra. Ravin arrived moments later and pointed in the direction of the same trees Tavesin had found her in previously.

"She is there."

Tavesin could sense her presence now that he was near. He broke into a trot and hurried to her location, praying she was well. Ravin kept pace with him easily with his much longer strides.

"Arra!" Tavesin called breathlessly as he spied her disheveled red-brown hair.

She looked up and managed a smile through bruised lips. When her gaze met Ravin's, her initial good cheer was replaced by suspicion and unconcealed fear. "Taven, who is *he?*"

Tavesin halted several steps from her and chewed his lower lip, uncertain how much he could safely reveal.

Ravin bent to speak near Tavesin's ear. "She is herself, though I still advise caution. It's clear they haven't treated her well. Certain methods of torture can be…difficult to resist." To Arra, he said, "My name is unimportant. Your friend has asked for my aid, and I shall give it."

"You can trust him, Arra," Tavesin assured her.

Her eyes darted between them warily for a moment. "I came to tell you they've returned to the tower, Taven. The other Soulless and their army."

"We know, Arra."

Tavesin knelt down in front of her, wishing for the hundredth time that he had an aptitude for healing. Her injuries were more severe than he'd realized; several of her fingers were broken and bruises covered her fair skin. One of her legs was splayed outward at an unnatural angle, and he understood belatedly why she'd chosen to sit. He didn't believe she was able to stand.

"He's hurt you again."

Arra shrugged indifferently. "I wish he'd finish what he's started and allow me to have peace. I prayed you would come today, Taven. I need to say goodbye."

Tavesin blinked away tears as his heart lurched from her words. He wished there were something he could say to alleviate her fears, something he could do to erase her pain. When nothing came to him, he hung his head in defeat.

Ravin knelt carefully beside her. "You've endured more than most could have. I assume this is Garin's doing?"

Tavesin nodded. "He took her."

"He's a gods-damned despot," Ravin muttered darkly before he focused his gaze on Arra. "Has Garin told you anything else? Do you know of their plans?"

She shook her head. "I know only that he's been more enraged than usual of late. I don't believe the battle went in their favor."

"Thank you." Ravin turned to face Tavesin. "I suspect you'd like a few moments to speak with her alone. I'll be in the village, keeping watch."

Arra waited until Ravin was gone before she spoke again. "Taven, I cannot continue to risk coming here. If he learns…He will kill me. Despite my earlier words, I'm not ready to face Aeon. Not yet."

"I understand." He looked down and closed his eyes as despair settled like a cloud over him. "Arra, we've made plans… I can't tell you of them, in case *he*…"

She reached up and placed one of her mangled hands carefully against the side of his face. "I know, Taven."

He swallowed the lump forming in his throat and forced himself to meet her gaze. "I *will* come for you, Arra, and I *will* save you from him. You have my word."

A sad smile crossed her face. "I will pray for your success, Tavesin Drondes, and pray that I will continue to endure."

Tears streamed unbidden from his eyes as Arra winked out of sight. With Ravin's help, he would save her. He would keep his promise, no matter the cost.

The story will continue in War of the Nameless.

THANK YOU FOR READING THE TALISMAN OF DELUCHA!

If you enjoyed reading this book, please consider leaving a review. I hope you will continue the saga in book three, War of the Nameless.

Information about release dates will be posted on my website (www.ajcalvin.net), as well as shared via my newsletter. If interested, you can subscribe by visiting my website and clicking on the "Subscribe" tab.

ACKNOWLEDGMENTS

Like it's predecessor in the series, The Talisman of Delucha was a long time in the making. More hours than I can count were spent in the writing, revising, reworking, and polishing of this manuscript after it spent nearly two decades untouched.

I would like to thank my husband for his support and patience as I worked to complete this project. I was often scarce, but I believe the end product has been worth the time I sacrificed.

Another thank you goes to Jamie Noble, the artist who created the cover images for this series, and to Sheena Sampsel, the tireless editor who never complains about my many comma incursions and helped to make this story the best it could be.

And finally, a heartfelt thank you to all of my readers. Without you, writing would not be worthwhile.

NOW AVAILABLE

WAR OF THE NAMELESS
The Relics of War: Book Three

The god of death, called the Nameless by some, has been biding his time for millennia. His scheme to break free of his prison is nearing fruition, and with the aid of the Soulless bound to him, he seeks to regain his former power. The world has scorned him and it must face his wrath.

Emra Castledowns has gathered an army to combat the threat the Soulless pose. Beside her are Vardak, a skilled warrior, renowned amongst his people and the protégé of the god of war, and Ravin, the most powerful wielder of magic the world has ever produced. The wizards have allied with her, the Five Kingdoms have lent soldiers and arms, and even the gods—sworn to remain neutral during mortal conflicts—have begun to choose sides.

In spite of her army's might, the power the Nameless begins to unleash is daunting. The death god is a threat to the existence of every kingdom, every race and nationality—even the Soulless who serve him are not immune to his thirst for revenge.

ABOUT THE AUTHOR

A.J. Calvin is a science fiction/fantasy novelist hailing from Loveland, Colorado. By day, she works as a microbiologist, but in her free time she writes. She lives with her husband, their cat, Magic, and a fairly large salt water aquarium.

When she is not working or writing, she enjoys scuba diving, hiking, and playing video games.

For more information on the author and news about her writing, please visit her website at www.ajcalvin.net.